Zane looked up at her. All the protective layers she'd erected that day teetered under the blue intensity of his gaze.

After a long second, he crossed the short distance to her side in one step. He sat on the edge of her mattress.

For several seconds they stared at each other. Kinsey felt as though she was going to explode.

"You look beautiful tonight," he said as he ran a lock of her hair through his fingers. "Of course, you always look beautiful."

"For all the good it does us," she whispered. When he leaned over her and kissed her cheek, she turned her face. "Don't."

"Sorry," he said, and slowly sat up. He didn't leave, however, just sat there, still and silent, one hand on her shoulder as he stared into the room. Finally he looked down at her again.

"Last night I asked you to give me one more day. That day is now over. I think you should drive away tomorrow and let me finish this."

COWBOY
INCOGNITO

BY
ALICE SHARPE

MILLS & BOON

Published in Great Britain 2015
by Mills & Boon, an imprint of Harlequin (UK) Limited,
Eton House, 18-24 Paradise Road, Richmond, Surrey, TW9 1SR

© 2015 Alice Sharpe

ISBN: 978-0-263-25305-4

46-0515

Harlequin (UK) Limited's policy is to use papers that are natural, renewable and recyclable products and made from wood grown in sustainable forests. The logging and manufacturing processes conform to the legal environmental regulations of the country of origin.

Printed and bound in Spain
by CPI, Barcelona

Alice Sharpe met her husband-to-be on a cold, foggy beach in Northern California. Their union has survived the rearing of two children, a handful of earthquakes, numerous cats and a few special dogs, the latest of which is a yellow Lab named Annie Rose. Alice and her husband now live in a small rural town in Oregon, where she devotes the majority of her time to pursuing her second love, writing.

This book is dedicated to the newest member of
our family, Tyler Lawrence Shumate.
Live long and prosper, sweetie.

Chapter One

Kinsey Frost loved her adopted home of New Orleans no matter what the weather threw at her. Since moving there a few years ago, various storms had flexed their muscles and she'd kind of enjoyed the drama of it all.

However, on a summer day like this, when the humidity hovered close to a drizzle and no breeze blew off the Mississippi River, mixed feelings tended to sneak their way in. Add a crowded hot sidewalk, time restraint and a sore back from climbing up and down a ladder all day and she was about five seconds away from hailing a cab to take her the six blocks home. She was painfully aware she had an hour to take a shower, change her clothes and return to the gallery she'd just left.

That was cutting it close and she decided on the spot that once she had cleaned herself up, she would drive back to the gallery instead of walking as she usually did.

To take her mind off her wilting condition, she focused on her fellow pedestrians. As an artist, she was always interested in people watching, even when they had their backs to her. Directly ahead walked a woman who had twisted her hair into an intricate knot and secured it with what looked like red chopsticks. In front of her two businessmen in lightweight suits argued about something, their profiles twisted with emotion. Then came a woman wearing a pink dress who held the hands of two little girls. Twins? Probably, as they were the same size and wore identical clothes.

Looking even farther ahead, Kinsey caught a glimpse of a tan Stetson hat. She tilted her head to see on whom it perched and found a tall guy with dark hair touching the back of his shirt collar. A black leather vest stretched across broad shoulders. Through the legs of those between them, she caught sight of jeans and black boots.

This was not Bourbon Street. Few tourists visited this area at five o'clock on a Friday afternoon, fewer still dressed like this man. She watched him for another half block, struck by his steady gait and the aura he emitted of knowing where he was going and what he was going to do when he got there. She couldn't help being curious about his ultimate destination.

Life was full of interesting people with fascinating stories you never had a chance to know. Right now, for Kinsey, the far more pressing issue was time. The gallery was holding an opening-night show for an "outstanding new talent." That's what the owner called anyone to whom he dedicated wall space and a wine-and-cheese party. In Kinsey's opinion, this time he was dead-on right. She'd spent most of the day hanging one beautiful painting after another, striving to suit both owner and finicky artist. No doubt there would be a fair amount of hand-holding required that evening.

The light on the corner changed and the crowd up ahead slowed down to wait it out. Kinsey had lost track of the cowboy, but now he caught her attention again. He stood at the edge of the sidewalk, slightly apart. The giggling antics of the two little girls apparently caught his attention and he turned. As though he sensed Kinsey's stare, his gaze darted from the children straight to her.

The word *handsome* didn't do him justice, didn't begin to hint at the smoldering warmth of his eyes, the curiosity, the intelligence. His tan was deep, his eyes an unexpected blue, his brows straight and dark. He appeared to be several years her senior, maybe in his midthirties, and she'd bet a bundle he was better looking now than he'd been a decade before. That's what bones like his could do for a man…

Very slowly and with more than a taste of speculation, his sensual lips twitched into a smile as he returned her appraisal. Dazzled and a bit embarrassed to have been caught staring, Kinsey immediately looked away.

And that's how she came to be facing the bicyclist speeding down the middle of the sidewalk, scattering pedestrians like a stiff wind blowing through fallen leaves. She hastily stepped out of the way as he whizzed past, the yellow vest the company's pedaling messengers wore flying out behind him. The matching helmet obscured his features. Kinsey twirled to face the corner and shout a warning, but it seemed everyone had already sensed something amiss. Someone dropped a shopping bag and someone else screamed. The woman with the children grabbed each girl by a hand and dragged them to the shelter of a recessed doorway, but one of them pulled free. Laughing as though caught up in a game, she shot out onto the sidewalk.

The weirdest mixture of slow motion and fast-forward came over Kinsey as she soundlessly watched events unfold. The child suddenly stopped dead in her tracks, struck now by the approaching danger but obviously afraid to move. The cowboy dashed to sweep the girl out of harm's way. The cyclist veered closer to them and then like a flash, unexpected and unreal, he let go of the right grip and shoved the still-moving cowboy, connecting with his shoulder, upsetting his precarious balance. The push propelled man and child toward the street at the same instant a cab cut the corner too close and the cowboy stumbled into its path. The cab stopped abruptly, the driver's face through the windshield one of abject terror.

The screech of brakes and blare of horns masked the collective gasp of the onlookers. The cyclist had gone down, too, but he'd rolled to his feet and now went to the aid of the fallen. As he hovered over them, the momentum created by the flow of traffic speeding by in the other direction caused his yellow vest to whip around his torso like the wings of a wounded butterfly.

The crowd began moving again. Kinsey hesitated just a second, then dashed into the street, heedless now of her aching muscles and sweating brow. As she closed the distance, the cyclist hopped up, ran to his bike, somehow managed to mount it and pedal away down the sidewalk like nobody's business.

The child, still caught in the cowboy's slack embrace, whimpered. The man lay still as death. Kinsey leaned over them as the woman in pink appeared, screaming something in what sounded like Swedish, while the little girl who hadn't been injured sobbed uncontrollably by her side. Kinsey set her fingers against the man's throat and felt the flutter of his heartbeat, saw the flickering of his lashes. The child's eyes were open, but her skin was pale and she looked dazed. Someone touched Kinsey's shoulder.

"I'm a doctor," a middle-aged woman said. "Please, move aside, let me see them." Kinsey stood and backed out of the way, one hand covering her mouth, unaware of the bloodstains on her white jeans.

AMBULANCES SHOWED UP and soon after, the police. The taxi driver had finally emerged, white faced and shaken. One policeman led him away from everyone else for an interview. Kinsey was questioned along with the other onlookers. Of course, officials were very anxious to hear about the cyclist, and Kinsey discovered she was one of only two people who'd actually seen the shove. Attention of the others seemed to have been focused on the child or even the taxi. Kinsey could offer very little description of the aggressor as it had all happened in such a blur and the helmet had hidden his features.

They wanted to know if it looked as if the cowboy and the cyclist knew each other, or if the child had been the target. They wanted to know if she could recall anything that implied malice. As she watched the ambulance crew load the child and man into separate vehicles and drive away, she blinked rapidly. "Nothing," she admitted. "Except the shove, of course."

By luck, someone had been using their phone to record the twin girls and had caught the incident. Hopefully, the video would reveal things that had happened too fast for the human eye to spot.

"We're going to go to the hospital now to find out more about the victims," one of the officers told Kinsey as he wrote down her name and number in his notebook. "If you think of anything, anything at all, call me."

"What about the company the messenger worked for?" she asked. "Speedy Courier, isn't that the name? Maybe they can identify which of their messengers were on this street today."

"We're checking into that," the officer assured her. He handed her his card and she scanned it quickly. His name was Edward Woods. He nodded at her and walked away toward his car. A second later, Kinsey called out to him.

"Detective Woods? There is something," she said. "Your footsteps just now…" Her voice trailed off as she fought to organize her thoughts. "When the courier ran off, I heard the slap of his shoes."

The detective's shoulders shrugged with uncertainty as to her point.

"I see these messengers all the time," she explained. "My mother lives in one of those beautiful old houses a couple of miles farther up the avenue and the gallery I work at is only two blocks from here. I shop at the little grocery right up the street… Anyway, all the couriers around here dress the same. Their vests are always zipped. This one wasn't. Plus, they all wear black formfitting bike pants and specialty sports shoes, you know?"

Light began to dawn in Woods's eyes. "Sports shoes," he repeated. "With rubber soles."

"Yes. I think this guy was wearing loafers. His feet made a sound just like yours did. He might have been in slacks, too, maybe tucked into dark socks. I can't quite recall."

"You still can't remember anything about his face?"

"No."

The detective sighed.

As she headed home, Kinsey used her cell to arrange backup for the gallery show. The time when she should have returned had come and gone, and once again, a sense of urgency propelled her toward her apartment. The door closing behind her gave a fleeting sense of security and the desire to sit in front of a fan and catch her breath almost overwhelmed her. Instead of giving in to it, she took a hurried shower, pulled on a black dress, pinned up her damp hair and returned to the gallery.

The opening party was in full swing by the time Kinsey found a parking spot and walked through the door.

Her boss, Marc Costello, caught her eye and gestured for her to join him. Together, they moved to a private alcove, greeting guests before bending their heads to speak.

"I heard about what happened out on the street," Marc said. He was about fifty with a shock of silver hair and looked the part of a gallery owner right down to his black turtleneck worn under a stylish black silk jacket. Not exactly summery New Orleans attire, but that wasn't what he was interested in anyway. "Are you all right?"

"I'm fine," she assured him.

"I have to tell you something. Right about the time of that accident, your boyfriend, Ryan Jones, was in here. He was asking a whole lot of questions."

Kinsey instantly conjured an image of Ryan: curly blond hair, bittersweet-chocolate eyes, a nice smile. She'd met him several weeks earlier when he came into the gallery to buy a painting for his office and wound up taking Kinsey to dinner instead. Since then, she saw him whenever his New York engineering firm sent him to New Orleans to work on a levee project they'd contracted. "What kind of questions?" she asked.

"Stuff about your background, where you'd grown up, things like that."

Kinsey's brow wrinkled. "What did you tell him?"

"Nothing. You haven't exactly told me a whole lot, you know. I just said something about what a hard worker you are. He said he knew that. Then he started asking questions about your family, specifically, your mother."

Kinsey swallowed hard. "My mother? What did he want to know?"

"Let's see. How old she was and how long had she lived here and where exactly did she live and work…stuff like that. I told him the truth, that I'd never met her, that she was kind of a recluse. He left a few minutes later after getting a phone call."

"That's…odd," Kinsey said. She'd spent years looking after her mother who at times was a social misfit. The thought of a friend asking questions behind her back— well, it was disquieting.

"I thought so, too. That's why I'm telling you." He took a deep breath and added, "On top of that, I'm afraid we have a more immediate problem than a snoopy boyfriend."

"Don't keep calling him my boyfriend," she protested. "We haven't known each other that long and he's only in town—"

Marc held up a hand. "Yeah, yeah, yeah, you know what I mean. Our star artist is holed up in the ladies' room."

Still reeling over news that Ryan had been asking about her family, Kinsey shook her head. "How long has she been in there?"

"Forever. Someone from the newspaper showed up and wanted an interview and she refused. Turned all shy, refused to have her picture taken or anything. Thank goodness you're here. She's supposed to say something meaningful about her muse in five minutes. Remind her that's why I'm doing this show, to sell her work, not be her therapist."

"I know, Marc. I'll get her back out here."

"Tell her the newspaper guy left."

"Did he?"

"Yeah. I tried to get him to stay, but art shows aren't exactly a huge draw, even when the paintings are as good as these."

The opening seemed to be well attended, for which Kinsey was thankful. She'd sent out over a hundred invitations and it looked as if about half had decided to come, packing the narrow, trendy space with well-dressed people sipping wine. Of course, it was a heck of a lot cooler in the gallery than it was outside, so maybe that helped account for some of the attendees.

As she moved through the room, greeting people as she went, she noticed several discreet sold signs. That should make Marc happy.

Once inside the ladies "lounge," Kinsey found Ellen Rhodes sitting forlornly on a velvet bench, staring at her hands.

"Congratulations, you're a hit," Kinsey said with a giant smile.

Ellen looked up with nervous blue eyes. "I can't do this. I don't like all these people looking at my work."

"Isn't that the point of a show?" Kinsey asked gently.

"I didn't know it would be like this. So many people…"

"You've already sold several paintings," Kinsey said. "You're a hit."

"I just want to go home."

"Listen, I get it, you're not into the publicity side of things, you're not a media hound. But Marc has a lot at stake here. He believes in your work or he wouldn't have offered you this show. Most artists work for recognition, you know. Buck up, now."

"You sound like my mother," Ellen said, but at least there was a little snap in her voice.

"That's because I'm channeling my own," Kinsey said. "I've heard versions of this speech my whole life." Like when she'd come home from a school she'd only attended a month to find her mother packing…again. No matter how much Kinsey pleaded to stay in one place, they inevitably moved on. When Mom got it in her head it was time to go, they went. Period.

Until a few years ago, that is. As soon as Kinsey had

announced her independence and settled down in New Orleans, her mother had followed suit. She now took care of a sickly elderly man who had once been wealthy but was no longer, and she seemed almost content.

"Is that newspaper guy still out there?"

"No. Marc gave him an interview and he left." Kinsey's cell phone rang and she slipped it out of her pocket, answering hesitantly when she didn't recognize the number. She listened for a minute or so before responding in a soft voice.

"Is everything okay?" Ellen asked as Kinsey pushed the end-call button.

Kinsey dropped her phone into her evening bag. "Huh? Oh, yes. And no." She made a decision and added, "I'm really sorry, but I have to leave."

"You can't," Ellen squealed.

"I have to. That was the police."

"The police!"

"They want my help with an accident victim. I have to go to the hospital right away."

Ellen started to protest, but Kinsey hustled her back into the main gallery and steered her toward Marc, who couldn't hide the look of relief that flooded his face.

"Are you feeling better?" he asked Ellen.

"I was until Kinsey said she's leaving."

Marc's smile drooped as he turned his attention to Kinsey. "You can't leave. You just got here."

"I'm sorry, but the man who was hit earlier this evening is conscious and the police asked me to come see him."

"Why you?"

"They didn't say."

"But you don't even know him!"

"I know," Kinsey agreed. "I'll be back as soon as I can," she called as she raced outside, car keys in hand.

A half hour later, she stepped out of the elevator onto the third floor of the hospital. She immediately spotted Detective Woods standing at the end of a short corridor as though waiting for her.

"I can see I took you away from something special," he said with an appraising glance at her dress. He himself wore the same light blue sports jacket he'd worn earlier.

"I was at a work-related event," she explained.

"Well, it was good of you to take time out for this. We appreciate it."

"I don't know what I can possibly do to help," she said. "Is he in this room?"

The detective glanced at the door in front of them. "Yes, but I'd like to speak to you for a moment before we go in. Can I get you a cup of coffee or a glass of ice water?"

"No, thanks."

The hospital had placed two chairs by the window at the end of the corridor and he gestured for her to sit. "First of all," he began as they settled into the chairs, "you were right. The cyclist you and the others saw wasn't a messenger for Speedy Courier. The real one claims he'd just finished a delivery and was stooping to unlock his bike when someone bashed him over the head. He'd left his helmet looped over the handlebars while he made the delivery. Anyway, when he came to, he found his bike, helmet and vest were missing. He has no idea who did it. He showed up back at the Speedy office to report it about the same time we showed up asking questions."

"So the guy we saw was a phony," Kinsey said.

"Yep. We're retracing the real messenger's trail to see if anyone he made deliveries to noticed anything peculiar.

By the way, he's a very thin, small young man. I imagine the thief couldn't get the zipper up on the vest and that's why it was open. Oh, and the phone video showed just what you surmised. The guy was wearing slacks and loafers."

"The real messenger is okay?"

"He's got a bump, but he's fine."

"And how about the little girl the cowboy saved? Is she all right?"

"Released an hour or so ago. The woman with her and her sister was the new au pair. I think she was more traumatized than the kids. By cowboy, are you referring to our John Doe?"

"That's how I thought of him," she said, nodding toward the room. "Because of the hat and everything. Wait a second, John Doe? You don't know who he is?"

"No."

"But his wallet—"

"Is missing. We think the cyclist must have taken it. And before you ask, no cell phone, just a key chain with six keys on it."

Was that what the cyclist had been doing while everyone thought he was trying to help? Stealing the cowboy's identity? It had to be. She racked her brain for an image of him pocketing something and came up blank, but he'd had his back to her and that bright vest flapping around him. "Did the taxi driver see anything?" she asked.

"He claims just about everyone on the ground was out of his line of sight. I had someone check that out and he's telling the truth, they were too close to the front of the cab for the driver to see what was going on."

"Wait a second," Kinsey said as she finally made sense of what the detective had said a couple of sentences earlier. "You said the cowboy is conscious. Can't he just tell you his name?"

The detective shook his head. "He doesn't remember who he is. In fact, he doesn't remember anything. And we have no way of knowing if this condition is recent or ongoing because no one has come forward to ask for a missing man, let alone one fitting his description."

Kinsey sat back on the chair a second. "If this amnesia just started because of the incident today, is there a chance it could go away by morning?"

"The doctors say it's anyone's guess. He could start remembering his identity in five minutes, five days or five years. Apparently lots of people with head injuries forget segments of their lives, usually just the few minutes preceding their accident. Anyway, chances are good someone who does know him will show up sooner rather than later. For now, we only have one lead."

"And what's that?" Kinsey asked.

"You."

Kinsey perked up immediately. "Me? What are you talking about?"

"Your name was written on a piece of paper we found in his pocket. Can you think of a reason for that?"

"None," she said.

"And you're sure you've never seen him before?"

"Pretty sure," Kinsey said. "I guess it's possible I ran into him sometime in the past. I've lived in a fair number of cities all across the country." Even as she spoke, she found herself doubting it could be true. John Doe, for lack of a real name, was an arresting-looking man. Would she have forgotten someone who appealed to her on such a gut level?

Woods sighed as he got to his feet. "Would you come

with me to meet the guy? Maybe it will jar a memory if you hear his voice."

"Of course," Kinsey said, ignoring the pounding of her heart. She had no idea why she felt so nervous. Sweaty palms defied the hospital's efficient air-conditioning system.

Suppressing a shiver, she followed Woods into the room.

Chapter Two

Despite his throbbing head, he fell into a black-and-white world of disjointed collages. It was a relief when a noise shook him out of the nothingness of his dreamworld. Even as he gingerly rubbed his eyes, he recognized the sound the door made when it opened and closed.

He looked up, expecting to see the cop who had asked him questions earlier or one of the doctors or nurses who were taking care of him. He did not expect to find himself staring into the velvety-brown eyes of a small woman wearing a formfitting black dress that revealed creamy smooth shoulders and a modest hint of cleavage.

He lifted his gaze back to the oval perfection of her face and hoped that he and she were longtime lovers, that she would run to him, throw her arms around him and whisper his name in his ear before planting her succulent red lips right on his. He wanted a name. He wanted an identity. He wanted his past, and maybe she was the key. If so, she made a heck of a sexy key and he was prepared to earn his memory back one succulent kiss at a time.

Her response to his gaze was a nervous twitch of her lips. He tried a reassuring smile, but that stretched the three stitches in his left cheek and he grimaced.

The woman did not look as though she loved him. Hell, she didn't even look as though she knew him.

"You must be Kinsey Frost," he said.

Now she just looked spooked. Her eyes grew wide. "Do you know me?"

"I don't even know me," he admitted. He nodded toward the cop standing behind her. "Detective Woods told me they found the name Kinsey Frost on a piece of paper. I just assumed you're her."

Some of the uneasiness fled from her face. "Oh, I see."

"I'm hoping you have answers for me," he added.

She shook her head. "I'm sorry. Today is the first time I ever saw you. I'm sure of it." She narrowed her eyes as she looked him over and nodded. "You were walking ahead of me down the sidewalk and you caught my attention because of your hat. But I don't know you."

His hand flew to his head. "I was wearing a hat?" He directed his gaze to Woods. "Where is it?"

"It fell off when you tumbled into the street. A car going the other way nailed it."

"What kind of hat?" he asked.

Kinsey supplied the answer. "A tan Stetson. It looked kind of new and very nice."

He glanced down at his hands. He'd already noticed calluses and deeply tanned skin, along with old scars, on his knuckles. "Workingman hands," he said softly. Not the hands of a teacher or a doctor. The hands of a man who got down and dirty on occasion, and instinctively, he knew at least that much about himself. He looked up at Woods. "And I was wearing cowboy boots. That's what the nurse said."

"That's right," Detective Woods concurred. "Plus, you don't sound like you're from around here. In fact, you don't have much of an accent at all. We're checking hotels to see if any of their customers are unaccounted for, but it's questionable anything will come of it. There are thousands of rooms in this city. It's unlikely anyone has missed you yet, unless you didn't show up for an appointment or something. The big question is why you were carrying Ms. Frost's name. What's the link between you two?"

"I hope that's a rhetorical question and you aren't expecting an answer from me," he said. He looked at Kinsey again. "It's up to you."

Her hand brushed his arm. "I'm sorry," she said. "I can't imagine why you were carrying my name."

"In addition to working at the gallery, you're also an artist yourself, aren't you?" Woods asked.

She turned to look at him. "Yes."

"Could he have gotten your name from a third party in relation to your work?"

"I guess so. I've done several portraits for people in New Orleans since I moved here a couple of years ago." She glanced back at him with a question in her eyes. "Maybe one of them gave you my name and you were trying to find the gallery to talk to me."

"He was walking away from, not headed to, the gallery," the detective pointed out with a frown.

"People sometimes have a hard time finding the place. It's very narrow. Maybe he walked right past it."

"We'll question people on that street as time and manpower allow," the detective said. "Including Marc Costello. But as you know, it's a long one with several businesses and homes farther along…it's going to take a while. I'd appreciate it if you would also make a list of the people you did work for so we can ask them if they might have given your name to the…victim." The detective shook his head as he looked at the bed. "Sorry, I'm not sure what to call you."

"Don't worry about it," he said.

The detective scanned his notebook briefly before directing a comment to Kinsey. "When I questioned you right after the incident, you said he was walking with determination, that he appeared preoccupied."

Kinsey nodded thoughtfully.

"That doesn't sound like he was searching for something to me."

"I guess it doesn't," Kinsey agreed.

The detective opened a small manila envelope he pulled from a jacket pocket and shook out a set of keys.

"Those are the keys you showed me earlier," he said. "The ones they found in my pocket."

"Yes," Woods said. "I wanted you to hold them, look at them, see if they jog a memory." He pointed at the fob, a small disk decorated with a red tractor and the words *Red Hot, St. George, Utah.* "We checked on that, by the way."

"It sounds like a strip club," he said.

The detective laughed. "Yeah, that's what we thought, too. What it really is, though, is a nickname for a small tractor. We found the dealership that carries it, name of Travers's Tractors. They're not missing anyone, but we did fax the police there your photo. They showed it to the staff at the dealership…didn't get any hits, but a couple of people are on vacation, so they'll try again in a few days. They also have a couple of other stores in their chain and they said they'd ask around and get back to me, but we're also contacting them. Keep in mind that sooner or later someone will wonder what happened to you and report it to the police." His phone rang and he stepped away from the bed to answer it.

Kinsey gestured at all the machines. "Are your other injuries serious?"

"Not as bad as they could have been," he replied, glancing at each key in turn.

"Were you out long?"

"I woke up in the ambulance."

"And you didn't know who you were? That must have been terrifying."

He ran his fingers over the tractor logo and shook his head before meeting her velvety gaze again. "It wasn't like that. What I was aware of was that I didn't know where I was or what had happened to me. There was an oxygen mask over my mouth and nose and my head hurt. I felt confused. I guess there are just certain instances when you decide to wait it out and see what happens. I mean, I could hear the siren, there was a guy sitting next to me who smiled and I was obviously being cared for. That was enough. At first."

"So you have a concussion?"

"And apparently a hard head, too. There's bruising and scrapes, a few stitches, stuff like that, but no broken bones, just this fog where my brain used to be. Thank goodness the taxi didn't hit me or the child I had in my arms."

"The child you saved," Kinsey said.

He smiled, ignoring the stress on the stitches. He liked the way her voice softened as she spoke, the look in her eyes as she met his gaze. "Anyway, the doctors said I was lucky." He paused for a second. Truth was, he didn't feel real lucky right that moment. He'd gladly exchange a broken arm for the return of his memory. "Thanks for trying to help," he added. His gaze followed a few strands of dark hair that had pulled loose from the pins atop her head and trailed down along her cheeks, brushing her collarbone, framing her face. She looked as if she'd stepped out of a dream, and he had another gut feeling about himself. He was a sucker for brunettes with red lips. "You were at a party or something, right?"

Her smile lit up her eyes. "The dress gave it away, huh?"

"More or less."

"We were hosting an opening show for a local artist at the gallery," she said. After a slight pause, she added, "I wish I knew what to call you. John Doe seems kind of impersonal."

"You're artistic," he said. "Give me a name, something that you think fits."

She narrowed her eyes as she studied his features. Then she smiled. "My father died before I was born, but my mother told me that he read constantly and what he liked best were Westerns. She said his favorite author was a guy named Zane Grey. How about we call you Zane?"

"Zane," he murmured. "I like it. Okay, thanks."

She nodded as the detective returned. It was obvious he'd overheard some of their conversation when he raised his eyebrows and said, "Zane?"

"My new alias."

"It fits you," the detective said. "Well, Zane, we've found the bike the fake courier used abandoned in a hallway of an old building due for demolition. I'm going to go check it out. The doctors want to keep you here for several days."

"Who's going to pay for that?" he asked.

"Don't worry about it."

"I don't think I can handle being cooped up in this place for long," Zane admitted. "I think I may be an outdoor type of guy."

Woods narrowed his eyes. "Try to remember that someone took a huge risk today to steal your wallet and probably a cell phone. He pushed you into traffic in front of a crowd of onlookers. It could have just as easily wound up with him in the street as it did you and the child. That underscores this person's recklessness."

"I wonder what was worth such a risk," Zane mused.

"We may never know."

"Did the video help you identify the man who attacked Zane?" Kinsey asked.

The detective shook his head. "He never turned around and looked at anyone." He glanced at Zane again. "Listen, you're safe here. And if you remember anything at all, call me. I left my card on the table by your phone."

Zane had been holding the keys, turning them over and over in his fingers. The detective nodded at them. "Are they bringing back any memories?"

"No," Zane admitted. "Afraid not." He started to hand them back, but the detective held up a hand. "No, that's okay. We made copies, you hold on to those. The doctor said something familiar might jog your memory, and those keys are about all we can offer. That and what's left of your clothes in the cabinet over there."

"The keys are easier to hold," Zane said.

"Exactly." Woods nodded his goodbye to Kinsey and hurried from the room.

Kinsey took a deep breath. "I guess I'd better go, too. It was nice to meet you, Zane."

"Do you have to leave?" he asked. Then he smiled. "Of course you do. You have to get back to work."

"I could stay for a few minutes," she told him.

A panicky knot in his gut followed a moment of pleasure. What in the world did they have to say to each other? He couldn't talk about himself, he couldn't talk about places he'd visited or things he'd seen because he didn't know, he wasn't sure.

She leaned one hip against the bed and looked at him expectantly.

"So, you noticed me because of my hat," he said when no other topic sprang to mind.

That's right," she said.

"But we didn't exchange a word?"

"Not one."

"Did I notice you?"

She looked almost embarrassed. "Kind of. I mean, our eyes did meet one time and you smiled at me."

"I bet I did," he said.

"And then everything started to happen."

"Yeah, the detective told me. Listen, be honest," he added, straightening up and trying to appear dignified. He was finding out that hospital beds weren't designed to make a man look virile and strong, and for some reason, that's how he wanted to look for her. "Did I appear to be a cowboy, you know, a real wrangler type, or did I look like someone who wanted to be a cowboy?"

"You mean, did you look like the real deal or a poser?"

"Exactly," he said, nodding.

She thought for a second. Even doing nothing but thinking looked good on her and it gave him a chance to admire the sweet curve of her lips and the shape of her earlobe.

"Well?" he prompted.

"This is just an impression, you understand. Your clothes looked expensive and new, but you wore them like you'd been born in them. To me, you looked like a guy who was on a mission."

He thought about that for a minute. "Do I look like the kind of guy who asks you to paint his portrait?"

"Not really, though everyone is different. Anyway, maybe it's not your own portrait you wanted painted. Maybe it was someone in your family. Your wife or your kids."

He held up his left hand. "No ring, no white line where one has been."

"Lots of hardworking guys don't wear rings," she told him. "Maybe you work with big equipment, like at a mill or something. And if you have a wife, she must be wondering where you are."

"One would hope," he said, and they stared at each other for a few seconds, the silence broken when the door opened and a petite blonde nurse bustled into the room.

"Time for our meds," she chirped.

Kinsey straightened up. "I'd better go," she said.

Zane heard a note of relief in her voice. How could he blame her? He caught her hand and squeezed it. "Thanks again, Kinsey."

She stared at their linked hands for a second before raising her gaze to his face. "When your memory returns, let me know, okay?" She took a pen from her purse and scrawled her phone number on the back of the detective's card.

"If you're in this neck of the woods tomorrow, drop in and say hi," he told her as she handed him the card. "For all intents and purposes, you're the only friend I have." He winced and shook his head. "Did that sound pathetic enough?"

"You're going to be fine," she told him, her dark eyes soft, her voice barely a whisper.

The nurse handed Zane a small paper sleeve with a pill nestled inside. She picked up his water glass, shook it until the ice inside rattled. "I'll go get you more water. Back in a sec." As the door closed behind her, Kinsey spared Zane one last smile and then she was gone, too.

He laid his head back against the pillow and studied the pill. He hoped this was the one that would help him sleep and he welcomed the prospect. Maybe tomorrow he'd wake up a new man…or rather the man he used to be.

But before he took that pill, he was determined to

get on his feet and walk. Something inside urged him to remain strong and vigilant. He hoped the nurse didn't give him any flak.

As KINSEY WALKED to the parking garage, she dug her cell phone from her purse. She'd silenced it when she arrived at the hospital and now she turned the sound back on.

As expected, there were several calls from Marc. Not expected were the three from her mother. Marc's messages were all the same: come back to the gallery! Her mother left no messages. And there wasn't one from Ryan, either, who always called when he got into town. The absence of that call coupled with his earlier questions made Kinsey nervous, but why? There was probably a harmless explanation, and she intended on finding out what it was. She called Ryan's cell number and left a message when the phone switched immediately to voice mail.

By now the show at the gallery was over. The crew engaged to clean up after the gala would be hard at work. Kinsey called her boss, half wondering if he'd fire her on the spot.

"It all turned out okay," Marc said. In the background, Kinsey heard voices and the tinkling of glass. It sounded as if Marc had gone out to eat after the show. "We sold eight of her paintings. Everyone loved her once she lightened up."

"I'm sorry I had to leave," Kinsey said as she unlocked her car door.

"Couldn't be helped," Marc said. His voice was muffled, as though he had covered the phone to speak to someone else, and she waited a second or two before he got back to her. "Listen, it's time to order and I'm starving. I'll see you tomorrow."

Food. When had she last eaten, lunchtime? Her stomach growled.

She contemplated calling her mother and decided against it. There was one phone in the old house. Her mother was and always had been something of a night owl, but the man she took care of would be asleep by now and Kinsey didn't want to wake him.

Those three calls were worrisome, though. Had Ryan somehow found out where she lived and, heaven forbid, had he visited her?

That would not do. If there was one thing Kinsey knew, it was her mom didn't like strangers. Frances Frost was obligated now to Mr. Dodge, but the poor old guy couldn't live forever. Sooner or later, she'd be free to wander off again and perhaps if pushed, would do so sooner rather than later.

Three calls meant something had gotten to her. Kinsey knew she'd never be able to sleep if she didn't see her mom in the flesh and make sure everything was okay. At the last second, she stopped at the small grocery located about midway between the Dodge house and the art gallery to pick up something—anything—to eat. She was met at the door by the Chinese owner, Henry Lee, who was getting ready to turn the open sign to closed.

"Can I grab something really quick?" she asked. "I'm famished."

"Sure," he said, allowing her to enter though turning the sign to discourage further patrons.

Kinsey grabbed a premade po'boy sandwich and a bottle of iced tea. A basket on the counter held bananas and apples and she added one of each.

"I heard the show was a good one," Mr. Lee said as he totaled her purchases.

"I didn't get to attend much of it," Kinsey admitted as

she handed over a twenty-dollar bill. "You heard about the accident down the street?"

"I heard one of those courier guys went berserk and drove into a crowd of people," Mr. Lee said as he counted out Kinsey's change. "I can't tell you how many times one has come close to clipping me."

Kinsey gave Mr. Lee an abbreviated rundown of what had really happened, causing the man's faint eyebrows to arch in surprise. But then his forehead wrinkled. "Did you say the victim wore a cowboy hat?"

"Yes, a tan Stetson. Why?"

Mr. Lee swore under his breath. "I knew there was something I wanted to tell you. A man was in the store earlier today. A cowboy. I swear, he stood right where you are asking questions about someone named Smith. Mary Smith. I think that was the name. Maybe it was Sherry. Anyway, I told him I didn't know anyone by that name. Then he asked about Mr. Dodge's housekeeper."

"By name?"

"No. He called her a housekeeper."

"What did you tell him?" Kinsey asked, trying to remain unflappable. She wasn't sure Henry Lee knew she was even related to the Dodge housekeeper.

"I didn't tell him anything. You have to understand that back in the day, Bill Dodge used his money to do a lot of good in this neighborhood for people like me. You'd have a hard time meeting a kinder man, and I wouldn't send trouble his way for anything. He deserves to live out his life in peace, and as far as I'm concerned, that housekeeper of his allows that to happen. Without her to shoo people away, that worthless nephew of his would walk off with half the house. Anyway, the cowboy guy asked a couple of questions. He was holding up the line in back of him and people were getting restless. He asked about other contacts he could talk to. I recalled seeing you and the housekeeper chatting with each other one day—it's the only time I ever saw that woman talk to anyone in here—so I wrote your name on a piece of paper and said you might know something. Frankly, I was trying to get rid of him. He got busy on his cell phone, I suppose looking you up, then he left. That's it."

"Did you indicate my connection to the gallery?"

"No. I just gave him your name and told him to phone you. You have to understand, it was really crowded in here. I didn't have time to be answering questions, especially when the Gastner sisters started arguing about which one of them got the last box of beignet mix. Half my customers walked out. I completely forgot about the man until right now."

"Did he mention any facts about himself? You know, like where he was from or his name, anything at all?"

"No. I don't think so. I was kind of distracted."

"You need to tell the police about this," Kinsey said. "Ask to speak to Detective Woods."

"I will."

"It could be important," she added. At least she wouldn't have to make a list of her former clients now that this issue would be cleared up. "But maybe you could leave Mr. Dodge and his housekeeper out of it."

"Gotcha," he said with a nod. "I was going to do that anyway because I don't want to trouble Bill."

She left a few minutes later, her head swimming with all that had happened today and what it could possibly mean. Back in her car, she unwrapped the po'boy and took a bite. Was it possible Zane and Ryan were somehow connected, or was it coincidence that two men had asked questions about her mom on the same day and that one wasn't responding to her calls and the other had come close to being killed?

Surely Ryan would realize Marc would report his questions to Kinsey. She was tempted to think it was out of character for Ryan to go behind her back, but truth be known, she wasn't sure exactly what kind of character he had. He'd come on pretty strong, but now that she really thought of it, he hadn't shared much about himself. She knew he was working on a levee project, but she didn't know which one.

Seamlessly, she shifted gears to think about the man she'd given the name Zane, but for a second, she couldn't get past his blue eyes. Paul Newman eyes, with the same frank evaluation going on behind them. It was pretty obvious now that he hadn't wanted Kinsey to paint his portrait because he hadn't asked Mr. Lee directly about her.

On the other hand, she knew just how she'd like to capture him if she did have the opportunity. The sexy twinkle of his eyes, the slight cleft in his chin, his cheekbones and lips. She'd pose him straight on, his rock-hard torso and broad shoulders encased in a trim T-shirt to reveal his muscular arms, head slightly bent forward, thinking about horses or tractors or engines or whatever it was a guy like him thought about when he contemplated life.

Like his wife? Like his girlfriend of thirteen years? How about his six kids?

Hey, this was a fantasy. She could give him any life she wanted because it was doubtful she'd ever see him again.

In fairness to both of them, he'd also exhibited traces of humor that appealed to her, and she hadn't missed the speculative nature of his perusal of her. She knew he was brave and selfless because of the lightning-fast way he'd stepped in to save the little girl, and she knew he was resilient because of how quickly he was attempting to put this behind him and move on. How horrible it must be for a man of action to be frozen in one place and in one moment. It must be like walking out of a warm, cozy room into a blizzard and having the door slam and lock behind you.

Bill Dodge's house was an old Victorian painted a ghastly purple that Kinsey imagined had actually improved as the sun faded the color and the trees matured and concealed the full impact of all that paint. The roofs were steep and Kinsey knew the top floor and attic were seldom used anymore. At eighty years and ailing, Mr. Dodge was too feeble to climb the stairs and slept in a downstairs room that had once been his den. Her mother slept in the housekeeper's room located behind the kitchen. The arrangement seemed to work for both of them.

Kinsey climbed the stairs onto what had once been a beautiful wraparound deck, screened in for summer sleeping when the house was too hot. The screens were torn now and the deck was wobbly. The neighborhood was still good, and while this house had probably once upon a time been a showpiece, now it was like the poor, shabby relation. In some ways, the house reminded Kinsey of an elegant woman who slept on a park bench—still lovely, but rumpled, worn, tired.

At least there was a slight breeze blowing now, making the air bearable. Kinsey wished she'd gone home first to change out of her cocktail dress into shorts because she'd known the downstairs of this house could get stifling. Hopefully, she'd be out of here and on her way home in a few minutes. The day seemed to have lasted a week and she was tired.

Before she announced her presence, she took a deep breath. Dealing with her mom was never easy, and doing so when something had prompted her to call three times suggested trouble.

As Kinsey raised her hand to knock, the door flew open.

Chapter Three

Zane. The name was growing on him, settling into the creases of his very empty brain.

Kinsey Frost's face flashed in his mind and he suspected there was a silly grin on his face as he reconstructed her. She was so darn pretty. There was something else about her, too, something kind of sweet and innocent. Or maybe his response had more to do with the fact hers was the only face he could conjure that wasn't related to people employed to take care of him. She'd come to help out of kindness and perhaps curiosity, which was totally understandable, considering they were strangers.

But, brother, she'd looked hot in that dress with her ruby lips and wavy hair....

Was she attached to someone else? For that matter, was he? On one hand, if he had a wife, hopefully she'd expect him to return to her and come looking for him when he didn't. The flip side was this pull toward Kinsey. If he had his phone he could do an online search of her name and find out more about her. Frustrated and bored, he went the old-fashioned route and found a phone book in the drawer by the bed. He just wanted to see her name, just to reassure himself he hadn't made her up. There was a map in the front of the book and he found her street, Hummingbird Drive, curious as to how far away she was.

Not more than two or three miles, he discovered, and for some reason, that created a warmth in his heart where it had only been cold before.

Hummingbird Drive. That's where a woman like her should live, he decided. Someplace that sounded as small and lovely and vibrant as she was.

Feeling way too restless to stay in bed, he'd pushed his IV stand around the looping corridors right after Kinsey left and then again after dinner when the sedative they gave him had little effect. He was supposed to spend a week here? The idea made him crazy. But if things didn't change, where exactly did he go next?

He finally decided to give sleep another chance and settled back into the bed, but the oblivion he'd so looked forward to continued to elude him. Eventually, the hospital began quieting down. A nurse gave him another pill, and it was with relief when he felt his eyelids grow heavy. He stirred sometime later, awoken by the telltale swishing of the door that alerted him someone had entered his room.

He lay there for a second, expecting a cheery voice to announce it was time to check his blood pressure or take his temperature, but the room was eerily silent and the shadows too deep to make out a human shape.

"Who's there?" he asked.

The silence remained and Zane realized he must have woken up as someone left his room. Maybe a nurse had come in to take his vitals and found him sleeping soundly. Either that, or his drugged brain had created the noise.

Settling back against his pillow, he soon fell asleep again. This time he actually had a dream with substance. A wolf chased him through tall, golden grass. He panted from the effort to escape merciless fangs. And then suddenly, he was hanging from a tree, a noose around his neck. The tree was big and black with sprawling branches that scratched at the underbelly of the clouds. Its roots spread below him like an old man's hands clinging to the cracked earth. His neck hurt. He reached up to yank the rope away. He couldn't breathe.

His eyes finally opened but the nightmare didn't stop. A man stood over his bed, two big hands around Zane's neck. The pressure increased as the man pressed down harder and harder, grunting with the effort to strangle Zane who, between blankets and tubes, couldn't move. And he couldn't budge those merciless hands from their deadly grip, thumbs pressing into his windpipe.

The light suddenly went on. "Hey! What's going on?" a female voice yelled.

The hands instantly released Zane, who grabbed at his throat and gasped for air. He caught a glimpse of a man with shaggy white hair, horn-rimmed glasses and a bushy white mustache. The guy instantly turned toward the woman and pushed her hard. She went down amid a clatter of trays and equipment and the man disappeared out of the room.

Zane finally untangled himself and got out of bed. The nurse who had been knocked down struggled to sit up. He bent to help her just as an orderly arrived. "What are you doing to her?" the orderly demanded, trying to loosen Zane's grip on the nurse's arm.

"Tom, don't be silly, he's trying to help me," the nurse said as she finally got to her feet. She was a solidly built middle-aged woman with a no-nonsense approach. Her forehead was bleeding, but she paid it no attention. Fury raged in her eyes, but her expression changed to one of horror as she looked at Zane's throat. "Oh my gosh," she said. "That man was trying to choke you." She directed her next comment to the orderly. "Don't just stand there, Tom. Alert Security. Have them call the police."

The orderly took off back down the hall.

"The man who attacked you looked like Mark Twain," the nurse said as she blotted her forehead with a cloth. Her gaze dipped to Zane's neck again. You'd better get back into bed."

Zane shook his head and wished he hadn't when the room spun. "I think I'll sit for a while. I'm not anxious to lie down again."

"The stitches on your face look red. I'm calling the doctor right now."

"Please, I'm fine."

She pushed the intercom button that hung around her neck, speaking into the unit, asking for the doctor who showed up quickly and checked Zane over. He seemed to be about Zane's age, with fine blond hair and a boyish smile. He was the same doctor who'd checked on him earlier.

"Y'all are having yourself a heck of a day," the doctor said in a rich Southern drawl.

"That's one way of putting it."

"I'll stick a bandage on those stitches, just for the night. I don't think it needs to be redone. Open your mouth now, let's take a peek at your throat."

Zane did as ordered. He'd noticed his voice was deeper than it had been and his throat felt raw. "I'll prescribe some soothing spray," the doctor said. "Not much else we can do unless you want us to up the pain medication for a while."

"No," Zane said. "Thanks, anyway."

The doctor chuckled. "I took a look at all your X-rays. You have a fair number of healed breaks. Seems like you might lead quite an active life in some capacity. But you apparently mend well, so I suppose a little bitty concussion and a torn ligament or two won't be much of an obstacle to you."

The doctor left soon after. The nurse had yet to go tend to her own cut and hovered close by, obviously distressed that something like this had happened on her watch.

"I'll get your meds," she said at last.

"No, thanks. I don't want any more medicine."

"Did you know the man who tried to choke you?" she asked.

He gave her a look and she shook her head. "Sorry. I'm kind of rattled. For a second I forgot about the amnesia."

"Don't worry about it."

Detective Woods himself showed up a little later. He listened with narrowed eyes as Zane and the nurse related what they'd seen.

"Was he apprehended?" Zane asked at last.

"No one saw anyone who even vaguely resembled the man you two have described," Woods said. "We'll take a look at hospital video…" His voice trailed off as a security guard entered the room. He carried what looked like a white mop head in his hands.

"We found this on the second floor, stuffed in a trash can," he said, and Zane realized they were staring at a wig. "We also found one of them novelty masks, you know, the kind with the bushy eyebrows and glasses and a mustache. I put it in a paper bag for you." He now raised the bag proudly.

Woods snatched the bag away. "Next time just leave things where you find them and let us take care of it," he said. "I'll get someone to go check out that can, meanwhile, please make sure no one else touches it. And put the wig in another sack. I'll need to print you."

"I guess that explains the Mark Twain vibe," the nurse said as the guard left.

"And how he was able to leave the hospital without being noticed," Woods added.

The nurse, sporting a bandage on her forehead, insisted Zane climb back into bed. He met her gaze directly. "No," he said.

"You've had a traumatic event. I know the doctor said you'll be all right, but it's time for another sleeping tablet and you need to be in bed to take it."

"No more medicine," Zane said. He knew he was drawing a line in the sand but he'd had it.

"Really, sir."

"No, listen," Zane said. "You undoubtedly saved my life tonight. I'm very grateful to you and I promise to be a good patient starting tomorrow, but for right now, I need time to sit and digest everything that's happened and I don't want to be bothered by anything or anyone. I'm fine, the doctor said so. Go coddle someone who needs it, okay? Please?"

She produced a reluctant smile. "I'll check on you in a while."

He just nodded.

Woods shook his head as the swishing door behind the nurse sent chills racing down Zane's spine. His gaze dipped to Zane's neck and back to his face. "How are you feeling?"

"A little sore, a little confused, a little scared, to tell you the truth," Zane admitted. "And mad."

"I'm going to arrange to have Security post someone on your door. You'll be safe here."

Zane had heard that before. He gave a vague nod and waited until Woods had left the room, deep in thought but with a growing sense of conviction.

He knew what he had to do.

The closet Woods indicated earlier did indeed hold

what was left of his clothing: two black boots, size eleven. That was it. Zane didn't know if his other clothes had been destroyed when he fell or confiscated by the police to search for fingerprints or some indication of the man who had attacked him on the street and stolen his identity, phone, what have you. He stuck the boots on right over the socks the hospital issued. After grabbing Woods's card and his own keys off his tray table, he opened the outside door.

The hall was clear except for a nurse engrossed in entering data into a computer mounted against the wall. Her back was to him. As quietly as he could, he pushed his IV stand the opposite direction, ignoring stiff, aching muscles and a headache he suspected would fell an ox. He'd seen a break room on one of his loops around the hospital floor and he made for that now.

His luck held. The room sported a table and chairs, a coffeemaker, fridge and microwave, but no people. He easily removed the IV from his arm and abandoned the stand in a corner. He found a pair of scrubs hanging on a hook and hastily put them on, adding a white lab coat that someone had left draped over the back of a chair. His keys and Woods's card went into the pocket. The hall was still empty. He knew the elevators were right across from the nurses' station so he used the stairwell, undoubtedly following the same path the man who had tried to choke him had taken an hour or two earlier. When he opened the door on the lobby floor, he half expected to find a security guard waiting for him, but the cavernous space was almost empty. A second later, he said good-night to the guard on duty at the exit and walked purposefully away from the hospital as though he did so every night of his life.

Was he really leaving without telling a soul where he

was going? Was this what an innocent man did after a murder attempt?

What else was he supposed to do? Docilely lay back in his bed until his room was surrounded with police and security guards and he might as well tuck himself away in a jail cell?

No way. Depending on other people didn't sit well with him, not when the stakes were high and not when another gut feeling told him he knew how to take care of himself. It would be tricky defending himself against an unknown foe. Reason said that tonight was the culmination of something ongoing. He had no recollection of where he'd been or what he'd been doing. The killer would be back unless Zane managed to disappear until his memory returned, and that's just what he planned to do.

But where does a man without a penny, without an identity, without a friend in the world, actually go?

The keys jingled in his pocket as he walked and he took them out as he passed beneath a streetlight. Red Hot. A tractor dealership in Utah. Apparently no one had recognized his photograph. But maybe seeing a living breathing human being would be different.

If he remembered his geography, Utah was about four states away from New Orleans. A couple of thousand miles or so. It would take days to hitchhike there.

Well, it wasn't as though he had anything else to do, was it? He kept walking.

KINSEY STOOD ON the front porch of the house facing her mother, Frances. The abrupt door opening had caused her to stumble backward in her heels, and now she held on to a flaking post to steady her nerves.

What a day.

"Where have you been all night?" Frances demanded. "I called three times. Why are you all dressed up?"

Kinsey knew she and her mom shared certain similarities in appearance. Both were on the petite side, though Kinsey was a couple of inches taller, both curvy, both with deep brown eyes. Kinsey's hair was her natural shade of dark brown while Frances had dyed her hair her entire life. Currently reddish-brown, silver roots showed in the center part. Over sixty now, the years had started to show in the lines on her face and the sag in her shoulders. Kinsey had never understood why her mother settled for backbreaking, low-paying employment as she was well read and intelligent. Frances had stressed that no job was more or less noble than another.

Where they differed was internal: Kinsey open and curious, Frances suspicious and very much a mind-your-own-business woman. Kinsey artistic, sketching her way through life, as proficient at mixing paints as her mother was at whipping up pancake batter.

"We had a show," Kinsey said, deciding on the spot to skip the details about the bicycle and the cowboy. "Let's go inside."

"We better not," Frances said, softly closing the door behind her. She and Kinsey were now almost lost in shadows. Just a sliver of moonlight and the light filtering through a nearby window helped them see each other. "Bill is finally asleep," she added. "He's had a tough day and I don't want to chance waking him and get him coughing again."

"Were you waiting for me? I almost had a heart attack when the door opened like that."

"I was afraid you were *him*," Frances said, glancing behind Kinsey as though expecting someone else to materialize. Kinsey actually looked over her shoulder, but there was no one there that she could see. On the other hand, she couldn't see much.

"*Him* who?" she asked, her mind leaping straight to Ryan. Had he said or done something upsetting? What? What could he possibly say or do? "What's going on?"

"It's Bill's nephew, Chad. Bill got a note from him saying that he was coming today or tomorrow. I've been on edge ever since reading it. Bill doesn't want him here."

"Oh, dear," Kinsey commiserated. She knew her mom didn't get along with Chad. "Can you call him and tell him that?"

"Neither Bill nor I know his phone number. I don't think he wants anyone to know how to reach him. That way, he can call all the shots. The last time he came, he accused me of stealing Bill's coin collection. He prowls around here making demands."

"Like what?"

"He wants me to show him all the things he remembers his uncle used to have, things like those coins and stamps and heaven knows what. And when he isn't taking inventory, he's eating, and guess who he expects to do all the cooking?"

"What can I do to help you?" Kinsey asked. For the life of her, she couldn't think of a darn thing.

Frances took a deep breath. "When I couldn't reach you, I called James Fenwick."

"Mr. Dodge's attorney?"

"Yes. You've met him."

"Guy about fifty, kind of stuffy?"

"I wouldn't describe him that way," Frances said. "He's been very kind to Bill. Lately he's been helping him go through his collection of books."

Kinsey could easily picture the room Mr. Dodge used as a bedroom. Every wall was covered with floor-to-ceiling shelves and each of those housed a wide array of books. She felt bad that she'd been less than flattering in her description of James Fenwick and now she mumbled, "That's very nice of him."

"Yes, it is. He's one of the few considerate people left on the planet. Anyway, Mr. Fenwick is out of town on business, but he'll come straight here when he drives home tomorrow. He said he'll leave before dawn."

"Good. What if I come by before work just to make sure things are okay until he gets here? Would that help?"

"Yes. Thank you. I know how busy you are."

"I wanted to ask you something, Mom," Kinsey added. "Do you know a woman named Sherry or Mary Smith?"

Her mother shook her head. "No. Why?"

There was no way in the world that Kinsey was going to add more stress to her mother. She omitted the fact that people had been asking about Bill Dodge's housekeeper— she'd tell her that tomorrow when the poor woman wasn't so overwhelmed. "No reason. I just heard the name."

Frances nodded. "Come early, okay? Bill is better in the morning and always enjoys your visits. And heaven forbid, you don't want to run into Chad."

Though Kinsey had never met Mr. Dodge's nephew face-to-face, she did know his name was Chad Dodge. If her mother was any judge at all, Chad was a greedy, demanding man. Everyone knew he was set to inherit this house when Bill Dodge died, but apparently he wasn't content to wait.

Fatigue dragged at Kinsey as she agreed to be back bright and early in the morning. Her feet in the stacked-heel sandals hurt like blazes, her hair drooped down her sticky neck. Frances stepped back to ease open the front door and listen intently, her profile vivid in the stream of light flowing from within the house. Though still attractive, the years were taking a toll and Kinsey glanced away.

"I hear Bill coughing," Frances said. "I have to go."

"I'll see you tomorrow," Kinsey said. "Try not to worry too much."

Her mother slipped inside and closed the door behind her. Kinsey heard the slide of the dead bolt. It was a relief to collapse back into her car, start the air conditioner and polish off the now-tepid iced tea.

Fifteen minutes later, it was an even greater relief to turn onto Hummingbird Drive, a charming name for a decidedly ordinary-looking road. She pulled into her parking spot behind the house and got out, juggling the apple and banana she hadn't eaten yet, longing for the privacy of her own space in the apartment above the detached garage and the cool softness of her bed.

A voice from the shadows made her drop both pieces of fruit and she whirled around to find herself facing a large man. Even as she gasped, he moved into the light and she saw who it was.

With a hand on her chest, she blinked unbelieving eyes. "Zane?"

He had knelt to retrieve the fruit. "I didn't know for sure where you lived," he said softly as he straightened up. "I knocked at the main house, but no one is home."

"My landlord is up fishing in Alaska," she said. "My place is above the garage." She couldn't make sense of his being here. "Why aren't you in the hospital? You sound funny." She saw now that he wore hospital scrubs with a white lab coat. That didn't make any sense, either.

"I wasn't followed here," he said. "I made sure of that."

"Followed? What's going on? Wait, do you remember things about yourself?"

"No," he said. "No, that's not it." He looked directly

into her eyes and her breath caught from his intense gaze that easily penetrated the dim light. "May I come inside for a few minutes?" he asked in that newly hoarse voice.

She wasn't sure what to do. It seemed insane to invite a stranger inside her home, especially one twice as big as she was. But she picked up no violent vibes directed her way. "I have to admit I'm curious about what's going on and why you're dressed like that, so I'll bite, come on in."

He followed her up the outside stairs and waited while she unlocked the flimsy little lock on her door, which, come to think of it, needed to be changed to a stronger one. When she turned to face him in the light of the room, she gasped again.

"What happened to your throat?" she asked, eyes wide.

He didn't answer immediately. His gaze seemed to fly around the room, from one wall to the next, one painted canvas after another, as though he couldn't quite take them all in at one time.

All those paintings in so little space probably came across as too much, but when you had a lot of paintings and limited wall space, they tended to add up.

"Did you create all of these?" he asked.

"Well, not the landscape, that's a Vincent van Gogh print, and the lilies are Monet…well, all the people, yes."

"You're amazing," he said, his gaze finally settling back on her face. "Who are all these people?"

She shrugged, unwilling to be distracted. "What happened to your neck?" she asked again.

He set the fruit on her table, then ran a hand through his hair. He seemed to exist in a perpetual state of sexy. It was just the way he was put together, the way he moved, his mannerisms and the expression in his eyes. But now bone-weary fatigue vied with that innate magnetism and seemed to win. "Mind if I sit down?" he asked.

"Help yourself," she said as she locked the front door.

He settled on her lime-green love seat. The apartment consisted of a kitchen/living area and a small bedroom/bath. Most of time it seemed pretty roomy, but Zane was at least six foot two and possessed a kind of commanding presence. She'd noticed this hours earlier when he stood on the sidewalk. "Would you like something cold to drink?" she offered as she started the electric fan in the window.

"Some water would be great," he said, and she fetched him a glass before perching on a counter stool.

After finishing his drink, he started in on his story. When he got to the part about waking up to find someone choking him, she almost fell off the stool.

"It has to be the same person as this afternoon," she said. "I'll never forget the brazen way he pushed you. Is the nurse okay?"

"She's fine."

"Thank heavens she came into your room." With a shudder, she added, "I can't believe you took out your own IV." She and needles were not the best of friends.

He rubbed his face with his hands as though trying to stay awake. It was the middle of the night by this time and she sympathized and shared his fatigue although his presence had driven most of hers away.

"And you have no idea what he looked like because of the disguise?"

He nodded. "That's right. Even his size was hard to gauge because it all happened so fast."

"But why did you leave the hospital? I don't get it. Woods told you he planned on posting a guard."

"I'm not entirely positive why I left," Zane said. "I guess I thought my chances were better on my own than being stuck in that place. Besides, what did I do to get in this kind of trouble? I'd kind of like to find that out before the police do. Anyway, I didn't know if they'd actually let me leave if I asked—I still don't know whose going to pay my bill, for instance. So I sneaked away and that's also more or less why I ended up at your house. I was going to borrow your phone and call Woods to try to explain, but I just decided against it."

"Why?"

"I guess I don't want him bugging you, and I don't want him trying to get me back into the hospital. He's a smart guy. He'll see my boots are gone and talk to the guard on duty and learn I walked away out of choice and he'll put two and two together. Maybe I'll call when I get out of town."

She nodded. His logic sounded reasonably sane to her. Well, at least as sane as escaping police protective custody to take your chances with a man who tried to kill you—twice.

"But I do need to borrow twenty dollars," he added. "I'll pay you back, I swear. If I'm going to hitchhike to Utah, I'm going to need something to eat along the way and I don't have a penny. Eventually I can probably hock my boots—well, anyway, how about it?"

"Of course," she said immediately. "The money is yours. And I'll pack you a lunch to take with you."

"That would be great. Thank you."

"Turkey on sour dough?"

"Anything you have," he said, "will be appreciated."

"I'm going to change clothes first, then I'll make you a lunch. Are you hungry now?"

"No."

Biting her lip, she added, "Zane, I should tell you that I found out why you had my name in your pocket. The grocer down the block from the gallery gave it to you because you were in the store asking about someone named Sherry or Mary Smith. Is there any chance that rings a bell?"

"None."

She hit her forehead with her palm. "Why didn't I think of the internet?" She retrieved her phone. A moment later, she shook her head. "Get this. There are over forty-seven million hits for Mary Smith." She tapped the tiny electronic keypad again. "Over six million for Sherry Smith. Without an age or a career or a location, it's impossible." She fooled around a little more with the search engine, typing Mary Smith, New Orleans, and the same for Sherry Smith. Nothing that appeared relevant in any way showed up.

"Well, Mr. Lee promised he'd call Detective Woods and tell him about your being in his store," she said with a sigh. She didn't mention the fact that she'd asked Mr. Lee to keep Bill Dodge and his housekeeper out of it because she felt guilty about that. Zane needed all the help he could get and she had no right to deny him the turning of every stone. She just needed some time to try to make sense of things.

She closed the bedroom door behind her and quickly slipped out of her clothes, exchanging the dress for shorts and a T-shirt. She left her feet bare, splashed water on her face and went back into the main room where she found Zane still staring at the paintings that surrounded him.

"Aren't you kind of warm in all those clothes?" she asked, and then felt her cheeks grow pink at the way those words could be taken.

He apparently didn't read anything in her voice but what was there—concern for his comfort. "No, I'm fine."

She sat down on the stool for a moment. "Zane, right after you asked about the Smith woman, you were hurt by an impulsive crazy person. I bet if we asked Woods where the real courier was robbed, it would turn out to be close to the grocery store. I think your attacker was in that store. Maybe he followed you." She stopped short of finishing the sentence—*or maybe you came in together.*

Was that possible?

"I was also hurt right after the grocer gave me your name," Zane said, smothering a yawn and apologizing for it. "I can't make sense of any of it and that's what's so frustrating."

"It'll come. I'll go make the sandwiches." She padded into the adjoining kitchen and got to work. She made him two generous sandwiches, found an ice pack in the freezer and a bottle of sweet tea in the refrigerator, included the apple and the banana she'd bought earlier and threw in a few granola bars for good measure. She'd been to the bank earlier that day so she knew she still had a couple of ATM twenties in her wallet.

When she turned to look back in the living room, she found Zane had fallen asleep with his head thrown back, his hands lying on the cushion next to his thighs, his legs sprawled in front of him as though he'd finally surrendered to his long, arduous day. His breathing seemed steady and deep and, without the impact of his gaze, he appeared wan and worn out. She bent to shake his shoulder and he turned slightly at her touch, his breath warm against her hand, but didn't waken.

Up close like this, the bruises on his throat looked like bloody fingerprints, red and ugly, grotesque in their cruelty and intent. A bright red dot of blood had seeped through the bandage over the stitches on his cheek.

She straightened up without touching him again, staring down at him for a moment, moved by his plight, touched by his decency and scared for his life. And totally intrigued.

How were they connected, where did her mother fit into this? Did Ryan have something to do with what happened? Could he have been the phony cyclist? She didn't think so, but was she positive?

No answers, not tonight, anyway. She quietly put the bag of food in the refrigerator, dimmed the lights and with one last look at the gorgeous man asleep on her love seat, closed the bedroom door behind her.

Five minutes later, she slept.

Chapter Four

The sun was just peeking in the window when Zane sat up straight. The room did a one-eighty and he grabbed his head as he blinked a few times. Where in the hell was he?

The dozens of pairs of eyes staring endlessly from the paintings covering the walls brought the last few hours crashing back like a rogue wave on a beach. Unfortunately, that's all that came back. His mind was still as empty as a purloined vault. It looked as if his loss of memory wasn't the overnight variety.

He glanced at the closed bedroom door behind which he imagined Kinsey slept, turning suddenly when a noise at the front door jarred him fully awake. He was on his feet and ready for action when Kinsey let herself inside, stopping abruptly when she saw his aggressive stance.

"Sorry," he said, relaxing his muscles. "I guess I'm a little jumpy." It was the first time he'd spoken since waking. His voice was as raspy as it had been the night before and each word seemed to rake the inside of his throat.

"You didn't wake up when I left," she explained, the alarm fading from her eyes. Dressed in a cool blue wispy blouse and white pants, she looked as though she belonged on top of a mountain or in a meadow or something. He could only imagine what he looked like.

"I went out to buy coffee at the little place on the

corner," she said as she offered him a twelve-ounce container with a heady aroma. "I thought you might appreciate a cup. I'm afraid I have to be at my mother's place in thirty minutes, which means we have to leave here pretty soon."

With heartfelt thanks, he accepted the proffered coffee and took a deep whiff as he slipped off the plastic sipping lid. She sat down on a nearby chair and stared at him a few seconds. "How are you feeling? How's your throat?"

"I'll live," he said.

"I hate to say this, but those bruises look worse today than they did last night. And the abrasions on your forehead and cheek…well, anyway, it might be hard to win the trust of a Good Samaritan who gets little more than a glimpse to form an opinion of you."

"You're referring to motorists who might be going my way?"

"Yes."

He touched his neck. Neither the scrubs nor the lab coat he'd filched from the hospital had a collar he could use to conceal the marks his attacker had left. "I don't have much choice," he said. "Speaking of that, do you think you could drop me off close to the interstate on your way to your mother's house? It might be easier to hitch a ride from there. I'll stand somewhere where people can get a good long look at me and sense what a stalwart fellow I am."

"I have an idea," she said, leaning forward. "Let me loan you the money for a bus ticket."

Nothing about her, from her old car to this barely furnished apartment to the decent but inexpensive clothes on her back, suggested Kinsey was rolling in dough. "That's okay," he said softly. "I don't want to go further in debt. The twenty you're going to loan me will get me by."

She nodded, perhaps relieved but too nice to show it.

She took a sip of her coffee and spoke again. "I have something I have to tell you," she said, sliding him a nervous glance.

"Is there time? Shouldn't we be leaving?"

"Yes, but you have to know this. Remember last night when I told you the man at the grocery store was going to call Detective Woods and tell him that you'd been in that day asking about a woman?"

"Sure," he said.

"What I didn't tell you was that he said you also asked about an elderly man in the neighborhood. Specifically, you asked about this man's housekeeper."

"I wonder what that was about," he said, noting the way she avoided his gaze and clutched the paper cup in her hands. Finally, she looked at him again. "I asked Henry, he's the grocer, not to tell the police about the housekeeper."

"Why?"

"Because she's my mother."

He set his cup down on the chest Kinsey used as a coffee table. "I don't quite understand," he said.

"And I don't have time to explain," she said, her expression worried now. "Anyway, Henry said you asked about the housekeeper right after you asked about Smith. I mentioned this to my mother last night and she claims she's never heard of anyone with that name and I believe her, but that's why you had my name. Henry either knows Mom and I are related or thinks we're friends. He gave you my name to get you out of his store because you were holding up the line and he needed to break up a fight over a box of beignet mix."

Zane stared at her a minute. Was this for real? It sounded like something out of an old sitcom. "Okay," he said at last. "So all that happened, but why can't your mother just tell Detective Woods what she told you, she doesn't know the woman, end of conversation."

"You don't know my mother," Kinsey said.

"Obviously."

"And I don't have time to try to explain her now." She glanced at her watch, and stood abruptly. "It's getting late," she said as her phone rang. She dug into the small purse she wore across her body and emerged with the cell phone. She scanned the caller screen impatiently and he thought he saw disappointment on her face. The look disappeared as she hit a button and slipped the device back in her bag. "That means you have to go, too. I can't leave you here—"

"I know," he said as he stood. His body screamed in protest at the abrupt action, reminding him of what he'd been through fewer than twenty-four hours before. "Do we have enough time for me to splash some cold water on my face?" he managed to say, his voice more hoarse than ever.

"Of course," she said.

At her bedroom door, he turned. "I'd like to go with you to your mother's place."

"No way," she said, her attention back on the phone.

"Kinsey, think about it. Maybe your mother knows me or of me. Maybe that's why I asked about her. Or how about the guy she works for? Maybe one of them will recognize me, give me a name and a family, an identity."

"That's not likely," Kinsey said, shaking her head.

"But it's the only lead besides that tractor dealership in Utah. I have to try."

Her nod seemed reluctant. He continued on his way before she could change her mind.

THE CALL HAD BEEN from Marc. It wasn't uncommon for her boss to call her with a short list of errands to perform when she opened the gallery, but right now that prospect didn't interest her.

Ryan still hadn't returned her call. She'd looked up his company's number before leaving for the coffee that morning and programmed it into the phone. The original plan had been to call after she dropped Zane off by the interstate, but his announcement that he was going all the way with her nixed that.

She punched in the New York number now. It was answered on the first ring by an actual human being, which seemed amazing considering it was a Saturday morning. The greeting was breezy but followed by a long pause when Kinsey asked for Ryan Jones. The man on the phone finally said, "Would you repeat that name?"

Kinsey did, with the explanation that Ryan was in New Orleans that weekend working on their levee project.

Another pause. "I'm sorry," the man said. "I don't know anyone named Ryan Jones."

"He's one of your engineers," she protested.

"I'm actually the owner of this business," he explained. "I came in early today to work on…well, you don't care about that. Listen, we're not all that big an operation, so I know every one of my employees. There is no one here named Ryan Jones."

Kinsey thought for a second. "Maybe he's with your New Orleans section."

"What New Orleans section? We don't have one."

"You have no contracts down here at all?"

"None. I'm afraid someone has given you false information."

"Is there another A and P Engineering firm in New York?"

"No," he said gently. "Just this one. I'm sorry."

"One more thing. Do you know someone named Ryan Jones in another capacity, like a neighbor or someone at a club or maybe a business associate, you know, something like that?"

He seemed to think for a few seconds. "No," he finally said. "Sorry."

Kinsey murmured something and clicked off the phone, glancing up when Zane cleared his throat. He took one look at her face and moved toward her. "Are you okay?" he asked.

She stared into his crystal-blue eyes. Ryan had lied to her about his job and probably everything else. He'd asked questions about her mother and then he'd disappeared right around the same time that Zane took the stage. But it hadn't been Ryan who had pushed Zane— she was almost positive of that, even though she hadn't seen the attacker's face. Ryan was too tall to be that man and he didn't move in the same way.

So perhaps Ryan was Zane's adversary. Or were they in cahoots? If so, in what capacity and most important, why did her mother seem to be in the middle of it? She pulled up the pictures she'd taken, almost all of paintings she'd admired or people whose faces had intrigued her. She finally found what she was looking for, a photo of a painting of the Mississippi River. She'd taken the picture at a street show a few weeks before. Ryan had walked into the frame and she'd inadvertently caught his profile.

She handed the phone to Zane. "Does this man look familiar to you? Could he have been the man in the hospital, for instance?"

Zane studied the image for a second. "I can't tell. You think he's connected to me?"

"I don't know. Maybe," she answered honestly as she took her car keys from her bag.

"Is he someone important?"

She shook her head. "I don't know that, either."

KINSEY PULLED UP in front of the garish Victorian and parked behind a blinding-white luxury sedan. She had a feeling Bill Dodge's attorney had arrived at the house first and couldn't help wondering in what shape she would find her mother.

"This is some house," Zane said as he looked around.

"Yeah."

"It doesn't really fit the neighborhood anymore, does it?"

"Not really," Kinsey said, but she was distracted. Nerves and trepidation made her throat dry. "The land it's sitting on is the real value."

"I bet," Zane said.

They'd climbed the rickety stairs by now and Kinsey grabbed Zane's arm. "Do me a favor, okay?"

"Anything."

"Just go along with whatever story pops into my head to explain the fact you're in hospital scrubs."

"What are you going to say?"

"I haven't the slightest idea," she admitted. Maybe they should come up with a plan. She was about to suggest this when the door opened and they found themselves face-to-face with an average-sized man in his midfifties with perfectly styled graying hair. He held a briefcase in one hand. They caught him midsentence and he stopped talking at once.

"Hello, Mr. Fenwick," Kinsey said.

"Kinsey, you're looking well." James Fenwick's gaze left her face immediately and traveled up to Zane's. Kinsey had called him dour the night before, but now she looked at his tanned skin and the expectant smile curving his lips and he seemed a little less formidable than he had before.

Kinsey's mother was right behind Fenwick. She, too,

looked at Zane, but instead of curiosity, her expression reflected fear. As long as Kinsey had been aware of her mother's emotional state of being, meeting strangers was always fraught with this initial reaction of distrust.

"Who is this?" Frances Frost demanded, narrowing her eyes and frowning. "What's wrong with his neck?"

"I had a riding accident yesterday," Zane explained as his hand flew to his throat. "While playing polo. Anyway, my horse's flying hooves almost took my head off." As Kinsey gaped at this explanation, Zane cleared his throat. "You look familiar. Have me met before, Mrs. Frost?"

"No," she said firmly. "I've never seen you before right now. Your clothes...are you a doctor?"

"Yes," he said easily. "Yes, I am."

"What are you doing here with Kinsey?"

"Zane is a neighbor," Kinsey said. "He needed a ride to work this morning."

Frances waved all this aside. "Come with me," she told Zane. "Bill's cough is worse. He won't let me call his doctor, but since you're a doctor and you're here anyway, you can take a look at him."

"Now, Frances," James Fenwick said gently, "this young man isn't Bill's doctor. Bill's situation is too serious to fool around with, you know that."

"Yes, I do know that. But Bill's doctor isn't here and this man is." Kinsey could tell her mother was digging in her heels.

"I don't have any...equipment," Zane said, "but I'll be happy to talk to him if it will make you feel better."

The two of them disappeared inside the house.

"Your mother is a woman of strong conviction," Fenwick said.

"You mean she's stubborn."

"Not a bad trait in this day and age when everyone rolls

over." He seemed to smile at Kinsey's mom's quirks. "Is your friend really a doctor? I didn't want to say anything, but it looks as though he slept in his scrubs and he hasn't shaven. What's his name? Zane what?"

"Doe," Kinsey said. "Zane Doe. And he looks a little worn-out because he worked half the night and has to go back and his shower was broken." She stopped herself before throwing in any more made-up details. "So, Mr. Fenwick, have you talked to Bill and my mother about Bill's nephew's impending visit? They were both pretty upset about it yesterday."

"I did talk to them," Fenwick said as he checked his watch. "I'm going to have to run. I have a meeting in thirty minutes. Don't worry about your mother. She'll call me the moment Chad appears and I'll be back here within fifteen minutes. I won't allow that rascal to make trouble, I promise you that."

"I know you're good to Bill," Kinsey said.

"Yes," he said, and then added in a soft voice, "And I don't like to see Frances upset. She's a special lady."

Flabbergasted, Kinsey nodded.

"Well, nice to see you, Kinsey, take care, say goodbye to your mother for me, will you?"

Kinsey nodded again. As she crossed the porch, she heard Fenwick's car door slam. The sound of his revving engine followed her inside.

She found everyone in the den that Bill Dodge now used as his bedroom. The walls were still lined with row upon row of books, though there were also signs that sorting had begun. Kinsey knew from the times she'd studied the spines that just about every area of interest was covered. Many small libraries would like to have such collections.

Bill had mounted her Christmas gift to him on a prize

piece of wall real estate, one of the few empty spots to be found. It was a painting Kinsey had done using an old photograph of Mr. Dodge back when he fished the river. In it, he wore a hat punctured by dozens of fishing flies and he carried a pole, but she'd also tucked a small book into his breast pocket with only the word *Huckleberry* showing. Kinsey felt very honored that he liked the painting so much.

"There's my girl," Bill said as she entered the room. "Frances was just going to get me and the good doctor a cup of herbal tea. Sit down here and keep me company while she's gone."

The pictures on the wall showing him standing next to various dignitaries through the years revealed Bill Dodge had once been a tall man with hair as dark as Zane's was now. Time and illness had softened all the edges, wrinkled his skin and faded his vibrancy.

None of that affected the kindness of his expression. Having never known her father and growing up with a paucity of adult men in her life, Kinsey enjoyed the way Bill Dodge doted on her. She sat by his chair, marveling that anyone who looked so frail could project so much curiosity. His freckled skull sported few hairs, his eyebrows had all but disappeared, but the lively depths of his blue eyes revealed an active mind and inquisitive nature. She knew he'd started his adult life as a fireman, retired from that, went to college, became a teacher and then graduated from that into real estate before running for city council. He'd been a major influence in one small pocket of New Orleans's history. He'd fished, sailed, bound books and dabbled in glass blowing. In short, he'd been quite the Renaissance man.

"I'll help with the tea," Zane offered.

Frances tried to wave him away, but he blithely

pretended he didn't know what she was doing and followed her from the room.

"Are you terribly upset about your nephew coming for a visit?" Kinsey asked, not really trusting her mother's take on the situation. Frances regarded a door-to-door salesman as an interloper. A houseguest must really annoy her.

"Well, you see," Bill said, pausing to cough into a handkerchief. Her mother and Mr. Fenwick were right, the cough sounded ominous. "I hadn't seen Chad in years and years when he showed up here and tried playing the doting nephew." More coughs racked his frail body and Kinsey put out a hand to grip his shoulder. He put his head back down on the pillow and closed his eyes.

"He's your sister's son, right?" she said, hoping to do all the talking so he wouldn't have to. "Mom said she was almost a generation younger than you and that after she died, her husband moved away with their son."

"He came for visits…once in a while," Bill said. He opened his eyes. "I have something for you." He gestured toward the far wall. "Package in the top drawer of that old chest. Fetch it for me."

Kinsey did as he asked, finding what he wanted tucked away under clothes she'd never seen him wear. She handed it to Mr. Dodge before reclaiming her seat. "Why are we whispering?" she asked.

"Because I want to give you this without your mother around," he said as he presented the tissue-wrapped package back to Kinsey.

"Why?" Kinsey asked as she took it.

"I don't want to get into an argument with James Fenwick. Just not strong enough to fight all of them. He insists we catalogue everything. And if anyone tells Chad that I'm giving things away, he'll turn more belligerent than ever. He's got quite the temper. Best I just do what I want without anyone throwing in their two cents."

This long speech seemed to have exhausted him again. Kinsey suspected that he'd probably given away the coin collection that Chad accused her mother of stealing. Kinsey instinctively felt her mother could fight her own battles and that Bill Dodge was the one who deserved to live the rest of his life in whatever way he wanted.

"Do you think Mom rats on you to your lawyer?" she asked.

"Of course not," he scoffed, and then coughed again. To Kinsey's untrained ears, the cough sounded deep and disturbing and she suddenly understood her mother grabbing onto Zane when she was told he was a doctor. "But I know she occasionally confides in him," Bill added with a wheeze. "She could mention the fact I've been giving my books to special friends and then Fenwick would start in. I don't have an argument in me. Go ahead, unwrap it."

Touched by the very fact he was bestowing an obviously important possession to her, she lifted the tissue to find a small five-by-seven-inch book with gold-leaf writing on the cover. Kinsey ran her fingers over the embossed title as she read it aloud, *"Female Artists of the Twentieth Century."* She opened the pages to find reproductions of works and biographies of artists she'd both heard of and never knew existed. The edges of the paper were gilded while the binding was constructed of spectacular red leather embossed with tiny artists' pallets. "This is beautiful," she said, raising her gaze to meet Bill Dodge's. He smiled with joy. "Thank you, Mr. Dodge. I'll treasure this."

"You'll be in the next edition if they make one," he said. "Front and center, Kinsey Frost, portraitist extraordinaire." They heard footsteps approaching and he added,

"Tuck it in your handbag now. Our secret. Man my age needs a secret or two."

Kinsey hastily closed the book and squeezed it into her small cross-body bag as Bill leaned close with a couple more whispered questions. "Is that young man really a doctor?"

Kinsey shook her head. "How did you know?"

"I've been around a lot of doctors lately. Why is he dressed like he is?"

"He has no other clothes," she said and wondered what Bill would make of that comment.

"So he's in trouble," Bill stated.

She nodded.

He sat up straighter as the other two entered the room. "Took you long enough," he said, but the comment was followed by an attack of coughing that brought Frances racing to his side.

"No offense to you, Doctor," she said to Zane, "but I don't think Mr. Dodge's cough has a thing to do with allergies like you said. I'm calling Bill's real doctor."

"That's a good idea," Zane said as Frances left the room. He looked at Bill and added, "Sorry, sir, but she's right, you know."

Bill's eyes were watering. His breathing sounded ragged and his face was pale.

"I suppose she'll do what she wants anyway," Bill said. Zane asked to use a bathroom and Kinsey told him where it was. As soon as he left, Bill caught Kinsey's hand in his. His voice had withered considerably and now the whisper didn't seem so much a choice as a necessity. "Go back to that same dresser…bottom drawer…jeans, shirts… you know, for your friend. About his size…once upon a time. Take what you want…I won't need them…again."

"Thank you," Kinsey said and did as he requested. The

clean clothes were all neatly folded and she haphazardly chose several items and stacked them on a chair. The long dialogue had wiped Bill out and she helped him sit up in bed to ease his breathing.

Eventually her mother arrived. "The doctor said to call an ambulance and take him to the hospital. He'll meet us there."

The next half hour passed in a blur. Zane disappeared with some of the clothes and returned looking informal but spectacular in faded jeans and a black shirt. They stowed the rest of the items in a small satchel that Frances pointed out during one of her trips between the front door and Bill's bedside. She completely ignored the fact that Zane had morphed from a crumpled "doctor" to a regular guy.

"I feel funny leaving my mother in the lurch," Kinsey told Zane. "I'd better drive her to the hospital and stay with her until Bill is safe."

"Yes, of course," Zane said.

"I can drop you off."

"I'd appreciate that. The hospital isn't far from the highway, is it?"

"No."

"Then just take me there and I'll walk over." He looked straight into her eyes. The power of all that dazzling blue made her heart race. "This means goodbye."

"Not the way I wanted," she said. She hated any goodbye, there had been far too many in her life, but this one, done prematurely and in haste, really sucked. "Be careful," she added. "Let me know when you remember who you are. Promise me."

"I promise," he said, his fingers grazing her cheek.

They were alone except for Bill, whose eyes were closed. Kinsey was surprised and yet not surprised when

Zane leaned down and touched her lips with his. Her racing heart almost exploded.

"Just as ripe and juicy as I knew they would be," he whispered, and kissed her briefly again. They stepped apart as the sound of the ambulance siren exploded into their consciousness.

THEIR NEXT GOODBYE was done on the run. Kinsey was spared watching Zane walk away as her mother propelled her into the hospital. They found seats in the waiting room. While Frances tapped her foot and sighed repeatedly, Kinsey found a corner and called Marc, explaining where she was and that she might not make it in to work at all.

"No problem," he told her. "Violet and Brent can cover for you. We'll see you when we see you."

"It might be a few days."

"Like I said, no problem."

Kinsey looked at her mother as she walked back to her seat. Her mother's gaze was fixed on the closed steel doors of the emergency room. She looked as frightened as she did worried and, for the first time, Kinsey wondered if it ever occurred to her mom that when Bill died, she'd be out of work and a home. Of course, it must have. It would hardly be the first time one of her jobs ended and she had to start over again. How did she do it?

After four hours of endless waiting interspersed with occasional assurances that things were progressing and they should be patient, a doctor finally appeared and explained that Bill's condition had stabilized but he wanted to keep him overnight. Frances could see him once they transferred him upstairs.

Kinsey was preparing herself for an all-night waiting-room vigil when the door blew open and James Fenwick appeared. He pocketed the cell phone he'd been holding to his ear. "I've just heard, I've been in and out of meetings," he said, grasping Frances's elbows. "Is he okay?"

She explained what they had learned and he assured her that he was there to stay. When she expressed concern about Bill's nephew arriving to an empty house, Fenwick shook his head. "The place is locked, right? If he finds his way in, so be it. We'll worry about Chad when we have the time. Okay?"

Frances slumped against James as she nodded. She appeared close to tears. Kinsey was about to offer comfort when Fenwick's arm stole around her mother's shoulder and he squeezed her. She smiled up at him and in that instant, Kinsey knew her mother had finally created a family of sorts that didn't require Kinsey's total attention. The thought was amazing: a little sad in a weird way, and joyous in a hundred others. It seemed a trumpet should blare or confetti should fall—something, anything, to mark this totally unaddressed but major transformation. Hallelujah.

Kinsey touched her mom's arm and got a distracted glance. "Oh, Kinsey. James is here."

"I see that," Kinsey said.

"You can leave if you have other obligations," Fenwick said. "Your mother won't be alone."

"I know you're incredibly busy," her mother said. "There must be a million things you need to do. Don't worry about me."

"Okay," Kinsey said. "Tell Bill not to scare me like that again, okay?"

"I will. And thank you for sitting here with me so long."

"I love you, Mom."

The two older people declared their intention to find the cafeteria for a late lunch before going to Bill's room.

Kinsey declined the offer to join them and, feeling lighter than she had in so long she couldn't remember, left the emergency room.

And then she remembered that Zane was gone, this time for good.

Chapter Five

Zane's left leg throbbed. When he'd changed into Mr. Dodge's old clothes, he'd found bruises from his knee on up. That made sense, considering he'd landed on that side when he was flung into the street. But now, between walking and standing so long, his endurance was spent.

What was taking so long? Maybe he should move on to plan B.

Instead, he found a nearby patch of green and lowered himself onto the grass, using a landscape rock to lean against. Not bad, he thought, better than standing with nothing to look at but pavement and cars. The sun felt good on his battered cheek, seemed to sink down under his skin and massage the dull ache in his head and the wounded nerves of his neck and shoulders. He closed his eyes and tried to think positive thoughts.

He must have dozed, for suddenly he was awake and looking up at the only face on the planet he wanted to see.

Kinsey's eyes were huge as she studied him. "What are you doing here at the hospital? You should be all the way out of Louisiana by now."

He got to his feet as gracefully as he could manage. "I couldn't leave," he said, brushing himself off. He'd moved too fast and his head spun. Kinsey shot out an arm to steady him and he winced. "How is Bill?"

"Holding his own," she said. "Have you been out here all this time?"

"Yeah. I started walking back to the highway and then I suddenly knew I had to make sure you didn't need help before I left. You've done so much for me."

She smiled, hugged him briefly and stepped back. That brief hug was the first time she'd put her arms around his torso, the first time she'd been that close to the strong maleness of his whole body, and she was suddenly burning with awareness. "Why didn't you come inside? Why stay out here where it's hot and sultry?"

"That particular hospital holds some unpleasant memories for me. I like being outside better."

She opened her car. "Get in, I'll give you a lift to the road." Eventually, she merged into the far-right lane. "Remember, you promised to let me know when you figure out who you are," she said as the on-ramp approached.

"Pull over to the side of the road," he said. "No reason for you to go any farther. I can walk up the ramp." He hoped his voice didn't reveal how reluctant he was to leave her side. Hot pangs of loss ate away at his stomach as he grabbed the bag with all the grub she'd fixed him the night before, and turned back for a last look at her. To him she always seemed full of light and now he realized she was achingly familiar in a way no other person was. He fought the idea that it wasn't just because he could remember no one else. It was her. "Here I am thanking you again," he said and hoped she blamed his thick voice on his battered throat. "I don't know what I would have done without you."

"Another goodbye," she whispered. "Our third or fourth."

He was surprised to hear in her voice the same longing he felt inside, to belong, to connect. "Then we won't say goodbye this time," he said.

She reached across the space between them with both hands and gently turned his collar up. "That looks better," she whispered. "Good luck. Be careful."

"You, too," he said.

A smile trembled on her lips. Her lips, the same succulent red lips that had been driving him crazy since the first moment he laid eyes on her.

This time, she was the one who initiated a kiss, but this one wasn't quite as chaste as earlier. This one echoed the same notes of longing her voice had contained and he responded to it at once.

She couldn't know how much he had anticipated this moment when they kissed for real, she couldn't possibly guess at the thunderclap her lips set loose in his brain. He kissed her back, again and again, lost in the gentle but blinding tension, the noise in his head deafening him to everything.

What was he doing? He had to act now or he'd chicken out. He tore himself away from her and all but threw himself out of her small car. The door slammed closed behind him as, without another word, he purposefully put one foot in front of the other, not looking back, not daring to linger.

KINSEY SAT IN the car and watched Zane's retreat. Her lips still burned. Damn, that man tasted and kissed just as good as she'd known he would.

Did he realize that he limped? Did he have any idea how the past events had compromised his voice and his endurance? He hadn't mentioned a thing about the vicious attempts on his life; surely he hadn't dismissed them.

But what if he had? What if the man who had tried to kill him had been watching them all morning?

Don't be crazy, she scolded herself. Zane had been a perfect target in the parking lot for hours. He'd slept through her approach. If she'd been the bad guy, he'd be dead.

Unless the parking lot was too public for something like that. What if he was biding his time? What if he sat nearby right now, in one of the cars parked right over there or hovering unseen in the traffic behind her? What if he was just waiting for her to pull away and then he would pick up Zane. And Zane, who had never seen the man's face, would climb in to meet his doom. That would be it, third time's a charm, the culprit could be successful.

The premonition was too great to ignore. She put the car in gear. As she drove up the ramp, she checked her rearview mirror. Every other car now seemed to hold a predator. At the sound of her approaching engine, Zane turned with his thumb out. He looked startled when they made eye contact and she slowed down. He opened the passenger door and stared at her.

"What—"

"Get in," she said.

"But—"

"There's a truck coming. Please, just get in."

He did as she asked and she sped up as the truck whizzed around her while blaring its horn.

"Kinsey, what are you doing?" Zane asked.

"I'm driving you to Utah." She darted him a glance. "You're in no shape to hitchhike. There are coated aspirin in the glove box and a bottle of water in with your food unless you drank it already."

"I have some left," he said. He found the medicine and shook three out into his hand. After he swallowed them he stared at her. "Be honest with me. Are you doing this because of our kisses?"

"No," she scoffed. "Good heavens, I'm not fourteen."

He sighed impatiently and she took the hint and started talking. "You were asking about my mother before you were pushed into the street. What you don't know is that my boyfriend of sorts was also asking about my mother that same afternoon on that same street."

"You have a boyfriend?"

"A sort of boyfriend. Except now I find that he isn't what he said he was."

"How does he explain himself?"

"Who knows? He isn't answering my calls."

After a lengthy pause, he sighed. "If my head didn't hurt so much, I'd shake it in befuddlement."

"There's a connection of some kind, I mean, between you and the man I know as Ryan Jones. At least I think there is. And my mother, of all people, seems to be at the epicenter of it all."

"So that's why you're driving me to Utah. Listen, why don't you just foot me a bus ticket like you offered. Sooner or later, my memory will return and I'll pay you back."

"Is the thought of my company for a couple of days really so terrible?" she asked with a quick glance.

"You know it's not that," he said. "This is just too big a commitment considering…everything."

"But it's not, Zane, that's what I'm trying to tell you. Somehow I feel that your destiny is entwined with mine. Let me come with you."

"What about your job?"

"The gallery doesn't have anything major planned for two weeks. Marc will be okay, I'm not his only employee. Besides, I just have to do this. I have to protect my mother."

"By leaving her all alone in New Orleans?"

Kinsey shook her head. "Mr. Fenwick seems kind of attentive."

He rubbed his forehead without comment.

"You have to understand," she added. "I spent most of my life in very close contact with my mother and there were no men allowed. Zero, zilch. I thought it was because she'd been so devastated by my father's death that she'd sworn off love."

"How did he die, Kinsey?"

"In a bus crash up in Maine. He was coming home from a construction job. His body was burned beyond recognition. Mom said they had to use dental records to identify him. It took a few weeks, so the accounts all list him as unidentified. That seemed like a terrible injustice when I was a kid. Anyway, she finally agreed to take me to the site when I was about fourteen. I'm not sure what I expected to find all those years later, just some kind of remembrance for my dad and the other ten people who died that day. But, of course, there was no trace of the tragedy." Her heart flip-flopped in her chest. Was she still holding on to that moment of childish disappointment?

"I'm sorry," he said gently.

She smiled. "It all happened a long time ago. I built him up in my head—there were so few mementos of him, as though Mom couldn't bear to be reminded—anyway, and now here she is acting coy with another man. It's a little jarring."

"Does it bother you?"

"No. It's her life. She deserves to live it after devoting so many years to me." She sighed and added, "That's enough about my history."

"Well, we sure as hell won't have much of a conversation if we depend on what I know of my past to keep us occupied," he said.

She cast him a thoughtful look. "How does it feel to leave New Orleans? Like a giant weight is being lifted from your shoulders?"

She saw him shrug and it looked good on him, just the way everything else did. A shrug called attention to his shoulders and they looked outstanding encased in the black cotton of his new-to-him shirt. Add the self-deprecating smile that lit his eyes until they glimmered with blue light and she was mesmerized. "Not really," he said. "In a way, leaving feels like I'm abandoning the only sliver of history I possess." After a deep sigh, Zane's fingers braised her thigh. "Correction. It feels like I'm abandoning half the bits of history. You're the other half and you're here, and okay, I admit it, I'm glad."

"Good," she said.

"And with any luck, we're leaving a would-be killer behind."

"Hmm…" she murmured, recalling how spooked she'd been when she'd watched him walk away.

"What's he look like?" Zane asked.

"Who?"

"Your sort of boyfriend."

"Tall like you, curly blond hair, brown eyes." She sighed and added, "Enough about me. I'm starving. Is there any food left in that sack?"

"One sandwich," he said, digging into the bag and producing it.

"Want to share it with me?" she asked as he unwrapped it for her.

"No, I ate mine an hour or two ago. Then I ate the apple and the banana. This sandwich is yours."

As she drove and munched, she noticed Zane's head

nodding and encouraged him to get comfortable and close his eyes. "The fastest way to get to Utah from here is to travel up through Shreveport, over to Dallas, and then on to Albuquerque. St. George, Utah, is about a hundred miles northeast of Las Vegas. It's going to take over twenty-four hours of driving."

"How do you know all this?"

"We traveled around a lot when I was growing up. Now, get some sleep, okay?"

He finally did as she suggested, and for over three hours, Kinsey drove in peace and quiet. She just hoped it wasn't the kind of peace and quiet that precedes a storm.

ZANE WOKE UP when the car stopped. He looked around as he blinked himself into full consciousness. Kinsey had pulled into the parking lot of a wood-shingled joint promising the best barbecue in Louisiana. Judging from the enticing aromas adrift on the very faint breeze, it might actually turn out to be the truth.

"Feel better?" she asked him.

"Yeah, thanks for the nap," he said. "Where are we?"

"On the other side of Shreveport. You slept through the worst traffic, but I'm hungry again and I need to walk around. I thought we could get something to eat and then hit the road again."

"Sounds good."

The restaurant was bustling and the bar area was filled with people having a raucous time. After the quiet of the past twenty-four hours, this assault of noise and color and vibrancy actually felt good to Zane. After freshening up, they were told to choose a table and found a small booth located near a window.

Kinsey ordered half a rack of ribs and sketched on the back of the throwaway menu while awaiting delivery of their food. The image of their waitress began to emerge, then the bartender's with the handlebar mustache. Next, with just a few strokes, she captured the images of three men sitting at the bar.

"Who are all those people in the paintings hanging on your walls?" he asked.

"Just people. Faces I saw, people like that bartender and our waitress. A few of them were friends from when I was younger. I went through a stage of looking at old school pictures and then attempting to age people to see what they would look like now."

Their dinner finally arrived and Kinsey attacked it with gusto. His throat wasn't quite up to that yet—the sandwich had been hard enough to get down. He settled on sides of soft food that presented fewer challenges, but he got a kick out of her obvious pleasure with the ribs. The amusement suddenly turned into something else when she licked sauce off her fingertips. He found the sight of her tongue teasing her lips spellbinding.

"What's wrong?" she asked.

"Not a thing."

"Why are you looking at me like that?" She switched to a Wet Wipe to finish the cleanup. It was more efficient but not nearly as entertaining.

"I've become obsessed with your lips," he confessed. She didn't say anything for a minute and he wondered if he'd alarmed or offended her.

Then those wonderful lips curved into a smile. "I love your eyes."

"Really?"

"Your mouth isn't bad, either."

They stared at each other for a long, quiet moment until the tension between them burned Zane's skin. He had no memory of his character, of what kind of man he was, although he was willing to bet he was a one-woman kind of guy. His body was telling him Kinsey was that one woman. She wasn't only real because she was damn near the only person he knew; she was real because he could feel her inside his bones. "Too bad you have a sort of boyfriend," he finally said.

"Too bad you might have a wife and half a dozen kids," she countered.

"On the other hand, your sort of boyfriend has disappeared, right? And even if I am married in real life, right now, in my head and heart, I'm free."

When her eyes narrowed and she frowned, he gently stroked the back of her hand. "I'm just joking around, Kinsey. Don't look so worried."

"It's what you just said about Ryan," she said, leaning forward. "I've been assuming he's been avoiding me. But now that I think of it, Marc said Ryan left in a hurry after getting a phone call. As far as I know, that's the last anyone saw of him. What if the same person who's been attacking you attacked him? And what if they were more successful?"

"So maybe Ryan and I were working together on something and had a common enemy?"

"Exactly. I'm going to call Detective Woods." She slid out of the booth and walked outside the restaurant. Through the window, Zane saw her dig her cell phone from the small purse she still wore strapped across her chest. He asked for their check and paid it with the twenty Kinsey had loaned him, before walking outside just as she was severing the connection.

"Did he say anything about me running out on him?" Zane asked.

"He was annoyed, but I don't think he was too surprised. He told me to tell you he heard back from the other three tractor stores, two more in Utah and one in Idaho. Nobody there recognizes you, either. He also showed your picture to the grocer and he confirmed it was you. Anyway, I told Woods about Ryan. They haven't had any murders where the victim fits Ryan's description, but he seemed glad to maybe have another piece of the Zane Doe picture."

"If he can see a picture in all this, he's a better man than I am. Let's get out of here. How far away is Dallas?"

"A couple of hours give or take."

"How do you feel about me driving the car?"

"I feel fine about it. But until we get out of town, why don't I drive? I actually went this way last year when I attended an art show, so I'm familiar with the roads."

"That's fine," he said. "I'd probably get us lost in five minutes."

"Stick with me," she said.

"That's my plan." After paying the tab and leaving a tip, he had about fifty cents to his name and that was only because he hadn't eaten much. It was irritating to have no money. He had a feeling being broke wasn't normal for him. Look at his boots, for instance. They screamed expensive. And there was that comment from Kinsey about the pricey clothes he'd been wearing.

He laughed to himself. For all he knew, he'd spent his last penny on fancy duds to impress some girl or maybe he stole those items or they belonged to this Ryan fellow he was mixed up with.

Who knew?

THAT MOMENT IN the restaurant when she and Zane had stared hard at each other had rattled Kinsey more than she cared to admit. Her funky green car really was on the small side and he was a large guy. She was super aware of him being only a few inches away, and repeatedly cautioned herself to remember he may well be attached to someone else.

It was more difficult to rein in her emotions than it had ever been before. How many times had she found a guy interesting, only to discover she and her mom would be pulling up stakes and starting over? Goodbye followed goodbye until she thought she'd grown numb to them. The result of that was a certain resignation. She could live without love.

Besides, what did love lead to? Marriage. And what was the point of a marriage if not to provide a home for children? Face it, babies required a level of selflessness Kinsey wasn't sure she was up to. In so many ways it seemed to her she'd already raised a child: her mother. She was finally free, why couldn't she just be happy with that?

The answer was sitting next to her. How had everything changed with the arrival of a man without a name or a past or even a safe future? How had he done it? Did she dare grow more attached to him? Wasn't that a perfect blueprint for misery?

These thoughts raced through her head. Though she'd only driven a couple of miles since the restaurant, it seemed as though they'd been back in the car for an hour. She was exhausted. Thank heaven the traffic was easing up and Zane could take over.

"There's a bridge up ahead," she murmured. "I'll pull over after we go under it and you can drive."

"Great," Zane said as he peered through the windshield. "I wonder what that's all about," he added, pointing at the top of the bridge.

Kinsey darted a glance where he gestured. The bridge didn't seem to have any moving traffic. A lone white truck stood out against the rapidly fading light. It was stationary, parked directly above their lane. Leaning on the railing looking down was the indistinct figure of a man.

"God, I hope he's not going to jump," she said as the car neared the bridge.

Suddenly, Zane reached across Kinsey and grasped the wheel, turning the car hard to the right. Kinsey stomped down on the brakes. Overhead, a shower of shrapnel hit the hood and the top of the car before they found the protection of the bridge itself. They hit the sidewalk curb, bounced into a pillar and then back onto the road. Cars whizzed past, honking alarm, apparently unaffected by whatever had fallen. Dead headlamps, ominous popping noises and sluggish steering announced the run-in with the pillar had come with a price. Kinsey yanked hard on the wheel, struggling to control the vehicle, though she could barely see where they were going, thanks to the spiderweb of cracks now crisscrossing the windshield.

"Pull over!" Zane shouted, and once again lent his muscle to hers. They rolled from beneath the bridge, emerging on the other side and to the oasis of a small turnout.

Zane was out of the car in a flash. Kinsey followed suit. She had no idea what had hit them, although it seemed to her that there were too many thumps and crashes to be a single body. And yet, in the corner of her mind, she could see one large oblong object falling toward them before all hell broke loose.

Had that oblong shape been a human being?

Zane took her hand. It was dark under the bridge, though car headlights revealed the broken glass from her little green car. They moved carefully along the sidewalk, dreading what awaited them. Debris in the road showed up as weird shapes they couldn't immediately identify.

"Over there," Zane said, pointing at a long object sitting

on the verge beside the road. Kinsey held her breath as they approached.

She expelled her breath when she saw it wasn't a human being. "It's a box," she said, taking in the long rectangular shape. It appeared to be metal, three feet long, twelve or fourteen inches wide, twisted now, the lid clasps open, the lid itself askew. It didn't look as though it had been there long as the grass beneath and around it showed no signs it had begun to grow up around the sides and no rust had attacked the myriad of dents and scratches.

"A toolbox," Zane said.

"And all that stuff on the road…those are tools," Kinsey added. "That maniac threw a toolbox off the bridge. He could have killed us!"

They both looked up toward the top of the bridge at the same time. It was darker than it had been, but the bridge lights had flickered on. There was no longer a truck—or a man—in sight.

"What are the odds we would be in the car happening to pass under the bridge at that exact moment?" Zane said, lowering his gaze to connect with Kinsey's. She didn't miss the edge of sarcasm in his voice.

They both fell silent as their minds worked overtime, or at least that was Kinsey's excuse for the chill that cut through the humid air. She'd felt this same way just the day before when she'd stood on a New Orleans sidewalk and watched a fake messenger push Zane into a busy street. The sound of approaching sirens, along with the sight of pulsating lights, assured them another driver must have called the police.

"Here we go again," Zane said softly.

Kinsey was just glad he was still holding her hand because her knees felt like cooked noodles. She didn't think the fact that the box hurled toward their car spewing missiles of destruction had anything to do with coincidence. And she couldn't believe Zane thought so, either.

Chapter Six

"Had to be kids," Sheriff Crown said with a slow shake of his head. "Parents let them run wild nowadays. What starts out as a prank can turn deadly in the blink of an eye."

They'd been driven to the sheriff's office. The deputy who had responded to the call stood in the doorway. "You think it might have been the Owen boys, Sheriff?"

"Could have been," the sheriff said. "Their daddy has a big old white truck. You better drive on out there." An older man with a gray mustache, he appeared to be at the end of his lawmaker career. He sat back in his chair and shook his head again. "You folks were mighty lucky."

"They pretty much killed my car," Kinsey said. Zane had to agree. The police tow truck had hauled it to a garage that wouldn't be open until the next day. Zane suspected Kinsey's insurance would total it outright.

But for now they were stuck. There was no way in the world Zane could pay for any of this, not the car, not a hotel, not even breakfast tomorrow morning, at least not right this minute. And Kinsey was not rolling in money. He marveled at how composed she looked in the midst of this disaster. Maybe, like him, she was counting her lucky stars that the toolbox hadn't landed on her windshield. If it had, he doubted either one of them would be sitting here.

He felt positive the sheriff was on the wrong track thinking this was the act of misguided, rambunctious kids looking for excitement on a Saturday night. Zane would bet his life that the guy on top of that bridge had been waiting for Kinsey's distinctive green car and the passengers it contained. It was the same kind of spontaneous deadly act as the other two attempts, using the means at hand, in this case a toolbox that had probably rattled around in the back of his truck for ages.

Zane knew why he wasn't telling the sheriff about his suspicions. He didn't want to get tied up in statements and red tape. He didn't want to sit in this small burg of a town waiting for the law to figure things out while their assailant had time to plot his next move.

The question got to be why Kinsey was going along with the sheriff's suppositions. Why wasn't she launching into a recital of the events leading up to tonight?

She suddenly stood up. "Sheriff, we've told you everything we know about what happened."

He looked down at the paper on his desk. "Lone man, white truck. You don't know what kind of truck and you didn't see anything about the man you can identify. Is that about right?"

"It all happened so fast," Kinsey said.

"That's not much to go on," the sheriff grumbled. "Course, we do have the toolbox to check, and the tools might produce some prints or something else that ties them to someone around here." He pulled at his mustache and added, "Funny thing about that bridge. It's not used much anymore. Once upon a time it led to the Chemco Company back parking lot, but Chemco got involved in a big lawsuit five, six years ago. When they closed up shop, they boarded up the property, so now the bridge doesn't lead anywhere."

"That's why we didn't see any moving traffic up there," Kinsey said.

"And that's why I figure kids are behind this. I put that in the plural because they tend to run in a pack. You might have missed seeing the others. Anyway, they'd know about the bridge. They probably thought it would be funny. Once they set their plan in motion, they undoubtedly got scared and took off like bats out of hell."

Kinsey nodded as though agreeing. "I wonder if we could leave now. You have my phone number if you need anything else."

"Yeah," he said, and rattled it off as though double-checking he had it right. Then he turned his attention to Zane. "You didn't leave me an address or a phone number."

"He lives with me," Kinsey blurted out. "We're engaged."

"And what about the fact you aren't carrying any identification?" the sheriff asked with a pointed look at Zane's still-bruised neck.

Zane adjusted his collar. "I didn't realize I'd forgotten my wallet until we were hours from home. Seeing as I'm still light-headed from that polo accident I told you about, I didn't plan to drive, so I didn't figure it was a problem."

"Sheriff," Kinsey added, "Albuquerque is still a long way from here. My girlfriend is going to be crazy disappointed if we don't show up for her twenty-sixth birthday party."

"You can't drive your car until they get it fixed," the sheriff pointed out.

"I know that. I left my charge card information for the garage with instructions I'd call to hear the damages and okay the work depending on what my insurance company says. For now, could you tell us where to rent a car?"

"Aren't you kind of rattled after what happened?"

"I'm fine," she said firmly.

The sheriff stared at her a second, then at Zane, who did his best to cover his surprise upon hearing Kinsey planned to rent a car. Maybe she was washing her hands of the whole thing and going home. Part of him hoped that was the case.

And a bigger part didn't.

Finally, the older man slapped the top of his desk and nodded. "Deputy Norton will give you a ride to the rental place. You could head on back to Shreveport for more choices—"

"I'm sure we'll find something here," Kinsey interrupted. She put her hand on Zane's shoulder and added, "Come on, honey, it's time to get back on the road."

Zane got to his feet, stumbling just a hair as he put his weight on his left leg, the injury exacerbated by the sprint back under the bridge. Kinsey gripped his arm and steadied him. They picked up the satchel of Bill Dodge's clothes, Kinsey's bag of art supplies she swore she never left behind, and started toward the door.

"You two take care of yourselves," the sheriff called.

Muttering thanks, they escaped while they could.

WITHIN AN HOUR, they were under way again.

"What bothers me is how he—whoever he is—knew about that bridge," Zane said.

"I know," Kinsey whispered.

"How could that be unless this dude is local?"

"I don't know. Maybe he worked at Chemco sometime."

"So he followed us all the way from New Orleans,

waited around while we ate dinner, drove ahead to the bridge and then dumped the back of his truck on us?"

She shrugged. "I guess. Either that or it's those kids the sheriff is so fond of."

"I can't quite buy that."

"Neither can I." She sighed. "But maybe the delay coupled with the different rides in different police cars will throw him off."

He was quiet and she decided not to pursue that line of thought. Zane had hardly been traveling in a straight line since this whole ordeal had begun, and yet, whoever was after him seemed to be one step ahead or behind, depending on your point of view.

"You must be really tired," he said.

"I am. Are you okay to drive?"

"Sure. There are lots of big signs directing me to Dallas. I'll get us there."

"And from there to Amarillo," she said around a yawn as she found a good spot to pull off the road.

While Zane acquainted himself with the car, she took the opportunity to call her mother. It was getting late, but her mom answered on the first ring.

"James brought me home from the hospital a half hour ago," she said. "He wanted to come inside, but he looked so tired. When I went to my room, I found it had been searched."

"By who?" Kinsey asked, but added, "It doesn't matter who. Call the police. Leave the house immediately."

"Don't be silly. It had to be Bill's snoopy nephew. I loaded Bill's shotgun and walked through the whole house. No one is here and I can't see that anything was taken."

Ignoring the image of her tiny mother hauling a shotgun around an old mansion with four floors, if you counted the attic and the basement, Kinsey repeated her warning. "Please, leave for the night. Go to a hotel."

"Nonsense."

Time to give up on that, Kinsey decided. "How is Mr. Dodge?"

"His breathing is better, but we all know it's only a matter of time. He wants to come home. Maybe tomorrow, they said." She paused for a long second and Kinsey imagined her mother's moist eyes. "I'm not sure what I'll do when he dies."

"You always warn me not to look too far ahead," Kinsey said softly.

"Yes, that's true. Listen, why don't you give me a lift to the hospital in the morning and say hi to Bill. He always loves seeing you."

"Well, actually, I can't," Kinsey said.

"The gallery?"

"Not exactly. See, my doctor friend—"

"Wait just a second. That man is no more a doctor than I am. Did you see his hands? Those are not the hands of a professional. What's going on?"

"I didn't intend to mislead you," Kinsey said, which was a half truth at the very best. "Things just kind of got out of hand. You don't need to worry about me."

"I've been worrying about you since the day you were born," her mother said. "I sacrificed just about everything for you."

Kinsey had never heard her mother say anything about sacrificing everything and it jarred her. What did she mean?

"Tell me about this man."

"I just met him yesterday," Kinsey said. "He was in an…accident. He can't remember his name. I'm trying to help him. We're on our way to Utah where he has a kind of a lead."

After everything that had happened, Kinsey didn't think she'd ever gotten around to admitting to her mother that Zane had been asking specifically about her before his injury. She wasn't about to bring it up now, especially since she was still trying to figure out the unspoken antagonistic edge of this conversation. Her mother made leaps of her own, however. "Why was he asking *me* so many questions this morning?" she demanded. "What does that cowboy want with me?"

Kinsey paused before stammering, "Why…why do you call him a…a…cowboy?"

"Those boots," her mother said.

"Lots of ordinary people wear boots, Mom."

"He left here in a Western shirt and jeans wearing those boots and looked totally at home. The way he walked, that swagger! And you heard him talk. Even his tan and his haircut announce who and what he is. That man is a cowboy, Kinsey, no matter what silly story he's feeding you. And you can't trust a cowboy. They're dangerous. They want one thing and one thing only. Please, wherever you are, just come back to New Orleans. Wash your hands of him."

"What do you mean the way he talks? What about it?" Kinsey asked. And since when did her mother lump cowboys into the same group as sex offenders?

"Come home," Frances Frost repeated.

"Not yet."

"Now!"

"I stopped taking orders quite a while ago," Kinsey said softly.

"You're just like your mother!" Frances sputtered.

"I'll take that as a compliment. End of story."

"You said it, not me," her mother snapped and the line went dead.

Kinsey slid into the passenger seat, still dazed by the conversation. When Zane touched her cheek with a gentle caress, she almost jumped out of her skin.

"Hey, are you okay?" he asked. "Is something wrong at home?"

I sacrificed just about everything for you…

"Kinsey? Just tell me. What's wrong? Do you want to go back?"

"No," she said. "Do you?"

"No. But I feel very uncomfortable with you going into debt helping me, and if that's compounded with family problems, you need to pick your priorities."

She nodded. Internally she knew that she had chosen what was right and necessary.

He cupped her chin, leaned across the midconsole and brushed her lips with his. Instant fire reminded Kinsey she might not be thinking totally with her head.

As he started the car, she leaned back and closed her eyes. She'd dealt with a lot of confusion in her life, the by-product of her mother's personality and tumultuous lifestyle. But this took the cake.

KINSEY'S EYES DRIFTED OPEN. The reassuring sounds and motion of the moving car almost lulled her back to sleep, until the bright sunlight bathing her face registered in her brain. She sat up abruptly.

"Morning," Zane said. She looked around. The countryside zooming by was dry, rural, a hundred shades of brown. How had she managed to sleep through the entire night? "What time is it?" she croaked.

"Almost seven." He glanced at her again and added, "Someone needs a cup of coffee."

"You can say that again. Where are we?"

"Just outside of Amarillo, headed to Albuquerque. We'll be in St. George by midnight, even with a couple of stops."

"Maybe we should spend the night in Vegas and finish up tomorrow morning," she said. "Otherwise, we may not be able to walk when we get there."

"You're probably right."

"I can't believe you drove all night," she added as she tried to do something with her hair.

"I was wide-awake and anxious to avoid any more falling objects."

"So, nothing happened?"

"Not a thing. I don't think anyone is following us. We do need fuel, though, so keep your eyes peeled for a gas station."

A moment later, she gestured at a billboard beside the road. "Look. Five miles to the Armadillo Roadhouse, home of Dave's famous flapjacks."

"Do you like flapjacks?" he asked her.

"Doesn't everybody?"

"I'd like them better if I was the one buying them for you," he said.

"We'll find out who you are and then you can hit up your friends and family to repay me," she said breezily. There was no reason for him to obsess about this as there wasn't a thing either one of them could do about it. Her card would stretch a bit further, and then they'd have to think of something else. But that was another catastrophe away.

She looked at her phone to see if she'd received any messages while she slept. Neither her mother nor Ryan had called. She knew her mother's reason was out-and-out stubbornness; it was Ryan's fate that worried her. The confusion of the night before resurfaced.

THEY CLEANED UP in the restaurant bathrooms, ate breakfast and filled the car with gas. Kinsey called the hospital and learned Mr. Dodge was being released later that day. At least that much was going right in the world.

Her next call was to her insurance company, then the repair shop. The last call was followed by a moan.

"What did you learn?" Zane asked as he buttered the pancakes that had just arrived.

Kinsey looked at her small stack, her appetite gone. "The repair shop gave me a number I'm pretty sure the insurance company will deny. That means they'll total the car and give me what their tables tell them it's worth, which isn't enough to actually replace it. Damn."

Zane shook his head. "I was afraid of that. Well, look on the bright side. Maybe I'm rich."

"My car problems are not your fault," she said, and took a bite. Dave's flapjacks were pretty darn tasty.

"If it was an attempt to kill me, I think that's my fault," he said.

"I don't. Let's not talk about it, okay?"

"Sure."

Back in the car, Kinsey drove while Zane dozed fitfully beside her. Her goal was to clear her mind and just go with the flow. She was no stranger to road trips—that's how she and her mother had moved around for years. But then she'd been a child, relying on an adult's decisions, and now she was an adult and Zane was depending on her to keep all the balls in the air.

Ever mindful that someone could be trailing them or driving ahead, her gaze darted between the rearview mirror and the road. She made her hands remain steady on the wheel as she drove under bridges. The saving grace was that it was light outside.

Worries about killers and having no car began to creep in as mile after mile of desert passed outside the windows. She wished Zane would wake up and talk to her, but he looked reasonably comfortable huddled down in his seat.

Her mother was right—he did look like a cowboy.

As the afternoon wore on, Zane's peaceful slumber seemed to be waning. She saw his hands twitch on his thighs, his lashes flutter against his cheeks. She became truly alarmed when he clutched his throat and cried out. A moment later, his eyes flew open and he looked around as though trying to figure out what was going on. His expression was wild.

"You were having a bad dream," she told him. "Do you remember what it was about?"

He blinked several times. "It's kind of vague," he said, his fingers still at his throat as though the choking had just happened. "There was a giant black tree. That's all I can remember."

"Sounds like something out of a kid's nightmare," she said.

By the time they rolled down Las Vegas's brilliantly lit main street, Kinsey's muscles were knotted from all the sitting. For once, she wasn't hungry—all she wanted to do was move.

They checked into a small motel off the beaten track. The room held a single bed that they both stared at. Kinsey was thinking it was going to be hard to curl up in a bed with Zane mere inches away and get any kind of sleep at all. She didn't know what he was thinking, but by the smoldering look he cast her way, she figured it was along similar lines.

"Maybe we should get out of here for a while," he said.

"Good idea."

The evening was very warm without any of the river breezes that sometimes helped cool things down in New Orleans. They found a casino with a cheap buffet, then followed their ears to a band playing old rock songs from the sixties.

"I need to move around," Kinsey said, looking at the small wooden dance floor.

"I'll give it a try," Zane said.

"Is your left leg up to it?"

"I'll just pretend I'm moving," he said and did just that as Kinsey flexed tight muscles. She loved the familiar beats, singing along with the band when she knew the lyrics and earning a round of applause from a couple of older guys taking a break from keno.

"How do you know the words to these songs?" Zane asked as they came together for a slow dance.

"It's my mom's favorite music," she said close to his ear. It was heaven to be held against his firm chest, to have his warm breath on her neck and cheek, his hand planted on her lower back. She closed her eyes and let the rhythm soothe away the long hours in the car.

"You're very close to her, aren't you?"

Kinsey thought about that for a minute. "Yes and no," she said. "She was the center of my universe because there were so few other constants."

"How about grandparents?"

"My dad was an orphan and Mom's parents died before I was born. I was all she had."

"Well, at least she had you."

"Yeah. But that's a big load for a kid to carry, you know, to be everything. It's harder than it sounds."

"I bet it is," he said, looking down into her eyes, and

they both smiled. "I wonder what my childhood was like," he added.

"You'll reclaim your memories," she said softly, her gaze on his mouth and the perfect shape of his lips. She'd tasted them several times now, but that didn't mean she didn't want to sample them again.

"And if I don't, I'll have you," he said, and she wasn't sure if he meant in the figurative sense of memories of her or actually having her—at his side, in his bed, sharing his life.

Once again she cautioned herself to slow down. Zane was an enigma and would be until he found his place in the world and remembered why he was in New Orleans, why he'd asked about her mother, what he knew about Ryan.

Soon enough, it was time to return to the motel. They took a cab in the hopes that if they had a tail, it might throw them off. Once back in the room with the dead bolt in place and curtains drawn, they took turns using the shower. Zane had some of Bill Dodge's garments to change into and Kinsey had grabbed a long beach cover-up off a sale rack in the casino basement. It was a weird shade of orange, which probably explained its cheap price tag, but at least it was clean. By the time she was ready for bed, Zane had already chosen a side. She took the other. She was nervous and excited and full of cautionary tales that ran through her head like the ticker tape she'd once seen in an old movie.

"It feels great to lie down," Zane said as his hand found hers and clasped it.

"I wish I knew if you were married," Kinsey said and then wished she hadn't. Why couldn't she just shut up and scoot over to her side of the bed and go to sleep?

"I do, too." He turned on his side, facing her. Their

faces were close, their hands joined. Every inch of Kinsey's body ached with awareness and desire, and by the tone of Zane's breathing, she knew he was in similar distress.

"I can't believe I've ever felt this way about anyone else," he said, his fingers caressing her arms.

"I know I haven't," she said. "You're making me want things I never wanted before."

"Like what?"

"A future with one person."

"And children?"

"I don't know."

"I like kids," he said.

"Why?" she asked.

"The usual things. Their innocence, their trust. What they represent when it comes to playing life forward. On a gut level I guess I feel they're what matters, they're the point of it all." He paused. "Why are you uncertain?"

Kinsey's mother's comment about sacrificing everything rang once again in her mind. Now she wondered why it came as such a surprise. Was it because Kinsey had always felt as if she was the one called upon to make concessions, helpless to lead a normal life because of her mother's idiosyncrasies? "I guess in a way I feel like I've already raised a child," she murmured. "My mother."

"Nurturing a brand-new baby would be way different than dealing with a grown-up," he said.

"I would hope so," she responded with a chuckle, but it died in her throat as his lips touched her cheek.

"I want to kiss you," he murmured against her skin.

"You just did," she answered softly.

"Not like that," he said, moving closer still, his arm sliding under her shoulders, pulling her against him. He licked her earlobe, nuzzled her throat, showered a dozen moist kisses on her neck, on her shoulder, across her clavicle. Her breasts throbbed with a wanton pulse that drummed inside her body like a jungle beat. By the time his lips touched hers, she was half gone, and she returned his kiss with the pent-up longing of every moment she'd been aware of his existence.

She wanted his gentle, warm hands to touch every inch of her and she could tell by the erection pressing against her thigh that his longings equaled her own. It felt like destiny. The ticker-tape machine fell silent, warnings ceased; she was his for the taking. Even the fact that this zero-to-ninety reaction had happened in mere moments and with a man who remained a virtual stranger failed to rouse her consciousness.

And then he paused as though similar thoughts had detonated in his brain. The slight hesitation was enough to reawaken Kinsey's common sense.

If they kept racing down this particular mountain, they would end up having sex, right here, tonight. And tomorrow when he rediscovered a wife? They would have to live with this act, with this decision.

The sex-hungry part of her brain whispered: *you would have this night to remember. Isn't that enough?*

He rolled over on his back and swore. A sigh passed his lips next, and then his cheek grazed her shoulder.

She sat up abruptly, unable to bear his touch, though she hungered for it with every ounce of her being. His hand landed on her back and she flinched. "I'm sorry," he whispered. The bed creaked as he sat up behind her. His arms circled her and he spoke against her hair. "This is my fault."

She didn't even try to respond.

"You're right about me," he continued, "about not knowing what obligations and responsibilities I already have in my life. I shouldn't have started this, it was weak to give in to the lust I feel for you when I have absolutely nothing to offer, not even tomorrow."

"I didn't exactly try to stop you," Kinsey said softly.

His lips touched her shoulder. "Stick with me for another day, Kinsey, and forgive me for putting you in this position."

She turned her head a little and closed her eyes. She was as much at fault as he. She nodded and he hugged her. When he lay back down, he pulled her with him and she tried to relax by his side.

She'd known better than to let herself get mixed up with him at this stage of his quest. She'd ignored her common sense. She wouldn't do that again.

Chapter Seven

They set out early, but the night before had been restless and uneasy. It took two hours to drive to St. George. Nestled in a valley and surrounded by red cliffs, it was larger than Zane had expected and very pretty with its green trees and steepled white buildings.

"Getting nervous?" she asked. She'd been polite but reserved during the whole drive, a parody of her former warmth. Last night had been hard on both of them.

"A little," he said. "I could walk into a tractor dealership in a few moments and someone could call me by name."

Kinsey nodded toward her small handbag on the console between them. "Dig out my phone and look up Travers's Tractors so we don't get lost."

"Sure." He opened the clasp, but there was a book stuffed inside the bag, making a search tricky.

"I'm sorry," she said after glancing at him. "It's not in there. It should be in one of the pockets on the outside."

"What book is this?" he asked.

She glanced at him. "It's an art book Bill Dodge gave me because it concerns women artists. I think he must have rebound it himself. I wanted to ask him, but things got out of hand and I didn't get a chance."

"What I can see of it is very pretty." He closed the

main bag and discovered the phone where she'd said he would. He found it oddly comforting that he knew how to use the device. So why didn't he know anything about himself and the people he loved?

He glanced at Kinsey. *Please, let there be no one else,* he said inside his head. His biggest fear was that he'd find a wife and children waiting for him and he would not remember them. He'd have to stay with them, but his heart would beat for Kinsey. She would go back to her life, and he would have to find a way to come to grips with his.

He directed Kinsey through the quiet streets to the other side of town. For some reason Zane couldn't explain, neither one of them seemed worried today about an assailant. He noticed Kinsey rarely checked her mirrors and his heart hadn't skipped a beat every time they drove beneath an overpass.

"There it is," he said, looking ahead at the green sign with the words *Travers's Tractors and Farm Equipment* written in white. His throat felt dry and he turned up his collar although the bruises had grown dark now and hiding them was nearly impossible.

Kinsey pulled into a large parking lot that held a few trucks.

"Let's get this over with," he said, opening his door.

The store consisted of a big showroom filled with tractors and attachments. The only other people were a salesman showing an elderly couple a mower, and another salesman who approached them with a huge smile. "Howdy, folks," he said, putting out a hand. "My name is Ted Baxter. You looking for a tractor?" As they shook hands, Ted frowned and then nodded. "I've seen you before," he said.

Zane's pulse quickened and he felt Kinsey's body tense. "You have?"

"Sure. I remember now. The police faxed us your photo. Am I right? That's you, isn't it?"

Hope that he'd be recognized by the first person he met flared and died within a few short sentences. "That's me," he said. "I hoped that walking in here might trigger someone's memory."

"I'm real sorry for your predicament."

The elderly couple walked past them toward the door, deep in conversation. Their salesman drifted over to Ted's side and stared at Zane in a way that suggested he, too, recognized him from a photo.

"Can you tell us where your other franchises are located?" Kinsey asked.

"Sure. Heck, I've got a brochure in my office."

Zane had taken the key fob out of his pocket and showed it now to the two men. "Before you get that brochure, do either of you recognize this?"

"Red Hot," Ted said as he turned it over in his hand. "That's a small tractor made by Bolo, kind of the sporty model. There, in the corner, that's what they look like. But I've never seen a key ring—"

"I have," the other salesman said. "About four or five years ago. They ran a promotion when the model first came out. We had these little disks printed for all the stores. Someone made a mistake and this branch's address ended up on every one of them. Manufacturer cut us a deal, so we used them anyway."

"All the stores?"

"Yeah. Most of them just made up little fake keys with their own branch's location. Those never lasted long."

"So you don't know which store this came from?" Kinsey persisted.

"No. Sorry."

Ted ran off to get the brochure. Back in seconds, he

turned the pamphlet over where five franchises were listed. "It had to come from one of these," Ted said.

The other salesman looked at the list. "Wait a second. How about the Falls Bluff branch?"

"What Falls Bluff branch?" Ted asked.

"Falls Bluff, Idaho. Wait. I forgot—you weren't here four years ago. Right after the Red Hot promotion began, the branch in Falls Bluff closed its doors. I heard that someone bought the property and opened their own farm equipment business. Some of the same people might still work there, though."

"Do you know the name of the new place?" Zane asked.

"No, sorry, I don't. It was on Festival Street, though. I doubt you'll miss it."

Five minutes later, they were headed north on their way to Bryce Canyon where they would find the next Travers's Tractors, and from there to Salt Lake City, then into Idaho—Twin Falls first, then Falls Bluff, final destination Coeur d'Alene.

BY THAT NIGHT, they were both travel weary. Utah had been a bust and they'd forced themselves to keep going until they got to the Idaho border. Since it was way too late to worry about things like debt, Kinsey bought them both clean clothes at a department store just minutes after hearing her car had been totaled. She would receive well under a thousand dollars for the little lime bug and it rankled.

Tomorrow they would go to three more stores, but Kinsey had kind of given up hope and she could tell that Zane had, too. They were weary of sitting, asking the same questions in almost identical venues, looking over their shoulders and eating fast food.

There'd been no sign that day that anyone was interested in them, and Kinsey began to think that maybe Sheriff Crown had been right about the bored kids.

She asked for and received a room with two double beds and locked the dead bolt. She sat cross-legged on her bed for an hour and sketched from memory the woman who had waited on them, an angelic-looking teenager with the unexpected tattoo of barbed wire and tiny red hearts encircling her neck. Even conquering that didn't lighten her mood and she finally lay back on the pillow.

All the while she'd been drawing, she'd been glancing over at Zane lounging atop the other bed clad only in boxers and a T-shirt. He'd borrowed a newspaper from the office, stretched out on his stomach and started the crossword puzzle. Memories of his strength and gentleness tugged at every part of her body.

He seemed to sense her attention and looked up at her. All the protective layers she'd erected that day teetered under the blue intensity of his gaze. After a second, he crossed the short distance to her side in one step. He had long, straight legs, not quite as tan as his muscular arms and commanding face. He sat on the edge of her mattress.

For several seconds they stared at each other. Kinsey felt as if she was going to explode.

"You look beautiful tonight," he said as he ran a lock of her hair through his fingers. "Of course, you always look beautiful."

"For all the good it does us," she whispered. When he leaned over her and kissed her cheek, she turned her face. "Don't," she whispered.

"Sorry," he said, and slowly sat up. He didn't leave, however, just sat there, still and silent, one hand on her shoulder as he stared around the room. Finally he looked down at her again. "Last night I asked you to give me one more day. That day is now over. I think you should drive away tomorrow and let me finish this."

"You keep forgetting about my mother," she said. "You were asking questions about her. I need to know why so I can protect her."

"It's more than that," he protested. "Whoever took my wallet knows where I live. He might have swiped a cell phone, too, which would reveal even more about me. We have to stay alert and be prepared for the worst if we actually find out where I'm from."

"You're talking about another ambush?"

"He could be there before us."

"I'm staying with you until Coeur d'Alene," she said. "I have a feeling about that place. Let's get some sleep, okay?"

Before he got back in bed, he snatched the chair at the desk and levered it under the knob.

In the morning she called her mother and found out Bill was home and the dreaded nephew had shown up full of demands. "He treats this place like it's his already," Frances fumed. "Always prowling around, looking for something. And he grew a beard. All that red hair—he looks like a Viking. Anyway, where are you now?"

"Idaho. Just a couple of places to check."

Frances was silent for several beats before she said, "Idaho?"

"Yeah," Kinsey said. "One of the few states we didn't live in."

"We were there for a few months when you were three. You just don't remember. I have to go. Chad is taking apart Bill's desk." The phone clicked off.

Zane had come into the room. "Your mother?" he said.

"How did you know?"

"You get a certain look in your eyes after you talk to her." Kinsey actually cracked a smile.

The Twin Falls Travers's Tractors was a bust, just like the others. They reached Falls Bluff by noon, their expectations rock bottom. The town's namesake seemed to be the flat-faced mountain that sported a waterfall located to the north. Evergreens covered the hillsides surrounding the town, while open plains baked in the sun.

The city was tiny and Festival Street was easy to find. So was the green-and-white sign repainted with the name Shorty's. The interior didn't resemble a Travers's outlet. There were no cubicles, no open floor space. Every inch seemed to be crammed with shelves displaying must-have country equipment and goods.

There was no one in sight, so they bided their time, unsure how to attract attention, listening to a country-western station on the radio. Finally, they heard a noise coming from the back and turned in time to see a young woman enter the room carrying a forty-pound sack of feed. She dropped it next to the counter and slapped her hands together. Strawberry-blond pigtails on either side of her head made her look younger than a probable age of twenty. Looking right at Zane, she called, "Hey, Gerard, I didn't know anyone was out here. Hope you haven't been waiting long."

The song on the radio seemed to fade away as a moment in time stretched endlessly inside Kinsey's head. This girl knew Zane. Was this it? His name was Gerard?

"Just in town, thought I'd stop by," Zane said. It appeared he wasn't going to announce amnesia if he didn't have to.

"He's showing me around," Kinsey added. "I'm visiting from New Orleans." The girl didn't respond to New

Orleans, so apparently it wasn't a place she associated with Gerard.

"Long as you're here, do you want to pick up Pike's order?" She rounded the counter and opened a box, riffled through receipts and read aloud. "Galvanized fencing staples, half a dozen sacks of oats and molasses horse feed, dog food and two reels of utility chain. Oh, and he wants a dozen calf bottles." She looked up at Zane and added, "I have most of the order put together out back. You can pull your truck around to the loading doors."

"I don't have the truck with me," he said and Kinsey could see he was angling his head to get a look at the order. The salesgirl noticed him doing this and handed it over. Kinsey looked, as well.

The order was made by someone named Pike Hastings and was billed to the Hastings Ridge Ranch, Falls Bluff, Idaho.

How was Zane, or rather, Gerard, related to Pike Hastings?

The girl must have been a mind reader. "Tell your brother everything is here whenever he wants to come into town and get it."

"I will," Zane said, his voice kind of hollow.

The girl turned her attention to Kinsey. "Did you know Lily from before she got married?"

Lily? Was this a sister or was this a wife? More to the point, was this Zane's wife? Kinsey bit her lip and tried not to look as shaken as she felt. She murmured, "No, I didn't."

The mention of a woman and the word *married* in the same sentence seemed to affect Zane in the same way it had her. He quietly handed the order form back to the girl, who plopped it in the box. Kinsey could feel the tension coursing through his body and she suspected he needed to get out of that store and decompress. She knew she did. "It's about time we get back," she said vaguely, waving in the direction of the door.

Zane seemed to suddenly recall the key fob that had played such a big part in this ritual, and he took it from his pocket. "Do you have any more of these?" he asked, showing the girl the Red Hot tag.

She shook her head. "I've never seen one of these before."

"I must have picked it up somewhere else," he said. "Well, see you later."

"Give Lily and Charlie my best."

"Sure thing," Zane said.

PIKE, LILY AND CHARLIE. Three names he should recognize, three people, one of them his brother. Who was Charlie? And Lord, was Lily his wife? Was Charlie his son or father or another brother?

For a minute or two, they both sat side by side in the cocoon of the rental car. Zane finally cleared his throat. "That girl seemed very sure I was Gerard Hastings."

Kinsey looked over at him. Her tongue flicked across her luscious candy-apple lips, her huge eyes glittered like dark water trapped in a cool well. "She did. You are."

"But that doesn't mean Lily is my wife. She didn't actually say that."

"No, she didn't. But you know what, Zane—I mean, Gerard. Wow, that's going to take some getting used to."

"Tell me about it."

"What I was going to say is that for your sake, I hope one look at her and you'll remember who you are and what's important to you. You'll remember who you love."

"I think I know who I love," he whispered with a quick glance into her eyes.

"Don't say that. Listen, all we can do is find out." She took her cell phone from its pocket and brought up the map. Two minutes later, she said, "Here it is. Hastings Ridge Ranch, Route 109." She plugged her phone into the car charger and added, "Twenty miles from here lies what is apparently your home. You'll finally learn the truth."

He stared at her until she lowered her gaze, stuck the keys in the ignition and started the car.

The truth. Would he be able to live with it once he found it?

Chapter Eight

The countryside flattened out as they drove east of town. Zane—he simply could not think of himself as Gerard yet—studied each house, farm and ranch as they sped by. How many hundreds of times he must have traveled this road and yet nothing looked familiar. When they pulled around a yellow school bus, kids waved through the windows. Had he ridden that bus or one like it to school? How far did his past go back here?

The thought that the man who had attacked him might be waiting at the ranch added another level of tension. Even when there ceased being people or houses and the scenery turned into bucolic vistas, his stomach stayed tied in a knot. Kinsey seemed as distracted as he was, which he supposed meant she was just as nervous.

Had he left this place in a huff? Would his family welcome him back or be shocked he'd returned? He didn't know if he'd been away a week or a month. The girl at the store hadn't seemed surprised to see him, so probably not that long. She also hadn't reacted to the mention of New Orleans. Had his destination been a secret and, if so, why?

"It shouldn't be far now," Kinsey said. "It sure seems to be out in the middle of nowhere, doesn't it?"

"Yes," he said uneasily. Did this mean it was a poor ranch struggling to make ends meet? How was he ever going to pay Kinsey back in a timely manner if that was the case?

At the top of the next hill they looked down into a valley of sorts. No buildings were visible from the highway, but they did see a long road accented with a line of power poles bisecting the floor leading to another hill a mile or so away. A small red car drove toward them along that road, a cloud of dust in its wake.

Kinsey stopped the rental at the point where the paved and the gravel road intersected. A herd of cattle, these with calves by their sides, looked up at them, mooed their disapproval and moseyed away from the fence.

"Are you ready for this, Gerard?" Kinsey asked, gesturing at the approaching car.

"Not Gerard, not between us, anyway, not until it means something. And I'm about as ready as I'll ever be. Let's get out and ask the driver if we're at the right place." He stepped from the air-conditioned comfort of the sedan into the summer heat of the day. The smell of animals and dried grass filled the air. A minute later, the red car pulled alongside their rental and the door opened.

A small dynamo of a woman wearing jeans and a T-shirt waved when she saw them. While her expressive dark brows framed equally dark eyes, her hair was very blond and spiky short. Beaded earrings dangled toward her shoulders. "Gerard, I didn't know you were back," she said. "Have you seen your brothers yet?"

Just like that, he learned he had more than one brother. "I...I just got back," he said. Was this Lily?

"What happened to your throat?" she gasped. "And your cheek. Were you in a fight? I thought that was Chance's area of expertise."

It was hard to miss the derogatory tone in her voice. Who was Chance? And who, exactly, was this woman?

"No, not a fight," he said. "I had an accident."

She studied the marks a moment and narrowed her eyes. "That must have been quite the *accident*. It looks to me like someone tried to choke you."

Zane wasn't sure what to say that wouldn't reveal his memory loss and he didn't want to do that right now. Kinsey must have sensed his feelings for she jumped into the silence. "My name is Kinsey Frost," she said, extending her hand.

"Lily Kirk," the woman said and shook Kinsey's hand. "Are you a friend of Gerard's?"

"Yes," Kinsey said.

"I see by your license plate you're from Louisiana."

"The car is a rental," Kinsey said without volunteering any additional information.

Zane, who'd been fooling with his shirt collar, added, "Kinsey and I met a few days ago. She gave me a ride home."

"Where's your truck?"

"I'm not sure," he said.

"That makes no sense." She shook her head. "Never mind, it's none of my business." She glanced at her watch, then peered down the road. "The bus is late. Poor Charlie is stuck on that thing for forty-five minutes coming and going to summer school. It's only for three weeks and heaven knows he needs to be around other kids, but I still feel sorry for the little guy."

She wore a ring on her left hand, but it was hard to tell if it was a wedding band or something else. Zane wondered if she was married to one of his brothers. The last name was wrong, but many women didn't automatically change their name upon marrying.

"We passed a bus about ten miles back," Kinsey said.

"Good, then it'll be here any minute. The gal who drives that bus knows these roads like the back of her hand."

There was no way to ask the next question that wouldn't be abrupt, so Zane just put it out there. "Is there anyone new at the ranch, say, within the last two days?"

"One guy."

"When did he get here?" Zane asked.

Her eyebrows knit together as she thought. "Not long. What's today, Tuesday? Maybe since Sunday. I guess he asked around town and found out who was hiring. Pike's the only one who talked to him that I know of. He said the guy is a drifter on his way to New Mexico and needed a few weeks' work because he ran out of money. That's all I know. Why?"

"I was just wondering," he said. He glanced at Kinsey and read what she was thinking in her eyes: the timing was pretty darn suspicious. Was this man there for them? Striving to sound casual, he added, "What's he look like?"

"I don't know. I've never met him. Oh, wait. Pike says he has a red beard and I think he said he was about thirty." Kinsey looked startled by the description. Meanwhile, Lily tilted her head as though a thought had just occurred to her. "Where did you run off to, Gerard? No one here knew. Chance just said that you left right after the wedding but wouldn't tell him where you were going or how long you'd be gone. Of course, he could be lying through his teeth and who would guess?"

Zane didn't have the slightest idea what Lily was talking about, but there was the name Chance again and said with the same derision. He tried to look confident as he said, "I'm not trying to be secretive. I'd just like to explain it later, okay?"

She lowered her gaze for a second, then looked back.

"I'm sorry I said that about your brother. Sometimes I forget my place."

Grumbling engine noises preceded the arrival of the school bus. It ground to a halt beside them and as Lily walked toward the door, a small boy with fair hair and freckles appeared on the stairs. He was a slightly built kid who wore torn pants and a red-and-white-striped shirt. He jumped off the bus as though exiting a burning building.

"See you tomorrow, Sue," Lily called as she waved the bus off. She looked down at the child and shook her head. "Oh, Charlie, those are your new jeans! How did you get a hole in them already?"

"I don't know," Charlie mumbled.

"Come on, fess up. What happened?"

"Nothin'."

"Charlie, did someone push you again?"

"No," the boy said quickly.

Lily put her hands on her hips. "It was Trevor, wasn't it? I'm going to call his mother."

"Mommy, no!" Charlie said in a panic. "No! Everyone calls me a baby." Suddenly the boy seemed to realize they weren't alone. He looked from Kinsey to Zane and the threatening flood of tears vanished. "You're back!" the child cried.

"Yeah," Zane said. "I'm back."

"I'D LOVE TO paint that woman," Kinsey said as she followed Lily's car down the gravel road. Zane figured Kinsey kept a good distance between them in case Lily's tire threw up a rock. He knew she was nervous about the rental. "She's really pretty, but it's not that. There's something haunting behind her eyes. Did you notice it?"

"No," Zane said truthfully. It was impossible not to recognize Lily's charm and quirkiness, beauty even, but he hadn't looked closely at her, not really. "Her hair is sure blond."

"Bleach," Kinsey said. "It's a good look for her. Different."

"Yeah," he said. Right now, he was just anxious to get to the end of this road and find out what came next. He didn't know if the land they were passing was part of the Hastings ranch or if the ranch existed down one of the smaller roads they'd passed.

Fenced pastures lined either side of the road, the land beyond glowed golden in the afternoon sun, changing from rolling mountains dotted with bright green trees to the high mountains beyond with their permanent cover of evergreens. Every once in a while they would top a rise and catch a glimpse of a river twining its way far below. Cattle grazed everywhere.

They also caught glimpses of houses, some old-fashioned and some very modern, all far off the road and secluded from one another. Each had an assortment of outbuildings and barns.

"Do you remember any of this?" Kinsey asked.

Zane stared out at the rows of mown hay that lay drying in the sun before the hay baler came along and did its work. He didn't know how he knew this, he just did. "Not really. It all seems vaguely familiar. You know, I really don't think Lily and I are married to each other. And she didn't ask if my wife knew I was home. I can't tell you how relieved I am."

"You two could be in the middle of a terrible marriage, I guess, but she didn't treat you that way."

"No, she seemed more or less indifferent to me." He took a deep breath and touched her leg. "There's only one woman in the world I want to be attached to, Kinsey. You know that, right?"

She cast him a serious look. "I know that's what you think now. I know that we're immensely attracted to each other and that if you're single, I can guess what we're going to do about that attraction. But I also know your life right now is one-dimensional. For all intents and purposes, you're four or five days old and I am the single familiar face in a sea of strangers. That could change."

"And you don't want a broken heart," he stated flatly.

"No, do you?"

"No." Though he suspected that one or both of them were going to end up with just that.

They were silent a few seconds and then Kinsey added, "Why didn't you just tell Lily the truth and ask for her help?"

"I don't know for sure," he said.

"I got the impression she's no one's dummy," Kinsey added.

"So did I. I guess I just want to tell my family all at once. There's so much I need to explain, and so much I need explained to me. Lily mentioned a wedding and a guy named Chance and don't forget the new wrangler, which makes me remember you acted kind of weird when she described him."

"That's because she used the same words my mother did to describe Chad Dodge. But it can't be him. I talked to my mother this morning and she was yelling at him. I swear, so much has happened since this morning, it seems like three days have passed."

Zane rubbed his forehead. They grew quiet as they drove by a crew mowing the tall fields of hay, four combines working in harmony across a huge sweep of land. Were any of them family members? While he studied their far-off action, Kinsey crested yet another hill. Her intake of breath earned his attention.

"Holy cow," she said.

The river they'd glimpsed all along made a turn in the valley below them. The acreage on the peninsula that the U-shaped bend created looked green and fertile, with fields rolling to the bank and a road extending down to the river. A big old wooden house sat in a protected alcove. It appeared to be surrounded with concrete and rock decks, most of them covered to provide relief from sun or snow. All the work buildings sat off a distance. Some of them looked very old while others gleamed with new paint. Sunlight glinted off the meandering blue water.

"If that's the Hastings ranch, your chances I can actually repay you for everything you've done just went up," Zane said.

"It's beautiful here," she whispered.

"Beautiful enough to make a portrait artist stick around and try painting a landscape?"

She spared him a brief glance. "We'll see," she said.

KINSEY PULLED UP behind Lily's car, which was parked next to a vibrant fenced garden bursting with squash, beans and corn. The air smelled of herbs. The sound of running water echoed across the land while the drone of insects and the distant braying of cattle added other dimensions. All and all, it smelled, felt and tasted like summer.

They were immediately beset upon by a trio of dogs who woofed and wagged their greetings nonstop. Two seemed to be shepherds with black-and-white fur, perky ears and mischievous eyes. The third looked like a Lab mix, kind of a rusty brown. All of them paid their respects to Kinsey but focused most of their canine love on Zane.

He knelt and petted each in turn, suffered the occasional tongue washing with a smile and ruffled soft ears all around.

"They like you," Kinsey said.

"Who doesn't love a dog?" he replied. He looked up at her with eyes bluer than the vast sky above and added, "Did you have a dog when you were a kid?"

"No," she said. How did you have a dog when you never owned a house? Not many of the rentals her mother could afford allowed pets and Kinsey had been denied as much as a goldfish.

Zane straightened and they both surveyed the house. Up close it remained the sprawling log structure they'd seen from above, but it loomed even bigger.

"I have work to do," Lily called as she ushered Charlie up a short flight of stone steps to a small deck complete with a narrow wooden bench. The child yanked open the door and scooted inside the house, but Lily paused before following her son. "Are you guys eating with us tonight or are you going back to your house?"

The question seemed to stump him. He looked at Kinsey, who wasn't sure what to say, then back at Lily. "Thanks, we'll eat here if you have enough."

"Are you coming in now?"

"Uh, no. I want to look around."

"Gotta say hi to Rose, I bet."

"Yes, where is she, do you know?"

"The barn," Lily said. "Where else would she be? Honestly, Gerard."

He squared his shoulders. "Where is everyone…else?"

Her brow furled as if confused. "Your dad is on his honeymoon and your brothers are out in the east field doing a health inspection on a group of heifers. There's no one else here except me and Charlie."

"What about the new ranch hand? Where is he?"

"Probably out with the mowing crew. How would I know? Chance doesn't exactly discuss work details with me, you know. I'm just the hired help."

"Will there be a chance for me to talk to my brothers before dinner?"

Lily hitched her hands on her waist and narrowed her eyes. "I know I'm too mouthy for my own good, but wow, you're sure acting strange. In about three hours, just like always, whoever is here will collapse in the library to look through the mail. You usually join them, lately, anyway, well, since…" Her voice tapered off, she glanced at Kinsey, then away. A second later she turned and walked into the house.

"I wonder what that was all about," Zane said.

Kinsey shrugged.

"She apparently works here," Zane said. "She's obviously not my wife. And apparently, I don't live at this house."

"Yes," Kinsey said and wondered if it meant anything that Lily hadn't mentioned a wife at home waiting for him. It was impossible to know without asking and it was clear Zane wasn't going to ask until he saw his brothers.

He shook his head. "It's all too much. No way do I want to go inside and make small talk for three hours. Let's go find the barn."

"What about the possibility of an ambush?"

"We'll keep our eyes open."

"Okay, I'm with you."

The dogs frolicked around their legs as they headed toward the most obvious building. It turned out to be relatively new and set up for horses. There was no one about—even the stalls were empty except one. Within this space resided a swaybacked mare with a graying red mane. The horse looked as if she was getting on in years, and though the outside door of her stall stood open, she contentedly munched hay from a holder. A sign over her stall read Rose and looked as though it had been made a long time ago with a wood-burning kit.

"I don't think she's going to have a lot to tell us," Zane said as the mare ambled up to him. He reached out to touch her and she closed her big brown eyes. Kinsey got the profound feeling that the horse recognized Zane and that there was affection between them. Or would be when Zane finally remembered his past and became Gerard again.

As she took out her phone, Zane ran his head down the old mare's face. "You're a sweet thing, aren't you?" he said gently. She nuzzled his neck and made a deep grumbling sound in her throat. After a few minutes, they exited through the door on the other end of the barn and found a shaded pasture with a dozen horses grazing on grass. "Who are you calling?" Zane asked as Kinsey once again attempted a call.

"Detective Woods. There's no reception, though."

"Why Woods?"

"Don't you think he should know your identity? It will change the way he conducts his investigation."

"If we wait until tomorrow, I might have actual details to share," he pointed out. "Like maybe the license number of my truck or travel dates he can check. Maybe one of my brothers knew my plans. Lily intimated that Chance doesn't always tell everything he knows."

Several glistening animals had looked up at them and one, a lovely black gelding, trotted to the fence, his mane and tail flying out behind him. The horse came to a stop opposite Zane. Snorting, he stretched his head over the top railing and bumped Zane's shoulder with his velvety nose. Zane laughed as he leaned against the fence, the horse's big black head right beside his own. They were joined a moment later by a smaller horse, dappled gray, with a delicate head and huge liquid eyes. She sniffed Kinsey's hair.

Zane laughed again. Honestly, he might not remember being Gerard Hastings, but it was as if he'd started to come back to life the minute his feet hit Hastings's earth. "You know, I have to assume these horses are mine to ride whenever I want," he said. "I know you're not really dressed for it, but do you know how to ride a horse, Kinsey?"

"Kind of. It's been a few years, but maybe it's like a bike, maybe you don't forget."

"That's what I'm banking on. Let's saddle up these two and take off toward the ridge behind the house. It beats finding someplace to hide until eight o'clock tonight. And if that new wrangler gets word we're here, I'd just as soon be a little harder to find."

Kinsey looked down at the white pants she'd washed out in the sink the night before, and the black shirt she'd bought the day before that. The sandals weren't great for riding, but she should be okay if the horse didn't step on her. "After you," she said with a sweeping gesture of her arm.

THEY FOUND ALL the equipment easily, as the barn was a model of organization. Though the dogs settled in to watch the saddling process, they didn't follow when Zane and Kinsey led the rides from the barn.

Knowing the horse had a far better chance of finding the right trails, Zane provided gentle pressure to go in a general direction but left most of the decisions to the animal. In that way, they entered a wooded area where the air was noticeably cooler. They soon came across a small tributary stream that fed to the river. Once they'd waded across, the land began to rise. Eventually, the woods thinned out.

Zane felt no sense of fear out here. He began to re-think the whole bridge incident. Had they jumped to a false conclusion? Had there been just too much going on to think clearly or was his thinking slow because of his compromised physical condition?

One thing that wasn't slow was his heartbeat when he turned in the saddle and looked back at Kinsey riding the little Arabian mare. When she looked up and met his gaze, her ruby lips curved. Now that he was home, even if it turned out he wasn't attached to another woman, would she go back to New Orleans and her mother and her job and her life? She had to have friends and connections in Louisiana, while she had none here. Why would she stay? To get to know him? To be with him, to be his lover? Would that be enough for her?

The trees continued thinning as the land stopped climbing, and now they could see through the branches to a broad field dotted with the huge umbrella shapes of oak trees. This was the top of the ridge, he figured, and more than anything he'd seen yet, it struck a chord with him.

Something drew him west and he went with his gut. The horse was a smooth ride, full of energy and strong. He could hear the hooves of Kinsey's steed behind him and glanced over his shoulder to make sure she was still in the saddle. Not only was she there, she was smiling, apparently enjoying herself as much as he was.

Within a few hundred feet, an odd sense of familiarity slowly turned to one of dread. A minute later, gut clench-ing, he realized what it was.

The dream he'd had in the hospital: *the rolling gold*

grass, the chase, the looming tree with the gnarled claws as roots. The choking, gasping…

Here it was, the tree, not bare and black, but leafy and vibrant and yet menacing. Branches thick as rum barrels ran parallel to the ground like suspended bridges, more animal than plant. The towering tree made his skin crawl and he didn't know why. The horse had come to a halt and now he slid out of the saddle, boots hitting the ground, careful not to stand in the shade it cast, uneasy and nervous.

Was someone else here? Was this response really to a tree or to the sense they were being watched, followed? He turned suddenly. Where was Kinsey?

Right behind him. He'd lost track of her for a few moments, hadn't noticed the sound of her horse approaching or felt her presence as she dismounted.

"What's wrong?" she asked. Her dark eyes reflected his confusion.

He shook his head as he allowed his gaze to take in a 360-degree view. There was no one else around and very few hiding spots. "Nothing." How could he tell her he'd been spooked by a tree? "Let's see what's over there," he added, and pointed farther west, willing to go almost anywhere as long as it took him away from here. He climbed back on the black horse, waited for Kinsey to mount the Arabian, and together they took off toward the distant mountains.

Within a couple of miles, his breathing returned to normal and he began to question the reaction that had taken him by surprise. The land once again changed character, and evidence of human occupation started to appear. At first it was the fact the trails turned into roads with rutted grooves that wagon wheels must have dug in the past. Then it was old wooden fences rotting on their rock-pile posts, abandoned roads leading into the distance and signs that a railroad had once existed although the tracks were now overgrown. They reined in the horses when they saw several structures up ahead and heard the sound of a river. Crossing a rickety bridge, they found themselves in a cluster of buildings lining either side of a street.

"It's an old ghost town," Kinsey murmured as they slowly rode between the decrepit wooden structures. Here and there a bit of paint remained, the BAN of a bank, for instance. Cracked glass in the dark windows and decaying wooden sidewalks were decorated with what appeared to be new no-trespassing signs. They rode silently to the end of the town and stopped before reaching an array of rusting mining equipment.

Kinsey cleared her throat and he looked at her. Her fine dark hair had come loose from her ponytail and swept across her forehead and cheeks. Her lips, as always, resembled heart-shaped candies, her eyes burned with curiosity and her skin had attained a slight blush from the sun. For a second, he thought of what he knew of her childhood and what he'd seen and heard of her mother and he wondered how she'd managed to come out of it so whole.

"I'd like to investigate this place but it's getting late," she said.

"I know." It was a relief to Zane to leave the old town, though he was uncertain why. Avoiding the tree that had so impacted him, they found the path they'd traveled through the woods.

It was almost eight o'clock.

Time to find out who and what he was.

Chapter Nine

After unsaddling the horses and calming down the dogs, Zane raised his hand to knock on the door Lily and Charlie had used to enter the house. Kinsey caught his fist before it connected. "This is your family home, remember?" she said.

He looked down at her and smiled. "No, as a matter of fact, I don't."

"Very funny." She grabbed the knob and turned it. The dogs stayed on the porch as though they'd been trained to.

They entered a mudroom full of outerwear hanging on hooks. Racks below were stacked with boots, while a ledge above held a variety of hats. It appeared as orderly as the barn had. Judging from the size of the shoes and clothing, the space was used mainly by men.

Kinsey opened the connecting door, when once again Zane paused. Though his confidence had impressed her from the very first glance she'd had of him and had seemed to double once they got to the ranch, things had subtly shifted. Sometime earlier, back when they broke out of the woods and came across that beautiful old tree, he'd grown thoughtful and then hesitant. Even the ghost town, which she'd found fascinating, had seemed to creep him out, and if it wasn't from conscious associations, then what was the explanation? Something subconscious?

They entered what turned out to be the kitchen, a large room with two gorgeous rock walls and a wide wooden island. Lily looked up from her task at a granite drain board. The tray beside her held a dozen hollowed-out potatoes. She paused from dicing chives. "Hey, where did you guys disappear to?"

"We went riding," Zane said.

"Really? Where did you go?"

"Around."

Lily's brow furrowed and Kinsey leaped into the ensuing silence. "We rode up through the woods to a plateau and from there to a neat old ghost town."

Lily stopped what she was doing as her gaze swiveled to Zane. "You took her *there*?"

"Yes," he said. "Why?"

"No reason," Lily said, dropping her gaze. She picked up a chunk of cheese and a grater. "Chance and Pike are in the library waiting for you. Frankie drove into town, some kind of emergency or other. You know him."

"Where's your son?" Kinsey asked.

"Charlie fell asleep right after his dinner. I feed him early in the summer."

They left the kitchen without further comment. The next room was a dining room with a very long table running down the middle, set with plates and silverware at one end. Framed photographs above a sideboard caught both of their attention and they paused to look.

"That's you," Kinsey said, pointing at a dark-haired boy of about fifteen sitting astride a red horse. "And I bet that's Rose back in the day. She has to be twenty-some-odd years old."

"These other kids must be my brothers," Zane said. He pointed at a lineup of boys that ended in a man of about forty. "That must be our father," he added. "But where is our mother? There are no women on this wall."

"Or signs of one living in the house, aside from Lily, that is," Kinsey said. "Maybe your mother died some time ago and your dad just remarried."

Lily came through the door and seemed surprised to find them lingering in the dining room. She set a bowl filled with greens on the table. "If you want to talk to your brothers about something, you'd better get to it. Dinner will be ready in about a half hour. The roast is in the oven, so I have some time. Would you mind if I listened in?"

"Of course not. You seem to be an integral part of the household."

She gave him the look Kinsey was beginning to know followed almost every conversation she had with Zane. The woman knew something was wrong.

They followed her out of the dining room into a spacious entry. A broad staircase rose on the left side complete with polished banister it wasn't hard to picture Zane and his brothers sliding down when they were kids. Lily quickly led them into the library, which, appropriately enough, held shelves of books.

The only other home library Kinsey had ever seen was Bill Dodge's, with its mass of volumes that reflected his eclectic reading taste. This selection was not nearly as huge and, judging from the few titles that jumped out in a quick glance, not as varied. However, the books were not what really caught her attention.

Two tanned, weathered-looking men occupied the room. One was standing by the window with a glass of amber liquid in his hand and he turned to face them, though his gaze quickly shifted to Lily as she crossed to a bar located in the corner. He turned back to Zane and raised his glass before draining it in one swallow. There was an unmistakable devil-may-care aura about him, an edge of recklessness impossible to miss. He was easily as tall as Zane and just as good-looking in his own way.

The seated man was younger by a few years. A pair of dark-rimmed glasses perched on his nose, while longer, lighter brown hair drifted down over his eyebrows. He didn't give off Zane's steadfast earnestness or the other man's rakish quality; instead, he seemed more intense and private. Maybe it was a combination of the bookish glasses coupled with the stack of half-opened mail scattered across a table in front of him that reminded Kinsey more of a college professor than a cowboy.

These men had to be two of Zane's brothers. Though they were very different in appearance, the muscles and self-assurance emanating from all of the gathered Hastings men stood out. There wasn't a wedding ring in sight except for the gold band on Lily's hand.

"About time you decided to come home," the standing man said. "George Billings bought four hundred calves this afternoon. We need to go round them up from the Pine Hill pasture and get them to the pens for loading by Friday."

Zane nodded.

The man set aside his empty glass. "Where are my manners?" he said, his gaze drifting to Kinsey.

"What manners?" Lily mumbled without looking up.

He ignored her as he took Kinsey's hand. "I'm Gerard's good-looking brother, Chance. The quiet one on the couch is Pike. And you are?"

"Kinsey Frost," she murmured. Chance had a dazzling smile and a charming way of making a woman feel beautiful that probably got him pretty much anything, or anyone, he wanted.

However, between Chance's lingering eye contact

and Zane's glare, there was enough testosterone floating around the room to fuel a rocket.

Pike took off his glasses as he stood up. His eyes were blue like Zane's but darker. "Evening, ma'am," he said. He turned to Zane and added, "Where did you run off to after Dad's wedding? One minute you were here, the next you were gone."

"That's what I need to talk to you about," Zane said. "But first of all, what do you know about the new guy you just hired?"

Lily looked up. "You asked about him earlier today."

"Yes, I did."

Pike folded his glasses into his breast pocket. "You must mean Jodie Brown. We're always shorthanded this time of year and everyone in town knows it. I guess he asked around and someone gave him our name. Why?"

"He's been here since Sunday?" Zane said.

"Yeah. I met with him in town on Saturday evening and he said he wanted to start the next morning. What's going on?"

Kinsey took her first deep breath in quite a while. If Pike had met face-to-face with the wrangler on Saturday evening, then there was no way that man could have dumped a toolbox on her car way back in Louisiana that same night.

Zane seemed to reach the same conclusion. He took out the key chain with the Red Hot medallion and showed it to both his brothers. "You guys recognize this?"

"Sure," Chance said. "I picked that up a few years ago when I was down in Twin Falls at a farm equipment convention. You swiped it from me when I got home. Why are you asking? Don't you remember?"

Lily had been pouring drinks while the introductions were made and she arrived with a glass for Kinsey and one for Zane. Zane took a long swallow. Kinsey took hers to a chair by the window and sat down.

"No, I don't remember," Zane said. "In fact, I don't remember anything that happened before last Friday afternoon."

Both brothers wrinkled their foreheads and said, "What?" in tandem.

Zane took a seat near Kinsey. "Here's the thing. I've lost my memory. The only reason I made it back to Idaho is because Kinsey helped me trace that key fob all the way from New Orleans. The girl at the feed store in town recognized me. I know this must sound crazy but it's true. I don't recognize anyone in this house or this ranch or this state."

"What were you doing in New Orleans?" Pike asked.

"I don't know," Zane said. He set the glass down and shifted his gaze from one person to the other. Kinsey's heart went out to him as his brothers mumbled disbelief.

It was Lily who spoke first. "That's why you've been acting so odd. That's why you rode up to the… I wondered. Does this have something to do with your neck?"

"Yeah," Zane said.

"Tell me."

Chance flashed her an annoyed look. "Aren't you supposed to be cooking dinner or cleaning something? That is in your job description, isn't it? This conversation is personal."

"Dinner is cooked," she snapped back. "And Gerard invited me."

"Leave her alone," Pike added. "Stop being a jerk."

Chance tore his gaze from Lily and zeroed in on Zane's neck. A low whistle escaped his lips. "I didn't even see all those bruises. Have you been in a fight? Aren't you always telling me to have a cool head? And what do you mean you don't know why you were in New Orleans? Why would you go there?"

"I was hoping one of you could tell me that," Zane said.

Pike sat back down on the sofa. "We don't know why you left. It's been about a week. You took off right after Dad and Grace left for their honeymoon. You looked like a man on a mission, but you didn't share any details, like why you were leaving during mowing or where you were going."

"Did I say when I'd return?"

"Not to me," Pike said.

"Nor me," Chance added.

"How about a woman named Mary or Sherry Smith?" Zane added. "Does that name ring a bell?"

"Not a one," Pike said and Chance agreed. "Are you telling us you don't remember being Gerard Hastings at all?"

"That's what I'm telling you," Zane said.

"You don't remember Dad's last wedding?"

"Nope."

"Or Grace?"

"That's the woman your…our father married, right?"

Chance chuckled. "Dad calls her lucky number seven."

"Your father has been married seven times?" Kinsey blurted out.

"Yep, that's why none of us boys really look that much alike. We each have a different mother."

"Where are they all?"

"Frankie's mom took off and disappeared a few years back," Chance said. "Mine is in Atlanta, Pike's mom lives in California with her movie-star boyfriend and his daughter."

"And Gerard's?"

"She died when Gerard was a baby."

"Wow," Kinsey said softly. "Is this new wife nice?"

"She's a little on the strange side, but at least she isn't twenty years old like the one before her. That creeped me out," Chance said.

"Grace is a nice woman," Pike added. "She's just had a hard time."

"Twenty-five years ago. Get over it already."

"There are some things you don't just get over," Lily said softly.

Kinsey saw impatience on Zane's face. This conversation wasn't answering any of the questions he wanted addressed. "Do I have a family?" he asked. "A wife, children, an ex-wife, a current girlfriend?"

"You don't remember Heidi and Ann," Pike said with an uneasy sliding glance at Chance that chilled Kinsey's heart.

Zane sighed deeply. "Who are Heidi and Ann?"

"Oh, God," Chance groaned. He backed up until he tumbled into a red leather wing-back chair and leaned his forehead against his hand.

Pike was the one who explained. "Ann was your wife, Gerard. And Heidi was your little girl."

"Was?" Zane said. "Where are they now?"

After a prolonged hesitation, Pike sighed. "There's no way to sugarcoat this. They're both dead. Man, I'm sorry."

"When did they die?" Zane asked in a hollow voice. He'd been prepared for the possibility of his having a family, but not this.

Again, Pike responded. "Heidi died two years ago last Friday. She was six years old. Ann died the next day."

"Were they in an accident?"

"More or less. Let's talk about that later. Tell us what happened to you."

"Do you have a picture of them?" Zane persisted.

"Are you sure?"

"I'm sure."

Pike got up and walked to the desk. He picked up a framed photograph and brought it back to Zane. Kinsey leaned toward him to see the photo, though she noticed it took him a few seconds to do so himself.

It was a family portrait taken on a snowy day. Zane stood behind a lovely woman with dark hair, his arms around her waist. She held a little girl of two or three in her arms, a charmer with dimples and twinkling brown eyes.

The woman looked a lot like Kinsey.

"I don't remember them," he said softly.

Kinsey put down her untouched drink and stood up, drawing the attention of everyone in the room except Zane, whose gaze still searched the photograph in his hands. She had to get out of here. Town was less than an hour away. She could get a room for the night, start back to New Orleans in the morning.

"Tell us what happened to you," Chance demanded.

Kinsey took a deep breath. She wasn't needed here. She looked down when Zane's fingers brushed hers. "Would you mind giving them a quick run-through of the last few days while I pull myself together?" he asked.

"Not at all," she said, and knew she wasn't going anywhere, not yet, not tonight. She moved to the sofa, where Pike sat down beside her. Chance pulled his chair closer and Lily perched on the arm of the sofa near Pike. In a quiet voice, with as little drama as possible, Kinsey told them about the attacks on the sidewalk and the hospital, Zane's questions about her mother and the heavy toolbox thrown off a bridge.

"That's why Gerard wanted to know about our new hired hand," Chance said.

Lily looked frightened, of all things. "Having someone come after you is terrifying. No wonder Gerard is jumpy."

"It is scary," Kinsey agreed. "But as far as the wrangler goes, the timing is wrong, it couldn't have been him."

"You're really not positive the bridge attack was directed at you in particular, is that right?" Pike said.

"Yes. We need to call the sheriff and ask what he's uncovered."

"I'm going to keep my eyes on Jodie," Chance said.

"Where's Gerard's truck?"

"No one knows," Zane said as he finally looked up from the photograph. "How did my wife and daughter die?" he asked.

Chance got up from his chair, walked to Zane's side and gripped his brother's shoulder. "Don't do this to yourself. Dad will be home tomorrow afternoon. Maybe seeing him will jar your memory and you won't have to go through this again. Give it until tomorrow."

"I can't," Zane said. "Tell me how they died. Please."

It was Pike who took a deep breath. "Heidi climbed up where she didn't belong. Something happened…we don't know for sure. Anyway, she fell. Ann tried to get to her but apparently slipped in the process and hit her head. If we'd found them sooner, I don't know. No one knows for sure."

Zane's stare was intense as he focused on one brother then the other. "Did Heidi fall from a tree? Did she fall from the one up on the plateau?"

"The hanging tree? No, why do you ask that?"

"It was just a feeling," Zane said.

"You have a thing about that tree," Chance said. "Always have."

Kinsey cleared her throat. Zane seemed too distracted to even ask why they called the big oak the hanging tree.

She glanced at Lily who quickly looked down at her hands. Her earlier reaction to their ride suddenly made sense. "They died in the ghost town, didn't they?" Kinsey whispered.

"Yeah," Chance said. "That's right, they did."

UNABLE TO FACE sitting around a table and enduring any more stares and questions, Zane asked for and got directions to his own house. It turned out it was located down the road that ran parallel to the river.

"What do you think of my brothers?" he asked Kinsey as their headlights startled a small herd of deer.

"I think they're nice," she said. "What do you think?"

"They're different from each other," he said. "I get the feeling Pike takes care of business and Chance gets into trouble whenever he can."

"Me, too," she said.

"He and Lily sure seem to dislike each other."

"Do you think?"

"Yeah. Don't you?"

"I'm not sure," she said.

He yawned into his fist. It was twilight by now, and so consuming had this day been that to Zane it felt as if a month had gone by. In the back of his head he knew that dismissing Jodie Brown as an assassin was premature, and from what he'd overheard Pike and Chance saying, they agreed. Since no one had any idea what Zane had gotten himself into, how could they judge how many people wanted him dead or even if there was a conspiracy? On the other hand, he now carried Pike's revolver.

It appeared his house was newer than the main house and less than half the size. Built partway up the gentle slope to the river, the view promised to be wonderful once daylight came.

An automatic light went on as Kinsey parked inside a carport next to a newer blue SUV. Zane was too tired and emotionally wrung out to take in many details, but as they moved to the front door, he heard animals in the nearby fields. Pike had assured him they'd been taking care of his horses, feeding his chickens and milking his cow. They might as well have told him they'd been airing out his magic carpet. Nothing had any relevance to him.

He opened the door with the key Pike had pointed out and held it for Kinsey to enter first. As usual, she carried her painting-supply tote over her shoulder and a small brown bag in her arms. It was filled with the few garments she'd purchased along the way to flesh out her limited wardrobe. Zane was still mostly living in Bill Dodge's old clothes and set the satchel and Kinsey's belongings on the bottom step of an open staircase leading to the second floor. Then he made sure the lock on the door was engaged and the dead bolt slid closed.

Kinsey had been flipping on lights and now he looked around the house, straining to remember anything, yearning to feel a flicker of recognition that would bring his family back into focus. He'd dreaded the house being a mausoleum filled with pictures and sadness, but it wasn't like that. Instead, it had a kind of male clutter that felt comfortable, and though there was a picture album on the table, it was mercifully closed. He wasn't up to looking at faces he should remember.

He turned abruptly at the sound of Kinsey's inhaled breath. She was staring into the living room, a comfortable-looking space with overstuffed furniture and lots of golden pine. What appeared to be an antique grandfather clock occupied one corner, while the other held a locked gun cabinet.

But what had caught her attention hung over the unlit

fireplace. For one crazy moment, Zane wondered how Kinsey's likeness had made its way into his house. In the next instant, he realized it wasn't her. The woman in the painting was taller, less curvy.

"It's uncanny how much I look like Ann," Kinsey said under her breath, but he heard her.

"It's quite a coincidence," he said.

"Is it?"

He stared down at her. For days she'd been the eye of the hurricane for him, his compass. He'd grown to respect and like her. More, he'd started to envision a life with her, had wondered if love began with this aching desire never to be apart. He'd wanted her with him in every sense of the word. Finding out about a dead wife and child had jarred him and now it was clear, it had jarred her, too. He could see it in her eyes. "Of course," he said. "What else?"

"Don't you see?" she whispered.

"See what?"

"You were drawn to me because I look like your dead wife. Think about it. You were injured two years after her death almost to the day and the first woman you see who isn't a doctor or a nurse is someone so similar…"

"No," he said, grabbing her arms. "No."

She put her hands on his and leaned her forehead against his chest. "It's okay," she whispered. "It's not your fault."

He put his arms around her and held her so close he could feel her heartbeat. He'd been afraid of losing her because he was already committed. To lose her because a wife he couldn't remember was dead seemed the ultimate irony.

He tilted her chin and looked down into her eyes. He wasn't sure what he could say, but he did know what he could do. He lowered his face until their lips met. The kiss had a bittersweet quality to it that was new. Then suddenly he realized what was wrong. It was a goodbye kiss.

He pulled himself away and when her eyes opened to stare up at him, he claimed her lips again, and this kiss wasn't tentative or sweet or shy. Holding her around the waist, he lifted her from her feet, burning away her doubts and her hesitations, or at least trying to. He needed her, he wanted her, nothing had changed except everything, but that didn't affect the way he felt about her.

"Let me go," she finally whispered.

"No," he said. "I can't."

"Not forever, Zane, just for now. Put me down. Please."

He set her back on the floor and cupped her face in his hands. Staring deep into her eyes, looking for her soul, he whispered to her, "You have to understand something. Even when I remember my wife and our daughter and what happened to them, even when specific grief for them returns, I will continue to have the memories and feelings I have made these last several days with you. Those feelings won't be lost when the others return."

"You don't know that for sure," she said.

"Yes, I do."

They looked at each other as the big clock in the corner ticked off the seconds.

Finally, she sighed. "Let's just go to bed. Let's put this day behind us and figure things out tomorrow. Pike said your father will be back in the afternoon and maybe he'll know something that will help. For now, let's not talk or try to figure anything out except where to sleep."

He reluctantly loosened his grip and nodded. He picked up their bags and they climbed the stairs together.

The first room they investigated turned out to be a time bomb. It had obviously belonged to a small girl partial to bunnies and unicorns. He and Kinsey exchanged stricken looks. Without saying a word, he closed the door on what had to be Heidi's room. It didn't look as if it had been changed since the last time the child hopped out of bed.

The next room appeared to be a home office, the one after that the master suite. The room was stuffy. As Zane deposited their bags on a bench at the foot of the bed, he noticed a picture of himself and Ann on the dresser. Judging from his image, it had been taken several years before. Where had he met her? Had they married right away? How long had they been married before Heidi came along? Had they been happy?

He laid the photo facedown. She'd been gone from the world for two years. Contemplating where he was in the process of letting her go was futile.

"I can't sleep in here," Kinsey said.

He turned to find her staring around the room. "Because of me?" he asked.

"No, because of…Ann, I guess."

"Yeah. I feel the same way. There's one more door farther down the hall. Let's see if it's a guest bedroom."

The door opened onto a room very similar to the master room. It, too, had an attached bath. It was slightly smaller, nicely decorated and a little more intimate. "Will this do?" Zane asked Kinsey.

"It's perfect."

He withdrew Pike's gun from the back waistband of his jeans and set it on the shelf next to the bed, where it would be handy in case it was needed. Kinsey took the first shower and then it was his turn to stand under the hot, cleansing water. They climbed into the king-size bed at the same time. Within seconds, they'd rolled to the middle and embraced.

He'd steeled himself against succumbing to his feelings for her. The day had been so raw for both of them. But the fact was, he couldn't control his body or his imagination, either. He'd wanted to be with her since the night they'd met and now he knew he was free. But did she know that, too?

"Have you ever been in love, Kinsey?" he whispered.

"I thought I was once."

"With Ryan, that guy you told me about?"

"No, not him. It was back when I was twelve. The boy was thirteen. He didn't even know I existed. I thought he was very mysterious."

"Maybe I should try ignoring you," he said, kissing her ear. His fingers ran over the pearly satin of her shoulder.

She drew her head back to look at him, although he could barely even see the whites of her eyes. "I don't think you need to worry about attracting my attention," she said. "And you're plenty mysterious enough, as it is."

He kissed her again, this time on the lips. He didn't expect her to respond, but to his surprise she returned the kiss with the softest lips on earth. And when she parted them for his tongue, his whole body jumped to attention.

"Slow down," she whispered against his neck.

Was she telling him to back off? If so, something had to give. "This isn't going to work," he said softly as his hand slid over the tantalizing rise and fall of her waist. "I can't lie in the same bed with you and keep my hands to myself."

"I don't want you to keep them to yourself," she said, and as she spoke, she positioned her body closer to his, fitting her hips against his. She picked up one of his hands and moved it to her breast. "I just want you to slow down." Her warm breath against his skin drove him crazy.

Her hand slipped down and brushed against an erection he was powerless to contain. There was a layer of cotton between his flesh and her hand, but he was pretty sure he was about to spontaneously combust.

He brought his mouth down on hers again as he massaged her breast, delighting in the way her nipples grew hard. He tentatively lifted the strap holding up her orange gown and she moaned deep in her throat. With her help, he slipped the gown from her supple body and wished he'd left the lights on so he could see her.

But it was enough for now to just feel her. She slipped her hands under his boxers and pulled on them. Soon he was naked, too, and any thought of slowing down was obsolete and naive.

Deep, long, intense kisses led to exploration. Her curves felt mesmerizing under his fingers, and when he touched her intimately, she shuddered. Groans escaped his own lips and her fingers ran over the steel rod of his erection. The sound seemed to add fuel to an already enraged fire. Pressing kisses down her neck, he cupped the dense soft weight of her breasts. Before he could lower his mouth to suck on her nipples, she'd clasped his rear and slid a leg under him. He mounted her quickly, delirious now with sensations. Plunging himself inside her seemed to be the most natural thing in the world, and the way she raised her hips to accept him drove another nail in his ability to delay the inevitable.

Obviously, he'd made love before. He had no specific memories of doing so, but he had been a father. At that moment it was impossible to believe there had ever been anyone else, and as they moved together, all tangible thoughts ceased.

Their release came swiftly, thoroughly, both of them crying out in ecstasy before crumbling together.

After a few minutes, he switched on a small bedside lamp, anxious to see her face, hoping he would detect no regret. He found her staring up at him from the tumble of blankets at his side, her hair messed, her eyes dark and soft.

If what he felt throbbing in his heart and running through his veins wasn't love, what was? He reached for her and she came.

Chapter Ten

Kinsey woke up the next morning to find herself naked and alone in the bed. She'd slept in, but instead of jumping up, she lay there a few minutes basking in memories of the long night until she sighed deeply, sat up and looked around the room.

The vaulted ceiling rose high over her head while sunlight poured through the windows she'd opened during the night. The room was decorated with dashes of red, the curtains fluttered in the breeze. She thought back to the master room they'd abandoned, to the pile of male clothes tossed in a chair and the half-full glass of water on the nightstand that to her signaled Zane had left the ranch in a hurry the last time he'd slept in this house.

So, what had happened at the wedding or right after it that made Zane leave abruptly? Or had he been planning to go and stayed just long enough to see his father take wife number seven?

She spied her art tote on the bench at the foot of the bed. Yesterday had been the first day in years that she hadn't sketched or painted anyone. She'd thought about it when she glimpsed the pain hiding behind Lily's smile. She'd also thought about it when she entered the library and saw Zane's brothers. They were unique and yet cut from the same cloth. She couldn't wait to find out what Frankie, the one who had been absent, was like.

But she'd also thought about painting when she looked at the mountains, the fields, the horses. The ghost town begged to have its secrets revealed, though its worst secret of all, the deaths of Zane's family, made that impossible for her to even contemplate. For the first time in her life she ached to paint more than faces.

If she and Zane managed to get over the obstacles fate kept throwing their way, and if they managed to live through the assaults until the perpetrator was found, could she settle here?

This place was so different from New Orleans. Quieter, lonelier, the air dry instead of moist. The sky seemed three times as big, and the river, instead of being wide and lazy and muddy, was narrow and ambitious and cool. There would be snow in the winter and turning leaves in the fall. Spring would bring mountainsides of wildflowers, and everywhere you looked, at least on Hastings land, you would find cattle and horses. She'd even seen deer grazing in a meadow on the ride home from the ghost town, then again last night from the car. She'd glimpsed hawks soaring up in the sky and rabbits scurrying through the underbrush.

But the differences ran deeper and it wasn't just the scenery or the weather. Zane had grown up in that beautiful old house with four brothers and an endless stream of stepmothers. She had grown up in a series of cheap housing with one ever-present mother and no men. She'd always had something to eat and warm clothes, but she hadn't had acres of land to roam, dozens of animals to care for, a lifestyle set in motion since before she was born. She had never belonged to a piece of land, but Zane had and still did. This was a family ranch and that meant the family worked it.

After a shower, she dressed quickly, borrowing some of the cream she found on the vanity to soothe her sunburned face. Riding around yesterday afternoon out in the full sun without protection hadn't been the best idea she'd ever had. Then she went in search of Zane. She found him seated behind the desk in the room set up as an office. He looked up as she paused at the doorway and smiled at her.

"Morning, sunshine," he said as he got to his feet and approached her. The lazy, sexy look in his eyes, coupled with his loose-jointed gait, made her heart thump around. He paused right in front of her and lifted her chin. "You have a rosy glow this morning."

"I have a sunburn," she said, but she was thinking that she would never get tired of the way his eyes devoured her. Did feelings like that last? Zane's father had just taken his seventh wife. Did being raised in that kind of atmosphere encourage the concept to be content with one woman?

Why was she even thinking like this?

He lowered his head and touched her lips with his. All the emotions and sensations of the night before came flooding back, begging her to believe in fairy tales and forever. She allowed her head to dip slightly so she could brush her cheek against his knuckles.

"You look great," she told him. "I like the clothes."

He glanced down at his white shirt and the suede vest he wore over it. He hadn't shaved and the slight stubble glistening on his face beguiled her. "I found a walk-in closet full of my stuff," he said. "I seem to have a thing for vests."

She smiled as she recalled the first time she'd seen him. He'd been wearing a pliant leather vest and she'd admired the way it made his shoulders and chest look supremely powerful. And last night, aroused and commanding, the true depth of his strength had flooded her senses.

"I want to talk to you," he said. "Come sit down." He led her to the chair at right angles to the desk, whisked a yellow baseball cap decorated with an embroidered orange dog off the seat before sitting down in front of the computer.

"Have you remembered something?" she asked.

"No. But it's weird looking at the plaques on the wall, reading emails from people who are strangers, finding things like a baseball cap abandoned on a chair that I must have left there but have no memory of doing. It got a little overwhelming, so I called Sheriff Crown back in Louisiana. At least I remember what he looks and sounds like."

She shifted her weight forward. "Did the kids confess to throwing the toolbox off the bridge?" she asked.

"Nope. In fact, they have an iron-tight alibi."

"Did he question anyone else?"

"Yes, but got nowhere. He's convinced a local is involved but admits it's strange no one seems to know anything about it. He says 'pranks' like that usually get somebody talking, but so far, nothing."

She drummed her fingernails. "So the attack might still have been aimed at you."

"For all the good that supposition is doing us. Oh, and I also called Detective Woods."

"Did he mention if anyone fitting Ryan's description turned up the victim of a crime?"

Zane settled his hand on hers. "I asked. There's been no one. Hopefully, your friend is safe."

"Don't forget he might be your friend, too."

"I'm not forgetting," he said. "Anyway, I gave Woods my real name. He's going to search hotel records and see if he can find some trace of me. He has the make of my truck, the license plate and VIN numbers, so he'll check out the police impound yards, too, and call your phone if they find it. I have to admit that makes me nervous, though."

"Why?"

"Who knows what incriminating evidence might be lurking in my truck. I'd like to think I'm an innocent victim in all this, but I can't know that for sure until it's proven or I regain my memory. I just want to be there when the door is opened for the first time."

She sat forward. "Does that mean you're going back to New Orleans?"

"Eventually. How about you?"

"Pretty soon," she said. No matter what the future held, she couldn't just walk out of her apartment or family responsibilities. Besides, she needed some space and he did, too, whether he admitted it or not. Her place was at her own home while he needed to reestablish his identity here. This was all happening too fast.

A giant pit in her stomach warned her that parting with him was going to be pure unadulterated misery, worse now that they were lovers. By the time another few nights passed, how would she ever be brave enough to give him the space he needed?

"By the way, I found a notebook with my passwords in it, so I took a look at my bank records. I also found files in one of the drawers and scanned those. The upshot is that this is either a very profitable ranch or I am one hell of a financier. I can pay you back everything I owe you and help you replace your car."

"Don't worry about that right now…"

"Please, for the sake of my pride, just accept what I'm offering. This issue has been bugging me since the beginning. I have a nice fat checking account and a book of checks and I intend to repay you. Meanwhile, I own the SUV down in the carport, so let's pay the extra fee and turn in the rental to the local branch today or tomorrow. I'll buy you a plane ticket whenever you want to go home. Just let me know."

"Thanks," she said. Money, or rather, the lack of it, had been preying on her mind. It was a relief to know Zane could help. In a perfect world, she could gallantly refuse his offer and chalk generosity up to improving her karma; in the real world, she could not.

Her phone rang, which jarred them both. She got to her feet as she glanced at the screen. "My mother," she informed Zane. "I'd better take it."

He picked up the yellow baseball cap and pulled it over her hair. "I don't want you burned to a crisp today," he whispered. "I have plans for you tonight." He followed this with a kiss before pulling down on the brim. "I want to go back to the ghost town. Will you go with me?"

"Of course."

He smiled. "Talk to your mom. I'll go find the kitchen and rustle us up something to eat."

She punched on the phone as Zane left the room. It was amazing how empty a space could seem once he'd vacated it.

"Hi, Mom," she said, steeling herself for more ultimatums.

"Are you still in Idaho?"

"Yes. I'll be flying home soon, maybe as early as the weekend."

"What happened to your car?"

"A small accident. How are things with you?"

"Bill isn't doing well. He refuses to go back to the hospital or even allow me to call his doctor."

"Oh, man," Kinsey said. "He sure went downhill fast,

didn't he? Can Mr. Fenwick convince him to let you get help?"

"James says Bill actually has a right to conduct his death on his own terms. He has a point. It's just so scary."

"How about his nephew?"

"He disappeared again yesterday, but it's too much to hope it's for long."

"That's a lot for you to handle. How are you dealing?"

"James is a rock, thank goodness, since you're still off with that cowboy. You are, aren't you?"

"Yes. He rediscovered his identity but not his memory. Do you have a pencil handy? I want to give you the home number of my friend." She rattled off the number on the desk phone. "Cell reception is iffy here. Call me and leave a message if something happens, okay?"

"Okay."

They soon hung up. The conversation had been subdued, but it hadn't been antagonistic, for which Kinsey was grateful. A growling stomach reminded her she'd missed the last couple of meals. Time to find Zane and discover if he could cook.

"Your father will be home after lunch sometime," Lily told Zane. She was up to her neck in green beans and canning equipment. Already processed quart jars lined a towel-draped table, while a big pressure cooker released steam as a timer ticked nearby. A dozen sterilized bottles, one with a wide-mouthed funnel resting atop, awaited the pile of beans Lily chopped into two-inch pieces for the next batch.

"Do you know where my brothers are?" Zane asked her.

"Over getting the pens ready for the roundup on Friday. They said you should join them if you had the chance."

"You'll have to tell me how to get there," he said. She did and told him to take truck keys out of the mudroom. Zane asked Kinsey if she wanted to come with him and hesitated when she declined. "Go have some time with them," she said. "Maybe it will help you remember something."

"I don't like leaving you alone," he said as he squeezed her hand.

She gestured at Lily. "I'm hardly alone. Listen, I promise I'll stay right here at this ranch until you get back, okay?"

"I won't be long." He kissed her cheek and squeezed her hand.

"You two are close," Lily said after the door closed behind him.

Kinsey smiled. "You can tell?"

"He's letting you wear his lucky hat."

Kinsey had all but forgotten the yellow cap still perched on her head. "I don't think he remembers it's special."

"I know, but it is. He played Bulldog Football during high school. Anyway, I'm happy for both of you. He's a good man."

"I know," Kinsey said.

"It will be wonderful for him to have children again."

"I know he wants them very much," Kinsey said. "It seems to be a part of who he is."

"Is it part of who you are?" Lily asked with a swift glance.

"A family has never been a priority," Kinsey admitted. "Until now. Last night…well, yes, I think I'm finally beginning to understand the whole circle-of-life thing. Zane is teaching me. I mean Gerard."

"I don't mind what you call him," Lily said with a smile.

Kinsey had surprised herself with her answer and for

a moment felt a stir of panic. What if she built her dreams of a shared life with this man at this ranch and it never came to be? How would she go on?

And yet, what choice did she have but to see it through? Her heart had already traveled where her brain was afraid to tread.

Lily screwed a cap on a jar. "This batch will have to wait until I take care of Charlie and deliver lunch to the crew."

"How about the lunch? Can I make some sandwiches or something?" Kinsey offered.

"I already made chili and corn bread, and when I get back from running Charlie up to catch the bus, I'll grill chicken."

"That's a feast! What crew are you talking about?" Kinsey asked as she perched on a nearby stool.

"Sometimes they burn pastures after the grass is harvested for feed. It purifies the soil. It also, I might add, works up an appetite."

"I didn't see any smoke."

"You wouldn't. The field is over the mountain, miles from here. I don't know, maybe I bit off more than I could chew today. I shouldn't have tried to can this morning." She scurried to the staircase and hollered, "Charlie? Hurry up."

Kinsey heard the little boy protest, but Lily repeated her command before resuming her task.

"Have you been working here long?" Kinsey asked.

"About six months."

"Then you didn't know Zane's, I mean Gerard's, wife, Ann?"

"No. She was already gone by the time I came. I hope Harry's new wife can make it a home again, but from what Chance says, she's got issues of her own."

"Like what, do you know?"

"I've just overheard people talking. I guess she lost her family in a series of tragic events. That was a long time ago, but she hasn't really mended. I gather she feels responsible."

"That must be terrible."

Lily looked down at her hands. "Yeah. Guilt is an awful thing to live with. You'll like Gerard's father, though."

"What's he like?"

"Strong willed and opinionated, not my favorite traits in a male, but he took me in when I had nowhere else to turn. He's never even asked me to explain…things. Anyway, he's a chauvinist, sure. It's easier to dismiss in a man of seventy than it is in someone Chance's age."

"Explain something to me," Kinsey said. "Are you and Chance enemies or are you guys closer than you're letting on?"

Lily shrugged. "He wanted to date…I don't know."

"You didn't?"

"No. I've had enough of men like him. You know, all bluster and ego. He reminds me of…well, never mind, it doesn't matter."

Charlie tumbled into the room looking resigned to his fate. He glanced at Kinsey, then around the room. "Where is Uncle Gerard?"

"He's out working," Kinsey said. She turned to Lily. "I can drive him up to catch the bus for you."

"I appreciate the offer, but he'll require his daily pep talk," she replied. "If you could take the beans out of the pressure cooker when the timer goes off, that would really help. Oh, and the charcoal for the chicken is all laid out in the grill near the garden. Would you light it for me in about fifteen minutes?"

"Of course."

"Charlie, get your lunch box out of the fridge," Lily said as she grabbed her keys. She looked back at Kinsey and added, "Just use those tongs to lift the bottles out of the cooker and set them on that towel like the others, but make sure you wait until the pressure is at zero. I'll loosen the rings later. Thanks a bunch."

And with that, mother and child disappeared out the door.

Kinsey sat down at the table to wait for the timer to announce the pressure cooker was ready to open. The big room was humid from steam, but not entirely unpleasant. The minutes ticked by peacefully as the house seemed to settle around her. She thought back to the scrambled eggs Zane had made her for breakfast, and the way he'd flirted with her. Sharing a cup of coffee at his sunlit table in his very own house had seemed enchanting to Kinsey, like a piece of the giant puzzle called life had slipped quietly into place. There went the panic alarm again, and she smiled at her contrary thoughts.

She'd slipped her small purse across her shoulder that morning, and now she opened it without removing it from her body, taking out the book Bill Dodge had given her to help pass the time. It really was a beauty—he'd outdone himself on the binding. She opened it and found that he'd written something on the inside page. "For Kinsey," she read. "Remember, life is like a book—the important stuff happens between the covers."

She chuckled at the double entendre. Would she ever see him again? Suddenly she felt as if she was half a world away, living among strangers…

She turned a few pages until the timer finally went off. After fitting the book back in her bag, she opened the lid and carefully lifted the dripping bottles one by one. When they were all lined up without their shoulders touching, she began the search for matches and found them in a drawer by the stove.

It was warm outside but not as humid as inside the house. The three dogs ambled over as she walked to the garden, where she found a large chimney-style fire starter filled with newspaper and coals sitting on a bigger bed of charcoal. She'd seen these used before and knew the object was to light the newspapers and wait until the coals on top caught fire, then spread those over all the others.

This was going to take a few minutes, so after she lit the newspaper, she decided to investigate the garden. She let herself in the tall fence that must have been constructed to keep deer from munching their way through the produce. Though she didn't close the gate, the dogs held back. One wandered off toward the barn and the other two followed him.

It was a pleasure to walk the well-tended path. Rows of cornstalks and pole beans climbing up their strings heightened the feeling of isolation. Bright red tomatoes hung from trellised plants, while rows of peppers, eggplants and vines covered with cucumbers covered the raised beds. Yellow marigolds added color and beauty. She'd never been alone in such a lush, productive garden and found it tantalizing.

What would make it perfect, she decided, was a shade tree and a bench. How wonderful would it be to sit out here and read a book or try painting a still life…

Surely no one would deny her a tomato or two? She looked around until she found a branch covered with grape-sized fruit, and stripped three juicy specimens to pop in her mouth. The urge to find a basket and harvest everything in sight was overpowering.

Well, since she couldn't pick the fruits and vegetables, she could do the next best thing. She could draw them and luckily she'd brought along her art tote when they left Zane's house that morning. She turned toward the gate with the intention of grabbing a sketch pad and charcoal pencils but stopped short. A man stood a couple of feet away. A smile died on her lips as he raised his hand and revealed an ugly black gun.

"Who are you?" she gasped. "What do you want?"

His tongue darted over what appeared to be thin lips, although it was impossible to know for sure because of the reddish beard that covered half his face. Jodie! He shot a quick look over his shoulder as though he'd heard something. When he turned back to her, he licked his lips again. "You're coming with me," he said.

She wanted to run or scream but could do neither. It was as though her feet had grown roots in the fertile earth, holding her in place. He jabbed the barrel against her stomach. "Just do as I say," he snapped. His expression had gone from nervous to intense. He took a deep breath. "Listen. If you're good and quiet and don't give me any trouble, he won't have to watch you die. If you piss me off, he'll never forget what he sees."

He? Zane?

"What have you done to him?" she cried.

He grabbed her arm and pushed her in front of him, twisting her elbow behind her back. The gun poked against her spine. "Walk ahead of me. Don't try anything." His rough nails grated against her skin. She took a few steps and he stayed glued to her back.

"Hurry up," he demanded.

"Tell me what you've done to him!" she pleaded as they exited the garden. She frantically cast her gaze around the ranch, praying someone would see them and intercede. There just wasn't anyone. The dogs had reappeared and stood nearby, watching with big brown eyes.

The only thing that moved was the flame shooting out of the coal chimney.

"Walk over to that blue truck."

A rusted truck sat a few feet away, a squat, window-less canopy secured to the bed. "Open the door," he de-manded as he waved the gun at the passenger side. Maybe she'd have a chance to escape when he went around to get behind the wheel.

Or maybe he'd shoot her right here and now. But why? To get to Zane? It had to be. "What do you want?" she re-peated as she opened the door. "Just tell me."

He pulled her back against his chest, raised the gun to her temple and hissed hot air against the back of her neck. His body felt as hard as a concrete pillar, the arm wrapped around her waist as unyielding as a steel cable. "Did you honestly think Block would let you walk away?" he said. "Did you think he wouldn't find you, that he wouldn't hunt you down? Did you think he'd let you steal the only thing in the world he cares about?"

"Who is Block?" she cried. "I don't know who you're talking about."

"Don't play dumb with me," he said. Her pulse seemed to jump against the cold metal as he guided the gun down her neck, slowly and methodically, down between her breasts, to her belly. She struggled to breathe, to think. Every nightmare she'd ever had shot through her head. "You are about to have a very fatal accident," he whis-pered. "And after you're dead, Block will get what he wants, what is his."

"I don't know anyone named Block. Please."

"You're playing with me," he growled against her skin. "That means I play with you, too." He abruptly thrust his tongue into her ear, his free hand twisting the strap on her purse up around her neck. She grabbed at his hands to keep from being strangled and threw her head back into his, hoping to knock him out cold. His teeth came down hard on her earlobe and she screamed.

"Bitch!" he barked as he pushed her against the truck.

Warm blood dripped down her neck. She tried dodging away, but he caught the strap again and yanked it hard. Then he brought the gun down on her head. She raised her arm to protect herself. "You're making a mistake," she screamed. "Stop!"

The next blow connected with her temple. She tried to grab something to steady herself, but she couldn't make her fingers work. Her body hit the ground with a thump. A gray rock filled her entire field of vision until it, too, faded away.

Chapter Eleven

Zane found his brothers where Lily had told her they'd be. Both were working on the pens located in the middle of a vast field surrounded by acres of sloping hillsides. He understood that the pens, shoots and ramps would be used by a group of cowhands to gather and contain cattle, to sort and load them onto trucks so they could be taken to their new home, though he had no actual memory of ever doing any of the work himself.

Chance told him to shovel aside the deadfall and debris that blocked several of the gates while he replaced a rail. "It's odd giving you directions when you've been doing this stuff your entire life," he said with a wink. "You're the oldest, you're usually the one bossing everyone else around."

"Yeah, well, I'm not exactly myself," Zane said.

Pike tossed a broken board into the back of his truck. "Still can't remember anything, huh?"

"No." He wiped the sweat from his forehead with a handkerchief and added, "Have you ever heard me mention anyone named Ryan Jones?"

Chance paused mid–hammer stroke and appeared to think. Eventually he shook his head. "No."

"How about you, Pike?"

"Can't say as I have. Who is he?"

"Someone in New Orleans. A friend of Kinsey's. It doesn't really matter. But let me ask you this. Didn't it seem funny to you guys that I would leave the ranch during a busy time of year and right when Dad had just gone off on his honeymoon?"

Pike shrugged. "Sure it did. You're usually not the secretive type. But you've organized things here pretty efficiently and we have adequate help."

"I organize things around here?" Zane asked.

Chance laughed. "Like I said, Gerard, you're kind of bossy."

The name still sounded like a character out of a book to Zane. He dug in his shovel. "What about our father?"

"He thinks he's the brains, but he's been deferring to you, and to a lesser degree the rest of us, for years. Man, he isn't going to believe you don't remember any of this."

Zane glanced up at the blazing sun. Why in the world had he worn a vest? He glanced at the watch he'd put on after finding it on top of his dresser that morning. "As soon as we're finished here, I need to get back to Kinsey. I don't like leaving her alone."

"That's fine," Pike said. "Tomorrow we're going to round up the rest of the calves over at the Bywater pasture. We could use your help."

"Sure," Zane said. Maybe Kinsey could borrow a pair of boots from Lily—they looked about the same size. Then she could go with them.

"Anyway, you don't have to worry about the new wrangler, Jodie," Pike added. "I sent him and a few others up to the ridge to bring down the herd and sort out the calves. They're getting really big. It's a good thing we found a buyer."

"So Jodie isn't on ranch land?"

"Well, define ranch land," Pike said. "This place is

strung together like a patchwork quilt. We own most of it, we rent some of it, we lease other parts. Anyway, just rest assured, Jodie is about ten miles south of here and won't be back for hours."

"Even if he wasn't, no one gets past our iron maiden," Chance said.

"What iron maiden?"

Pike threw another piece of wood. "That's what Chance calls Lily."

"That's one of the names I have for her," Chance said. He hammered in a nail on the gate he was repairing and added, "I also call her irritating, defensive, secretive…in fact, if she wasn't so easy on the eyes, she'd have no redeeming qualities."

"She's got a cute kid," Zane offered.

"Charlie's okay. A little wimpy, maybe. How he got that way with Lily for a mother is a mystery."

"Dad likes Lily," Pike said. "So do Frankie and I. You're the only one with a problem."

"Frankie is the youngest, right?" Zane asked. "Is he back on the ranch today?"

"He didn't show up," Chance said. "Frankie isn't exactly dependable."

"He's trying to change," Pike said.

"He needs to try harder," Chance grumbled.

Zane concentrated on his job for a few minutes, but a growing sense of uneasiness made it hard. He didn't want to walk out on a job half done, so he redoubled his efforts until a half hour later, the last rail had been replaced and the gates were all operational. "I'm heading back," he announced.

"I'll ride with you," Pike said as he tossed tools into the back of the truck.

Chance banged in another nail. "I'll be right behind you guys. I want to finish up here first."

Zane let Pike drive as it was obvious his brother knew the lay of the land a lot better than he did. "Last night you called that big oak up on the plateau the hanging tree. Why is that?" Zane asked as they set off toward the ranch.

"Because of the three men who died hanging from its limbs."

"Three? When did this happen?"

"A long time ago." Pike slid him a look. "You saw the ghost town. It used to be a pretty prosperous mining town. Then four men robbed the bank the night a big payload came in. The citizens formed a posse and ran them down. They brought them back to that tree and hung them up to die. Their bodies weren't cut down for months. And after that, the town died."

"Yikes," Zane said. "But you mentioned four thieves."

"One of them, a guy by the name of John Murdock, escaped. The story goes he got away with all the money and was never heard from again."

"Chance says I've always been obsessed with that tree. I don't know if it's true, but I do know I had a profound reaction to it yesterday and I've dreamed about it a couple of times."

"Everyone but Dad and Chance get the willies around the tree. The whole town calls us Hanging Tree Ranch, not Hastings Ridge. But in your case it runs deeper than that. A bunch of older boys tied you to the tree when you were about ten. As I've heard the story, it took Dad until the middle of the night to find you and by then you'd been stuck for hours listening to coyotes, absolutely terrified. That leaves an impression."

"No kidding. Do we own the ghost town?"

"Yeah. You've been lobbying to plow it under for obvious reasons. Dad wants to take it apart board by board and resell the lumber to a decorator in town. Apparently there's a market for old wood."

His voice trailed off and Zane figured it was because he didn't want to reopen the subject of Ann and Heidi, but he soon realized he was wrong. His brother had let up on the gas pedal. His gaze followed a dust trail going down a road running at right angles to the one they were on. Pike glanced at Zane.

"That looks like Jodie's old beater truck."

"Are you sure?"

"Pretty sure."

"But you sent him miles away from here."

"Exactly. He said nothing about not going. This isn't the road we typically use to get off the land. It leads up into the hills, eventually to the ghost town. I can't imagine what he's up to, but he came from the direction of the ranch. Maybe he went there to tell someone he was moving on. Drifters do that, you know. Let's go check out the house. Jodie might have said something to Lily. We could clear this up in a minute or two."

Zane turned in his seat to watch Jodie's truck racing away in the other direction. They picked up speed as the road evened up and within ten minutes were parking by the garden next to the SUV they'd driven from Zane's house a couple of hours before. Zane was struck with the horrible feeling he was too late, but too late for what? He jumped out of the truck before it came to a full stop. "Kinsey?" he yelled as he ran. He tore through the kitchen door. The room was empty and quiet, still filled with jars of beans and little else. He stood still for a second, then yelled Kinsey's name again. The silent building seemed to hold its breath and he knew in his bones she was not inside this house. A shiver snaked down his spine.

He hurried back outside right as Lily pulled her red car to a stop. The smile slid off her face when she looked at Zane and Pike. "What's wrong?"

"Kinsey isn't here," Pike said. "Did she say anything to you about leaving?"

"No. She promised—"

"Look at this," Zane interrupted. A yellow baseball cap lay on the ground. The cap was jarring enough, but even more alarming were the scuff marks in the dirt and the fresh tire tracks leading away from the ranch.

"That's your Bulldog hat," Pike said.

Zane picked it up. "Kinsey was wearing this." He turned it over in his hands but froze when a bright red smear along the band caught his eye.

The two brothers exchanged a one-second stare before they both sprinted back to the truck. Pike got behind the wheel, gunned the engine, made a wide turn and took off back down the road, turning when they came to the spur that would put them on Jodie's trail.

Enough time had passed that the dust had died down, making it anyone's guess if Jodie had continued up this road or not. All Zane could think of was that red smear and he looked at it again. His gut and every other instinct in his body told him this was Kinsey's blood. He couldn't imagine how the hat would end up in the dirt unless it had been torn off her head, a possibility supported by those ominous scuffle marks in the dirt. It was inconceivable to him that she would have lost it without knowing. And there was that blood...

"We'll find him," Pike said with a slap on his shoulder.

"I know." He looked out the window at the rolling hills and felt sick inside. Jodie could be almost anywhere. Maybe they should call the police and try to get some help.

"If they took her to get to you, then she may be the bait in a trap," Pike said.

"It doesn't matter," Zane said. He'd been staring out the window as he spoke and now he sat forward. "Slow down, Pike. Go back a few yards."

Pike backed up the truck. Two tracks of flattened grass led off across a field, their bent stalks shimmering gold in the heat. Pike immediately followed the trail.

"What do you figure? He's got a good twenty-minute lead?"

"At least," Zane said. "Probably more like thirty minutes. Is it possible he's headed to a major highway?"

"It's possible. It's a little out of the way but definitely possible, especially if he thinks we might be following him."

The land began to climb until they finally flew over the top of the ridge. Zane recognized the plateau they'd ridden to the day before. Up here the ground was harder to read, rockier and scattered with downed trees and gullies. There were no longer any clear impressions of tires to follow.

Off in the distance, gazing past clumps of trees, he could see the imposing shape of the huge old oak. "I have a feeling about that tree," Zane said.

"Then we'll go look," Pike said as he veered that direction. They had to slow down because of the rocks, but Pike kept with it. Zane leaned out the window and tried to see something, anything that would help. Was he letting the creep factor of the tree get to him? "Kinsey, Kinsey," he whispered into the wind, then he sat up straighter. "I see something blue under the shade of the tree."

"Big enough to be a truck?"

"Yes. It's not moving. Why would he park there?"

Pike didn't answer, but Zane could easily come up with a perfectly innocent answer. Maybe the guy was eating lunch in the shade of the tree. Maybe Kinsey was back at the ranch somewhere. Maybe he'd jumped to conclusions...

The ground finally evened out and they were able to travel faster. The blue truck was growing more defined, as was a figure moving around beside it. By the size of the person, Zane knew it wasn't Kinsey, so it must be Jodie. If the guy was just out for a ride, he'd stay where he was and find out what all the drama was about. That seemed to be the case for a few seconds, and then suddenly the man disappeared around the back of the truck. When he reappeared the next time, he was climbing into the driver's seat. The truck wallowed over the roots before it took off, making a wide circle to head south.

"I can intercede his path," Pike said and slowed down to make a wide turn.

"No," Zane said quickly. "Something's on the ground. Drive to the tree. Hurry."

Pike aborted his turn and they all but flew over the remaining distance. Try as he might to discern what Jodie had left behind, the intense shade of the tree and the twisted depth of the roots concealed the truth. Pike finally hit the brakes a good distance away to avoid those roots and Zane popped open his door. He ran with his heart in his mouth and then stopped abruptly as the ambiguous shadows on the ground evolved into Kinsey.

She lay sprawled, her clothes bunched around her body, her hair almost covering her face, smaller in this state than he'd ever seen her, her skin delicate and pale and covered with blood. For one interminable moment, he thought she was dead, but then he heard her moan. A second later, he knelt by her side.

Pike came to a grinding halt beside him. He, too, knelt. "Oh my God," he whispered. "What did he do to her?"

Zane felt her hands. They were cool to the touch. He smoothed her hair away from her beautiful face and saw that her right earlobe was torn. She cried when he tried to pull down her shirt and straighten her legs. Her eyes fluttered open and she looked at him. Tears immediately trickled down her cheeks.

"Where does it hurt, baby?" he whispered.

She licked her lips.

"There's water in the truck," Pike said and ran off to get it. Zane slipped off his vest and folded it under her head. He tried once again to make her comfortable, checking for broken bones as he did so, finding to his relief that a majority of the blood was on her face and seemed to come from the torn lobe and a gash across her forehead.

Pike was back in a minute and they wet a handkerchief to drip warm water onto Kinsey's lips. She'd drifted off for a few seconds, but as the water touched her, she opened her eyes.

"Zane?"

"I'm here, honey. What happened?"

"A man," she said.

"It was Jodie. Did he hurt you anywhere I can't see?"

"My ribs," she said very softly. "My head."

"You're okay now," he said. Who the hell *was* Jodie? And why had he taken Kinsey and then abandoned her here? What was the point?

In a way, he didn't care. Kinsey was beaten and bloody because of his selfish desire to have her close to him. He would find Jodie and one way or another, exact revenge for what the man had done.

But there was another question just as compelling. How had he, Gerard Hastings, provoked such violence? He had to find out. Someone had to know.

First things first. "Come on, sweetheart," he murmured to Kinsey. "We need to get you to a doctor."

She looked into his eyes but didn't speak. Together, he and Pike helped her stand, then Zane scooped her gently into his arms. Pike wandered away with his cell phone as Zane carried Kinsey to the truck. The back was too full of tools and discarded lumber to use it as a bed for her, so he carefully helped her settle in the front seat, then he scooted in after her. She collapsed into his arms as Pike got behind the wheel. Pike handed him Kinsey's shoulder bag, her wallet and the small art book. "I found these tossed aside," he said. "They're hers, right?"

"Right," Zane said as he took the proffered items. "Who did you call?"

"Chance. He's taking off to look for Jodie."

"If he finds him, the bastard is mine," Zane said.

KINSEY KNEW SHE was safe and for the moment that was enough. The cocoon of Zane's arms lulled her as the truck ambled along slowly in deference to her injuries. They finally hit smooth pavement and the speed increased.

The urgent-care facility contacted the police. By the time they showed up, Kinsey's ribs had been taped, her forehead gash closed with the proper bandages, her earlobe stitched and her body laced with antibiotics and a tetanus shot. She was told in no uncertain terms that she should go home and go to bed at once, that in a bigger city with an actual hospital, she would have been admitted for at least an overnight stay.

"Hey, Gerard, long time no see," Officer Robert Hendricks said as he came into the treatment room. The two men shook hands. Kinsey thought the officer's expression reflected a certain surprise at Zane's lack of response to his overt friendliness. "Where's Pike?" he added. "I heard he came in with you."

"He did. He got a call from Frankie, who's been in town a couple of days for some reason. Sorry, I'm unclear on the details."

"You don't know why Frankie is here in town?"

"No, do you?"

"No, but I better look into it. Damn, I hope he hasn't slipped back into trouble." He turned his attention to Kinsey. "Are you up to telling me what happened?"

She was sitting in a reasonably comfortable chair, her hand firmly clasped in Zane's. It was impossible not to notice the way the officer's gaze kept straying to their linked fingers.

"It started in the Hastingses' garden," she began. All she could think of was Jodie's threat. "He told me if I came quietly, Zane would not have to see me die, but if I caused a fuss, Zane would never forget how Jodie killed me." She swallowed a lump and took a deep breath. "Then he started in on someone named Block."

Zane took the floor for a moment and explained what they'd already been through in New Orleans. He also confessed his amnesia. "The Block name means absolutely nothing to me," he added. "I'll ask Pike and the others about it when I see them."

Hendricks nodded as though a light had gone on in his head. "You have amnesia?"

"Yes."

"Well, that explains why you're looking at me like we've never met."

"I'm sorry," Zane said. "How well do we know each other?"

"High school, college, you were my best man, my wife and I were Heidi's godparents."

"Oh, hell," Zane said. "I'll buy you a beer when I get back to normal."

Hendricks laughed but soon turned serious again. "Okay, Ms. Frost. What did Jodie say about this Block?"

Jodie's voice came back, as did the sensation of his hot, sour breath against her neck. It was the exact words that were jumbled and she shook her head in frustration. "I can't remember exactly how it went," she admitted. "The impression I got was that Block was angry with me for taking something that was special to him. Jodie said I would die in an accident and then Block would get back what was his. It was all so confusing. Up until then I thought this all revolved around Zane…I mean Gerard. When I said I didn't know anyone named Block, Jodie got angry. He…he ran the gun down my chest…I don't know, I thought for a moment he was going to rape me. I tried to get away. He bit my ear. I don't remember anything after that until he pulled me out of the truck. He took my handbag and he tore it apart as I tried to sit up. He took the cash, but there was hardly anything left. I wondered if this was some kind of bizarre robbery, but the money seemed incidental to him. He threw all my things into the field and started yelling at me."

"What did he yell?" Zane asked.

"I don't know. He was impossible to understand. The kicks began and I just tried to protect my head. After a really hard blow to my side, he said he was going to find a rope in the back of his truck and tie me to the tree for the buzzards." She glanced up at Zane. "I thought about you finding me like that, what that would do to you." Unbidden tears burned behind her nose. Zane hugged her shoulders and smoothed her hair.

She took a deep breath. "But all of a sudden, he gave me a last kick, got in his truck and left in a hurry. I couldn't believe he was going away. The next thing I knew, Zane and Pike were there."

"Does anyone have a picture of him?" Hendricks asked.

"If you have a piece of paper and a pencil, I might be able to give you something better than a verbal description," Kinsey said.

"She's a portrait artist," Zane explained. "A very talented one."

"My lucky day," Hendricks said as he hustled out of the room to find supplies.

AFTER LEAVING HIS family at the ranch, Zane drove on to his house where he helped Kinsey up to the second floor. She sat gingerly on the bench at the foot of the bed while he carefully removed her clothes. Black-and-blue marks had begun to appear, each one representing a punch or a kick. He clenched his jaw so she wouldn't see how angry they made him.

"My orange gown—"

"I'll get it for you." He found the garment beside the bed where he'd tossed it the night before after almost ripping it from her body. He pulled it over her head and helped her into the bed.

"You're safe now, you know that, right? I'll be here," he told her as he helped her find a comfortable position and covered her with a light blanket.

She caught his hand. "I want to go home," she said. "I don't want to be here anymore."

He swallowed his disappointment. Of course she wanted the comfort of her family and her own four walls, but the doctors had told him she shouldn't fly for a few days. He leaned over to kiss her forehead. "I'll take you home any time you say," he whispered against her cheek. They would drive. It wasn't as if they hadn't made the trip before. "We'll leave tomorrow if that's what you want."

"That's what I want."

"Okay, sweetheart. That's what we'll do. Try to get some sleep."

Her grip tightened. "You aren't leaving me, are you?"

"Of course not," he said. He wanted to add that he would never leave her side again, but he wasn't certain that would strike her as an attractive thought. Maybe leaving here meant leaving him.

Within a few minutes, her grip grew slack, her breathing even. The next thing he knew, he was opening his eyes on a room where the light had significantly changed. He glanced at the clock and sat up. He'd fallen asleep sitting up and over two hours had passed. He stood when he realized what had woken him was the sound of an engine outside.

His first instinct was to grab the gun off the shelf, and he did this before creeping across the heavily shadowed room to the window. It was crazy to think Jodie would dare come back to the ranch, but his heart beat in his throat anyway. Then he recognized Pike's truck. He tucked the gun in the small of his back and raced downstairs to open the door before Pike could ring the bell and disturb Kinsey.

"How is she?" Pike asked as he came through the door.

"She's asleep right now, but I wouldn't be surprised if she has nightmares about this for weeks."

"I'm real sorry. I feel bad that I hired that jerk. I should have insisted on references. We've never had trouble before, so I guess I got complacent."

"You didn't know any of this was going on," Zane said. "In retrospect, I should have hunted him down last night and I shouldn't have left Kinsey behind—"

"We both feel responsible," Pike interrupted. "And it does Kinsey absolutely no good at all."

"I know it doesn't. She wants to go home. I can't let her make the trip alone."

"I understand," Pike said. "We'll get along without you. Dad is home now, he plans on riding out with us to Bywater, so don't worry about it."

"I have a favor to ask," Zane added.

"Shoot."

"I need someone to take Kinsey's car to the rental place and settle the bill. Of course I'll repay it."

"I know you will. I'll take care of it. How are you going to get to Louisiana?"

"I'll take the SUV. Hopefully when we get there we can find my truck. I want to give the SUV to Kinsey since I'm responsible for the destruction of her car. Which leads me to ask something. The ranch appears to be profitable. I'm a little startled at how much money I have."

"The ranch is profitable," Pike said, "but you're twice as rich as anyone else. Your mother's father died a couple of years ago and left you a small fortune."

"That explains it."

"Like I said, Dad got home a couple of hours ago. We've filled him in on what we knew so you wouldn't have to start at the beginning again. Lily was going to come stay with Kinsey, but she got busy cooking, so I came instead. Dad wants to see you."

Zane looked toward the stairs. Reason said Kinsey would sleep through his absence and that Pike was just as capable of protecting her as he was. Nevertheless, he didn't want to leave.

"I've been meaning to ask if the name Block means anything to you," he said. "Jodie mentioned it to Kinsey during the abduction."

Pike shook his head. "It doesn't ring any bells. She doesn't recognize it either?"

"No. One more question. What's up with Frankie and why aren't any of the rest of you married?"

"That's two questions," Pike said. "It's hard to keep in mind that you don't remember everything about us. Frankie has been in and out of trouble his whole life. I guess there's one in every family and in our family, it's Frankie."

"I thought it was Chance."

"No. Chance is a player in some ways and he never walks away from a fight, but he doesn't tangle with the law."

"And Frankie does?"

"Afraid so. He used to run with an unruly bunch of losers. Lately he's been trying to sort himself out. Listen, you have enough to worry about right now. I'll take care of Frankie."

"How about the married part?"

Pike flashed a tentative smile. "That's harder to explain. Things just haven't worked out for any of us. Maybe it has something to do with the parade of women Dad marched through our childhood. Maybe that left a bad taste in our mouths when it came to marriage."

"Yet I married," Zane reflected.

Pike looked toward the stairs. "Yeah, well, you seem to have a knack for finding exceptional women."

After the past several hours, Zane had grown to like and trust Pike. For the first time since arriving at the ranch, he thought he might be able to belong here again, to care about these people even if his memory never returned. "Thanks for all you did today," he said. "I'll go down to the ranch house, but I won't be long. I want to be here when she wakes up."

"I'll sit in your office," Pike said, "so I can hear if she needs anything."

"Thanks." He took the gun from his waistband and pressed it into Pike's hand. "Take care of her."

"I'll keep her safe until you return."

Chapter Twelve

He found everyone in the kitchen, sitting around the big maple block counter. Lily stood at the stove stirring a pot of what smelled like marinara sauce, while Charlie perched on a stool nearby watching her. Chance was sorting mail and the man who had to be his father sat as though he'd been expecting Zane.

"What the hell is this I hear about you having amnesia?" he demanded.

It was pretty easy to see parts of himself and his brothers in his father. Harry Hastings had Chance's forehead and full head of hair, though his was mostly white. On him, Pike's dark blue eyes and straight brows looked stern instead of thoughtful, and though Zane was decades younger, his father's general physique was much the same. There was also a belligerent twist to his lips that seemed to be all his. It announced clearly he didn't like obstacles and would not tolerate any funny business.

"Hello to you, too," Zane said.

Harry Hastings grunted at Zane's reply. "I heard some little gal was injured by one of our wranglers. Is she okay?"

"She will be," he said.

"Can't believe something like that could happen on Hastings soil. Damn negligent of Pike to hire him."

"Pike didn't know," Zane said. He looked around for some sign of the new wife. "Where's your bride?" he asked.

"She wanted to stay in town until she's boxed up all her stuff for the move out here. Damn woman has been living alone in a tiny house for twenty-five years. You wouldn't believe how much crap she has. Anyway, we'll take a transport and the horses out to Bywater tomorrow. I predict your memory will come back as soon as your butt hits a saddle."

"If that was true, it would be back now," Chance said. "Gerard rode out to the ghost town as soon as he got here."

Harry's brow furrowed. "Why did you go out there if you didn't remember Ann and Heidi?"

"I didn't plan on going there. It's just where we ended up."

"We?"

"Me and the woman who was hurt today. Her name is Kinsey Frost."

His dad grunted. "Well, a day working cattle will put you right as rain, mark my words."

"Actually, I won't be here tomorrow," Zane said. "Kinsey wants to go back to New Orleans. I'm taking her."

"New Orleans?" he snapped.

"That's where she lives. That's where I lost my memory. Do you know why I was in New Orleans while you were on your honeymoon?"

"No idea. You never said a word to me about it."

Zane fought off disappointment. His father had been his last hope. "Listen, Jodie Brown gave Kinsey the impression someone named Block was angry with her for taking something he cared about more than anything in the world. He told her she would die in an accident. She hasn't the slightest idea…"

His voice trailed off because his father's attention had shifted to Lily, who had stopped stirring the sauce. She stood with her mouth agape, her gaze connected to Harry's.

"What's going on?" Zane asked. Even Chance looked up from the mail, apparently sensing the same sudden tension that Zane did.

Lily licked her lips. "Did you say Block? Jeremy Block?"

"She didn't hear a first name that I know of."

"Oh my God," Lily said, dropping the spoon into the sauce and lifting Charlie into her arms. She looked around the room as if she was searching for a way out of the kitchen, off the ranch, maybe off the planet.

"Is it him?" Harry asked.

Her voice, when she answered, sounded different. "It has to be. Jodie must be one of his minions." She met Zane's confused gaze. "Oh my God, Gerard, don't you see? He thought he was taking me. He thought Kinsey was me."

"You? Then you know Block?"

Harry Hastings got to his feet. He walked to Lily's side and put out his arms. "Charlie, how about you and me go find the dogs?"

Charlie all but leaped into Harry's arms and the two of them started for the door. Lily looked reluctant to part with her son and thankful for the help all at the same time.

By now, Chance had set aside the mail and was staring at Lily. "How could anyone confuse you with Kinsey? Granted, you're about the same size, but your hair…"

"Is really brown. I bleach it," Lily said. "I used to wear

it long, like Kinsey does. I wanted to look different, to disappear...he must have found her where he expected to find me." She swallowed hard. "How did he find me? I have to leave here. I have to go. Now. Tonight."

"Wait a second," Chance said as he stood. "Who is this man?"

She searched his face for several seconds before finally whispering, "Charlie's father."

"And what did you take from him?"

She seemed unable to speak, so Zane said it for her. "You took Charlie," he said. "You took Block's son."

Lily covered her face with her hands as sobs racked her body. Zane and Chance exchanged alarmed glances until Chance stepped closer. "You aren't going anywhere," he said gently. "You're safe here."

Lily looked up at Chance. "You don't understand. I'm not safe anywhere."

ZANE CLIMBED INTO BED after seeing Pike off, too wrung out from the day to even think about eating. The room was dark by now and Kinsey didn't stir when he slid between the sheets. As always, the proximity of her body aroused him. He held his hands in fists at his sides, determined not to disturb her. It promised to be a very long night.

"Aren't you going to make love to me?" she whispered.

He turned on his side. "You're awake," he said.

"I've been waiting for you. I want you to make love to me. You'll have to do most of the work, though."

"Are you sure you're up to it?" he asked as he stroked her cheek, careful to make sure it was her left one so he wouldn't inadvertently touch her bandaged earlobe.

"I'm sure. I want wonderful thoughts in my head, not ugly ones."

"I'm your slave to command," he said, sliding his hand down her throat until he hit the fullness of her breasts.

Their lovemaking was gentle compared to the night before, Zane being careful not to settle his weight on her bruised and cracked bones. He satisfied her needs and then his own, creating a pocket of potent warmth that seemed to drive away the demons. And when they both lay replete, she sighed deeply.

"I feel safe with you," she said, nuzzling his shoulder. "Tell me a story, okay? Let me hear your voice as I fall asleep."

He didn't want to tell her about Lily's revelations because he didn't want to burden her with thoughts of Jodie. That story could wait until morning. He couldn't tell her about his past because she knew as much about it as he did, but he could tell her about the places he wanted to visit. "Have you ever wanted to walk on an iceberg?" he began. "That takes a helicopter ride, I suppose. Imagine standing there on the tip of something so huge with the ocean in every direction. Or how about we travel down to Ecuador and then on to the Galápagos Islands. The wildlife there is something else." He paused for a few seconds and cleared his throat. "I've also given consideration to where we should honeymoon. How does Hawaii sound? Too ordinary? If so, maybe Tahiti or Australia or even the Bahamas. No, wait, maybe you'd rather go to Europe and visit art museums. What do you think, Kinsey?"

She didn't respond because she'd fallen asleep. He brushed her lips with his and she made a contented noise in her throat. At that moment he knew he had to have her, he couldn't let her go even if it meant leaving the ranch and his family.

Wouldn't his dad be thrilled to hear that?

It didn't matter. He'd apparently loved a woman once

before, and a child, too. Fate had given him a second chance and he wasn't going to blow it.

THE NEXT MORNING, Kinsey watched as Zane packed their bags. He'd just finished telling her about Lily's amazing revelation of the night before. It was reassuring to discover she and Zane hadn't been the intended targets, though the lingering malice and fear would take a while to deal with. She must have created doubt in Jodie's mind when she said she didn't know Block. After driving toward the road, he must have decided to check out her story by searching her wallet. And then, with the arrival of Pike and Zane, he'd cut his losses and left her.

Her phone rang and she glanced at the screen.

"Your mom?" Zane asked.

"Yes. I don't know if I'm up to this."

"Then don't answer it," he said. He looked back at her and his expression softened. "Do what you need to do, sweetheart. I'm going to go get some things out of the office. I'll be right back."

As he left, Kinsey answered the phone, doing her best to sound normal. "Hey, Mom," she said.

"I have news," Frances Frost announced.

"Is it Bill?"

"No, well, kind of. James has asked me to marry him right away, before Bill dies so Bill can know that I'm taken care of."

Kinsey stared out the window for a second. "Married. You're getting married?"

"Yes. Can you believe it? After all these years…"

"Mom, isn't it happening a little fast?"

"Fast? I've been a widow for twenty-five years. What's fast about that?"

"You know what I mean."

"Yes, I know what you mean. You're being cautious. But James has promised to take care of me. You have your life, it's time I allowed myself to have mine."

The statement reminded Kinsey of the time her mother had said she'd sacrificed everything for Kinsey. It was kind of troubling. "If this is what you want, then I'm glad for you," she said at last. "When's the ceremony?"

"Today. I wanted you to know."

Today! "Mom, we're actually about ready to leave for New Orleans. Could you possibly wait until I get there to, ah, share this with you?"

There was a substantial pause, then Frances spoke. "I can ask James."

"Would you? It would mean a lot to me."

"Then okay, we'll wait. But not for long, not with Bill coughing constantly."

"I'll need four days," Kinsey said. She knew they could get back in three, but she needed to have a little time to make sense of this once she got there.

"Okay. Let's say three o'clock four days from now, whether you make it or not, okay?"

"Thanks, Mom. I won't miss your big day. Is Bill's nephew still there?"

Frances lowered her voice. "He thinks I don't know what he's doing, but I can tell he's still searching the house. What in the heck is he looking for?"

"I have no idea. What does James think?"

"He says to ignore him. I'm trying. Have to go now. Keep in touch, honey, and hurry home."

Kinsey clicked off the phone and stared at the screen until Zane appeared in front of her and gently lifted her chin. "Are you okay?"

"We're going to a wedding," she said. "Mom is getting married."

"To the lawyer?"

"Yep."

"Are you good with that?"

"No. Two weeks ago she never mentioned his name. And now it's James this and James that. I'm afraid she's responding to outside influences."

"Like what?"

"Well, like my sudden desertion, for instance. And Bill's impending death. I think she's afraid to be alone."

"I imagine people marry for worse reasons," he told her.

"I guess."

"Maybe the lawyer has been lonely, too. Maybe he figures it's time to seize the day."

"You're probably right."

"I'm going to go put our things in the car. You'll feel better when you get there and see everything is okay."

He leaned down and kissed her lips and her heart raced. Every time he looked at her or spoke to her or touched her, it was more intense than the time before. She'd never felt about anyone the way she did about him. If her mother experienced even a molecule of that kind of desire, who was she to question it?

He turned at the door. "I'll be back in a few moments to help you down the stairs, okay?"

"Okay. Thanks."

As his footsteps faded, a chill ran through her body. All of a sudden she felt as though she was standing at a crossroad, buffeted by the inescapable winds of change. She hugged herself tighter.

Loss was in the air. She could almost smell it.

"I STUDIED A MAP," he announced an hour later when he left the main highway. "We're going to take as many smaller roads as possible. It might make the trip a little longer, but I'll feel better not being so damn obvious."

"But now that we know Jodie was after Lily, not you and me, what concerns you?"

He shook his head. "I'm not sure. Gut reaction to what happened yesterday. It might have been a mistake, but it served as a reminder that New Orleans could be deadly for us, and I just want to make sure nothing else hurts you. Ever."

She smiled. "Sounds good to me." She cuddled back in the pillows Zane had brought along in an effort to make her comfortable, wrapping a blanket around her legs to ward off the chill of the air conditioner.

"What did Lily say last night, you know, about Block?"

"Nothing much. Just that he was Charlie's dad. She was obviously terrified."

"Is she going to leave?"

"I don't know that, either."

"If Jodie is an example of how Block intends to reclaim his son, who can blame her for bolting? Does your father know this guy?"

"No. I asked him about it before I came home last night. All he said was that Lily was the grand-daughter of an old friend. When he heard she needed a place to retreat for a while, he offered her a job. He said it was obvious she didn't want to talk about what was wrong, so he left her alone. From what I've seen of the man, that must have taxed him. He's not exactly Mr. Hands Off."

"I hope Lily will be okay," Kinsey said before yawning into her hand.

The hours passed in a haze as she did her best to breathe in such a way that her ribs didn't hurt. After a light lunch, she fell asleep and didn't awaken until Zane announced they were getting a room at the first motel they ran into. The room they found was a lot nicer than either had expected, and the soft bed dominating the area looked like a slice of heaven to Kinsey. As always, being in Zane's arms was like a magic potion.

The day after that passed in a long, mind-numbing daze as they pushed the SUV and themselves hard.

They made it back to Louisiana by midnight of the next day, when Zane admitted he was too tired to drive another foot. He checked them into a ground-level room and excused himself to take a shower. Kinsey looked at her face in the mirror and almost gagged. No wonder she'd been asked so many questions about her injuries. Tomorrow they would be in New Orleans and she'd be her mother's maid of honor. Wouldn't she look fetching in the wedding photo?

She groaned at the thought and then groaned again when she realized she'd forgotten to call. It was late, but even if Frances didn't answer, at least Kinsey could leave a message. She placed the call and it switched to the answering service almost immediately.

"Hi, Mom, sorry I didn't call earlier. We're somewhere around Shreveport at the Red River Inn. I'm not sure how long it will take us to get back to New Orleans because we're traveling the scenic route, but I'll call when I get there and it will probably be sometime tomorrow, so you and I will have a whole day to go shopping for whatever you need. See you soon."

Zane came out of the bathroom followed by a billow of steam. Wet dark hair framed his amazing blue eyes, and his muscles, as he walked toward her, rippled with sensuous ease beneath his bare flesh.

She raised a hand to touch the bandage on her forehead and winced. He stood over her a moment, just about blowing her mind with the bevy of hot, damp masculinity hovering just a few inches away. Her pulse pounded in her throat. He sat down next to her, his powerful thigh touching hers. It was hard to catch a decent breath. Her imagination soared at the thought of being in his arms, of having him inside her.

He lifted her hand and brought it to his lips to kiss. "Does your head hurt?" he asked.

"No worse than usual."

"Then what's wrong?"

"I don't know. I guess I just got a breathtaking eyeful of how gorgeous you are and it reminded me I look like a zombie."

He stared into her eyes and smiled seductively. "Baby, baby, baby," he whispered as he touched her lips with his. "Glance down at my lap and you will find proof positive that you look perfect to me."

She did as he asked, looked up at him and licked her lips. "Care to prove it?"

"Thought you'd never ask."

THEY GOT A good start the next morning and, as usual, Zane left the major highways in favor of subsidiary roads. Kinsey had lived in Louisiana for almost four years now, moving there after college, but she'd never traveled these more remote highways. They were running alongside the Red River on a narrow road bounded on one side by the river and on the other by a slough. There was little traffic and as they drove, huge raindrops spattered against the windshield in the sudden deluge of a summer storm.

"It's so much different here than Idaho," she said as she reached into her purse to retrieve lip balm.

"Do you like it here better?"

"I don't know. A couple of days ago, all I wanted to do was get away from your ranch. It seemed so full of recent tragedy and intrigue. And then there was Jodie… New Orleans, in comparison, seemed safe, at least to me, but now, I don't know."

He glanced at her as she took out Bill Dodge's gift book. "Have you read that yet?"

"I browsed through it a day or so ago but I haven't actually read it," she said, once again opening the cover and reading Bill's dedication. "Zane, what are you going to do when you get to New Orleans?"

"Check with Woods about my truck, make sure you're okay with your family, go to a wedding…try to find answers." He paused for a second, and then snapped, "What the hell is that guy doing?"

She looked up from her book. A big orange truck barreled toward them, straddling the yellow line.

"Is the driver drunk?" Kinsey gasped.

Zane steered the SUV toward the nearest highway edge. Kinsey glanced over the flimsy-looking guardrail to see the muddy water of the slough. The sudden downpour had caused the water to move faster than normal. When she looked back up, the orange truck was closer and still coming on like a speeding train, way over on their side of the road. She realized it was the kind people rent to move their own stuff, ten feet high and half again as long. It looked humongous.

"Hold on," Zane yelled as he turned the wheel hard to avoid a head-on collision. Their vehicle slid along the guardrail metal against metal. But as the truck loomed over them, the driver must have yanked his wheel. The SUV, with nowhere else to go, burst through the guardrail and sailed over the embankment. Kinsey gasped as they landed ten feet out in the rushing water. The current immediately swept them along even as they began to sink. Muddy water poured through the open windows.

"Get out!" Zane yelled. "Hurry."

Kinsey tried to undo her seat belt, but her hands were shaking so hard she was clumsy and couldn't get the mechanism to release. The water continued to rise, soaking the thin blanket she'd wrapped around her legs. The belt finally opened and she jerked her body around to struggle with the door, but half of her was trapped. She turned back around to find Zane. What little she could see of him was disappearing through his window. She gave up on the door as the pressure outside made opening it impossible. The car had settled in the thick layer of mud on the bottom, leaving barely an inch of air at the top of the cabin. Floating pillows and debris obstructed movement in the murky water. She held her breath. What did she have? A minute? Two, maybe?

Strong hands clamped her arm and pulled again and again. Zane, it had to be Zane. She kicked free of the blanket at last and exited the car, breaking to the surface with a sputter, amazed she could take a breath, that she was alive. The current worked against her as she held on to Zane's shirt, relying on his superior upper-body strength to gradually guide them to shore. Other motorists had stopped. Someone threw a rope that Zane caught. He clasped Kinsey around the waist with his free arm. At last her feet found purchase on the slippery bottom. Together, they climbed the steep bank, Kinsey's ribs screaming with protest. The crowd reached out to help them over the guardrail.

Zane's arms had always provided a haven and this time was no different. They stood together as the pouring rain washed muddy water from their hair.

ANOTHER SHERIFF. ANOTHER tow truck, another few hours spent answering questions. Other motorists had noticed the orange truck's erratic path. Someone reported there was no license plate on the truck. One person swore there was a single driver, another swore there was a woman sitting by his side. Everyone agreed that as soon as Zane's SUV burst through the guardrail, the truck had gunned its engine and taken off.

Zane and Kinsey went through the motions of answering question after question that led nowhere. There wasn't any doubt to Zane that they had been the target, a fact proven when the tow company found a tracking device affixed to the undercarriage of the SUV.

Kinsey had left a message for her mother mentioning alternate routes and the one they'd taken was the most likely candidate. Still, to find and rent a truck like that and get it to the right place at the right moment seemed an impossible feat. And why would her mother do such a thing?

So, was it the nephew or even the lawyer? Zane didn't know enough to connect the dots.

Another rental followed their eventual release and they drove it as far as the nearest hotel, where they took hot showers and Zane re-dressed Kinsey's wounds. He sent all the wet clothing he'd salvaged from the car once it was towed out of the slough to the overnight laundry service and they both changed into the ubiquitous terry-cloth robes provided by the establishment. Zane knew that Kinsey was fading fast, trauma heaped on trauma, wounds affected by the latest situation. He wasn't doing a grand job of protecting her.

In something of a miracle, the little book Bill Dodge had given Kinsey had not washed out of the car and Zane had been able to save it. He spread it open on the counter in the bathroom to dry, blotting its pages with a hand towel, hoping to salvage something of the sentiment and beauty. He felt terrible that her keepsake was in its current sorry state.

He heard Kinsey on the phone, no doubt calling her mother. He caught only a few words and ducked back into the room to make sure everything was okay.

"That was James," Kinsey said. "Bill ended up at the hospital again and Mom is with him. James said she must have forgotten her phone in all the confusion. Anyway, he'll pass along a message that we're running behind schedule but will be there for the wedding tomorrow." She set the phone on the nightstand. "This means I'm going to have very little time to talk her into waiting a while before getting married."

He sat down next to her. "We'll get a real early start."

"Okay. Did you lock the door?"

"Yes, don't worry."

A few seconds later, she lay her head back on a stack of pillows, and a minute after that, she fell asleep.

After double-checking the locks, Zane settled in the chair by the window, staring at her, thinking. If only he could remember why he'd asked about Kinsey's mother, why he'd driven to New Orleans in the first place.

As the light faded in the room, he made a decision. Kinsey's mother must have the missing pieces of the puzzle. She might not know she had them, but his gut was telling him she did. It no longer mattered to him that she didn't want to talk or that it was her wedding day or anything else.

Tomorrow, he would find out what she knew or die trying.

Chapter Thirteen

"Wake up, sweetheart, we're almost at your place."

Kinsey roused herself from a restless nap and opened her eyes to find they had finally made it to New Orleans. She'd drifted off while examining Bill Dodge's book and it sat open in her lap. Though Zane had done a good job of trying to salvage it, she suspected it was a lost cause. The glue on the paper attached to the inside cover had been damaged and had begun to curl away. She touched it idly as she stared out the window and felt a bulge beneath her fingertips. Carefully, she peeled back the paper and withdrew an envelope with her mother's name written in water-stained blue ink.

"What's that?" Zane asked.

"Something for my mother. This is Bill's handwriting. He must have sealed it inside this book when he rebound it. I don't know why in the world he didn't tell me it was there or what it's all about, but I'm glad I'm seeing her today to give it to her."

"Maybe you should open it," Zane said. "After all, it was in a book he gave you."

"No way," Kinsey said. "I learned at an early age not to tamper with my mother's privacy. Hey, I wonder if there's anything in the back of the book." She flipped it over and lifted the cover. The paper had begun to peel away here, too, and she helped it along.

"Anything?" Zane asked as he slid a glance her way.

"Another piece of paper," she said as she unfolded it. This one didn't fade, he must have used a different ink."

"What is it?"

She was quiet for a second and then almost laughed. "It's a map of his house. It shows a secret room behind the bookcase in what was once his library. There's a red *X* as in *X* marks the spot. This must be where he hid everything. Good heavens."

Zane whistled. "Crafty old guy, isn't he?"

"Yes," she said, and placed the unopened letter and the treasure map within the pages of the book. For a second she stared out at the familiar streets. She'd changed more in the past week than she had in the past ten years and nothing looked or felt the same. Especially not the police car parked in her driveway. She and Zane got out of the rental and waited while a uniformed policeman approached them. "Is this your place?" the officer asked Kinsey as his gaze traveled between her wounds and bandages.

"Yes. What happened?"

"One of your neighbors reported hearing a noise last night. When they checked this morning, they found your door open and called us."

"Has anything been taken, can you tell?" Kinsey asked.

"You'll know better than we."

As he spoke, another car arrived and Detective Woods got out. "I heard about this on the police radio," he said by way of greeting. He shook Zane's hand and then demanded to hear what had happened to Kinsey, whistling when she and Zane finished their explanation. "Good heavens."

"Any word of Ryan Jones?" she asked him.

"None. How much do you know about him?"

"Not much. He apparently lied to me about where he worked."

"Chances are, if he lied about that, he lied about other things. He might be a con artist of some kind."

Kinsey glanced over at Zane. She knew he was still wondering if he and Ryan had been involved in something dicey—heck, so was she.

Woods addressed Zane. "We found your truck. It was in a parking garage. They waited seven days before calling us. We towed it to the impound yard."

"I'll come and retrieve it later today," Zane said. "Kinsey's mom is getting married in a few hours."

"The ceremony won't take long," Kinsey said. She couldn't picture them all sitting around and chatting afterward.

"Come see me after you get your truck," Woods said. "We have still shots taken from video both on the street and in the hospital. You can't see a face in either one, but maybe one of you will recognize something familiar that can help us identify the culprit or culprits. The wife and I are having a party this evening, so can you possibly make it before five? After we're done, you're welcome to follow me home, if you like. My wife makes a mean gumbo."

"Sounds great," Kinsey said.

They all climbed the stairs. Kinsey went inside first, but she didn't make it more than a few steps. It was obvious the place had been searched, less obvious if the intruder had found what they were after.

"Offhand, it just looks like someone was looking for something hidden in a drawer or under a carpet," she said.

"That's how it strikes me, too." Woods gestured at the paintings on the walls. "Did you do these, Ms. Frost?"

"Yes."

"I had no idea you were so talented."

Kinsey murmured her thanks as she glanced at the faces gazing down from the walls. Strangers, most of them, at least their inspirations were. The art itself had become more real than the subjects they depicted. And yet, somehow, those faces weren't front and center in her life anymore. Now she thought of Charlie's shy smile, Lily's haunted eyes, Pike's bespectacled intelligence and Chance's grin. And Zane, of course. Always Zane.

Eventually, the police left with admonishments not to stay in the apartment until the locks were fixed, an unnecessary warning. They changed clothes and Kinsey packed a few things to take with her. She had access to the owner's garage and Zane found boards and nails to secure the door.

He looked sophisticated and sexy in the tan suit he'd had laundered after their dip in the slough. It fit him perfectly, enhancing his broad shoulders, the crisp white collar framing his wonderful face. Kinsey chose a floral dress she hadn't worn since buying it months before. It fell in soft pleats to her knees, and the corseted midriff helped bind her ribs, making sitting and bending easier. She'd done her best to camouflage her injuries by carefully arranging her hair over her forehead and right ear. Zane's lingering appreciative glance reminded her of the first time they'd actually met and the way his blue eyes had delved right inside her soul to take up residence.

"I'm not going to try to talk her out of getting married," Kinsey said. I'm going to give her Bill's letter and all the other papers and keep my mouth shut."

He was quiet for a second before he spoke. "Kinsey, think about it. Regardless of the map, Bill writes your mother a letter of some kind and then binds it into a book he made a point of giving to you along with a cryptic inscription that could be interpreted as encouraging you to figure out how to find what he's hidden. Maybe what's in that letter is not something he wanted your mother to see while he was still alive. You may be doing her no favor by handing it to her on the brink of her wedding."

Kinsey opened the party purse into which she'd shoved the bare essentials, including the papers. What Zane said made sense. "You're right," she said, and slipped the stiff papers out of the envelope.

"Anything legible after being in the water?"

"Barely. It's a letter, all right. There are actually two pages—oh my, the second one is a will."

"Bill's will, I take it."

"Yes. It looks as though he's left everything he owns to my mother. It says something about betraying her trust and hoping she can forgive him. Here's something about retribution…" She scanned the letter quickly, her heart pounding as she began to make sense of what she read. "He says the house is full of treasures that he hid when his nephew started coming around and he had…doubts about something…no, I can't read what he had doubts about. There's something here about Mr. Fenwick…knowledge, it says. The rest of the words are blurred, but I get the feeling Bill is saying Fenwick knew about his plan to hide things. My God, Zane, if James got wind of this will then he would know my mother is about to be a very wealthy woman. Is that why he's been pursuing her so intently?"

"It sounds like it," Zane said as he pulled up in front of the Dodge house.

"Zane, do you think this had anything to do with what happened to you?"

He shook his head. "I don't see how, but it's awfully coincidental I was asking about her before someone tried to kill me. I'm not sure why I didn't pursue this more aggressively a week ago. You might not have been hurt…"

"Finding out who you really are was part of the process of getting to this point," Kinsey said. "Don't be so hard on yourself."

He put a hand over hers. "We have to warn your mother carefully, Kinsey. For lots of reasons."

"Yes, you're right."

"Don't put those papers back in your purse. If Fenwick catches on that you have them, that's the first place he'll look. He could very well have searched your apartment, you know. Tuck the papers in your dress somewhere."

She didn't take time to think how silly it was to do it. She just rolled the papers and the map and stuck them down in her bra. "How do you like my new curves?" she asked while batting her eyelashes.

He leered at her a moment and smiled. "I think I like the old ones better."

A NEIGHBOR MUST have been having a party, because there was simply no parking close to the house. They found a spot a half block away and walked, holding hands. Loud rap music blared from the party house across the street. Zane thought it would add an interesting twist to the middle-aged wedding about to take place.

James Fenwick answered their knock. "Come in, come in," he said. He was dressed in khakis and a knit polo shirt. Zane felt instantly overdressed, but perhaps Fenwick hadn't changed into his wedding duds yet. "You finally made it," he added.

"Yes." Kinsey looked around the foyer. "I'm sorry we're late. Where is everyone?"

"I have very sad news," he said, his expression growing

somber. "Bill passed away. I didn't want to tell you over the phone."

Kinsey tightened her grip on Zane's hand. "Oh, I'm so sorry," she said. "He was a wonderful man. I hope it was peaceful."

He nodded. "It was."

"Where's my mother?"

"That's the other thing I have to tell you." He closed the door, clicked the dead bolt and encouraged them to move farther into the house. He spread his hands as he continued. "Your mother and I decided to get married when we saw how quickly Bill was slipping away. Don't be upset with her, it just seemed like the right thing to do. She's afraid you'll be disappointed. Well, you know Frances. When she's uneasy, she cooks. She's making a big lunch. Come on back to the kitchen."

They followed him through the living room, where he pushed open the door leading to the old-fashioned kitchen. He gestured for Kinsey to enter before him. He followed close on her heels. Zane was taller than either of them and could easily see over their heads.

The only other time he'd been in this room it had gleamed and sparkled. Now, dirty dishes littered every horizontal surface. A narrow door across the room stood ajar. There was no sign of Frances.

"Where's Mom?" Kinsey asked.

"I don't know," James said.

"Why is everything so messy?"

James seemed flustered. "It's been hectic here lately. I could have sworn she was in here cooking."

"Where's Bill's nephew?" Zane asked.

"He went out."

"Are you sure?"

When James didn't respond, Kinsey called out. "Mom?"

There was no reply, but the open door beckoned Kinsey. "The basement is down there," Kinsey said as she flung it wide open. "Mom?" she called. "Are you down there?"

Zane moved to her side. "Remember your ribs," he said. "Let me go look."

"The light switch doesn't work," Kinsey said as she flipped it on and off with no effect.

"Must be a fuse," James said. "I'll try to find a flashlight. If she's fallen, she may need help right away." He called out, "Frances, can you hear me?" to no avail.

"I can see well enough to get started," Zane said as he took the first downward step. The first half of the steep stairs were sided on both sides by solid walls outfitted with a handrail. About two-thirds of the way down, one wall stopped abruptly, but there was still a railing for support on the open side. Zane had expected the light to improve at this point, but it didn't. He paused to look back toward the kitchen. Kinsey stood framed in the light at the top. "Tell James to hurry with that flashlight," he called.

Instead of answering him, she turned and suddenly James loomed beside her. It appeared they struggled. Zane started to climb back up to help. Before he could take more than a couple of steps, Kinsey shot toward him, her hands grabbing for the railings, her feet working overtime to catch up until the inevitable happened and she missed a step. A second later, she flew into Zane. Her momentum sent them both crashing against the open railing that broke under the onslaught.

They landed six feet below in a heap of humanity and splintered wood.

KINSEY RAISED HER HEAD and looked down at Zane's slack face. He'd taken the brunt of the fall and seemed to be unconscious. She moved off him and checked him as well as she could in the very poor light. "Zane, honey, wake up." He didn't move, but at least his breathing sounded steady and his skin felt warm. Was her mom down here, too? Why was it so dark? Had someone covered the windows?

She crawled to the wall where she could leverage her weight to stand. Gasping as her ribs protested, she clearly recalled James ripping her bag from her shoulder and shoving her down the stairs.

Was it possible he had also shoved Zane into the street over a week before? Of course it was.

Everything that was happening had to revolve around this house and its hidden treasures and her mother's inheritance. At least she could still feel the papers against her skin, but where did Zane fit into it?

Her phone had died in the slough, but what if James had acted impulsively and then run away? Maybe she could just walk upstairs and use the phone to summon help.

The lights came on suddenly, just about blinding her. She looked up the stairs to see two men standing in the open doorway. She quickly ducked out of sight. The men at the head of the stairs started speaking.

"Did you search her apartment? Was it there?" It didn't sound like James.

"Yes, I searched… no, I didn't find anything," James replied.

The other man swore. "I leave for a couple of days and look what happens. Did you even check Hastings to see if he was carrying a gun before you pushed him down there?"

"Give it a rest, Kevin. Everything is fine. You don't carry a gun to a wedding and that's where they thought they were going."

"But they missed out, didn't they?" the other man said. "I knew you'd marry the old broad before Dodge took his last breath. Had to make sure you were in her will, didn't you? It hasn't shown up, so now you got married for nothing. The house will come to me, just as we originally planned."

"And I'll get half," James said.

"Sure," the other man said breezily as the stairs squeaked. They'd begun their descent. Kinsey looked for a place to hide but stopped abruptly when she saw Zane. There was no way she'd leave him unprotected. She couldn't see her mother, but there were a couple of ancillary rooms down here. Maybe they'd locked her in one of those.

"I'll be a widower by midnight," James added. "And let me remind you that we wouldn't have to get rid of all three of them if you'd done a proper job of it in Shreveport. Either time, I might add."

"You're the one with connections up there. You were part of the legal team for Chemco, not me. You should have gone and done the dirty work. Besides, you had two chances to get rid of Hastings, too, and you bungled both of them."

"Not my fault. I had to act fast when I heard Hastings asking about the Dodge housekeeper. No time to plan things properly. And the hospital attack would have worked if that damn nurse hadn't shown up when she did."

The men paused where the railing had given way and stared down. Kinsey did her best to meet their gaze with defiance. She saw that the new man was younger than James and carried a gun. Even from six-plus feet away, she could see the arrogance burning in his green eyes.

"Kinsey," he said. "Wish I could say it was nice to see you."

In that instant, she recognized his voice. But the man she associated with that voice had curly blond hair and dark brown eyes. "Ryan?" she said, confused.

He shook his head. "Kevin Lester, alias Ryan Jones, alias Chad Dodge. Heck, by now I answer to almost anything. Go ahead, call me Ryan."

"What's going on? Where's my mother?"

He stepped off the last stair and looked down at her. "How about a kiss for old time's sake?" he asked and started to claim one.

She slapped him. A piece of his beard came loose and dangled from his chin.

He reached up and plucked it off. "Hair dye, applications, optical contacts…you can learn a lot in prison if you pay attention, and I did. That's where I met Bill Dodge's real nephew. By the time I got out, I knew more about Chad Dodge then I did about myself. When Chad overdosed, I was able to convince Bill Dodge I was his long-lost nephew."

"Until you got cocky and aroused his suspicion," the lawyer chided. He looked at Kinsey. "Bill asked me for guidance. He didn't trust his nephew, so he'd hidden all his valuables, but he wouldn't tell me where. I told him to tread gently because his nephew had a hot head but that I would hire a private investigator and have Chad verified. Of course I did no such thing.

"Anyway, Bill was determined to change his will to benefit his loyal housekeeper. He wanted advice about how to protect her inheritance if it was proven she'd committed a capital crime. That got me curious, but about then he stopped talking. He wouldn't even let me draw up the will, said he'd do it himself and make sure it was safe."

"Crime?" Kinsey asked. "My mother a criminal? What in the world are you talking about?"

"That's what I wanted to know. That's why I sent *him* to get friendly with you," Fenwick said with a nod toward Ryan. "When that didn't work, I decided to warm up to Frances."

"And then we lucked out," Ryan boasted.

"That's right," Fenwick said, nodding. "I hardly ever go in that little grocery store down the road, but there I am one afternoon when Hastings waltzes in and starts asking questions about Mary Smith and the Dodge housekeeper. I had to know why he was interested in your mother, so I stole his wallet and phone. Thanks to that, I was able to figure out where Hastings was from and that narrowed my search. I finally figured out what was going on and I knew that if Bill Dodge made Frances his beneficiary, she needed to stay lost to the world at least until she made a will of her own. Hastings had to go."

"But you guys screwed that up," Kinsey said softly.

"Yeah, well, once we found out Hastings had amnesia and that you and he were getting close, it seemed like we might skirt by until Bill died, Frances inherited and she died. Then we could disappear substantially better off than we are now."

"You had to make sure my mother married you before she knew about the money. Otherwise, she'd leave most of it to me."

"Exactly."

Kinsey was determined not to ask this man what he thought her mother had done that would land her in jail. If Frances had committed a crime, it went a long way toward explaining why she'd spent Kinsey's life looking over her shoulder, restless and suspicious. Kinsey wanted answers, but not from this jerk.

Ryan nudged Zane with his foot. "Time to wake up, sleepyhead."

Zane groaned as his eyes flickered open. He tried to sit. Kinsey knelt to help him. Ryan grabbed her arm and pulled her away. "Leave him down there. Fenwick, check for a weapon."

A moment later, Fenwick finished a quick search. "He's clean."

"Where's my mother?" Kinsey demanded.

"In the washroom," Fenwick said over his shoulder.

"You'll have time to catch up while we wait for it to get dark," Ryan said. "James, get the tape."

James took a roll of duct tape off a nearby shelf. As he did that, Ryan put a stranglehold around Kinsey's throat. "You, Hastings, get up nice and slow or the lovely Ms. Frost won't live long enough to say goodbye. Walk over there toward that closed door. There's a washroom back there. Move it."

Zane shuffled off in the commanded direction. Kinsey was afraid another head injury following on the heels of the first had exacted a devastating toll. He opened the door to the small room full of laundry equipment and one other human. Her mouth covered with a strip of tape, ankles bound together and hands secured behind her back, Frances sat on the floor by the washing machine, her eyes growing huge as she looked from Kinsey to Zane and then to James Fenwick.

With the gun still pointed at Kinsey, Fenwick taped Zane the same way he had Frances except for the mouth, and then it was Kinsey's turn. He tore the tape from Frances's lips. "Yell all you want, dear wife. It's a big old house, no one will hear you. You have some explaining to do to your daughter before you reach the pearly gates."

"After it's dark, we'll take a road trip to the swamp,"

Ryan said as he turned off the overhead light. "Friend of mine owns an alligator farm. You'll love it there. At least, at first you will." And he closed the door.

Chapter Fourteen

The only light in the small room came from the front-loading dryer after Zane managed to open the door that activated the interior bulb. Then he and Kinsey took turns trying to release each other's wrists, but the tape just stuck harder the more they struggled. Frances sat nearby, oddly subdued.

"Mom?" Kinsey said. "What's going on?"

"James is a maniac," Frances said. "I've been down here for two days. He's convinced Bill left his house and treasures to me. That's what he and that phony nephew of his have been looking for. A will."

"We have it," Kinsey said.

"You do?"

"Bill gave it to me. Zane and I found it this morning."

"Well, it doesn't matter now," she said. "James and I signed wills leaving everything to the other right after we were married."

"We also found a letter Bill wrote you. It was meant to be an apology because he'd betrayed your trust and told Fenwick the truth you'd confided in him. What truth, Mom? I don't get it."

"I do," Zane said.

Kinsey turned to face him. "Really, Zane? You've figured it out?"

"Most of it. There's something else. It's time to start calling me Gerard."

She stared into his eyes, suddenly understanding the difference she'd sensed in him after he recovered from the fall from the stairs. "Your memory is back?"

"Splotchy but improving. You two scoot as far over there as you can. I'm going to be making some noise."

"It won't help," Frances said. "This part of the basement is as good as soundproof."

Kinsey scooted over, as did Frances, when it became clear Zane didn't intend to yell for help. Instead, he raised his bound legs and brought his shoes down on the open dryer door. He did this four or five times, then took a rest, breathing hard for a moment. "I know why I was in New Orleans," he said with a glance at Kinsey over his shoulder. "I remember who sent me and why." His gaze shifted to Kinsey's mother. "It was to see you, Frances."

She shook her head.

"Your daughter sent me."

Kinsey jerked. "I sent you? Huh?"

He twisted his body around to face her. "Kinsey, I suspect this woman's true name is Mary Smith. She's not your mother."

"What are you talking about?" Kinsey said, looking from Zane to Frances.

"Right before my father's wedding, his bride showed me a letter she'd just received. It was from a man in New Orleans who used to know her family. He swore that he'd seen Mary Smith in his neighborhood. He didn't know what name she was using, but he had heard that she worked for a rather well-known man in the area, a guy by the name of William Dodge."

"This has nothing to do with me," Frances said. "Kinsey, don't listen to him."

Zane continued as though she hadn't spoken. "Trouble was, Mary Smith was supposed to be dead. Grace had to know the truth, but she didn't want to tell my father. She begged me to come look into it. That's why I drove here. To find Mary Smith and hopefully, a girl named Sandra."

Kinsey could feel the shakes starting in her body's core. "Sandra?"

His voice grew gentle. "Mary Smith is your grandmother, not your mother. She shot and killed your father, kidnapped you and disappeared from Idaho. Then she arranged your fake deaths so the authorities would stop looking for her. That's why your life was so nomadic, that's why she was always anxious. She's been running for almost twenty-five years. Your given name is Sandra."

Frances had buried her face against her bent knees.

"Wait a second," Kinsey said. "Your new stepmother is my…my mother?"

He nodded.

"But I have a birth certificate and a social security card saying I'm Kinsey Frost."

"Frances, don't you think you owe Kinsey an explanation? You can't hide from this any longer."

Frances looked up. Her tear-stained face terrified Kinsey. "It's true," Frances whispered. "After I…took you, I got a job caring for a sickly baby about your age. When she died, I stole her identity and gave it to you. I changed my name so we'd match and just avoided situations where I had to prove who I was. I did it because I had to."

"You had to?" Kinsey repeated. "Why?" She blinked back tears. "Why?"

"To save you," Frances whispered.

"Save me from what?"

Frances shook her head and pressed her lips together. Kinsey's throat tightened. "I can't hear any more right now," she said, and then in an abrupt turnaround added, "What about my father? I mean the one who died in a bus crash."

Frances took a shaky breath. "Your grandfather died years before you were born. I had to give you a father. When I read about the unidentified man on the bus, I decided to use him."

Unspent tears burned behind Kinsey's nose. Everything was made up. Her name wasn't her name. Her birthday wasn't real. Her mother wasn't her mother, the father she'd mourned had never existed. "I don't believe any of this," she whispered.

Zane looked at her again. "I'm sorry, Kinsey. I wish it were different. I have to keep trying to break this door."

"I know," she said.

Once again he raised his legs. Kinsey could only imagine the strain and stress of what he was doing as time after time his feet slammed down on the dryer door. The machine was old, but the hinges held.

He took breaks now and again, scooting next to Kinsey, putting his face close to hers. As time passed and the hope of creating some way to cut their bonds began to seem increasingly remote, he whispered into her ear, "I want you to know I love you," he said. "If we survive tonight, I want you to be my wife."

"But you must remember Ann and Heidi now. Are you ready to move on?"

"I never thought I would be," he said. "I thought I'd just hurt forever. And then I met you. I know we both need time to...adjust to everything. I just wanted you to know how I feel. I hope you feel the same way." He kissed her gently. "I can't bear the thought I might ever lose you."

"You won't," she said. "Never."

"Okay, love. That's settled. Now, this is what we're

going to do. We're going to sit back to back and use each other to get to our feet. Can you do it?"

"I'll try."

It was harder than she thought it would be because of the muscles she needed to use that were connected to her cracked ribs, but stifling a scream of pain, she managed. "Now what?" she said.

"I'm going to sit on that damn door and you're going to sit on my lap."

With that, he dropped himself down hard on the dryer door. Kinsey inched her bound feet close to join him, but it proved to be unnecessary. The door groaned and ripped off of the machine. Zane fell with it to the floor. Sure enough, the metal hinge had torn away from the dryer and jutted out in all its snaggletoothed glory just waiting to saw through some duct tape.

"You go first," Kinsey said. Zane managed to get on his knees and back up to the busted hinge. A minute later, he was free.

"Now what?" Kinsey said as they all stood. They'd removed most of the tape, but Frances had been sitting for over two days and hadn't eaten or drunk anything in that long, as well. Moving stiffly, she drew a handful of water out of the laundry faucet and drank it down like it was champagne.

Zane caught Kinsey staring at Frances and wondered what she was thinking. Having just recovered the memories and emotions, both good and bad, that define any individual, he considered what was worse: to have no memory of what you'd lost or to have to redefine everything you thought you knew. He hoped he could help her see that many of the people and things she'd believed in were still real, but he knew it was going to take her time to work through it all. At least she wouldn't have to do it alone.

He glanced at his watch and saw that it was almost six o'clock. Darkness was still hours away. "Is there another way out of the basement?" he asked.

"Just windows," Frances said. "You'd have to break them, they don't open."

"And they must be boarded up," Kinsey added.

"I'm going to look around," Zane said. "You two stay here." He didn't miss the uneasy look that passed between the women as he turned the knob on the door. It had been locked from the outside. Shoving his shoulder against it, he applied thrust and weight and heard the gratifying sound of an old lock giving up.

The lights were off in the basement, so he moved slowly to avoid running into something. He wouldn't chance the stairs for the simple reason it was obvious the door at the top was closed. Opening that door and walking into the kitchen seemed foolhardy at best. If he was shot, Kinsey and Frances would be sitting ducks.

He stood there for a second, trying to orient himself. The washroom was at the back of the house, but this part of the basement was right under the living area. He needed to be quieter now than he'd been before. He felt his way carefully to the outside wall and reached up to feel the rough texture of old wood. Sure enough, someone had nailed boards over the glass.

After numerous attempts and failures, he finally found one board that wasn't nailed in as well as the others. He pushed a nearby box beneath the window to improve leverage and managed to pull and twist it free. That provided adequate light to see that there were four windows in a row, all boarded up. Each was about eighteen inches high and a couple of feet long. He needed to find a tool to help himself and fumbled around for several moments until an old golf club caught his attention.

And that's when he heard a tapping noise coming from the window he'd partially uncovered. The noise came again and he realized it originated outside. He had no idea who or what he'd find, but as he didn't have a whole lot to lose, he used the gold club to pop off another board.

A man had crouched down to be able to see through the window. Zane couldn't believe it when the heavily shadowed figure materialized into Detective Woods. Woods pantomimed his reluctance to talk, pointing overhead. Zane realized they were directly under the kitchen.

And yet, this was something of a miracle and what was the saying, fortune favors the bold? Using the head of the golf club, he tapped on the glass until it shattered, wincing at the noise it made. The windows were from before the age of safety glass and jagged pieces gleamed like vampire fangs. He took off his jacket and tried to brush some of them away as Woods leaned in close.

"I came looking for you when you didn't show up at the impound yard or my office," he said. "After the last week or so, I figured almost anything could have happened."

"James Fenwick and the man Kinsey knew as Ryan Jones are upstairs and they're armed. They're behind everything. They're waiting until dark to get rid of us. We have to get out of here."

"I knocked on the door first," Woods said. "No one answered, but I knew they were in there and that got me curious. When I saw your rental parked down the block, I decided to do a little snooping. These boarded-up windows looked suspicious. Where are the others? Anyone hurt?"

"They're close by. I'll get them."

"Hurry. I'll call for backup and work on this glass."

Zane rushed back to the washroom. He found Kinsey and her grandmother standing apart, not looking at each other. "Come on," he urged. "We have a way out."

They didn't need coaxing. The three of them arrived back at the window to find that Woods had draped his suit coat over the sill. Zane helped Frances climb on top of the box. With Zane shoving from behind while Woods pulled from outside, Frances twisted her body sideways to fit through the jagged opening. She was almost out when a startled scream jumped from her throat. She swallowed it back almost immediately. "I'm sorry, I'm sorry, I cut my leg."

"We'll take care of it in a minute," Woods said. "Stay low and quiet." He turned back to Zane. "Let me work on this piece of glass before Kinsey and you come through."

"Hurry," Zane urged as Kinsey stepped onto the box. He caught her hand and pressed it against his lips. "I love you," he said.

As she looked down at him, a smile spread her beautiful ruby lips. "I love you, too."

"I think I got it," Woods said. "Give it a try."

As she began to hoist herself up, Zane heard a noise coming from the top of the stairs. The door was still closed, but the light came on. Zane ran for the stairs, climbing two at a time, rushing as fast as he could. If either man entered the stairwell, they'd catch Kinsey in the act of leaving. He had to stop them.

James appeared right as Zane burst into the kitchen. Zane slugged him square on the jaw and caught his shoulders as he slumped. The other door opened. Ryan paused midstep, but he recovered quickly and the semiautomatic he'd flaunted in the basement appeared in his hand. Zane did the only thing he could think to do to keep from taking a bullet in the gut. He shoved James Fenwick at Ryan with every ounce of strength he still possessed.

The gun went off before both men hit the floor. Zane was already in motion, following them. When he caught a glimpse of the gun in Ryan's hand, he kicked as hard as he could. The gun spun across the room.

Zane scrambled to retrieve it and held it on Ryan as Ryan shoved James's limp body off of his. They stared at each other while a pounding on the stairs preceded Detective Woods's abrupt arrival in the kitchen, weapon drawn. "You're bleeding," he said after a quick survey.

Zane glanced down at his side. His white shirt was stained red where the bullet that had killed James Fenwick had apparently passed through his body and nicked Zane's rib cage. "Just a graze."

"Please, sit down before you fall down. I've got him."

Zane shook his head. "Not until I see Kinsey."

"She'll be out front by now."

Zane stepped around James Fenwick's body without a second glance. He opened the front door and saw Kinsey and Frances standing next to a squad car. Kinsey turned. For the first time in over two years he felt whole and complete again.

And the reason was running toward him.

"I'm nervous," Kinsey admitted as Zane turned onto ranch land. He stopped his truck in front of his father's house. To the world, legally, they were Sandra and Gerard, but to each other, the old names were the ones they used.

"I don't blame you, sweetheart," he said, "but I think you'll like Grace when you get to know her."

Even as he spoke, the side door opened and a delicate-looking woman with graying brown hair appeared. Kinsey didn't need anyone to tell her that she was looking at her mother, who rushed out onto the porch and then stopped. She clasped her hands together and held them against her chest as though struggling to keep her heart from leaping from her body.

Kinsey got out of the truck and walked up the stairs. She wasn't sure what to say or how to act. Even thinking of anyone other than Frances as her mother felt wrong somehow.

Grace reached out and took Kinsey's hands. "Sandra," she said softly. "Oh, my dear, I can hardly believe it's you."

They sat down on the narrow bench, searching each other's faces. Finally Grace cleared her throat. "How is my mother holding up? I know it's been two weeks since, well, everything happened. I wanted to come to New Orleans, but I wasn't sure it was the right thing to do…"

"Please," Kinsey said softly. "It's okay. It's been a really busy two weeks. Anyway, Frances is being extradited back to Idaho. I'm not sure what charges they'll bring against her. It's hard for me to believe she actually murdered my father."

Grace's grip on Kinsey's hands tightened. "About that…you need to understand something. I was different back then. Selfish and stupid…into drugs…my marriage was a joke. Greg was…difficult and high all the time. He kept making me ask my mother for money and she always came through, except for the last time, when she refused. She said we needed to grow up and take care of our baby, get sober…of course, she was right."

They were talking about Frances, or technically, Mary. Kinsey had to constantly remind herself about the truth of the relationships she'd taken for granted her entire life. The falsehoods and lies still roamed her mind and heart like a pride of caged lions.

"That last day I was passed out in the bedroom," Grace continued. "Greg and you were in the living room. The police said he'd just finished cleaning his gun. All the supplies were still on the table. And he was high as usual. Mom came to the house to pick you up and take you back to her place. She took care of you a lot, almost all the time. Anyway, Greg was furious with her for not giving us the money we'd asked for. They got into an argument… I know because their yelling woke me up. You wouldn't stop crying. It was terrible.

"I tried to get up to help, but I couldn't get my balance… I was too wasted. I heard Greg tell my mother to leave. She pleaded with him to let her take you with her, that you were crying and needed a clean diaper. He said she would never see you again, period. Again I tried to get control of myself, but I couldn't focus. Your cries became screams. I guess Greg took out his aggression on the most innocent person in the room. My mother shouted for Greg to stop hitting you. She begged him. And then there was a gunshot…it got real quiet."

"You don't have to finish this," Kinsey said in a shaky voice.

Grace swallowed hard. "Yes, I do. Eventually I made it out to the living room. Greg lay on the floor, his revolver next to him. The door was wide open. You and my mother were gone."

Kinsey wiped tears off her cheeks. Zane was suddenly standing beside her. He handed her a clean folded handkerchief. A sense of peace flooded her body as he gently smoothed her hair.

"I'm sorry to have to tell you all this," Grace whispered. "I'm sorry you have to know what your father and I were like. I didn't protect you. My mother did in the only way she thought she could. I want you to know that

I've spoken with the district attorney and begged him to consider all the facts before he brings her to trial. But if it comes to that, I'll speak out for her."

"Thank you for being so honest," Kinsey mumbled, and then she spontaneously hugged her mother. "I know it can't be easy for you," she added.

Her mother straightened up but kept her hands around Kinsey's. "I don't expect you to forgive me or your grand-mother for what we've done to your life, but please know it wasn't intentional. Until two weeks ago, I thought both of you were dead. When I got that letter and Gerard agreed to go see what he could find out, I never dreamed I was sending him into such danger. I just had to know. I've lived my life in shame and guilt."

"I think you both have," Kinsey said. "Maybe it's time to stop."

Grace hugged Kinsey this time and that caused a new flood of tears. Finally she spoke again. "I've talked to your father, Gerard, and he promises me we'll help my mother financially. How do we go about getting decent legal help?"

"It's taken care of," Zane said. "The lawyer who drew up Bill's will made sure the inheritance came to her. His practice will defend her if it comes to trial. As for fi-nances, there was a room built behind library shelves crammed with art and old books, antiques, even a crusty old trunk of gold doubloons—Bill was quite a collector. She'll be okay."

"And the man who almost killed you?"

"Which time?" Zane asked with a fleeting smile. "The lawyer pushed me into the street and tried to choke me in the hospital, Ryan threw a toolbox on top of us and forced us into the slough."

"I was thinking about the shooting."

"Ah, Ryan. Aka, Chad Dodge, Kevin Lester and a bunch of other names. The police have enough on him to keep him behind bars for decades."

Someone inside the house yelled Grace's name and Kinsey stood. "Is that Lily?" she asked. "I've been worried about her."

Chance showed up in the open door. "Don't you know?" he asked. "Lily is gone. She left the same day you and Gerard did."

"Where did she go?" Kinsey asked.

Chance shook his head. "Just took off. Her and Charlie both. I don't know where they went. Frankly, I don't care."

They all looked at each other for a long moment, Chance's last declaration hanging in the air like acrid smoke. And then Zane put his arm around his brother's shoulder and Chance's bravado slipped off his face.

Kinsey closed her eyes for a moment, unable to bear any more emotion. She heard retreating footsteps as everyone apparently went inside the house, but a second later, familiar hands clasped hers and pulled her against his chest. She opened her eyes and looked up at Zane.

"Let's go home," he said as he leaned down to kiss her.

"That sounds wonderful," she whispered against his lips.

Home. At last.

* * * * *

"If it's okay with you, I'll go out and check for footprints," Zach said.

Maddy smiled as she arched her neck and massaged it. "Sure," she said. "Why are you asking my permission?"

He snorted. "Are you kidding me? You told me in no uncertain terms that you were in charge here."

She eyed him with a raised brow. "You're telling me you're ready to take charge now?"

Zach felt as though her gaze were singeing his skin. He swallowed and shifted slightly, surprised that his body was straining in reaction to her teasing words. For someone who was not his type, she could take him from zero to uh-oh in no time flat. He forced himself to speak lightly, with no trace in his voice of the struggle he was waging to keep himself in check.

"Madeleine Tierney. When I'm ready to take charge, believe me, you will know it."

UNDER SUSPICION

BY
MALLORY KANE

Published in Great Britain 2015
by Mills & Boon, an imprint of Harlequin (UK) Limited,
Eton House, 18-24 Paradise Road, Richmond, Surrey, TW9 1SR

© 2015 Rickey R. Mallory

ISBN: 978-0-263-25305-4

46-0515

Harlequin (UK) Limited's policy is to use papers that are natural, renewable and recyclable products and made from wood grown in sustainable forests. The logging and manufacturing processes conform to the legal environmental regulations of the country of origin.

Printed and bound in Spain
by CPI, Barcelona

Mallory Kane has two great reasons for loving to write. Her mother, a librarian, taught her to love and respect books. Her father could hold listeners spellbound for hours with his stories. His oral histories are chronicled in numerous places, including the Library of Congress Veterans' History Project. He was always her biggest fan. To learn more about Mallory, visit her online at www.mallorykane.com.

For Michael. Love you.

Chapter One

The rain had finally stopped. Zachary Winter turned off the windshield wipers of his rental car as he passed the city limits sign for Bonne Chance, Louisiana. Now that the sun had come out, steam rose like tendrils of smoke from the blacktop road and clung to the windshield like shower spray on a mirror. He put the wipers on Intermittent. Rain in south Louisiana was seldom a relief, no matter what the season. Even in April, when most of the country was experiencing spring weather, an afternoon thunderstorm might cool the heat-soaked roads enough for steam to rise, but the tepid, humid air never seemed to change.

The last time he'd been here, in his hometown of Bonne Chance, was more than a decade ago. The name Bonne Chance was French for *Good Luck*. His mouth twisted with irony. Had his sad little hometown ever been good luck for anybody? He'd certainly never intended to come back. And the reason he was here now was not his choice.

He drove past two national chain grocery stores and a Walmart. "Well, Bonne Chance," he muttered, "I guess you've arrived if Walmart thinks you're worthy of notice."

As he turned onto Parish Road 1991, better known as

Cemetery Road, a pang hit his chest, part anxiety, part grief and part dread. He'd intended to get into town in time for Tristan DuChaud's funeral. Tristan had been his best friend since before first grade.

As he rounded a curve, he spotted the dark green canopy that contrasted with the dull granite of the above-ground tombs peculiar to south Louisiana. From this distance, he couldn't read the white letters on the canopy, but he knew what they said: CARVER FUNERAL HOME, Serving Bonne Chance for Over Forty Years.

He parked on the shoulder of the road, glanced at his watch, then lowered the driver's-side window. The air that immediately swirled around his head and filled the car was suffocatingly familiar, superheated and supersaturated from the rain.

One hundred percent humidity. Now, *there* was a hard concept to explain to someone who'd never been to the Deep South. How the air could be completely saturated with water and yet no rain would fall. He usually described it as similar to breathing in a sauna. But that wasn't even close. The air down here felt heavy and thick. Within seconds, a combination of sweat and a strange, invisible mist made everything you wore and everything you touched damp. And with the sun out and drawing steam from people as well as roads and metal surfaces, it could be disturbingly hard to breathe.

Getting out of the car, Zach shrugged his shoulders, trying to peel the damp material of his white cotton shirt away from his skin, but he knew that within seconds it would be stuck again. Then he took off his sunglasses. They had fogged up immediately when the damp heat hit them. Without their protection, however, the sun's glare made it almost impossible to see. He shaded his eyes and squinted at the small group of people who were gathered around the funeral home's canopy. Most of them were dressed in black. The men had removed their jackets and hung them over the backs of the metal folding chairs set up under the canopy.

He wished he could leave his jacket in the car but that was out of the question. He'd always found it more efficient to travel armed, in his official capacity as a National Security Agency investigative agent. Today, though, a storm had hit New Orleans about a half hour before the plane's arrival time and not even his high-security clearance could clear the runway in time for him to rent a car and make it to Bonne Chance for Tristan's funeral service. It looked as though he'd barely made it to the graveside in time.

He grabbed the jacket and put it on, then blew on the sunglasses to dry the condensation. He held them up to the light for inspection and put them back on.

As he walked toward the stately aboveground tomb that held at least three generations of the DuChaud family, he tried to sort out the people gathered there. Townspeople, family, friends like himself. But his sunglasses were fogging up again.

He approached slowly, breathing in the smell of freshly turned earth that mixed with the fishy, slightly moldy smell of the bayou, an unforgettable odor he'd grown up with and hadn't missed for one second in the thirteen years since he'd been gone.

Zach had pushed the speed limit as much as he could, considering what he knew about speed traps in south Louisiana, and still he'd not only missed Tristan's funeral, he'd almost missed the graveside service. It was just as well, he supposed. He'd dreaded seeing his classmates, most of whom had settled down in Bonne Chance like Tristan, and spent their lives working on oil rigs or fishing. He hadn't looked forward to answering their half-deriding questions about *life in the big city*.

Tristan DuChaud. His best friend, for as long as he could remember, was one of the finest people Zach had ever known. Maybe *the* finest. His gaze went to the carved stone of the tomb, its thick walls and ornate steeple soaking up all the warmth and sunlight and leaving Tristan's final resting place cold and dank.

It was strange and sad to be here, knowing his friend was gone. Especially since their last conversation had been a fight, about Sandy, of course. It had occurred two days before Zach, his older sister, Zoe, and their mom moved from Bonne Chance to Houston three days before Zach's fifteenth birthday. Sandy was mad at Tristan for some reason and she'd come to Zach's house to talk, just as she'd always done.

Tristan and Sandy had *liked* each other ever since third grade and everybody knew they'd get married one day. They were *that* couple, the one that would be together forever. But Tristan had always had a jealous streak, and that irritated Sandy to no end. Sometimes she'd egg him on by flirting with Zach, which infuriated Tristan, even though, or maybe because, he and Zach were best friends.

As Zach got closer to the grave site, the formless figures shimmering in the heat began to coalesce into recognizable people. The stocky man holding the Bible was, of course, Michael Duffy. His thick shock of light brown hair looked a little out of place above the black suit and white priest's collar he wore. Zach had heard from his mother that Duff had become a priest after the awful accident the night of Zoe's graduation, but he'd found it hard to believe that the fun-loving, hard-partying Duff was now a priest.

Duff raised his hand and the small group of people moved to sit in the folding chairs. Zach finally spotted Sandy, Tristan's wife—or widow. She looked as though she was doing okay, but for some reason, she was being led to the first chair by a woman he didn't recognize.

He studied the woman. She was about the same size as Sandy—maybe more slender. He couldn't place her. Was she a relative of Sandy's? Of Tristan's? He didn't remember ever seeing her before, and he would have remembered her. She had an intensity that he wasn't sure he'd ever noticed in a woman before.

The woman got Sandy settled then straightened and glanced around. She didn't seem to be looking for anyone in particular, but the tension that wafted from her like heat still reached out to him. He watched her, his interest piqued, not so much by her appearance, although she was attractive. He was interested in what she was doing.

Surveillance. The word popped out of his subconscious. He rolled it on his tongue. *Surveillance.* The woman was doing surveillance of the area.

As the woman checked the perimeter of the grave site, Zach noticed a subtle shift in her demeanor. She hadn't moved, but something about her had changed. When he'd first noticed her, she'd been alert, but she'd reminded him a bit of a mother hen, scurrying to keep up with Sandy, her chick. That impression had faded when she'd begun surveying the area.

Now there was nothing left of the mother hen. The woman was poised and taut in a way she hadn't been before. As he watched, she straightened, her entire focus as sharp and unwavering as an eagle that has spotted its prey.

As Zach watched her transform from protector to

predator, an electric hum vibrated along his nerve endings. He felt attuned to her, as though he knew what she was thinking, what she was planning. She stepped closer to Sandy, her weight evenly balanced between her feet, her focus unwavering.

He followed her line of vision and saw two men. Like many of the others, they were dressed in slacks and a shirt with no tie, as if they'd taken off their jackets because of the heat. But these two stood at the edge of the canopy with their hands in their pockets rather than sitting and they seemed to avoid looking at anyone directly.

Zach thought there was a family resemblance between the two, although the younger one looked as though he might still be in high school. So they were probably father and son.

He glanced back at the woman. He couldn't tell if she knew them, but he could tell that she was expecting trouble.

Her intensity fed his. His scalp began to burn. His senses focused to a razor-honed sharpness as time seemed to slow down. His entire body tightened and he instinctively shifted his weight onto the balls of his feet. An almost imperceptible vibration hummed through his muscles and tendons.

At that instant, as if his energy had reached her, the woman looked directly at him. A knife edge of caution sliced into his chest. He'd never seen her before, but in that instant when her gaze met his through the shimmering heat, he had a sinking feeling that before this day was over, he was going to wish he hadn't seen her now.

Her gaze slid away from him and back to the man and boy. Again, Zach looked, too. The boy was whispering to his father. He nodded in the direction of the woman and Sandy, and the older man shook his head no. He urged the son closer to the lined-up chairs as Duff called for everyone to bow their heads for prayer.

Duff began his supplication to the Lord without bowing his own head. As he spoke, he looked Zach up and down, nodded in recognition and tilted his head disapprovingly all at the same time. Zach stood still, clasped his hands behind his back and bowed his head. But he couldn't close his eyes. He kept the two men in his peripheral vision. If they moved suddenly, he wanted to know.

Once Duff said amen and raised his head, he held out a hand to Sandy to approach the dully gleaming casket, which was sitting on a wheeled cart, waiting to be placed into the DuChaud vault. Sandy stood, and her companion started to stand beside her, but Sandy stopped her with a small gesture. Alone, she approached the casket and laid a white rose on top, bowed her head for a brief moment, then turned and started back toward her chair. Then she saw him.

Her face, which had been set determinedly, dissolved into anguish at the sight of him, and tears filled and overflowed her eyes. "Zach," she whispered. "Oh, Zach, he's gone. Our Tristan is gone."

Zach took two long strides and gathered her gently into his arms. He closed his eyes and hugged her to him as if she were his long-lost sister. She clung to him the same way, and her slender shoulders shook as she cried silently. Zach held her while Duff gestured to Tristan's mother to come forward and lay a white rose next to Sandy's. After Mrs. DuChaud sat, the priest led the pallbearers past the casket to lay red roses on top, one by one, and back to their seats.

Then the priest laid his left hand on Sandy's shoulder and held out his right toward Zach. "Zachary Winter," he said. "I thought you swore you'd never come back here."

"There's only one reason I would, Duff. I mean, Father..." Zach had no idea what to call him.

Duff smiled and said, "It's Father Michael, but Duff is fine. Nobody around here dares to call me that."

Zach nodded uncomfortably, then leaned in closer to the other man as a couple came up to offer Sandy their condolences.

"What happened?" he asked in a low tone. "How did Tristan die?"

"From what I understand, he was walking along the catwalk on the bottom level of the oil platform with one of the Vietnamese roughnecks and he fell into the water near the drill mechanism."

"Oil platform?" Zach said in surprise as a knot formed in his stomach. "He was on an oil rig? What was he doing there?"

Duff's gray brows rose. "You don't know? Have you not talked to Tristan in all these years?"

Zach shrugged, embarrassed. "Not really. We didn't talk to anybody after we moved. You know, with Zoe being involved in the accident."

Duff grimaced briefly as he nodded.

"Nothing more than an email at Christmas. A comment on Facebook. You know."

"His dad was killed on a rig about two months before Tristan's high school graduation, so he dropped out and went to work on the oil rig to help his mother."

"But he was going to LSU. He was going to be a veterinarian. How could two months have made a difference?"

Duff nodded grimly. "I talked to him, but he was

determined. He saw it as a choice. Taking care of his family—he and Sandy were planning to get married right after graduation—or taking care of himself. He chose his family."

"Right." Zach's throat closed up. He felt sad and angry. Tristan had given up his education and the opportunity for a great career so he could go to work right away. The thought made Zach feel sick as he thought of all Tristan had given up. And for what? To end up dead at the bottom of the Gulf of Mexico?

"Wait a minute, Duff. Tristan had lived on boats and docks and floating logs on the Mississippi River and on the Gulf his whole life. He was the strongest swimmer I've ever seen. He couldn't have fallen overboard and drowned if he tried. What happened out there?"

"I wish I could tell you more but I can't," Duff said. "He went over with another guy, a roughneck. Maybe they were arguing or even fighting. Maybe they ran into each other in the dark."

"You know as well as I do it's never dark on an oil rig. What'd the autopsy say?"

Duff looked surprised. "The autopsy?"

Zach thought he'd hesitated for an instant. "The autopsy. Who did it?"

"I guess that would have been the ME, John Bookman. He's the medical examiner for the parish and chief of emergency medicine at the Terrebonne Parish Hospital in Houma."

"Okay. Houma is about twenty-five miles north of here, right?" Zach asked.

The priest nodded, then gestured with his head. "See Angel?"

Zach followed his gesture and saw Angel DuChaud, Tristan's ne'er-do-well cousin, talking to a small wiry man. Again, he was surprised. Three years older than he and Tristan, Angel had been the stereotypical bad boy all their lives. But he cleaned up nicely. His hair was styled and his suit fit impeccably, and hid his tattoos.

"The man he's talking to," Duff said, "is the parish medical examiner."

At that moment, Sandy turned around and took Zach's arm. He smiled at her and patted her hand.

"It's so good of you to come, Zach," she said.

"You know nothing could keep me from being here," he replied.

Duff took Sandy's hand from Zach's arm. "Sandy, walk with me over here. I want you to meet—"

Zach silently thanked Duff for distracting Sandy. He hadn't expected the parish medical examiner to be at Tristan's funeral, but he was grateful for the opportunity to ask him some questions. He walked toward Angel and, eventually, Tristan's cousin saw him.

When Angel spotted him, he waved. Zach sketched a half wave in the air and walked over to where Angel and the ME stood. Angel made casual introductions.

"You're the ME," Zach said to Dr. John Bookman. "Call me Zach. I was Tristan's best friend in school."

"I'm sorry. Terrible thing that happened to Tristan," the doctor said.

"Do you live here in Bonne Chance?"

"No," the doctor answered, eyeing Zach narrowly. "I live in Houma. Didn't Father Michael tell you that?"

Angel wandered away toward the DuChaud family crypt. Zach was glad. He didn't want him to overhear his next question. "I want to ask you about Tristan DuChaud's death."

Bookman's eyes shifted toward the casket, which was still sitting in front of the vault. But now the vault door was open. "I don't discuss my work, certainly not at a funeral."

"I understand. If I may…" Zach paused, wondering if what he was about to do was a mistake. After all, he was here not in his official capacity but just to mourn the death of his best friend and to show his respect for his widow. He decided it didn't matter whether it was a mistake. He needed to do it, for Tristan.

The question of what his boss would say flitted into his mind but he chased it out again. He'd worry about that later, if it came up.

He leaned in, close to the doctor's ear. "I'm with the National Security Agency." That was true. "We're investigating possible terrorist activity in the area." That was sort of true but not really. They *were* picking up chatter in the area around New Orleans and Galveston.

He went on. "I need to know what the cause of death was for Tristan DuChaud. Was foul play involved in his death?"

Dr. Bookman's eyes went wide, then narrowed again. He took a half step backward and studied Zach as if he were a slide under a microscope. After a moment, he asked quietly, "Did you say NSA? Shouldn't you be talking to the Coast Guard? They're in charge of the recovery."

"I need this information, Dr. Bookman."

Dr. Bookman fidgeted, obviously uncomfortable. "Do you have ID?"

Zach groaned but pulled his badge holder and ID out of his back pocket and handed it to the doctor and waited. The doctor discreetly glanced at it, looked at it again for a beat longer and then handed it back.

"You might want to meet me at the parish morgue after the service," he said quietly.

"No," Zach said. "I need to know now." He looked over at the groundskeeper, who was standing behind the cart that held Tristan's casket. "After the service could be too late."

Bookman followed his gaze. "I'm not comfortable with this. We should talk in my office."

Zach shook his head.

"Okay, but please remember that you are at the funeral of your best friend, and don't create a scene."

The medical examiner took a step away from the crowd. Zach followed him, his scalp burning at the doctor's statement. *Don't create a scene.*

"We don't have a cause of death," Bookman said.

"You what?"

"Lower your voice, Mr.—or is it Agent—Winter? You don't want to upset Sandy."

"Why don't you?" Zach asked quietly, afraid he knew the answer.

"Because we don't have a body."

Zach stared at him, then darted a glance at the casket.

"That's right. That casket contains no human remains."

"Son of a—" Zach stopped himself and rubbed his face. "You didn't recover the body?"

Bookman sighed. "I have remains."

"I don't understand," Zach persisted.

Bookman looked across the crowd at Sandy. Zach followed his gaze. "It's pretty simple. There's not enough of Tristan DuChaud to put in a casket."

"Not enough—" Zach felt queasy. He'd known that was the answer, but to hear it stated like that, in no uncertain terms, stripped him raw. "What do you mean, not enough?" he growled.

Dr. Bookman searched his face for a moment. "A

rather substantial piece of calf muscle, a piece of scalp with hair intact and…that's about it. Barely enough to provide identification. I can't afford to waste any of it by burying it in the ground. Now understand, I haven't positively identified these remains with DNA. I've sent the samples off, but it generally takes weeks, if not months, to get DNA back."

The doctor might as well have sucker punched him. The idea that all that was left of Tristan was a little muscle and a bit of hair. The back of his throat burned with nausea. "What about the other man?"

Bookman nodded. "He was pretty chewed up. There were several schools of sharks in the area."

Several schools of sharks. Zach tried to erase that phrase from his mind. "But you can identify the difference between him and Tristan, right?"

"On a superficial level, yes. I can. From physical attributes mostly. The Vietnamese man, according to his employment records, was five inches shorter than DuChaud. I would expect his torso, parts of which we recovered, to be smaller than DuChaud's. I would also expect the typical Asian features, whereas DuChaud was Caucasian. I'm relatively sure that the calf muscle tissue and the scalp with light brown hair belong to DuChaud."

"What's your conclusion? Any sign of foul play?"

"I can't answer that question. Right now, what I can say with relative certainty is that I have the remains of two men, one Caucasian, one Asian. There is enough of the Asian's torso present to be certain that he perished. The meager remains we collected for DuChaud are not conclusive at all, but judging from the damage to the Vietnamese man's body, it would be difficult to imagine that DuChaud could have survived."

Zach swallowed hard. "Wait a minute," he said. "You said difficult, not impossible. Are you saying there's a chance he could be alive?"

Bookman shook his head. "No. I'm not. The remains we have are not conclusive, but the men went overboard in a place and a situation that doesn't support survival. Not only was the drill mechanism and a large diesel motor right there, practically beneath them, but as I mentioned, there were sharks, too."

Behind Zach, the groundskeeper pushed the cart that held Tristan's casket. One wheel was rickety and it creaked with every inch of movement. He turned.

Sandy, who was standing next to Duff, started to turn around as well, but the priest kept his hand on her shoulder. With his eyes, he beckoned Zach.

"The Coast Guard has captured several of the sharks," Dr. Bookman went on. "They're sending me the stomach contents to see what additional remains I might be able to recover."

The queasiness rose in the back of Zach's throat again.

"Sorry about your friend," Dr. Bookman said.

Zach thanked him. He stepped quickly over to Sandy's side. He wanted to watch until the groundskeeper slammed the stone door and locked the bolt.

Actually, that wasn't what he wanted to do. He *wanted* to run over to the casket and rip it open. He wanted to see with his own eyes just exactly what was inside, if it wasn't his friend's body. But of course, he couldn't do that. He wouldn't. Sandy was there and he'd rather die than let her know that her husband's body was never recovered.

"Sandy," Duff said, "wasn't Zach one of Tristan's best friends?"

She glanced at him, not fooled for a moment, but allowing him to distract her from the sight of her husband's casket being pushed into the vault. "His *best* friend," she corrected, smiling at Zach.

He smiled back at her, and his conscious brain picked up on what he'd been aware of subconsciously since he'd first seen her. Sandy had always been slender, but the black dress she wore was formfitting and hugged a small but obvious baby bump. Tristan's widow was pregnant. His eyes burned and his heart felt broken into pieces. *Tristan had a child.*

Sandy's hand moved to rest on her belly protectively, and Zach realized he was staring. He looked up to see her smiling sadly at him. He opened his mouth to apologize or console her or something, but she shook her head. "It's okay, Zach," she murmured. "I'm doing okay. I'm about three and a half months along," she said, her voice quivering. "Tristan knew. He was sure it's a boy."

As he struggled for the right thing to say, he felt a presence behind him.

"Sandy," a voice said. It was the woman. "We need to get back to the house." She sounded exactly as he'd figured she would. She had a city accent. Maybe New Orleans, maybe another large metropolitan area. But one thing was for sure, it was certainly not a south Louisiana–bayou accent.

Turning, Zach met her gaze and saw for the first time that her eyes were blue. It didn't really surprise him. He didn't trust blue eyes.

Chapter Two

Her manner was no longer hostile, but it was decidedly chilly. Then she turned toward Sandy and within less than a heartbeat, her entire demeanor changed. A tenderness melted the ice in her eyes and her stiff shoulders relaxed. Zach shivered as the chill she'd aimed at him dissolved in the afternoon sun.

"You should lie down for at least a half hour while I put out the food and get ready for people to come by. Mrs. Pennebaker told me just now that she'd taken three more pies over and two buckets of chicken." She took Sandy's elbow and began to guide her away from Zach and Duff.

Sandy groaned. "How much do they think I can eat?" she said.

Zach was sure he'd heard a spark of amusement lighten her subdued tone for a second. Maybe she actually was all right. Or at least better than she looked, because she looked exhausted, crushed and on the verge of fainting, if he could tell anything by the paleness of her face.

"They know you're going to need lots of food, not only for yourself and the baby. Don't forget all the people who are going to be stopping by," the woman said.

"I know that. And I *don't* need to lie down. I'm fine."

As the woman led her away, Sandy turned back, reaching out to Zach. He took her hand.

"Come by, please? We— I haven't seen you for such a long time. You're not leaving right away, are you? And bring your bags. You're staying with me."

Out of the corner of his eye, Zach saw the woman frown. That stopped the polite protest on the tip of his tongue. Instead, he nodded. "Thanks, Sandy. I'd be happy to." He shot the woman a sidelong glance.

"Oh, Zach, this is Madeleine Tierney," Sandy said, then turned to the woman. "I'm so sorry, Maddy. I forgot all about introducing you."

Madeleine Tierney nodded at him without offering her hand.

"This is Zachary Winter. He's Tristan's oldest and dearest friend, practically since they were born."

Zach nodded back at her. "I'll see you at the house, Sandy," he said.

As the two women walked away, he took a few seconds to study Madeleine Tierney. She had on a dark jacket and skirt that was a little loose. Her shoes were plain and black with a medium heel. Her clothes seemed designed to keep people from noticing her.

While she waited for Sandy to get into the passenger side of a rental car, she swept the dwindling crowd one more time. She spotted the two men she'd been watching earlier. Zach checked them out again, too. They were walking down Cemetery Road toward town. When they passed the last parked car, Zach narrowed his gaze.

"See those two guys, Duff?" he asked. "Oh, sorry, Father Michael."

Duff waved his hand. "Don't worry so much about what to call me. I'm fine with Duff, except in church," he said. "What two guys?"

Zach nodded toward the men walking toward town.

Duff squinted at them for a few seconds. "Oh. Right. That's Murray Cho and his son. Pat, I think is his name. Why?"

"Were they at the church service earlier?"

"I'm sure they were. I don't remember seeing them, though." He frowned at Zach. "What's bothering you?"

"Just wondering how they knew Tristan."

"From what I recall, when they first moved here, Tristan let them use his dock. They're small-time fishermen."

"Commercial?" Zach asked.

Duff nodded. "They bought the seafood-processing warehouse from Frank Beltaine. I'm not sure if they've gotten their commercial license yet, but they're working on getting freezers installed. I understand they're going to start selling to the locals soon."

So the two men were part of the community. If they just got started, they probably didn't have much money. Maybe they were walking because they didn't own a car.

Zach thought about Madeleine Tierney, who had fed his suspicion of the two men. "So, who is this Madeleine Tierney? And why is she yanking Sandy around as if she was an untrained pup?"

"She's not yanking Sandy around. She's been renting a room at Sandy and Tristan's for the past few weeks." Duff used air quotes around the word *renting*. "Since Sandy's been pregnant, Tristan was working more and more hours on the rig. He was spending two, three weeks offshore and sometimes only a week at home."

"Aren't there regulations that control how much they can work?"

Duff nodded. "Usually, sure. But I've heard the rig

is shorthanded right now because of some virus going around, and the crews can work overtime if needed. Tristan was trying to save money so he could quit offshore and go to work as a veterinary assistant. Madeleine and Sandy struck up a friendship and Tristan thought it was a great idea for Madeleine to stay with her because he didn't like her being there alone."

"So who is she and where's she from?" Zach asked.

Duff shook his head. "I understand that she's an oil rig inspector who's been—"

"A what?" Zach was stunned.

"An oil rig inspector. Her dad was an inspector until he retired. Seems like I kind of remember a kid going on inspections with her dad. But I never paid much attention to the oil rigs before the British Petroleum spill."

Zach nodded. He understood. Bonne Chance was like many of the towns and villages along the Louisiana Gulf Coast between Mississippi and Texas. The townspeople were a mix of fishermen and oil rig workers, and the two sides had a kind of love/hate relationship with each other. The oil rigs attracted big fish, including sharks, but they were a strain on the delicate ecosystem of the sea. Plus, everyone was supersensitive since the BP oil spill, which nearly wiped out the entire fishing industry along the Gulf Coast.

Zach hated the rigs. His dad had worked the rigs until the day he apparently got sick of work and marriage and took off when Zach was around eight years old, leaving his mother and him behind. Now a rig had taken the life of his best friend. It didn't matter that he hadn't seen Tristan in thirteen years. The hole left in Zach's heart hurt just as much as if they'd never been apart.

"Zach?" Duff said, drawing his attention back to the

present. "I'll be at Sandy's in about twenty minutes, after I change clothes."

Zach nodded. Duff headed toward a new Mini Cooper. Zach turned his attention back to Madeleine Tierney, who was still hovering solicitously beside Sandy. She was looking up the road after the two men. As she watched them, she fiddled with the cross-body strap of the leather purse she carried. Something familiar in the subtle gesture, combined with the way she checked the clasp on the purse, stopped him cold.

He'd seen that exact set of gestures before. His weapons-training class with the NSA had included two women with whom he'd worked every day for twelve weeks. He'd watched them tuck their weapon into a specially made handbag and retrieve it time and time again. They had developed the habit of subtly locking and releasing the clasp of the bag, just as Madeleine Tierney was doing.

There was a concealed weapon in that bag. He'd bet a month's salary on it. He'd throw in another month's salary if carrying a concealed weapon were standard practice for rig inspectors.

Who the hell was she and what was her relationship with Sandy and Tristan? Judging by the bag and her handling of it, plus the way she'd kept an eye out for anyone suspicious, his guess was that she was a federal agent. Duff said she'd been here more than a month. Tristan had died five days ago, so she wasn't here because of his death.

Until he knew for certain who she was and why she'd gone to Tristan DuChaud's funeral packing a weapon, he wasn't going to let her out of his sight. She could be the key that would unlock the truth about Tristan's death. Even if that chance was one in a million, he couldn't afford not to take it. He'd stick with her until he knew everything about her.

He waited until she and Sandy drove away before he headed for his car, planning to follow them out to Sandy's house. But he stopped. No. There was one thing he needed to do first. He turned and looked at the grave site. Most of the people had gone. The casket was on a wheeled cart and the caretaker was just about to roll it into the open DuChaud vault.

Taking a deep breath, he walked over and asked the man if he could have a moment. The man stepped a few feet away. Zach bowed his head and put his hand on the cold metal of the casket. He knew it was empty, and yet it seemed appropriate to touch it as he said the only goodbye he might ever get to say to his oldest friend.

MADELEINE TIERNEY WAITED as the Cajun woman who had stayed at Sandy's house during the funeral fussed at Sandy. She turned the coverlet back on the bed. "Now you get under that cover, you," the gnarled little woman said. "And I'll tuck you in."

"I'm not sick, Marie Belle," Sandy had snapped irritably, but she lay down and let the woman tuck the coverlet around her.

Maddy had gladly stepped aside and let Marie Belle handle Sandy. Maddy hadn't had much luck convincing Sandy that she needed to rest for a while. On the other hand, even though Sandy argued, she listened to the little Cajun woman. And it was obvious by her pinched nostrils, pale face and sunken cheeks how exhausted she was. Her too-bright eyes were proof of the shattering grief that weighed her down, and the way her eyelids drooped was a definite indication that she needed a nap. She needed all the rest she could get, for the sake of the baby, if not for herself, Marie Belle told her. Meekly, Sandy agreed.

Meeting Marie Belle had given Maddy hope that she wouldn't have to deal with all the food that neighbors, friends and family had brought over. But no such luck. The Cajun woman needed to get home in time to boil a chicken for dinner.

Maddy told her to take some food with her, but the woman had shaken her head. "This food for Miss Sandy, yeah. T'ain't for me. You take care of that girl now. She needs rest."

Now, left alone in the kitchen, with Sandy resting in the master bedroom at the end of the hall, Maddy stared at counters stacked with pies, both homemade and bought, casseroles, bread and crackers and soft drinks and fruit. She opened the refrigerator even though she already knew it was full to bursting. She had no idea what she was supposed to do with all the food. She just hoped it was already cooked, because cooking was not her superpower. Sandy had taught her the basics of making scrambled eggs, but her best dish was still Marie Callendar's Fettuccini Alfredo with extra Parmesan cheese. The extra Parm was her special touch.

Cursing whoever had come up with the brilliant idea of sending food to mourners then showing up to eat it all, she checked the front door to be sure it was locked. She didn't want people coming into the house through two different entrances.

As soon as Marie Belle left, Maddy had gone into the guest bedroom and removed her Sig from her bag and placed it in the roomy pocket of her skirt, under the boxy jacket. An experienced law enforcement official or a seasoned agent might be able to tell that she was carrying a weapon, but it was unlikely that any of these folks could. She'd stowed her purse in the closet and headed back into the kitchen.

She was at a loss for what she could do to get ready for the onslaught of people who were on their way to Sandy's house. As she looked around helplessly, her thoughts went to the two men who'd shown up at the graveside service, dressed in clean, pressed slacks and shirts and yet looking out of place. Sandy had told her they were a local fisherman and his son, Murray and Patrick Cho. What bothered Maddy about them hadn't been their looks or their clothes. It was their attitudes that had worried her.

They'd avoided eye contact, seeming uncomfortable and yet almost defiant, as if they were expecting someone to ask them to leave. The son, Patrick, had stared at Sandy a lot. Once or twice his father had whispered something in his ear and Patrick had reacted with a sharp retort.

Thinking about them made her think about the other man who'd shown up at the graveside service but hadn't been at the funeral. The man with the sunglasses and the intense green eyes. She'd noticed him as soon as he'd taken his sunglasses off, while he was still standing next to his car. He was one of those people who command attention no matter where they go. He was tall, with dark hair and a lean runner's body. Just the type of body Maddy preferred in a lover. At least in a fantasy lover. She'd never dated a man with a body like that.

She blinked and shook her head. What had made her drift off into la-la land? She was on assignment—her first assignment. She hadn't anticipated that babysitting a pregnant widow and serving pounds of food would be part of the job, but she was a professional and she could handle anything that came her way.

Maddy glanced at her watch. Speaking of her job, maybe she had time to check in with her handler before all the people started arriving. She pulled out her phone. As she waited for Brock to answer, she spotted several stacks of red plastic cups someone had brought and left on the counter. She pulled one of the stacks toward her and twisted the tie that held the wrapper closed, but she couldn't get a good grip on it with one hand, so she stuck the package under her arm to hold it steady.

"Maddy, hi. How's it going?" Brock said. She knew very little about him, other than after military service he'd been in the CIA and had worked for an antiterrorist undercover agency for several years out in Wyoming after he retired from government service. She didn't know how he'd gotten from Wyoming to Washington, DC, or how he, as a federal retiree, could be working as a handler for Homeland Security undercover agents, but she did know she could trust him with her life, and that was enough.

"Hi. The funeral's over. That's the good news. The bad news is I have to be hostess for the entire town while they eat all the food they brought to Sandy's house." While she talked, she grasped the cups' packaging in both hands and tried to rip it, since she'd failed at getting the twist tie open.

"Right," he said. "You grew up in New Orleans. You ought to know Southern traditions," Brock said.

"I know them. I don't necessarily like them." With a frustrated grunt, Maddy ripped the plastic bag with her teeth. It tore straight down the middle and sent red cups rocketing across the kitchen island and onto the tile floor.

"Damn it," she whispered.

"What is it?"

"Oh, sorry, Brock. I was trying to open a bag of plastic cups and they just went sailing across the room."

"Do you have a report?"

"Yes, sir," she said, then took a breath. "Of course, I don't know everyone in town by name, but I do know their faces. I saw four people at the funeral that I'd never seen before." She bent over and snagged a small stack of cups that had landed right side up next to the refrigerator.

"Your assessment?"

"Sandy knew them. They were all members of the DuChaud family. She introduced me." Maddy rubbed her face and neck with her free hand. Tristan DuChaud's death hadn't left her unaffected. Although he was working undercover for Homeland Security just as she was, she'd never met him prior to coming to Bonne Chance.

After Tristan had reported that his cover may have been compromised and requested backup and protection for his wife, she'd been sent to arrange a spot inspection of the oil rig the *Pleiades Seagull* and slip him a secure satellite phone. But when she'd approached the rig's captain, he'd put her off, claiming a stomach virus outbreak making them too shorthanded.

While it left Maddy with her hands tied, it worked in Tristan's favor, as he could stay on the rig and work as much overtime as he could get, thereby having more time to eavesdrop on transmissions between the captain and his superiors and verify their conversations against the chatter the Department of Homeland Security had picked up about planned terrorist activity in the Gulf of Mexico.

It had already been established that much of the chatter originated from the *Pleiades Seagull*. On a rare week home with Sandy, Tristan had talked to his handler, citing several specific matches between unidentified chatter and telephone conversations that took place between the captain and an unidentified satellite phone.

His reports had prompted sending Maddy. By the time Maddy got there, Tristan was working practically nonstop aboard the rig. Once it was obvious that the captain was not going to allow Maddy on board, Brock had given her the alternate assignment of bodyguarding Tristan's wife, Sandy, cautioning her and Tristan not to let Sandy know that she was anything more than a new friend.

Maddy had been there nearly four weeks by the time Tristan finally got a week off. Between them, they'd convinced Sandy to let Maddy stay with her while he was working offshore. Tristan was happy because he wanted protection for his pregnant wife.

Maddy was not as happy. This was her first field mission and she wanted to be on the oil rig, in the middle of the action. She approached the captain a second time about a spot inspection. But again, he'd put her off.

Now Tristan was dead, and Maddy felt responsible. She blinked angrily at her stinging eyes. Stupid tears. She had always struggled with her weak side. The side of her that sniffled at funerals and weddings, and sometimes even Hallmark commercials.

"Maddy?" Brock said. "Continue."

"Right," she replied, blotting the dampness from her eyes with her fingertips, then grabbing for two cups that were slowly rolling toward the edge of the island. "There were fewer people at the graveside service. I saw three men who were not at the funeral. Two are Vietnamese fishermen, a man and his son, whom I had not seen before. Nor had I ever seen the third man." She stopped.

The third man. Once again, his image rose before her inner vision. His runner's body unfolding from the BMW. The sunglasses that he'd removed to reveal green eyes. According to Sandy, his name was Zach.

"Assessment?"

"Oh, right," she said, pushing thoughts of Zach out of her mind. "As I said, two of them were local fishermen, according to Sandy. Their names are Murray and Patrick Cho. They were respectful and dressed appropriately but seemed uncomfortable and somewhat belligerent, as if they were expecting to be grilled about why they were there."

"Did you get a photo of them or their vehicle? A license? Make? Model?"

"They didn't have a vehicle, at least not at the grave site. They walked back to town. And the entire time they were there, they didn't speak to anyone. They just stood and watched. A time or two they whispered to each other. Once, the younger one, the son, pointed at Sandy."

"Okay. Text me their names. I'll have them traced. What about the third man?"

"He was well-dressed and driving a BMW. I suspect it was a rental."

"So we can get ID on him."

"Absolutely. His name is Zachary Winter and apparently he's an old friend of Sandy's and Tristan's."

"Did you get a photo?"

Her hand tightened on the phone. "No. He was watching me the whole time. Sandy obviously cares a lot about him, but I don't think he's just a friend, though. He was too alert, too ready..."

"Ready for what?"

"Anything," she said as her imagination pitted Zach

against a burly gunman, whom he took down with his bare hands as a single drop of sweat slid from his hairline down his temple. "I'm sorry, what?" she asked. Brock had said something else but she hadn't caught it.

"Text me his name and the license number of his vehicle."

"I don't have the tag. He parked too far away." She saw a car pass the kitchen window, then pull over and stop. "Oh, hold on. Maybe I can get it right now. He just pulled up. I can see the tag out the window, if I can just read all the numbers." She angled her head a bit so she could see the license and read it off to Brock.

"I'll see what I can come up with. You get all you can from him and Sandy DuChaud."

"Anything from your end? Are you going to be able to get another agent hired onto the rig?"

"It's not looking good. We're trying to see if we can go another way to find out what Tristan overheard and if it's an immediate threat. We may pull you out, based on what we find."

"Oh," Maddy said as another car pulled up to the house. "I'd like to stay," she said. "Sandy's pregnant and alone here." A third car pulled up. "Here they come."

"Who?"

"Everyone in town. They're all here to comfort Sandy and eat the food."

"Stay alert."

"No problem," Maddy said, resting her hand on her pocket, where she'd concealed her Sig P229 handgun. "I'm always alert."

"Usually," Brock said wryly.

"What? What do you mean by that?" she retorted.

"I thought I was about to lose you twice in this conversation. First with the cups and then again when you described the stranger who is *ready for anything.*"

"Give me a break, Brock. I was just reporting what I saw." She felt her face grow warm. "It's been a long day."

"Maddy, we don't know yet what we're dealing with. But you know that you have to assume that—"

"Everyone is a potential threat. I know. Don't worry. I've got this under control." She did. She was confident and alert. As confident as she could be. Tristan's death was unexplained. It could easily have been an accident, as the drilling company said. Accidents were unfortunately not unknown on oil rigs. But there was another possibility. A very real, very ominous possibility.

Two months before, Tristan had told his handler that the captain was becoming suspicious of him. That's when he'd asked for backup and protection for his newly pregnant wife.

"Brock? I know we have very little to go on, but what if Tristan was pushed or knocked out and thrown overboard? He was sure that the captain had found out he was listening in on his phone calls."

"The director is having that looked into, but it's a pretty touchy subject right now, with elections coming up. No congressperson is going to be excited about the possibility of corruption going on in the offshore drilling industry."

"But a DHS agent died," Maddy said.

"No. An oil rig worker died. We're not disclosing his connection to DHS. Not yet. The director is insisting on moving slowly. He's got experts reviewing all of DuChaud's communications for any clues."

"Clues? He told his handler he needed backup and protection for his wife. Isn't that a *clue*?"

"Agent Tierney, I have told you what the director's position is," Brock said coldly. Then he went on in a kinder voice. "Listen to me, Maddy. The director is concerned. He'll be speaking with the top officials of Lee Drilling, the company that owns the *Pleiades Seagull*, very soon. In the meantime, we need you to take care of Mrs. DuChaud."

"What about getting onto the rig?"

"No. That's no longer your assignment. We're trying out some new technology, advanced listening devices, to pick up communications on the *Pleiades Seagull*. So you don't worry about the platform."

"New technology? Why didn't you use those before, instead of putting Tristan in danger?" she asked.

"Carry on with your revised instructions, Agent. I've got a meeting."

"Brock?" she said, but the phone was dead. He had hung up. She picked up another cup and straightened, wincing at the disapproval in Brock's voice. He'd been in military environments throughout his entire career and he felt that interactions between officers and agents should be handled with a certain protocol.

When she looked up, Zach Winter was standing at the French doors. He let himself in. His jacket was slightly damp with sweat and a little wrinkled, as was the white shirt under it, but he wore them as if they were bright as the sun and freshly starched. His broad shoulders stretched the material slightly and the open collar of his shirt revealed a prominent Adam's apple and long, sinewy neck muscles that hinted at a serious and strenuous fitness routine. Her gaze moved to the perfectly fitted dress pants, under which were long, muscular runner's legs that complemented his lean torso and long arms. If he'd been a little thinner or taller, he might have looked awkward and rawboned. But he wasn't thinner or taller. He was just about perfect.

"Um, mind if I come in?" he said.

Maddy's gaze shot back up to his. Her face burned but she ignored it and gave him a haughty look as she walked toward him. Her foot hit a cup she hadn't seen. "Damn it," she said, bending down to pick it up.

At the same time, Zach did the same thing and their hands touched. "What happened here?" he asked. "Who detonated the cups?"

She suppressed a laugh and glared at him as she grabbed the cup away from him. She moved to rise and found that Zach was already standing, his hand held out in an offer to help her.

She ignored it.

"I'm Zach Winter," he said.

Maddy realized that as perfect as Zach Winter was, she didn't like him. Didn't like his attempts to be charming or his too-familiar demeanor. "Yes, I remember from Sandy's introduction," she retorted.

He nodded. "So are you called Madeleine, Maddy or Ms. Tierney?"

Sudden, swift anger bubbled up from her chest and tightened her jaw. She started to say that Ms. Tierney would work just fine, when someone else appeared at the door. It was Father Michael. "Hello, Madeleine."

Maddy cleared her throat and gave him a faint smile. "Hello, Father. I'm still hoping you'll call me Maddy."

"Well, all right, Maddy." He clasped her hand warmly as he glanced around the kitchen. "I see Zach and I are the first to arrive. Where is Sandy? Is she resting?"

Maddy nodded, then looked at the priest assessingly. "So, how do you two know each other?"

Father Michael raised a brow at Zach then smiled at

her. "Let me introduce you to one of the most promising hometown boys ever to leave Bonne Chance. Zachary Winter. Zach, this is Madeleine Tierney." He smiled
sheepishly. "Maddy."

Maddy met Zach Winter's gaze. His name fit him.
It was sharp and cool, just like him.

"Sandy introduced us at the graveside service," she
said. "Hometown boy? Odd that no one seemed to recognize you except the Father and Sandy."

Chapter Three

Zachary Winter looked at Madeleine Tierney blandly. "I've been gone a long time. Odd that you're so hostile toward me at our first meeting," he responded.

"All right, you two," Father Michael said. "Try to get along. I'm going to watch for other guests to arrive." He went out the French doors onto the patio.

"Not hostile," Maddy said. "Just curious. When did you leave Bonne Chance?"

He frowned at her, then looked away. "I was fifteen," he said shortly. "Can I help you round up the stray cups before they all get away? We can stack them and start putting ice into them and nobody will know they almost escaped."

"Ice. Damn it," she muttered under her breath. She'd forgotten all about ice.

Zachary Winter held up a glistening, dripping bag of ice. She hadn't noticed that he'd been holding it.

"Thanks," she said as people started coming in the door, directed by the Father. "There's tea in the refrigerator, if you wouldn't mind pouring it. And the water from the door dispenser is filtered. Thank you."

He walked around the kitchen island and set the bag of ice in the sink, then began scooping up cups from counters and the floor.

Maddy turned to greet the new arrivals. For several minutes, she was busy inviting people in and directing them toward the cups of iced tea and water Zach was setting out. Before she knew it, a small cadre of women had taken charge of arranging food on the island and counters so the guests could help themselves. Everyone was milling about with loaded paper plates and talking to each other.

She should have been able to breathe a sigh of relief. Obviously, these folks understood exactly how a wake went. But she couldn't. She'd been worried about Sandy for days, ever since they'd gotten the news about Tristan. Thank goodness she was resting finally. She'd hardly slept the night before, worrying about the funeral.

Maddy didn't want anybody—and she meant *anybody*—bothering Sandy, now that she'd finally lain down. It didn't matter what anyone's relationship was to Sandy, Maddy wasn't letting them past the kitchen.

She looked around for Zach and saw him leaning against the wall near the door from the kitchen to the hall. He looked relaxed, holding a glass of water and watching people as they ate and chatted. Every so often, someone would walk toward the door. When they did, he'd straighten and take a half step away from the wall, blocking the door. He'd smile and say something that made the other person smile.

There was something not quite genuine about Zach Winter. The phrase she used when she was talking to Brock was *too ready*. And that was it. He should have been like everybody else here, polite, subdued, a little shocked by the death of a vibrant young husband and father-to-be. But Maddy knew there was a lot more behind those green eyes than just a man who'd lost his best friend.

Zach Winter was not like anybody else here. He might look like a slightly bored young executive, sad about his friend but counting down the minutes until he could politely leave. But as she watched him, it hit her. He wasn't standing there because he liked the view.

He was *guarding* the door. Zach was guarding the door that led to Sandy's room. That's why her two-word summation of him had been *too ready.* She'd sensed it all along. It was in his deceptively casual stance, his bland expression belied by the sharp green of his eyes. He'd appointed himself guardian over Sandy.

So then, the question became, was he a concerned friend being protective, or was he, like she, something more?

At that moment, Father Michael said her name. After checking out Zach one more time, Maddy turned to the father. He had taken over as host and was greeting everyone at the door. He'd made it his mission to introduce her to each guest as they came in. It was a genuinely nice gesture, even if Maddy was tired of trying to keep up with the names of everyone in town.

After about a five-minute steady stream of people, Maddy excused herself and walked around the island to get a cup of water. But even there she found no refuge, because the women who were cutting pies into slices and dishing up casseroles were talkative, too. She smiled and nodded for a couple of minutes, which was all she could take.

She headed over to stand by Zach. "Hide me, please," she teased, then said, "Thanks for keeping people away from the hall."

Zach smiled, not even pretending he didn't know

what she was talking about. "You looked nervous about the door, so I thought I'd help out by discouraging people from walking back there. But what do I tell them when they want to visit the bathroom?"

She gestured with the paper cup. "There's one in the laundry room. That door beside the refrigerator. Father Michael should be telling everyone when they come in."

"Oh, right. I remember that bathroom now. The ones who try to get past me want to 'peek in on Sandy.'" He checked the hall door to be sure it was latched. "How about Sandy. Is she asleep?"

"I doubt it, but she is lying down," Maddy said. "Hopefully, she's resting. She looked like she was about to faint by the time the graveside service was over."

"Sandy's a lot stronger than she looks," Zach commented. "Even pregnant."

Maddy blew out a frustrated breath. "I wasn't insulting her. Tristan asked me to be sure she was okay. I'm not sure she ever will be now."

"It's going to take her a while, but she'll be okay."

"Right. I guess I forgot who I was talking to."

"Pardon?" There was that quizzical smile again.

She gestured absently. "Tristan's best friend, right? Father Michael said you were born here."

He nodded again. After another swallow of water, he spoke. "Tristan's dad and mine were both offshore rig workers. My dad left us. Tristan's dad died as he was about to graduate high school. I hadn't talked to Tristan since we moved to Houston, but yeah." He paused and sadness clouded his eyes. "We were always best friends." He glanced over at her. "How much do you know about his death?"

She shook her head. "Not much," she said around a piece of ice she was chewing. "Almost nothing." *Stop,* she told herself. *Don't try too hard. Act like an ordinary citizen.* "It was an accident."

Zach's gaze had wandered, but it snapped back to her so abruptly that she was afraid for a second that she'd spoken aloud. "What about Sandy? Did she tell you what the authorities told her?"

"Some of it. I don't think they've told her much. Nobody saw what happened. The one thing that seems to have really devastated her is that they wouldn't let her see him."

Zach closed his eyes briefly.

"I saw you talking to the ME," she said. "You probably know more than I do. What did he tell you?"

"I just wanted to find out what happened."

She leaned closer. "He told you why they didn't open the casket, didn't he?"

He didn't answer her, but he didn't have to. The tension in his jaw muscle, plus his silence, answered her. She suddenly felt queasy. "Never mind—" she started.

Just then, a short sound like a muffled shriek came from down the hall, in the direction of Sandy's bedroom.

"Sandy!" Maddy whispered and started to whirl. Immediately she caught herself, remembering that the people in the kitchen could see her. Damn it, she'd left her alone too long. She'd gotten caught up in trying to keep up with the guests, and then she'd gotten caught up in arguing with Zach Winter.

"What?" Zach asked, his voice low. "What's wrong?"

"I'll be right back," she snapped. "Close the hall door." She managed to walk steadily until she heard the door close, then she rushed to the farthest bedroom. She grabbed her weapon out of her pocket with her right hand and reached out to open Sandy's bedroom door with her left.

Just as her fingers brushed the curved metal of the doorknob, Zach stopped her.

"Wait," he whispered, his breath tickling her ear. She felt the heat of his body as he reached around to stay her hand on the doorknob. His right hand moved and she heard the unmistakable swoosh of gunmetal against leather and smelled the faint odor of gun cleaner.

"What are you doing?" she hissed.

"We need to be ready for anything," he said.

We?

"Get behind me. I'll go in first," he said.

"What?" Maddy's mouth actually fell open. "Are you kidding me?" She wrapped her hand around the door-knob. "You stand back," she commanded, grasping her weapon. "I'm a federal agent. DHS."

He went completely still, and cool air brushed her overheated skin as he drew away. "You're what?"

She thumbed off the safety and whispered, "On three. One, two—"

"Okay, Maddy Tierney. I'm a fed, too," he muttered.

The four words nearly knocked Maddy to her knees. She had to concentrate with all her might to stay focused on the danger that could be lurking behind the wooden door. "Three!" she barked and burst into the room.

ZACH WAS IN full-on SWAT mode, which was what he called the combination of tension and hyperalertness that hummed through him. He'd had the best training in the world. When the NSA had decided to oversee their own undercover operations, they pulled in the best of the best as teachers. Special Forces experts from every branch of the military. After all, they were training mathematicians, accountants and computer specialists to be warriors.

Zach followed Maddy through the door, still a little shell-shocked by what she'd said and newly surprised by what he'd felt when he'd reached around her to stop her from bursting through the door. He gave her the lead and backed her up the way he would any commander. There was no advantage in forcing the issue of who was in charge and no time to waste. He slid sideways, his back against the wall, and surveyed the darkened room, all his senses tuned to the slightest indication of danger. On the other side of the door, Maddy did the same thing.

The hyperalertness he'd cultivated during his training gave him the ability to divide his focus without sacrificing any of it. So, as he assessed the room, a part of his brain assessed Maddy. The tension radiating from her was so perfectly honed, so specifically focused, that it felt as though it was melding with his, turning the two of them into one perfectly functioning supersoldier. It was a stronger version of what he'd felt when he'd first seen her scanning the perimeter of the grave site, looking for any danger.

Everything from the slamming open of Sandy's bedroom door to this instant had taken less than three seconds, but Zach knew that lives could be lost in much less time than that. Just as his brain determined there was no immediate threat, Maddy motioned for him to stay put. She crossed the room and checked the windows. They were locked.

Zach looked past her out into the yard. The sun had gone behind the clouds again, turning the day dark and foretelling more rain. Less than a hundred yards from the house, where the lawn ended and the overgrown swamp began, everything was cloaked in gray mist.

Maddy glanced through the open bathroom door, nodded, then turned to the closet. She looked at Zach, then gestured with her head for him to back her up as she opened the door. He moved into position and held his weapon at the ready as she jerked the door open. The rows of men's and women's clothes were neatly hung, with shoes lined up on the floor. There was no place for a person to hide.

"Clear," she said.

He took one last split-second glance around and holstered his weapon, then turned his attention to Sandy.

She cowered against the headboard of the bed, her eyes wide as quarters and bright with tears. When Maddy walked over and turned on the bedside table lamp, Sandy squinted in the sudden light. She didn't seem to notice Zach and she stared at Maddy as if she were an alien.

"It's okay, Sandy," Maddy said. "It's okay."

"Maddy," Sandy gasped. "I saw someone at the window. A man, maybe two. They were looking at me."

"Two men? What kind of men?"

Sandy pushed her hair back with a trembling hand. "I don't know. Men." She glanced at the window and seemed to shrink back into the pillows.

Zach looked through the glass again. The day was getting darker by the minute. If there had been people at Sandy's window, they could have disappeared into the opaque mist with just a few footsteps. "I'll go out and check around the window for footprints," he said.

"No!" Maddy snapped. "Not now. Wait until the guests are gone."

"Why? We need to check for prints before it starts raining again."

"You'll alarm them and then word will get out and everybody in town will panic." She leaned toward him and lowered her voice with a quick glance at Sandy. "If she really saw somebody and it has anything to do with Tristan, we can't risk the people in town knowing."

"Yes, ma'am," Zach said sarcastically, even though privately, he knew that her argument made sense. Tristan's friends and relatives would probably riot if they thought there had been foul play involved in Tristan's death. He looked at Sandy. "Sandy, hon. Tell me exactly what happened."

Sandy frowned. "I don't know exactly. Something woke me, like a noise at the window. Once I was awake, I heard voices. The room was dark and I forgot—" She stopped. "I thought it was Tristan. Then I saw a face, or two faces, at the window. They were looking right at me, but when I cried out they disappeared."

"And it couldn't have been shadows, or a dream?"

Sandy turned to him. "Zach?" she said, looking surprised. Then with a hurt expression. "You think it was a dream?"

He held up a hand. "Just asking. Tell me what you saw. Did you recognize either of the men?"

She shook her head. "No. I—I don't think so."

Maddy stepped in. "What did they look like?"

"Dark," Sandy said. "I'm not sure. I didn't get a good look at them. Maybe foreign? At first it was just one. Then a second man came up. He looked angry. I couldn't see their faces because they were in shadow. Oh, I don't know," she finished, shuddering. "They were there and then they were gone."

"What do you mean by foreign?" Zach asked, thinking about the Chos.

Sandy looked miserable and confused. Zach felt bad about grilling her, but he needed to know whether she had really seen anyone at her window or if she'd dreamed it. Had Tristan's death put Sandy in danger? Or had it merely caused her to have night terrors?

"Did they have weapons?" Maddy asked.

"Weapons? Why would they?" Sandy's wide gaze stared at her then turned to Zach. For the first time, she noticed the weapon in his hand. "Zach, is that a gun you're holding?"

"Sandy, listen to me," Maddy said, holding up her gun for Sandy to see. "I have one, too."

Sandy recoiled.

"Sorry," Maddy said. She stuffed it into her skirt pocket and sat on the side of the bed. She took Sandy's hands in hers. "Don't worry. The only reason I have it is because Tristan asked me to keep you safe. We heard you scream, so we ran in here to check on you. Now, I want you to relax, okay?" she said gently as Sandy's fingers tightened around hers.

But Sandy wasn't comforted yet. She'd turned her wide, frightened gaze to Zach. "Zach? What's going on?" Her voice rose and her face seemed to grow more pale. "Does this have something to do with Tristan?"

Zach swallowed. "I don't think so," he said.

Maddy jerked her head toward the kitchen, an unmistakable order for him to leave. Then she turned back to Sandy. "You have guests," she said kindly. Do you feel like talking to them?"

"Window?" he muttered.

Maddy's eyes turned cold as glacial ice. "No. Stick at the hall door until everyone is gone. Tell Father Michael to say that Sandy will be out in a few minutes. Tell him to give her ten minutes to greet people, then he should start encouraging people to leave."

He was glad to be dismissed. Tears were flowing down Sandy's cheeks and he had never learned what to do when a woman cried. He was happy to let Maddy take the lead for now. She'd probably be a lot better than he would at calming Sandy down and finding out whether the shriek they'd heard was the result of a bad dream or something sinister. And she was right about the door. They needed to keep the well-meaning friends and relatives corralled.

He holstered his weapon and backed out of the room, closing the door behind him. As he did, he heard Maddy's voice, low and soothing. Her voice didn't go with the intensity she radiated. But he liked it. A lot. He wished he could thank her for being so sweet to Sandy.

As he turned around to head back to the kitchen, he nearly ran into someone coming down the hall. "Whoa!" he said, holding out his hands.

"Oh!" the man exclaimed, but he didn't stop. He changed course, heading around Zach.

"Hang on a minute. Where do you think you're going?" Zach asked him.

"Hey, buddy," the man said warningly, then recognized Zach. "Oh, hey, Zach."

Zach looked at him more closely, trying to identify him. He looked vaguely familiar, but then so did about 80 percent of the people Zach had seen today. Bonne Chance was his hometown, after all, and in this part of Louisiana, a lot of people lived their entire lives less than ten miles from where they were born.

"It's Gene. Gene Campbell. I used to own the sports

equipment store…" He paused with a shake of his head. "Until Walmart came to town."

Gene Campbell. He barely recalled him. "Right. Where you going, Gene?"

Gene stared at him, frowning for a few seconds. "Oh. You probably don't know. Sandy's my niece. Her mom died years ago, if you remember. I thought I'd check on her. Is she sick, or what? She ought to be out here with her friends and family." He tried to pass Zach again.

For a good ol' boy just wanting to check on his niece, Gene seemed pretty determined.

"I remember you, but no. I didn't know Sandy was your niece. I didn't think she had any relatives after her mom died. Didn't that elderly couple take her in?" Zach said. When Gene didn't seem inclined to answer, Zach continued, "Anyhow, we're trying to let her rest. She was pretty upset after the service."

"Oh, yeah? When I saw her talking to Father Michael, she looked okay."

"What's new with you these days, Gene?" Zach put an arm across Gene's shoulders and turned him back toward the kitchen. "How are the kids?"

Gene shrugged. "How long's it been since you been here? My kids are married and I've got three grand-kids." He smiled. "They're the greatest gift in the world. How about you? Your mom doing okay?"

"Yeah. She's still in Houston. Doing great." Zach kept an ear trained on the bedroom behind him, but by the time he'd guided Gene back to the kitchen, neither Maddy nor Sandy had come out.

Just as Gene headed toward the kitchen island and the cups of iced tea, two elderly ladies peered through the door. "Is everything all right?" one of them asked.

Before Zach could answer, Tristan's mother scooted

around the ladies. "Everything's fine," she said to them. "Don't you think we should put out more pie?" She smiled sweetly.

As the ladies disappeared back into the kitchen, fussing about which kind of pie would be best, Mrs. Du-Chaud tried to slip past him, but Zach calmly and gently blocked her.

"Oh, Zach, sweetheart," Mrs. DuChaud said. She held out her arms and Zach gave her a hug. She was plump and pretty, and her genes had given Tristan his good looks, but right now her face appeared to be melting. Her skin sagged and her eyes had big purple shadows beneath them. The muscles of her arms and back when he hugged her felt flaccid. "You're all grown up. And so handsome. But, dear, you should go see Ralph tomorrow and get that hair cut."

"Mrs. D. I'm so sorry about Tristan."

"Thank you. Excuse me, Zach, I want to check on Sandy." Mrs. DuChaud shook her head sadly. "She's just devastated. Of course, so am I, but I've got my faith and my friends to help me. Sandy, though. Well—" she shook her head "—I just don't know."

Zach winced at her implication. Mrs. DuChaud had always had a critical tongue. "Maddy is in there with her. She…had a bad dream and Maddy's calming her down. She'll be out in a few minutes if she starts feeling better."

"Maddy? Oh. Madeleine Tierney. That woman. Who knows where she came from. But I thought I'd take Sandy a glass of water."

Zach double-checked her hands, but as he already knew, she wasn't carrying a glass. He raised his gaze and met hers without comment.

"I was going to ask her first," Mrs. DuChaud said.

"I must say, Zach, you've changed since you left—how many years ago? You used to be such a nice polite young man."

"Yes, ma'am," Zach said dutifully, still blocking the door. After a couple of seconds, Mrs. DuChaud sniffed and turned on her heel.

For the moment, nobody else tried to storm the bastions, although a few people looked at him curiously and one or two spoke to him while eyeing the closed door behind him. Finally, he had a moment to think for the first time since Maddy had dropped the Homeland Security bomb on him. She was an agent for the Department of Homeland Security, he thought. Not much surprised him, but that had. It explained a little bit of what she was doing here. But why had she shown up several weeks ago? And had her presence here had anything to do with Tristan's death?

Just at that moment, Maddy and Sandy came up behind him. He stepped aside as Maddy escorted Sandy into the kitchen, where it seemed as though half or more of the town waited to greet her and tell her how sorry they were.

With his new knowledge of her, Zach watched as Maddy guided Sandy through the cluster of people toward the ice water. She did a great job. She kept Sandy from having to say too much to any one person. Apparently, she was better at her DHS undercover job than at fixing and serving food and drink or handling a roomful of people. He smiled, remembering how nervous she was when he'd gotten there. She'd taken charge earlier like a veteran agent when she heard Sandy's cry of distress.

MADDY KEPT AN EYE on Sandy and was reassured by her steady stance and the way she greeted the guests.

She stepped back to give the young widow the spotlight. Turning her head, she looked over her shoulder at Zach. He gave her a slight nod and she acknowledged it with nothing more than a blink as she walked across the kitchen to join him at the door to the hall. To the left of that door was another door that led to the hall from the living room.

Maddy looked at the two doors, then at Zach. Without a word, she knew he understood. The two of them would stand guard together, simultaneously watching Sandy and keeping anyone from wandering through the house unescorted.

She stood near the living room door, her feet slightly apart, her arms at her sides. She flexed the fingers of her right hand. Zach leaned against the wall about four feet from the kitchen door, his arms folded and one leg crossed over the other, as if he had nothing better to do than hang out for a few hours. Maddy realized he was listening to the conversations going on in the kitchen.

Of course, people were talking about Tristan and what a nice young man he was, and how tragic it was that his life was cut off so suddenly and uselessly. Inevitably, though, some conversations turned to other topics, like safety on oil rigs, the current state of the fishing industry compared to the oil industry, even high school football rankings and whether the Bonne Chance Gators had a chance of getting to the state championships.

But Maddy's thoughts remained on Zach. She kept replaying the four words he'd muttered just before they burst into Sandy's room. *I'm a fed, too.*

"So what you said back there about being a fed, too. Just what did you mean?" she asked.

Zach was leaning against the door facing in his usual relaxed manner, his arms crossed. He didn't move, not even his head, but he sent her a sidelong glance. "You want to talk about that now?"

Maddy rolled her eyes. "Yes. Why not?"

"Just thought you would rather discuss it in private."

"I'd rather know who I'm talking to. I knew you were carrying the first time I laid eyes on you, but I need to know who you work for." She spoke in a low voice while she watched Sandy. "She's doing really well," she added.

"What? Oh, Sandy. I told you she's strong. I knew you were armed, too."

"Really? How?"

"That purse. You acted just like the female agents I trained with, fooling with the lock and keeping your hand on it."

"Okay, maybe I'll ditch the purse." Maddy rubbed her eyes. "Sandy may be strong, but she's also exhausted and grief-stricken. She hasn't slept since Wednesday, when she got the news about Tristan," Maddy said.

"Maybe she'll sleep tonight, now that she's—" He stopped.

"Now that she's what?" She glanced at him. "Buried him? Is that what you were going to say?"

He looked a little stunned. "Uh, no. I mean, yeah. That was it." He rubbed his face and squeezed his eyes shut for a second.

"You know, we almost didn't have a funeral. Sandy was extremely upset when they wouldn't let her see him," Maddy said.

"Well, you know why, right?"

"No. I figured maybe there were some, you know, injuries."

Zach stared at her. "Really? You don't know?"

"Look. I saw you talking to Dr. Bookman. He

wouldn't talk to me. Did he tell you anything?" Zach had been here only a few hours and he'd managed to find out something she'd missed.

He shrugged.

"Oh, come on. Just tell me so I'm up to speed." Her face and neck felt hot. It wasn't easy for her to admit she'd made a mistake. That she'd missed something. But the sooner Zach shared his information with her, the sooner she could be back on track. And nothing—certainly not a strong, handsome federal agent—would be able to knock her off her game again. She made a vow to herself that nothing and no one, not even Zach Winter, would distract her from her assignment.

"You don't know why they wouldn't allow her to see anything or let her have an open casket?"

Maddy saw the grim expression on his face. She took a deep breath and blew it out slowly. "Tell me," she said.

"The ME told me there weren't enough remains to put in a casket. The little bit they found was placed into evidence. Tristan DuChaud's casket was empty."

Chapter Four

Tristan's casket was empty. Maddy shuddered. "Oh, no," she said. "Poor Sandy. You can't tell her."

Zach's face went dark. "*You* can't tell her. And I swear if you do, I'll hang you up and skin you like a deer. Do you understand that?"

"Of course," Maddy said solemnly. "What else did he say? Did he have any word on cause of death?"

"Nope. No cause of death. Speculation is that he fell into the water from one of the lower metal catwalks. They said he and the Vietnamese guy with him may have gotten into a fight or were roughhousing or were drunk and fell overboard."

Maddy was shaking her head before he finished speaking. "That's not Tristan," she said.

"I know that, but how do you know that?" Zach's voice was low-pitched and toneless. The deadly seriousness of it made her shiver.

"Sandy told me. She's been in a bit of a haze ever since she found out about his death. She hasn't asked very many questions, but when Father Michael came to talk with her and told her some of what you're telling me, she said Tristan would never have fallen. I only met him twice during his weeks off, but I agree. He apparently lived here and boated and swam and climbed around the trees and the cypress roots all his life. I don't think he would have fallen, either."

"You're right. That's exactly what I said when the ME tried to sell me on the idea that he fell. Tristan would never have fallen off the platform. He was pushed."

Maddy stared at him as she ran the past few seconds over in her head. *He was pushed.* "That's it," she said. Her hand flew up to cover her mouth and tears filled her eyes. "That's it," she repeated sotto voce.

"What?" Zach snapped, frowning at her.

"It's the only thing that makes sense. He was pushed." She grabbed his arm. "And when Sandy starts thinking straight again, she's going to realize that. Oh, poor thing. How is she going to deal with that? With the fact that Tristan may have been murdered?"

Zach stood and started pacing. "If I have anything to do with it," he said through clenched teeth, "she won't have to, because before she figures that out, I'll have all the answers and we'll have whoever killed him *and* whoever ordered it done behind bars. Sandy won't have to face that unknown. She can at least have the comfort that the person who killed Tristan will be punished."

"You think you can do that? Okay. I think it's about time you told me who you are and who you work for," Maddy started, then realized she had raised her voice and a few people had turned to look. She smiled and cleared her throat, then spoke out of the corner of her mouth. "Please just tell me."

Zach blew out a frustrated breath. "I thought we ought to wait, but fine. I work for the National Security Agency, as an undercover agent." He pulled a badge holder from his back pocket and handed it to her.

She took it and glanced at it, then did a double take. After a few seconds, she looked up at him. "The National Security—" Her voice cracked. She stopped and took a deep breath and tried again to speak. "You mean the NSA? You work for the NSA?"

Zach's gaze narrowed. "That's right. The No Such Agency. Yes."

"But you're— You've got a gun." Her surprise morphed into incredulity.

"Try not to sound so impressed," he said wryly.

"But why? Why do you have a gun?" she asked, spreading her hands as if imploring him to explain. "I mean, okay. You're here because your friend died, and I know that you're concerned about Sandy. But really? What's up with the NSA? I thought they were all accountants and math whizzes, not undercover agents."

Zach scrubbed a hand down his face. "I'm a member of a division of the NSA that investigates possible terrorist activity, based on information the NSA gains from its listening activities. But I am on vacation right now. I'm not here in any official capacity. I'm just Tristan's and Sandy's friend."

Maddy stared at him for a long time, until he began to feel extremely uncomfortable. He rubbed his face again and was just about to ask her if he'd grown a third eye when she finally spread her arms again, palms out.

"So you're telling me you work *undercover* for the National Security Agency and you're licensed to carry a gun?" Maddy asked as her brain fed her a picture of nerdy guys in ill-fitting suits and taped-up glasses wielding guns.

"That's what I'm telling you," he said. "Want me to go over it a third time?"

Maddy shook her head. "No. I've got it. NSA," she said and chuckled without much mirth. "Who knew the No Such Agency was in the 007 business?" She shook her head. "So, what are you by profession? I'm guessing not a career soldier."

He lifted his chin. "I have a double PhD from Harvard. Math and forensic accounting."

"Ohh," she said on a chuckle. "Math and accounting. And how much experience have you had as an undercover agent?"

"Not much," he admitted, his jaw muscle flexing. "I've been on one mission, which turned out to be some kids that had hacked their favorite MMO game and changed all the villains' names to real terrorist names."

"MMO game?" she parroted. "I don't know what that is."

"MMO stands for Massive Multiplayer Online game." He waved a hand. "Don't worry about it. As I said, I'm not here in an official capacity." He looked at her. "Are you?"

Maddy ignored his question. "NSA undercover agents. Now I've heard everything."

"You've heard everything?" Father Michael said. "How about telling me some of it, because I believe I've still got a lot to learn."

"Oh, Father, you startled me." Maddy hadn't noticed him until he'd spoken.

"I just wanted to check with you before I go. Sandy is trying to make me take all the food with me." He nodded toward the kitchen counter where Sandy was packing up food in shopping bags. She looked up and smiled wanly.

"Good, because there is no way we will ever eat all that."

"Thank you, Madeleine—I mean, Maddy, for taking care of Sandy. And you," he said, turning toward Zach. "You keep these two women safe, you hear me?"

"Don't worry, Duff. I plan to," Zach said. Father Michael left, loaded down with food, and Maddy locked the French doors behind him. She sighed in a mixture of relief and exhaustion and rested her forehead against the door for a couple of seconds.

"Maddy, are you okay?" Sandy asked.

"Sure," Maddy said, turning around and smiling tiredly at her. "So," she said to Zach. "You call Father Michael Duff?"

"Can't seem to get used to Father Michael." He turned to Sandy. "Why don't you go back to bed? You can sleep late in the morning."

A faint shadow crossed Sandy's face. "I'm not sleepy," she said, then turned her attention to Maddy. "You're the one who needs to go to sleep. You look absolutely exhausted. Zach and I are just going to visit for a while."

Maddy looked at Zach, who gave her a brief nod. "Okay. I could use a shower. Maybe I will go to bed early, since Zach is here."

"Good. You've taken such good care of me. I appreciate it." Sandy held out her arms and Maddy hugged her briefly.

"You're sure?"

"Of course. I'm going to make up the Hide-a-Bed sofa in the nursery for you," she said to Zach. "Then we can visit. But first, I've got to pee, *again*. Apparently, when you're pregnant, the peeing never stops. Not even for a *funeral*." She stalked off down the hall.

Zach looked startled. Maddy looked at him. "That was a joke. Maybe she's doing better. Before she gets back I want to ask you something," Maddy said. "Do you believe what she said?"

"You mean that she saw someone at her window?

I have no idea. I don't know anything about pregnant women. Are nightmares or delusions common?"

"Don't ask me," Maddy snapped. "But you know her. So, do you believe her or not?"

"I believe she believes there were two men there. Do I think she actually saw two men sneaking around and looking in her bedroom window while there was a houseful of people here, including the sheriff? No. Not really. What about you?"

"That's pretty much what I think, too. But what if they were there? Who were they? What were they doing?"

"That's what I'm asking you. What about those fishermen you were watching so closely. Could it have been them? Does Sandy know them?"

Maddy frowned at him. "I suppose it could have been the Chos, and yes, she should have recognized them. But why would they be sneaking around the back of the house?"

Zach shrugged. "Why were you so suspicious of them?"

"Suspicious?" she repeated. "I was keeping up with everyone at the funeral service and the grave site. They weren't at the funeral service." She paused for a second, assessing him. "Neither were you, as a matter of fact."

He nodded without speaking.

"I actually can't imagine the Chos sneaking around Sandy's house, and I can't imagine Sandy not knowing who they were."

"Maybe she was half-asleep. Or completely asleep and the men at the window were nothing but a dream. What if it were a couple of oil rig workers? Maybe they knew Tristan and came to the funeral."

She shook her head. "One, if they were oil rig workers, they'd have to be off duty this week or they were sent by the captain. Two—" she held up two fingers "—if you work on an oil rig, you don't just ask for the afternoon off, grab a boat or order a helicopter and run over to the mainland. You should know this. Your dad worked on a rig, didn't he?"

Zach scrubbed a hand down his face. He was tired and he didn't want to talk about his family or his childhood in Bonne Chance. "He did, but he left when I was eight. I didn't know anything about oil rigs. All I knew was that he was gone most of the time and when he was at home, neither he nor my mom were happy."

"And three, as I told you, I kept up with everybody who came to the funeral and the graveside service," she finished. "There were no oil rig workers there. And if I missed someone, then Father Michael missed them, too. He paraded everyone who showed up past me and even though I don't know all their names, I did recognize them all."

It occurred to Zach that Maddy's knowledge of the oil rigs was good to have. Maybe he did get why DHS had sent her and why they'd hired her in the first place.

"I don't know," he said with a sigh as he heard the door to Sandy's bedroom open. "We need to take all this one thing at a time. If it's okay with you, after I talk Sandy out of making up that sofa bed, I'll go out and check for footprints. I'm afraid it's going to start raining again."

Maddy smiled as she arched her neck and massaged it. "Sure," she said. "Why are you asking my permission?"

He snorted. "Are you kidding me? You told me in no uncertain terms that you are in charge here."

She eyed him with a raised brow. "You're telling me you're ready to take charge now?" she teased.

Zach felt as though her gaze were singeing his skin. He swallowed and shifted slightly, surprised that his body was straining in reaction to her teasing words. For someone who was not his type, she could take him from zero to uh-oh in no time flat. He forced himself to speak lightly, with no trace in his voice of the struggle he was waging to keep himself in check.

"Madeleine Tierney," he said. "When I'm ready to take charge, believe me, you will know it." Then he turned and headed down the hall to the nursery, where Sandy was waiting for him.

"I'LL NEVER UNDERSTAND GUYS," Sandy said, setting a stack of sheets and pillowcases on the back of the sofa. "How can you still be best friends when you haven't spoken for over a decade?"

Zach shrugged. "We're guys," he said, then peered at her closely. "Are you okay, Sandy?"

She smiled sadly and shook her head. "No. How can I be okay? He's dead. I don't remember a time when he wasn't here—" She stopped and blotted a tear that was sliding down her cheek.

Zach nodded. "I know. I can't believe he's gone, either."

Sandy swiped at another tear, then frowned at him. "You two were arguing the night before you left."

"Not really arguing. It was just guy stuff."

"It was about me. Tristan acted jealous, but he never really believed I would cheat on him. But he did not like that you and I talked."

Zach smiled in recollection. "He was afraid I'd tell you all his secrets."

"And I want to thank you for doing that. I knew how to handle him because of the things you told me."

"You needed to know. Tristan is—was—a hard-headed idiot at times." He stumbled over the present tense and Sandy heard it. Her lower lip quivered.

"I'm so sorry you and Tristan never talked after you left," she said.

"Trust me, it was no big deal. I told him he ought to treat you better—treat you like his girlfriend, not another buddy to hang out with. I said if he didn't, he was going to lose you."

"Oh, Zach. That's why he slugged you, isn't it? What did he say?"

Zach's mouth curled into a smile. "He agreed with me."

"Agreed? But he split your lip."

He nodded. "Like I said, he agreed with me."

Sandy laughed. "He never liked being proven wrong." She started to reach for one of the sofa's seat cushions.

"Don't do that," Zach said. "I'll be perfectly comfortable stretched out here on the couch."

"It's no trouble," she said, reaching forward and trying to grasp the corner of a heavy seat cushion.

"Hey," he said, "stop that and sit. I need to hear all about this baby." He *needed* to hear all about the supposed accident that had killed his friend, but he wasn't going to make Sandy talk about that.

"And I need to hear how your mother is, and Zoe."

Zach sighed. "Mom's fine. She blossomed in Houston. She got a job at a big department store and is now one of the buyers, and she's become a total fashionista. She's a local celebrity because of her fashion style."

"Wow," Sandy said, her brows raised. "Double wow because you know the word *fashionista*."

Zach laughed.

"How's Zoe?"

His laughter faded immediately. "I haven't heard from her in a couple of years. Last I knew she was in Atlanta. She was married for a short while—I'm talking months. Mom said she's thinking about moving to New Orleans. I can't imagine why."

"Poor Zoe. Fox Moncour's death that graduation night really changed a lot of things in Bonne Chance, didn't it?" She paused. "I'm worried about how Tristan's accident will change things. I'm not sure I can stay here if the town takes his death as hard as it took Fox's."

Zach studied Sandy. Her gaze was on her fingers, which were playing with the corner of a pillowcase. He wanted to ask her how sure she was that Tristan's death was an accident, but he couldn't do that to her. Not on the day of her husband's funeral.

It was two hours later when Sandy went to bed and Zach went out to examine the ground around Sandy's window. As he'd predicted, it had started sprinkling rain, not hard enough to wash away footprints, but still, he hadn't found anything. The grass under the window was too lush and thick to show footprints.

In the nursery, he eyed the seven-foot-long sofa that was supposed to turn into a bed with just a tug on a lever. He'd told Sandy he would be just as comfortable stretched out on it.

Right now, he felt as if he could sleep on nails, he was that tired. He grabbed one of the pillows Sandy had brought him and tossed it at one overstuffed arm.

He turned the lights out and began unbuttoning his

shirt. He'd hoped to talk to Maddy some more, but she and Sandy had both been visibly exhausted. By the time he'd come inside from checking out the window, they'd gone to bed.

He was tired, too. As he'd explained to Sandy, his return flight was on Sunday, leaving New Orleans at 7:05 a.m., which meant he had to drive back to New Orleans tomorrow. She'd been disappointed and her eyes had gleamed with tears, but she'd smiled and told him she understood.

He flopped down on the sofa and stuffed the pillow behind his head, then threw an arm over his eyes and tried to relax. He wanted to get up early and spend some time with Sandy as well as talk to Maddy before he had to leave.

He had a method he used to get to sleep when he was too keyed up. He began to breathe deeply and slowly. Starting at his toes, he deliberately relaxed one muscle group at a time, moving up his legs and torso and out his arms to his fingers, then his neck and head and eyes. Usually, no matter how wide-awake he was, he'd be asleep before he got to his neck, sometimes before he got to his arms.

But within moments, it was obvious that tonight, his brain had no intention of slowing down. He managed to doze, but within seconds, some disturbing thing someone had said about Tristan would echo in his head and wake him up.

The first time he drifted off, it was his own voice, telling Duff that Tristan couldn't have fallen into the water and drowned. *Tristan lived on boats and docks and floating logs on the Mississippi River and on the Gulf his whole life. He was the strongest swimmer I've ever seen.*

By the fourth time, he'd barely fallen asleep, only to wake to the echo of the ME's horrifying statement, *There's not enough of Tristan DuChaud to put in a casket.* He gave up and sat up.

There was no way he could sleep. Not until he sorted out all the information in his head. He needed to think, therefore he needed to pace. The nursery didn't have enough room for him to take two steps back and forth, much less four or five. So he maneuvered around the baby bed in the middle of the room and quietly opened the door. Slipping out and up the hall to the kitchen, he ran a glass of water and drank it, then started to unlatch the doors to the patio and stopped. There were two tiny metallic plates between the top of the door and the door facing that he hadn't noticed before. It was an alarm. Obviously, it was not armed, because it didn't go off when he came in through the door, nor had the sheriff come roaring out to the house, called by a silent alarm.

He glanced at the window over the sink, then checked the front door. It appeared that all the doors and windows were armed. He remembered noticing a box on the wall behind the door between the hall and the kitchen earlier in the afternoon. He looked at it. Sure enough, it was the control for the alarm system, and it was off. Not just disarmed. Off. He made a mental note to check that everything worked and to make sure Maddy and Sandy knew how to arm and disarm it before he left for New Orleans.

He opened the French doors and slipped through them onto the patio, then closed them as quietly as he could. The air smelled like rain and the humid breeze on his skin felt a lot cooler than the steamy afternoon at the cemetery, although he'd be surprised if it was any lower than midseventies. He rolled up his sleeves and let the air pick up his shirttails.

For ten minutes or so, he paced and ran his fingers through his hair, rubbed his face and slammed one fist into the other palm as he went over everything he'd learned in the short time he'd been here.

Finally, he came to a conclusion. There was only one thing he could do, for Sandy, for himself and for Tristan. There was no way he was leaving in the morning. He sat down at the picnic table and dialed a familiar number.

"National Security Agency, how may I direct your call?"

Zach gave the operator the name of his immediate superior.

"Yes, sir. Just a moment, sir." He listened to the subtle beeps and clicks as she transferred his call.

He yawned. It had been a long day. He'd flown from Fort Meade, Maryland, to New Orleans, then driven over three hours to get to Bonne Chance. He'd barely had a chance to breathe before finding out the horrifying specifics of Tristan's death. He'd parried with Madeleine Tierney and helped her when Sandy screamed, and he hadn't even stopped to eat a sandwich or a piece of pie. And now it was midnight here, one o'clock in Fort Meade.

He doubted Bill was still at the office. He probably wasn't even awake. Sure enough, the voice that answered was dull with drowsiness.

"Yeah?" Bill said.

"It's Winter. I need a favor," he said. He heard bedclothes rustle as Bill sat up in bed with a groan.

"A favor?" Bill asked. "At one o'clock in the morning?"

"I need to take some vacation time."

"Vacation—that's what you called about?" Bill's voice was no longer sleepy. It was annoyed.

For an instant, Zach considered telling Bill everything he'd learned and everything he suspected. But he didn't. He knew what would happen if he mentioned Homeland Security to Bill. He'd be pulled back to NSA headquarters, and Bill would start a turf war with the Department of Homeland Security under whose purview chatter fell. So he gave Bill the story he'd decided on while pacing.

"My friend Tristan's wife is pregnant and she needs me to help her with his papers. You know, insurance and accounting stuff." Zach cringed at his lame reason. "I'd have to leave in the morning to make my Sunday-morning flight, so I wanted to check with you about staying a while, maybe a week or—"

"Yeah, yeah. Send me an email. I'm sure I won't remember this when I wake up. And just so you know—you could have arranged this before you left."

"Yes, sir."

"Good night."

"Good night, sir."

Bill hung up. Zach quickly typed an email and sent it, formally requesting the next five days as vacation.

MADDY WAS PRETTY sure she'd never felt so tired in her life. She'd spent a long time in the shower, letting the hot water run on her back and neck, her arms and body and, finally, her face. It was only when the water turned cold that she got out. She wrapped up in a terry-cloth robe, her limbs rubbery and her eyelids drooping.

By the time she'd gotten a pair of camisole pajamas on, she'd been more than half-asleep standing up. But as soon as her head hit the pillow, her brain started racing. Each time she began to doze, her brain kicked into high gear. Zach's voice hammered at her consciousness. *Who are you? Who do you work for? What happened to Tristan? Does Sandy know? What happened to Tristan? What happened? What—*

She sat up and clapped her hands over her ears, but since his voice was in her head, it didn't help. Why was she hearing Zach's voice asking questions he'd never asked her? She didn't know why, but inside her head he was relentless. Lying back down, she closed her eyes and pulled the covers over her head. That didn't help, either. Now that she'd covered her head, it wasn't just Zach's voice. Her handler Brock's voice echoed through her brain, too. *You're not focused. We may pull you out.*

"Shut up!" she whispered, sitting up. "Shh." She'd heard something. She held her breath and listened. It was a door closing. Two doors, like the French doors out to the patio. It wasn't Zach coming in from checking Sandy's window. She'd heard him earlier, before she'd gotten into the shower. Could it be Sandy?

She waited, but didn't hear anything else. If it were Zach or Sandy, getting a glass of water, wouldn't she be able to hear the water running? Maybe not, if the water were in a filtered dispenser on the outside of the refrigerator.

She got up and reached for her gun, but at that moment, she heard Zach clear his throat. Then she did hear the water running. It was Zach, and he was getting a glass of water, probably wearing nothing but his underwear, given the weather. No, she couldn't go out there. She didn't think she could bear to look at that body of his in nothing but briefs or boxers.

Pressing a hand over her racing heart, she lay down again and closed her eyes—tightly. What was the matter with her? Now her head was filled with a vision of Zach Winter practically naked, drinking a glass of cold water. He turned it up and guzzled it, and of course, a few drops escaped and ran down his chin to his neck, to his torso, to the waistband of those briefs—or boxers.

She moaned and moved her hand from her heart to her temple. Pressing hard, she tried to squeeze the Zach fantasy out of her head.

Brock was right when he said she seemed to lack focus. And from the way he'd said it, he suspected that Zach was the reason.

With a low growl, Maddy threw back the covers and got up. She hoped and prayed Zach was back in his room with the door shut, because if she ran into him in just briefs or boxers—well. Before that thought had a chance to finish, Maddy was shaking her head. She was *not* going to let a good-looking NSA agent knock her off her game. This was her first field assignment and she intended to ace it.

Despite her resolve, it took her a few minutes to decide to open the door and peek out. The door to the nursery was closed. Did that mean he'd sneaked back in without a sound? Or was he still out?

She slipped up the hall to the kitchen and got herself a glass of water. As she drank, she saw a dark form pacing back and forth on the patio. Her heart didn't quite jump out of her chest because she was pretty sure it was Zach, but she did stand perfectly still and watch, until she saw his face and body in a small patch of moonlight that peeked out from the clouds for a few seconds. She exhaled, having totally failed to notice that she wasn't breathing until that moment.

Then she stepped over to the door and opened it. Without the windows between them, she was able to see him a little more clearly, especially after her eyes adapted to the darkness. He wasn't undressed, but he had unbuttoned his shirt. When she saw that, her heart did jump out of her chest, or at least it felt as if it had. Then she opened her mouth and, because she'd made herself nervous thinking about his naked body and couldn't take her eyes off his bare chest and abs, she said something snarky and mean. "So, Zach," Maddy said. "Texting for a booty call?"

She grimaced, then nearly turned and ran when she saw him close his eyes in brief but very real pain. "In the home of my best friend's widow, on the day of his funeral?"

"Oh," she moaned aloud. "I'm sorry. I don't know where that came from. My evil twin, I suppose."

"Really?" His jaw worked. "Are you telling me that I've been talking to the *good* twin up until now?"

"Okay, I deserved that. I apologize. I didn't mean to say what I did. I was just—" She shrugged.

"Just what?"

"So, what are you doing?" she asked, trying to sound as if the prior exchange hadn't taken place.

"I'm not going to tell you."

She smiled and shook her head. "Can't blame you. Would it help if I answered some of those questions you said you had for me?"

His brows rose. "Maybe," he drawled. "What are you doing up anyhow?" he asked.

She saw his gaze take in her state of dress—or undress. The camisole pajama set she had on covered enough, she supposed. At least in the strict sense. But the material was thin cotton and although the top was dark blue, it still showed the shape of her nipples. She crossed her arms instinctively. Then when he smiled, she uncrossed them, felt exposed and crossed them back immediately.

When his gaze slid farther, down to the drawstring bottoms, she was thankful at least that they were long and not the short-short ones she'd started to buy. As his eyes lit on her feet, she had to force her toes to stay still and not curl in the pink flip-flops she wore.

"I was thirsty," she said, trying to pretend he wasn't checking out every inch of her. "And I was having trouble sleeping."

"Counting those sheep didn't help?" he asked, nodding toward her pajama bottoms, which had white fluffy sheep bouncing around on the same dark blue background as the top. She shrugged. "Guess not."

ZACH PERCHED ON one hip on the corner of the picnic table as he slid his phone into his back pocket. Then he went back to studying her. He'd already checked out the little pajamas and decided they were very sexy. He didn't even pretend that he wasn't ogling her body. He was too fascinated with the way the dim light from the kitchen played across her smooth, creamy skin. He was mesmerized by the little shadow created by the small bump of bone on the top of her shoulder. For one instant, he had the notion that it would be fun to chase that shadow—with his tongue.

He squeezed his eyes shut. He couldn't think of her that way. She was a Homeland Security agent. He wanted, needed, to find out what happened to his best friend. There was no place for sex here. No place even for just a flirtation.

Besides, there was almost nothing about her that he actually liked, except maybe that little shoulder bump. She was too confident, too sure of herself, too bossy, and she wasn't even that pretty. Okay, that wasn't fair, or true. He'd already decided that she was quite attractive, although not without flaws. She had nice hair, but her eyes were too big and her nose was too short and her mouth was too…something. Maybe too turned down at the corners? Maybe too pouty. Although, he had to admit that it was tempting. Very inviting.

He realized he was staring and she was becoming uncomfortable. His gaze lit on her right hand. Her fingers were drumming on her thigh. When she noticed him looking at her hand, she stopped and made a fist. He tried not to smile. He liked that he got to her. "You're an interesting person, Maddy," he finally said.

"So I've been told. Why do you think so?"

"How old are you?"

She took a long breath then sighed. "Is that what you wanted to ask me?" she said. "I'll just go back to counting sheep."

"At the funeral, in that dark suit, I'd have said thirty."

Maddy's jaw dropped before she had a chance to cover her surprise. "Well, I suppose I ought to be glad."

"Glad?"

"I dress that way on purpose, especially when I go on the oil rigs. It's easier if the guys think I'm older."

"I guess that makes sense. But right now, it's hard to believe you're not still working on your PhD." He tried not to smile.

"I have my PhD, thank you."

"In what?" he asked.

"Chemical engineering."

He nodded. "And you work for Homeland Security."

"Yes. Just like I told you."

"Why are you here?" he asked, folding his arms.

"Because I was assigned as backup for Tristan."

Zach went stone-cold still at Maddy's words. He had to play them over in his head more than once before he was sure what she'd said. "Backup," he repeated flatly.

"Oh. I'm sorry," she said, her face turning pale as her cheeks turned bright with color. "I didn't mean to blurt that out. You didn't know Tristan was working undercover on the *Pleiades Seagull* for the Department of Homeland Security, did you? I didn't mean for you to find out like this."

"Tristan, working for the government? That's not like him. And it sure as hell isn't like him to work on an oil rig. I remember he hated the oil rigs and that was back before we were in high school, before his dad died on one. Does Sandy know that you and he were—are with Homeland Security?" He rubbed his palm across the evening stubble on his face.

"I don't know," Maddy said. "I mean, no. I don't think so. She doesn't know about me. I'm pretty sure she doesn't know about Tristan. I can't tell you why he went to work for them. Maybe he was recruited because of where he lived and his particular skill set. They like to hire locals." She sighed and lifted her hair off the back of her neck, then shivered.

"You said you were sent here as backup for him? Why you? Did they send anyone else?"

"First of all, thank you," Maddy said wryly. "But no. I was sent because I'm an oil rig inspector. The plan was for me to conduct a spot investigation of the *Pleiades Seagull*, which, as an inspector, I'm allowed to do at any time. However, the captain of the rig can refuse if he has a good reason."

Zach didn't want to hear all this. All he wanted to know was what happened to Tristan and whether it was Homeland Security's fault. He wasn't sure what good it was going to do him or Sandy or anyone to know that, but right now, having that knowledge was the only thing that mattered to him. He gritted his teeth and tried to ask the right questions to get to the answers he needed. "I take it the captain of the *Pleiades Seagull* refused?"

Maddy nodded. "He stated that he was shorthanded because several crew members had contracted a stomach virus."

Zach looked out into the darkness toward the Gulf. A pale glow lit the sky from the oil rigs and boats on the water. "Why are you hanging around here now?" he asked.

"My secondary assignment was to protect Sandy. When Tristan requested backup, he also requested protection for her."

Zach whirled and grabbed Maddy's arm. "Protection? He asked for protection for his wife? That means he *knew* he was in danger. He *knew*! Why the hell did Homeland Security leave him out there alone?" He let go of her and pressed his temples with the heels of his hands, feeling as if he'd been kicked in the head. "If they knew Tristan was in danger, why didn't they pull him out?"

Maddy hugged herself. "I asked that same question. My handler, Brock, didn't answer me directly, so I have no idea what their plans were. But they did send me in. I was supposed to stay with Sandy and make sure Sandy was safe and let Brock know about any information I received from Tristan. It was only going to be another week or so before he'd have been back on shore for a week and DHS could find out his latest information and decide what to do."

Zach felt a lump growing in the back of his throat and his eyes were stinging. "Nice plan. How'd that work out for everybody?"

Chapter Five

Maddy's chin shot up and she glared at him while tears spilled from her eyes and flowed down her cheeks. She dashed at them angrily with her fingers. Her cheeks turned such a bright red that he thought her tears might sizzle and evaporate. "You go right ahead and be derisive and sarcastic. It's not going to make one bit of difference to me. I am fully aware that Tristan was killed on my watch. I will never—" Her voice cracked. She cleared her throat. "Never get over that. I should have been able to do something, even from here. I should have realized that he was too vulnerable out there on that rig alone."

She wiped a strand of hair away from her forehead with a shaky hand. "I should have called headquarters and made them get him off there."

"Would they have listened to you?"

"I don't know."

"Were you and Tristan able to talk while he was offshore?"

She shook her head. "No. Sandy didn't know that either of us was with Homeland Security, and Tristan had been caught eavesdropping on the captain twice. All I could do was listen in on their conversations and glean what I could from Tristan. He knew that the captain had his phone bugged from that end and that I was listening on this end. We had hoped that he could give me some carefully worded clues while he talked to Sandy, but we also knew that if it was a clue I could understand it would probably make sense to the captain of the *Pleiades Seagull*."

Zach's jaw was still tight. "That doesn't sound like a very good setup."

"It was a horrible setup. After the captain refused to let me on board to do an inspection, I was helpless, except as a bodyguard for Sandy. I even went back after three weeks and asked him again, hoping he'd be more cooperative. But he still refused." Her voice cracked.

"If he'd agreed in time, you think you could have saved Tristan?"

"I don't know. Maybe if there really was a virus on board, I could have forced the captain to evacuate the boat and fly everybody to the hospital in New Orleans. That way we'd have at least been able to get to Tristan and possibly remove him from danger, instead of hanging him out to dry."

"Is Homeland Security sending someone else to work on the rig in Tristan's place?" Zach demanded through clenched teeth.

"No. They have no way of getting another agent on the platform. The oil companies like to hire locals, preferably people who are already familiar with the rigs, but they'll take someone who has worked and lived on the coast of Louisiana all their life. From what I understand, Tristan was already working as communications officer on the *Pleiades Seagull*, so he was literally the perfect recruit for an undercover operation."

"Until he was murdered." Zach wasn't sure how much longer he could control his emotions. The more he heard, the more convinced he was that Tristan's death could have been avoided. He could still be alive, loving his wife and waiting for his first child to be born. Zach turned and looked out over the Gulf. He didn't say anything. Not because all his questions had been answered, but because he didn't trust his voice right now.

After waiting in silence for several moments, Maddy finally spoke. "Okay, so, I'm going back to bed, unless you've got more questions."

"Wait," he said, his voice raspy with emotion. For another half a minute he stood there, his back to her, trying to regain control. He hadn't seen Tristan in thirteen years, but he still felt as though a part of his heart had been ripped out. They'd been best friends throughout their entire childhood.

Finally he turned around. "Listen. I'm supposed to fly back to Fort Meade on Sunday, but I've asked my boss for a week's leave." He looked down, wishing he were stronger and braver. "I'm not sure why I did that. I have no authority. I'm just a government employee on vacation. Anything I do will be as a civilian, not as an NSA agent."

Maddy felt deflated. She'd hoped, one way or another, that she could convince Zach to help her figure out a way to bring down the people who had killed Tristan. She'd hoped he would talk to his superiors at NSA and they would get involved. Because she knew that all Homeland Security wanted from her was protection for Sandy. And Brock had hinted that they would probably be pulling her back to DC very soon.

She blew out a breath in frustration. "I don't get it. Why did you ask for vacation? Why didn't you tell your chief what's going on and request assignment down here? That would have made more sense."

Zach rubbed a hand down his face. "Because first, I can't prove that Tristan's death was foul play. All I've got is what I know about him. Second, the NSA is not in the business of solving murders. And third, even if they did decide to investigate Tristan's death, I wouldn't get the assignment. I've never been in the field before. I just finished training a few months ago. And last but maybe most important, I was Tristan's best friend all through childhood. That's a conflict of interest."

"So you decided to take a week's vacation? Why? Are you planning on going rogue?" Maddy felt laughter rumbling up into her throat. She tried to hold it back but she couldn't.

"I'm sorry," she gasped. "I don't mean to laugh. I'm just tired."

He glared at her, but she was right. It was kind of funny. Maybe he was *going rogue*, he thought, but he discarded that notion right away. He could call it that, but it didn't make it so. All he was really doing was planning a little amateur detective work while on vacation. He wasn't like some Special Forces officer in a movie who couldn't get permission to go back into enemy territory to save his friend.

He was a geek. His weapons were two PhDs and a gun he barely knew how to use.

"Laugh all you want. You're not much better. You're babysitting Sandy. Not that I don't appreciate you keeping her safe. But why are they leaving you here? Obviously you're not going to get onto the *Pleiades Seagull*."

"I'm planning to talk to my handler about that first thing in the morning. I need to report to him about the men who were supposedly peeping in Sandy's window anyway."

"Come on, Maddy. How long do you think they're

going to keep you here to guard Sandy now that Tristan is dead? The only reason they would is if they had any proof—" He stopped, cocking his head to listen.

"Wha—" she started, but he held up a hand, signaling for silence. He was suddenly as still and alert as a cat on the prowl. He lifted his head as if sniffing the wind.

Then she heard it. Someone, or some*thing*, was moving stealthily through the swampy area at the back of the house. The muffled footsteps and faint rustling of leaves and vines were subtle, but once in a while she could hear the sucking sound of a leg being pulled out of the sticky gumbo mud that made up the swamps of south Louisiana.

"Get down!" Zach snapped, grabbing her arm and pulling her down with him behind the picnic table. She lost her balance and fell on her butt, then scrambled up to her haunches.

He pulled his weapon out from the holster nestled in the small of his back and held it in both hands pointed skyward as he listened.

"What—" Maddy started, but he shook his head jerkily. She crouched there beside him, close enough to his left arm that she could feel the heat and the tension emanating from him in waves, and waited for whoever was sneaking around Tristan and Sandy's house to show themselves or slink away. She heard more movement disturbing the quiet air. She held her breath. The sounds were fading.

"Are we going after him?" she whispered, her mouth close to his ear.

This time the shake of his head was slow and deliberate. "No," he said finally. "I don't want to ask for trouble, either of the two-legged or the four-legged variety."

"Four-legged? You think it was an animal?"

He shrugged. "Stay down," he said as he rose slowly, still listening, still tensed and ready for anything. Maddy did her best to ignore the hint of rippling thigh muscles that were beneath the fine weave of his dress pants, right in her field of vision. *Long and lean and hard.* A shiver rippled through her.

What was she thinking? From the moment she'd first set eyes on him, all the practical sense and excellent intuition that made her a good rig inspector and a good undercover agent had blown away like dandelion spores on the bayou breeze. What had replaced her focus and single-minded determination was a searing fire deep within her, like lightning striking a methane swamp. She'd been shocked at her girlish response.

Thank goodness her training and personal determination kicked in when Sandy had cried out. She'd handled that well, even during those two or three seconds when Zach had leaned against her and stopped her from opening the door. The feel of his hot skin against hers and his breath on her cheek had registered but not distracted her from her mission, which was to keep Sandy safe.

But just moments ago, when she'd seen Zach on the patio with his shirt undone, she'd gotten swept up in the fantasy of him again, despite the fact that she knew as clearly as if he'd told her that she was not and had no hope of ever being his type.

Gathering every ounce of will she could muster, she pushed the feminine side of her to the back of her mind and forced herself to react like an agent, not like a *girl.*

"So," she said as she rose and eyed the blackness at the edge of the lawn that was the swamp. "What was it? A dog? An alligator?"

He stood, still and silent, for a few more seconds, still holding his gun at the ready, then he clicked on the safety, holstered it and turned to face her. "Dogs aren't generally that stealthy unless they've been trained. Alligators make a different sound."

"It sounded big."

He looked at her, one brow quirked. "Aren't you from New Orleans? And didn't you tell me you'd gone everywhere with your dad? You're not trying to say you've never been in the swamp, are you?"

She shook her head. "Nope. Never have. Never will—not on purpose anyhow. So, let's see. Maybe possum?"

Zach laughed. "Right. Try nutria, coyote or bear or bobcat."

"Bear? B-bobcat? Seriously? Are *they* stealthy?"

"Okay. Maybe not the bear."

Maddy groaned. "Great. So it's a zoo out here, only the animals aren't locked up." She expected Zach to laugh or at least chuckle, but he didn't. He gave her a solemn nod.

"Neither the four-legged kind nor the two-legged kind," he said. "So it might be a good idea if you keep that gun on you at all times."

There it was. The subtle reprimand she'd been expecting. She was on assignment and she'd walked out onto the patio unarmed. Her face flamed even as a chill crawled down her spine. "Right. Now what?"

"I'm going to bed. I've had a long day."

Zing. Another not-so-subtle slam. She should have beaten him to that punch. She should have said she was going to bed first. She kept relinquishing power to him when there was no need to. He'd already acknowledged her as commander at the door to Sandy's room.

"Sure. Me, too. I'm tired." She turned and headed inside, not waiting to see if Zach was behind her. About the time she got to the door from the kitchen to the hall, he spoke.

"Maddy?"

She stopped. "Hmm?" she said without turning around.

"Can I talk to you for a minute before we go to bed? I want to run something by you."

She looked back over her shoulder. "Now?" she said, faking a yawn, only to have it turn into a real one. "Can't this wait until tomorrow?"

"Nope. And close that door. I don't want to wake Sandy."

"Are we going to yell?" Maddy closed the door and turned, wondering what he had in mind. He stood right in front of her, his shirt still open. His abs were tight and rippled with muscle the way those of male models in commercials and book covers were. She'd always suspected those photos were touched up.

A thrill zinged through her and seemed to flip a switch deep inside her. She felt a sensuous throbbing in a very, very sensitive place. She took a deep breath and reminded herself that she wasn't his type.

He sent her a look that told her he knew exactly what was going on in her head and elsewhere. Again, her cheeks grew hot. Ducking her head, she went to the refrigerator for a cold glass of water. She took several swallows before she turned around to face him. She had to resist the urge to press the cold glass against her burning cheeks.

"Okay," she said briskly. "What can't wait until tomorrow?"

He leaned against the wall near the door to the living

room, crossed his arms and slanted one calf across the other. It was a deceptively casual stance. But Maddy, after only a few hours with him, knew that nothing about Zach Winter was casual. Not his words, not his demeanor and certainly not his stance. She was sure that underneath those perfectly tailored pants, the leanly sculpted muscles of his thighs and calves were taut and ready. If he had to, he could vault across the room in a fraction of a second and pull his gun while he was doing it.

"I don't like Sandy being here."

"What?" Maddy asked, thrown off guard by the statement. "Why not?"

"There's no reason she needs to stay here. She'd probably be happier up in Baton Rouge with Tristan's mother. It would probably be good for both of them. Mrs. DuChaud could use someone to fuss over and Sandy could use a distraction. She'll be more comfortable there."

"Because you're all about Sandy's comfort, right?" Maddy set her jaw. "What's going on, Zach?"

He just shook his head and leaned against the wall, lanky and carefree as a farmer after his last harvest.

"Come on. You take a week's vacation to stay down here, and the first thing you do is send Sandy away? What are you planning?"

He still didn't speak.

"Okay. I could be in bed, except that you said you wanted to talk to me. So, why aren't you talking?"

ZACH STRAIGHTENED AND STUCK his hands in his pockets. He looked down at his feet for a second then up at her. "Okay," he said. "I think Sandy is in danger. That's why I don't want her here. She's pregnant, she's grieving and she has no training in self-defense. She'll just be in our way."

"*Our* way?" Maddy echoed.

Zach ignored her. "You and Sandy are similar in height and your hair color is pretty close. Here's what I'm thinking. Let's say the doctor orders Sandy on bed rest for the rest of her pregnancy and says that she's having some kind of problem that not only confines her to bed but also quarantines her for her health and the health of her baby."

Maddy frowned at him. What he was saying began to make sense, but she didn't like what she was pretty sure he was getting at. "I don't understand."

"I want to get Sandy out of town secretly and put you in her bedroom, pretending to be her."

"You want to use me as *bait*?"

Zach shrugged. "I wouldn't put it that way, but if that's how you want to look at it…"

"It's not how I want to look at it," Maddy said. "It's how it is. You're putting me in Sandy's room in Sandy's bed, pretending to be Sandy. The definition of that is *bait*." She stood and smothered a yawn with her hand. "I think I'm fading. When are you thinking about doing this?"

"The sooner the better."

"Please tell me you're not wanting to do it tonight."

He shook his head. "I'm not sure I could do it tonight, even if I wanted to. But I'm going to have to talk Sandy into it and I can guarantee you she's not going to like it. So maybe we should regroup tomorrow."

"That works for me," Maddy said. "I'm really tired."

"So, I guess I'll see you in the morning."

Maddy looked at her watch. "Hate to break it to you,

but it's already morning. It's 3:00 a.m. I'll see you in a few hours."

"Where are you sleeping?" he asked.

She thought of a cute, slightly suggestive response, but she couldn't work up the energy to say it out loud. Besides, it would probably only end up being embarrassing if it went the way her previous attempts to be cute and sexy usually went. "In the guest room," she said.

"Why don't you sleep in Sandy's room. I saw a day-bed in there."

"Why? Are you thinking—"

He nodded. "I'd like one of us to be there with her, just in case anything happens."

"So, have you decided she wasn't just having a nightmare when she saw those two men at her window?" Maddy asked, searching his face.

"I think it could be dangerous to dismiss what she says she saw," Zach said grimly. He walked over and opened the hall door. "So I'll see you in a couple of hours."

"At least three," she said, yawning. At that instant, out of nowhere, came a high-pitched scream.

Maddy jumped and Zach drew his weapon. "Get your weapon and meet me in there. Approach with caution."

Zach vaulted through the open door at a run and headed toward Sandy's bedroom at the end of the hall. He heard Maddy's footsteps behind him and noted when she veered off into the guest room to grab her gun. He stopped at the edge of Sandy's door, holding his weapon in his right hand, supported by his left, just as he was taught. He knew he could shoot. He also knew he was not very good at it.

And he had no idea whether he could shoot a human being. Still, his gun was ready, safety off. He took a deep breath and decided that he was ready, too. As ready as he'd ever be.

He reached for the doorknob with his left hand, exhaled, then twisted the knob and shoved the door open.

The room was dark, very dark. He stood totally still, poised on the balls of his feet, prepared to dive, lunge or shoot, whatever the situation called for. He felt a fine trembling just beneath his jawbone. Praying he wouldn't lose his nerve, he felt behind him for the light switch, braced himself, then turned the lights on. The flash blinded him for a split second and left a red spot glowing in the middle of his vision.

Sandy's back was pressed against the headboard and her eyes were wide as saucers. One hand was pressed against her throat as if to stop more terrified screams.

Holding his weapon at the ready, he crossed the room, glancing briefly into the closet and the bathroom, and looked out the window. Nothing but blackness. He held his breath and listened. The only sound was the faint dripping of water off the trees and the house's roof.

As Maddy slid into the room, brandishing her gun, Sandy cried out, "Maddy! Maddy— Oh, my God, Maddy! I saw him."

"Zach?" Maddy said softly, the tone of her voice a clear indication that this time she was looking to him for leadership.

He nodded. A second later, he heard the quiet whoosh of a metal weapon being slipped into a leather holster. Then Maddy was on the bed and cradling Sandy in her arms.

"Who did you see, Sandy? The same men?" Maddy's voice was low and soothing. He was grateful that she was here. He wasn't sure how bad he would be at comforting his best friend's widow, but he knew he would be bad.

"No!" Sandy cried. "I thought it was them—at first—but it wasn't. Oh, Maddy! It was him. He was right there."

Zach carefully lowered his gun and slipped it into its holster as he watched Maddy slowly and gently calm Sandy down. It took her a while. At first, Sandy didn't want to be calm. She wanted to get up and run outside, or at least that's what Zach thought she was saying.

After a little while, her excited cries gave way to mumblings, which he couldn't understand at all. During all that, Maddy held her and whispered to her. Zach just stood there and watched until Maddy caught his eye and pointedly glanced toward the window.

Zach nodded. She was right. He needed to go outside and look around. It didn't take him long, and once again, he saw nothing. The thick grass under the window wasn't even bent.

When he came back into the master bedroom, Sandy was crying less and talking more coherently. Maddy still had her arm around her and Sandy was staring into space. But Maddy's penetrating gaze caught Zach's eyes and bored into his brain. She wanted him to listen. He stopped and waited.

"It really was, Maddy," Sandy said. She held a couple of tissues in her hand and kept wiping her eyes with them. "It really was him."

"Sandy, you're so tired, and there were people here until after eight o'clock. You probably heard them and they kept you from sleeping well. It's exhaustion. Did the doctor give you something to take if you can't sleep?"

Sandy shook her head and Zach saw her chin lift fractionally. He knew that look. She had no intention of letting Maddy or anyone else stop her from telling what she saw. "I saw him. I did. Oh, he looked awful."

She pulled away from Maddy and looked Zach in the eye. "Why is everybody telling me that Tristan is dead, Zach?" she asked, her eyes overflowing again with tears. "When I woke up a few minutes ago, he was standing right there."

Zach held up his hand. "Maddy, would you get her some water?"

Maddy nodded and got up. She turned toward the bathroom.

"From the kitchen," Zach added.

"Zach—" Sandy sobbed. "He was there, alive. Smiling at me."

But she wasn't smiling. Her face held a puzzled sadness that was about as painful as anything Zach had ever seen.

"He was soaking wet and so pale. He looked awful. I held out my arms for him but he disappeared. He must have had to hide, because one of those other men showed up at the window." She shuddered. "I think I screamed."

"Start at the beginning, Sandy. I need to know exactly what happened. What woke you up?"

Sandy relaxed a bit and pulled the covers up to her armpits. "I was lying here awake. I know I was awake because I was thinking about the funeral and how everybody had insisted on keeping the casket closed." She stared at her hands.

Zach saw a tear splash onto her thumb. He felt as if he should do something. Hug her. Wipe her tears.

Something. But all he did was wait, silently, for her to continue.

"He was standing right over there." She pointed to the window. "Like I said, he looked awful, but then I guess he's been through a lot."

Zach's eyes burned. He needed to stop her, to tell her that she'd been dreaming, that she couldn't have seen Tristan because he was dead. He didn't have the heart. Hell, he could barely stand to think about Tristan, much less have to convince his wife—his widow—of something he didn't want to believe himself.

But if not him, then who? Not Maddy. She was a stranger. He'd known Sandy for almost as long as he had Tristan. He had to be the one to comfort her, no matter how badly he botched it.

With courage he pulled up from somewhere deep inside him, Zach sat down on the bed. He held out an arm and Sandy moved closer. He slid his arm around her and pulled her to him so she was resting her head against his shoulder. "Sandy, sweetheart. We've known each other longer than anybody, except for Tristan and me. And you know you're my sister, as truly as if we had the same mother."

Sandy's shoulders shook with her tears. "I know. I love you, Zach."

"I love you, too, sweetheart. I need to tell you something. It's going to be hard for you to hear, and I'm going to do a really bad job of it, but you're strong. I know you can handle it."

At the word *hard*, Sandy looked up at him, fear and trust in her eyes.

"Go after him, Zach. He's out there, wet and cold and exhausted. He might even be hurt. Find him and bring him home to me. Please."

From the corner of his eye, he saw a movement in the doorway. It was Maddy with a glass of water in her hand. Zach inclined his head toward the front of the house, sending her a message to leave them alone. She set the water down on a table by the door and disappeared.

Zach pressed his lips to Sandy's bowed head as he blinked against the sting of tears in his eyes. "I need you to be brave."

Sandy went rigid, except for her hands, which trembled against his skin. "I don't want to be brave, Zach," she said. "I don't want to."

"I'll hold you," he said. "I'll hold on to you."

"Okay," Sandy said so softly it was nearly inaudible. "I'll try."

He pulled her closer, terrified at the trusting way she'd looked at him. His stomach was in knots and his eyes were blurry with dampness. He thought this might be the hardest thing he'd ever done. He'd sooner take a bullet than tell her the whole truth about Tristan's death. But she deserved to know.

He took a long breath. "Let me tell you what happened to Tristan," he said gently.

Chapter Six

Maddy stood frozen, just beyond the bedroom door. She couldn't leave until she'd heard what Zach was going to say. When she heard his heartbreaking words and Sandy's brokenhearted reply, she rushed into the guest room and closed the door quietly behind her.

She stood with her back against the door for a long time as Zach's gentle words to his best friend's widow echoed through her over and over, etching another scar onto her heart with each pass.

She doubled her fists and pressed them against her chest. She could barely breathe, the pain was so fierce. Tears coursed down her face and neck, drying before they reached her pajama top.

After a long time, she wiped the tears away with tissues, but even though the crying stopped, the pain in her heart still throbbed, more intense than anything she'd ever experienced.

"How?" she asked aloud. "How can anyone stand that much hurt and live?" She was talking about not only Sandy, but Zach as well, and she felt as though just knowing how much they were hurting might suffocate her.

Sandy's husband, her soul mate, the father of her unborn child, was dead, and she had to go on living.

How would she do it? Maybe she could stand it, for their baby. The baby would give her joy and heartache, blissful happiness and aching grief. After more than a month of living with her, Maddy knew that Sandy would survive. She was strong. She and her child would be all right.

Maddy dried the last lingering tears. She wondered if Zach would want to talk to her after Sandy went to sleep. She could stay up—maybe, if she made a pot of coffee—or she could try to go to sleep. Zach would probably have no qualms about waking her if he needed to talk to her.

Climbing into bed, she picked up one of the pillows and hugged it. She had a different view of Zach after what she'd seen him do. She couldn't imagine doing that, not even for her best friend. He was telling Tristan's wife the whole truth about what had happened to him.

It seemed at first blush like a cruel thing to do to Sandy, when she was already so devastated. But it was obvious Zach was doing the right thing. The look on Sandy's face told Maddy that he was doing the right thing.

Maddy's tension began to drain away as her mind followed Zach's reasoning. Years ago, he'd known Sandy almost as well as he'd known Tristan, she realized. And so he understood that she'd spent the days since Tristan's death in terrified confusion because no one would explain why she was being kept from seeing her husband's body. No one, not the medical examiner, not even Father Michael, had had the nerve to explain why.

Maddy's eyes welled with tears again. She swiped at them with her fingers, remembering the glimmer of dampness in Zach's eyes as he gestured for her to leave them alone. Zach was doing what a true friend did. He was helping Sandy to understand.

The sharp, cool NSA agent had a tender side, a side he would not want her, or anyone else, to see. He was a man, and men didn't weep. Not even over the death of their best friend.

But if he thought she wouldn't respect him for grieving, he was wrong. He didn't know that she'd seen her father crying over her mother's grave when she was eight years old. Zach didn't know that Maddy had learned that a man who would not cry was a man who could not feel—not the way he needed to in order to be a great leader.

Maddy turned over on her side, still hugging the pillow. Tears slid over the bridge of her nose and down onto the sheets. Sandy was truly lucky to have Zach in her life.

Just before she drifted off to sleep, Maddy thought about what her life would be like if Zach were in it.

FOUR HOURS LATER, Maddy came into the kitchen, freshly showered and wearing jeans and a sleeveless top. Her eyes were still puffy and she had a faint headache that she was hoping a couple or three cups of coffee would fix.

To her surprise, the coffee was made and smelled delicious. She looked out at the patio and saw Zach sitting on the far side of the picnic table with his back to the door, drinking coffee. He was facing the swamp.

She poured a mug for herself, added three heaping teaspoonfuls of sugar and headed outside. This morning she was carrying her weapon in the pocket of her jeans. As she stepped onto the patio, she saw Zach's gun sitting on the table next to a towel he'd used to wipe last night's rain off the table.

Without speaking, Maddy dried the table on the other side of his weapon and sat. She drew in a deep breath scented with mud and fish and seawater, then took a long swallow of her coffee. "Mmm," she murmured appreciatively.

Zach acknowledged her presence with a slight incline of his head before he drained his mug. Then he rose.

Maddy suddenly felt desperate to keep him there. She didn't want to sit out here alone with her thoughts. She wanted to talk to Zach. Wanted him to tell her that Sandy was just fine after he'd told her about Tristan. She wanted to hear that Sandy had agreed to go to her mother-in-law's house and leave the two of them here to battle whoever had killed Tristan, if anyone even had. "Don't go," she said, sounding pitiful.

"More coffee," Zach said gruffly, brandishing his mug as he hoisted himself up and headed for the house.

"I mean," she amended, clearing her throat, "come back, will you? Once you get the coffee? I want to—" She paused, trying to decide what to say. "—catch up." *That was lame.*

She half turned and saw him nod. With a sigh, she turned back around and watched the birds chase each other as she sipped her coffee. By the time Zach got back, she'd finished all but the last swallow. Instead of sitting on the bench, he climbed up and sat on the table with his feet on the bench beside her. He had on running shoes and old faded and frayed jeans that fit him in that perfect, comfortable way old jeans did.

Maddy leaned back against the table. "How's Sandy?" she asked.

"Okay." Zach's voice was still gruff. Maddy couldn't help but wonder if he'd slept any better than she had.

"You ended up staying with her all night, didn't you?" she asked. "Because I figured you'd have called me if you needed me to sleep in there. You're a wonderful friend."

He didn't answer.

"Is she going to go to her mother-in-law's? I mean, did she agree to?" she asked.

"See for yourself. She'll be up in a minute. I heard her moving around in her room just now."

"Oh," Maddy said, standing. "I'll start breakfast for her. She'll need to eat." She looked up at him and caught him staring at her. She knew her eyes looked swollen and bloodshot. She squeezed them shut for a second. "I hope my eyes aren't as red as they feel," she said. She took a good look at him. His eyes were red, too.

"I don't think they're as red as mine," he said, his gaze moving to the inside of his mug. "They look fine."

"Do you want some eggs and toast?"

He darted a look at her then back to his mug. "So you can cook now? Seems like it was just yesterday that you couldn't put ice into plastic cups."

She sent him an irritated look. "Sandy has taught me a few things since I've been here. How to make coffee and cook scrambled eggs. I already knew how to use a toaster."

He nodded sagely. "How about sausage or bacon?"

"None of that in the house," she said. "The smell makes her queasy."

"Okay. Eggs and toast it is." Zach stood and hopped down from the picnic table right in front of Maddy. He looked down at her with an odd expression on his face. "Thanks," he said.

Maddy turned to head into the kitchen. "Are you ready to eat now?" she asked over her shoulder. When she turned to look at him, she saw he had his cell phone out.

"Soon as I make a call," he said, then, "Damn. What's wrong with the service around here? I got a signal last night in the nursery."

"I think Tristan put in some kind of booster or something in the house. You may have to make your calls in there."

Maddy got out the eggs and bread from the refrigerator. She wasn't much for breakfast. Coffee sustained her until lunch and sometimes until dinner. But since she'd been here she'd been eating a piece of toast while Sandy ate her eggs. During the past week before they got word of Tristan's death, Sandy had been having less morning sickness and eating more.

Maddy broke and beat together four eggs. She figured Sandy could eat two and Zach could eat two. She decided to toast five pieces of bread. Zach might eat three. With butter and homemade fig jam, that should satisfy him. Shouldn't it?

As she was debating whether to add a fifth egg to the mixture, just in case, Sandy came into the kitchen. She went to the refrigerator and poured herself a glass of purple juice from a carton of tropical fruit punch. It was the only juice that didn't make her sick.

"Morning," Maddy said. "How're you feeling?"

Sandy sat down at the table and drank a few sips. "Okay," she said. "Something smells good."

"That's just butter heating in the pan." *Five eggs*, Maddy decided. "You sound like you feel better. I don't think you've thought anything smelled good since I've been here." She beat the eggs a few more times with her fork then poured them into the hot pan and began moving them around slowly with a spatula as they solidified.

"I'm okay, I guess," Sandy murmured and took another sip of purple juice.

Zach pocketed his phone as he came in, breathing in the smell of eggs and butter. Sandy smiled at him wanly, then lifted the purple liquid to her lips. She was freshly showered and dressed in a white sundress that fell loosely over her baby bump. She looked cool and pretty, if a little pale. "How're you feeling?" he asked her.

"I'm okay—" Sandy started, then she stopped. "No, I'm not! I don't want to leave!" Sandy said, slamming the glass down on the wooden table.

Maddy jumped.

"This is my home. It's— It was Tristan's home. Our friends are here. Our whole life is here. I don't want to go away." She was on the verge of tears, and the eggs and toast were growing cold on the plate in front of her. "Besides, what if—" She stopped, and tears started spilling out of her eyes and down her cheeks.

Zach stared down at his feet. He'd always had trouble being around a woman who was crying, mostly because he had no earthly idea what to do. His instinctive reaction was to fix it, any way he could, but he'd found out from long experience with his mother and several girlfriends that when the tears started, 99 percent of the time, no one could fix it. His usual reaction to a crying woman was to duck out of the room and wait. But he couldn't do that with Sandy.

First of all, he'd held her while she'd cried the night before. It would be rude and insensitive to run away this morning. Second, he was the one who had made her cry, and third, no matter how long it took for her to realize that she had no choice in the matter, he had to stand here and be the bad guy.

He knew what she'd almost said. *What if Tristan comes back?* He'd hoped that their talk last night would make her realize that whether the two strange men were real or not, her vision of Tristan had been a dream. But he supposed it was much too difficult for her to totally believe that yet, especially since Tristan's body hadn't been found.

But no matter how much she cried and protested, Zach was determined to get her away from Bonne Chance. He was not going to let anyone harm Sandy or her baby.

She would go to Baton Rouge with her mother-in-law, no matter how much she objected.

"But I don't want to be here, either," Sandy continued. "Those same people I love and want to live near won't leave me alone for five minutes to try to figure out how I'm going to do this without…Tris—" She sobbed, picked up the glass and slammed it down again. A little purple liquid sloshed out onto the wooden table.

"Sandy, listen to me," Maddy said, sitting down opposite her. "You've got to go. It's for your own safety and for your baby. You said you saw those men at your window. Think about what they could have done if they'd gotten inside."

"I *said*?" she repeated. "I *said* I saw them? What does that mean?" Sandy cried. "You don't believe me?" She looked from Maddy to Zach and back to Maddy. "Are you saying you think I dreamed it? Oh, my God, you think I dreamed the two men." She turned to Zach. "I know you think I dreamed that I saw Tristan and I do understand the things you told me last night. But please at least tell me that you don't think I'm crazy."

"Sandy, of course not," Maddy said. "Of course we don't think you're crazy. But the trouble is, we can't find any evidence that anyone was outside your window. We can't locate footprints in the long grass or find fingerprints anywhere. That certainly doesn't mean that the men weren't there. In fact, it means if they were there, then they're very good at covering their tracks. And *that* means you're not safe here."

"But you're sneaking me out of town. How are you going to make this work? Maddy, you're going to pretend to be me? You won't fool anyone. And you won't be able to keep them all quiet, either."

Zach looked up. "Sandy, don't worry about how we're going to do it. I need you to go to Baton Rouge with Mrs. DuChaud. I've got a twenty-four-hour guard from a private agency to make sure you're safe."

"A guard?" The tears gathering in her eyes began to roll down her cheeks. She swiped them away with the back of her hand. "Does Mrs. DuChaud know about this? She's not going to like having a guard on her house. I don't know why you're insisting that I can't take care of myself. When have you ever known me not to be capable of handling anything that came along?"

"Sandy, listen to me," Zach said. "I *know* you can take care of yourself normally. But you're pregnant and you're shocked and exhausted and grieving. This is not the time for you to be taking up the charge. You need to let Maddy and me worry about who's been sneaking around the house."

But Sandy pushed the chair back from the table and jumped to her feet. She rounded the table in two seconds flat and was in Zach's face. "Listen to me, Zach Winter. I know you think you're such a spectacular undercover agent, sweeping in here and *saving the day*, and you think I should just hop to do what you want me to. Well, do you know what the words *undercover agent* mean to me?"

She took a shaky breath. "They mean an empty casket being lowered into the ground, and crouching beside it, my husband's sad, heartbroken best friend, who's got this false *superhero* mask on whenever he thinks I'm looking at him. I have *always* fought my own battles, Zach. I want to fight this one *so bad*!" She doubled her fists and punched the air. "So bad that I can't even describe it."

He opened his mouth to speak, but Sandy wasn't finished and she talked right over him. "But I can't. As much as you want to keep me safe, I know that I have to keep him safe," she muttered, looking down and cupping her hands around her small bump. "So I have to trust you." She turned toward Maddy. "And you."

Maddy looked surprised. Sandy gave her a quick, sad smile. "Zach told me last night. He told me about his job and yours. I wish you had told me." She turned back to Zach. "I'll go, Zach. Promise me you'll make sure that Tristan didn't—didn't die in vain."

AROUND NOON THAT DAY, Mrs. DuChaud drove out of Bonne Chance and headed home to Baton Rouge. Sandy had agreed to lie down on the backseat with a light blanket over her until they were at least an hour out of Bonne Chance.

At the same time, Maddy packed empty suitcases in her rental car and drove it twenty-three miles to the next town, where she paid in advance for a week's parking in an enclosed garage. Then she waited at a coffee shop for Zach to come and pick her up and sneak her back into Tristan and Sandy's house.

Alone in the house after the two women had gone, Zach took a shower then headed downtown. He had about an hour before he needed to drive to Houma to pick up Maddy and sneak her back into Tristan's house under cover of darkness.

His first stop was at the doctor's office. The sign on the door read James Trahill, MD. Zach opened the door and found himself facing an old wooden desk with a middle-aged, wooden-faced woman sitting behind it.

"May I help you?" she asked without changing expression.

"I'd like to see the doctor," Zach said with exaggerated patience.

The woman glanced up at him over her reading glasses. "Problem?" she asked.

"I just need to talk to him."

"Name?"

"Zachary Winter." He waited. He didn't recognize the woman, but he figured she was about the same age as his mother, or maybe a little older, so she might know his name.

"Winter," she whispered as she picked the letters out laboriously on the keyboard in front of her. She painstakingly went through the dozens of questions needed by Dr. Trahill. By the time she'd finished, Zach felt as though he'd prefer Chinese water torture to her painfully slow typing.

Then she looked up at him with that wooden expression and asked again, "Problem?"

"Extreme anxiety," Zach said through clenched teeth. "Now."

The woman nodded and typed the two words, spelling them out in a whisper as she pecked. "Have a seat," she said.

Zach eyed the door behind her left shoulder. "Is he with someone?" he asked.

"No," she answered, still looking at the keyboard. Then she looked up at him, but she was too late. "No, wait. He's—"

Zach had already sidestepped her desk. He opened the door behind her. There were three doors in the hall. One was open. Zach looked in and saw a man in his forties with a receding hairline reading a chart through large glasses.

"Dr. Trahill?" Zach said.

"What?" The man looked up. "Yes?" He glanced at an appointment calendar then back at Zach. "Do you have an appointment?"

Zach shook his head. "No." He told him his name and whom he worked for and quickly explained what he needed.

"I'm not sure—" Dr. Trahill started.

"Look," Zach snapped, propping his fists on the desk and bending over the doctor. "I can have my superior call you and explain the importance of cooperating with me. It won't take long. A couple of hours, and he'll want you to read and initial a few forms. What I need is very simple. Just some advice. I want to make people think a pregnant woman is sick, sick enough to be in bed and, if possible, it should be dangerous for her to have any visitors, but wouldn't require hospitalization."

Dr. Trahill frowned. "What's this about? It sounds suspicious—"

"Did you hear what I told you? I work for the National Security Agency. The agency and I need you to work with us on this, Doctor. I'm sure you want to help your country, right?"

Trahill's lips compressed as he tapped the tip of a

ballpoint pen on his desk blotter. After a few seconds, his gaze met Zach's. "This is a little thin, but she could have a virus that compromises her immune system."

Zach liked the sound of that. "Compromises her immune system. You mean, she could catch something from her visitors."

The doctor nodded. "Very easily."

"That would be guaranteed to keep people away from her? They'd be afraid of infecting her and hurting the baby?"

Dr. Trahill nodded. "But if she truly were immunocompromised, I would have her transported to the hospital in Houma and placed in isolation, for her safety and her baby's."

Zach drew in a sharp impatient breath. "I get that, Doc. But I can't do this in a hospital in the next town. I need her here, in her own home. Now, my bet is that you can tell your receptionist out there about Sandy DuChaud's compromised immune system, and within less than an hour, the word will be spread all over town. Am I right?"

The look on the doctor's face told Zach that he was on target. The receptionist probably had a network better than Twitter for getting information out to her friends and neighbors.

"I still don't like this," Trahill complained. "What's this all about and what does the NSA have to do with it?"

Zach got in the doctor's face again. "Trust me, Doc. The less you know about this, the safer you and your family and, in fact, the entire town will be. All I can tell you is that this is a matter of *national security*. Do you understand that?"

Trahill nodded nervously.

"And if *that* gets out, Doctor, you will be tried for treason. Do you understand *that*?"

His eyes behind his big glasses grew impossibly wide, but he nodded. His Adam's apple bobbed as he swallowed. "I swear," he whispered, raising his right hand. "I swear, as God is my witness—"

Zach growled and turned on his heel. At the door, he turned back, figuring a little extra insurance wouldn't hurt. "Oh, by the way, we've got all your phones and hers—" he nodded toward the waiting room "—bugged. Not to mention many other phones in town. Remember, the only thing that needs to be talked about in town is that Sandy is sick and she can't have any visitors. Got that, Dr. Trahill? Because the NSA is listening to everything you say."

Zach left, tipping an imaginary hat to the receptionist as he passed her desk. He wondered if his assessment of the doctor as a timid man who was a closet conspiracy theorist was correct. It was a gamble. If he was a conspiracy nut, he'd be eating up all the intrigue and secrecy, savoring all of Zach's warnings until the danger was over and he could act the hero for being part of the secret mission. If he wasn't a nut, well—maybe he was a staunch patriot and would keep quiet anyhow.

Either way, it was done now. Within an hour, the whole town would be talking about *poor Sandy*, who was sick and quarantined in her own home, with her dead husband's best friend taking care of her. Each and every neighbor and friend would be trying to figure out ways to get a glimpse of her or give her a get-well card or just *speak to her for one second, to let her know we're all thinking about her.*

Zach liked the idea the doctor had given him of a reason to keep her quarantined. A compromised immune system. It meant that Sandy would be susceptible to all kinds of infections, as would her baby. It was a serious complication without any visible symptoms. So if anyone did catch a glimpse of Maddy masquerading as Sandy, there would be no clue that she really wasn't ill.

Chapter Seven

By the time Zach picked up Maddy in Houma and drove back to Tristan's house, it was dark. There was no enclosed garage, but Zach pulled into the driveway as close to the patio as he could get, so he could hurry Maddy inside with as little exposure as possible.

"Do you have the hair color and the blouses?" Zach asked her as she got out of the passenger side of the car.

"Yes, Zach. Right here. Just like when you asked me at the coffee shop. I'll color my hair tonight and wear one of these lovely oversize tops tomorrow. Is it okay if I don't wear maternity jeans?"

"What?" he asked, not quite sure what she'd said. Something about jeans. "Sure," he answered absently as he surveyed the front and side yards, making sure there was no one around. Tristan's house was eight miles from town and about a mile from a narrow, fingerlike bayou on the Gulf, at the end of a long, dead-end driveway, and he'd seen no cars out this way, but he still wanted to be 100 percent sure that he wasn't placing Maddy in any unnecessary danger.

He'd thought about standing guard through the night in case the men Sandy had seen at the window came back. His instinct was to take over and do lookout and guard duty himself every night and let Maddy sleep safely inside. But he knew that wasn't practical or smart. They needed to share duties so one of them didn't get too tired to be effective. After all, they were both specially trained undercover agents, capable of performing the same duties.

He didn't want anyone to see Maddy, and he sure didn't want to expose her to danger, but on the other hand, he hadn't slept at all the night before. If he didn't sleep tonight, he'd be worthless by morning.

Just as Maddy unlocked the French doors and went inside, Zach saw a flash of light from the back of the house.

"Maddy!" he cried softly.

She stopped and turned.

"Get into Sandy's bedroom now!" he whispered.

"What's wrong?"

"Saw something. Get in there in case they try to get in!" he commanded, drawing his weapon and pulling a high-powered flashlight from a small strap on his holster. "Shoot if you have to!" he added as she closed the French doors.

Zach moved toward the side edge of the house. He pressed his back against the wall and sidled along it until he reached the back corner. By then he could hear someone—or something—sneaking through the overgrown lawn. Carefully, he rolled sideways enough that he could get a glimpse around the corner.

A dark shadow, barely darker than the tangled jungle of vines and trees, was moving through the grass toward the swamp in a half crouch that left the upper third of its body exposed. The sky was cloudy enough to obscure the moon and a fine mist hung in the air. Still, Zach could tell that the shadow was human, but all he could see was a silhouette, so he couldn't tell if the person was a man or woman or if they were carrying a weapon.

All at once, Maddy was behind him. How he knew it was her, he wasn't sure, but when he half turned, there she was. "What is it?" he whispered.

"Someone's been in Sandy's room. It's a mess."

Zach cursed under his breath just as he heard more rustling movement out in front of him. "Get back inside," he commanded Maddy.

"Not on your life," she whispered harshly. "I'm sticking with you. You have no idea how many of them are out there."

"Damn it, Maddy—" he started, but a glint of light stopped him. "Did you see that?" he whispered.

"That flash of light? Was it a gun?"

"Maybe." He raised his weapon and aimed in that direction. "I'm a law enforcement agent and I'm armed! Stop! Stop right now or I'll shoot."

He heard the rustle of leaves and branches and the crunch of twigs and shells as the person picked up speed, headed toward the water. "Stop now! Stop or I'll shoot!" he cried, but the person kept running.

So he aimed carefully and shot a round that landed about three feet in front of the running shadow.

The person jumped and made a startled sound, then froze in place. Zach was ready. He aimed his flashlight directly at the head and turned it on. The intense beam lit a dark, narrow face with eyes that gleamed like small fires. Another startled sound, this one a deep grunt, echoed through the darkness. It sounded like a man.

"Stop! Right now!" Zach yelled, but the face disappeared from the flashlight's beam and the sound of feet and legs moving through underbrush got louder. "You out there. I *will* shoot again. Stop!"

Then Zach saw a flash and heard a blast. He grabbed Maddy and threw her and himself to the ground, all in one split second. He landed right on top of her a fraction of a second after he heard her almost silent *"Oof."*

The crunch of leaves and twigs hit his ears as the man sprinted through the tangled canopy of cypress and mangrove trees and oleander bushes that made up the overgrown swampland in south Louisiana.

Zach got his legs under him and started to rise, freeing his gun hand to take a shot if necessary, but his ears were buzzing and something warm tickled his right ear. Keeping his gun hand ready, he reached with his left hand to brush at his ear. His fingers came away wet and sticky. *Son of a bitch.* He'd been shot.

"Zach! You're bleeding."

Maddy's wide blue eyes stared up at him in horror. She reached up to touch his ear, but he avoided her hand and rolled off her. He'd instinctively held himself above her on his elbows and knees, but even so, the position was suggestive and uncomfortable. For him, it had gotten extremely uncomfortable, and he hadn't even been aware of his position or the sensations that had been aroused until he'd already rolled off her.

It showed that there were certain responses of the body that didn't require a conscious decision by the brain. Because if he'd had a chance to make a conscious decision, he'd have vetoed that particular position before he'd gotten himself into it.

Even as those thoughts flitted through his brain, he'd rolled up to his knees and was searching the dark perimeter of the yard for any indication of the man—or men—who'd broken into the house and shot at them.

Maddy flipped over onto her stomach and scooted around him, placing herself behind him again. He nodded. She'd done the right thing. She was armed, but he was tacitly in charge, and she had taken the secondary position without question or argument.

MADDY GRIPPED HER SIG as if it was her only lifeline. Seeing Zach bleeding had shaken her. The wound was just above his temple, and blood was spilling down the side of his face and trickling into his ear. She squeezed the handle of the gun more tightly, hoping her death grip would stop her hands from shaking. It helped a little.

She knew he wasn't badly hurt or he wouldn't be able to move as smoothly and freely as he did. But she also knew from first and second aid, that wounds, particularly head wounds, could exhibit delayed reactions. And she was sure he wouldn't allow her to look at his injury until the threat was gone.

So she stayed where she was and suppressed the urge to wipe the blood off his temple. He inched forward, holding his weapon pointed at the last place where he'd heard a sound. His left hand supported his right and he held the high-powered flashlight in the supporting hand, ready to flip on at a split second's notice.

He'd grown perfectly still and had angled his head to listen. She tuned her instincts as close to his as she possibly could. She drew herself up and tensed her muscles, ready for anything. Her blood burned and surged in her veins and her hyperfocused brain intensified and slowed every sound, every separate movement, as if the rest of the world was moving in super slow motion, and she and Zach were the only ones still in normal time.

To her, it sounded as if the person or people were running away. The sounds were fading. She glanced at Zach again. He angled his head so slightly she could have missed it, but she didn't. A thrill erupted deep inside her. He was thinking the same thing. It was a small thing, but she felt their connection.

They were in perfect sync, so attuned to each other that they might be one person. It was an exciting and extraordinarily intimate feeling. Yet nothing about it, not even the thrill that had arrowed through her, was distracting. In fact, it was a powerful and energizing sensation.

Zach turned his head and met her gaze. For an instant, they stood perfectly still. Then, as if they had a private, telepathic code, the two of them relaxed at the same time.

"Gone," Zach whispered.

Maddy took a step backward and Zach did the same. They moved back to the patio doors and slipped inside, still in sync, their shoulders barely touching. As soon as they were inside, they stood shoulder to shoulder, listening, watching, feeling. The house was empty; Maddy felt rather than heard or saw Zach nod.

"Clear," Zach said, lowering his weapon.

"Clear," Maddy agreed as she relaxed her right hand. It cramped and ached, she'd been holding the gun so tightly.

Still under the influence of their connection, Maddy turned toward him just as he turned toward her. Her eyes had adapted to the dark, and the lights from the oil platforms out on the water, combined with the lights from the town of Bonne Chance north of them, lent enough of a pale glow that she could make out Zach's form, if not his features, in front of her.

She took a deep, shaky breath.

"What was that?" Zach asked in a whisper.

"The intruders?" Maddy said, knowing full well they weren't what he was talking about, but here in the aftermath of their coordinated effort to protect the house and each other, she was shy about saying anything. If Zach let it drop, then she would, too.

"No," he said, shaking his head. "You know what I'm talking about."

"Yes," she whispered.

He took a step toward her, which put them toe to toe. His eyes glimmered with the pale lights from the south and the north. He was staring at her so intently that another thrill, a different kind of thrill, surged through her and settled deep, deep inside her.

He brought his hand up to touch her cheek, and the cold, jellylike texture of congealing blood from his fingers startled her until she remembered that he'd been shot.

"I need to clean that," she said, "and make certain you're okay. I'm sure there's some antiseptic around here somewhere," she said, but he pressed his thumb against her lips, stopping her words. "Not yet," he said softly, handing her a handkerchief from his pocket. "Just wipe it clean. It's only a graze. It's stopped bleeding already."

As she brushed the handkerchief across his skin, he kissed her. At first, his mouth was soft, his kiss slow and tentative. Maddy loved the feel of his mouth, which could look so hard, soft against her lips. But she wondered if she'd been wrong about him, about his need to be in charge. Was he really going to kiss her as if she were some fragile Southern belle? If so, she was not going to be happy.

He lifted his head to look into her eyes, his dancing with emerald green light, then he kissed her again, and this time there was nothing slow or soft about it. His mouth was hard, as she'd expected it to be. Hard and sensual on hers, demanding. He tasted her lips and she parted them so he could delve inside, deepening the kiss, until she was breathless.

The flame that had ignited in her the first moment she'd seen him flared. She gave him back his kisses, filled with as much yearning, as much need, as he'd shown her.

Then he changed the game again. Now he nibbled softly on her lips, her cheeks, the lobes of her ears, wispy tender nibbles that made her crazy with the need for more. Just when she thought she couldn't stand another ticklish brush of his lips against her nose and cheek, he grabbed her jaw between his fingers and thumb and ravished her mouth with hot, hard kisses that thrust and retreated, thrust and retreated, like the act of sex.

She gave as good as she got, kissing him back, grazing his tongue and lips with her teeth, darting her tongue in and out until his breaths rasped harshly in his throat.

"What is this?" he asked in a labored whisper.

Maddy drew back enough to free her mouth to speak. She didn't have to ask him what he was talking about, because she knew. They were still in sync. Still reacting in perfect tune.

"I don't know," she murmured. "Something happened out there. Something clicked. We were perfect. Connected somehow, so that together, we were better than the two of us alone. We were—" she laughed shyly "—like a supersoldier."

"I still feel it," he said, pulling her close and holding her tightly, pressing his lips against her hair.

"I know. Me, too." She lifted her head and kissed

him again. "It's like we know each other's moves. Almost know each other's thoughts."

Zach's chest rumbled with a low laugh. "Do you know what I'm thinking right now?" he asked.

"Yes, I do," she said with a soft smile. "And I think it's a wonderful idea." As soon as she said it, she felt him shut down, as if he'd flipped a switch.

"I'm not so sure."

Maddy winced. "What?"

"There were intruders in the house. We need to see what they took."

"Now?" she said. "Really? They're gone. Don't break the spell. I'm so ready for you my legs are weak. Please don't stop now." She kissed him again and again, then helped him remove his shirt and began nipping at his lips, his chin, then down to his collarbone and the firm planes of his pecs and breastbone. Then she turned to his nipples, those tiny erect nubs that made her mouth water just looking at them.

When she licked one of them, Zach groaned and grabbed her upper arms, trying to push her away.

"Hey," she said, trying to keep it light. "Don't push me away. These are two of my favorite things. And they're delicious." She grazed her teeth along the sensitized tip of the nipple. He arched and thrust his arousal against her.

"Oh, yes," she gasped. "That's it."

He thrust again, the hard length of him rubbing insistently against her.

"Zach, please," she begged. "Don't stop."

"Not sure I can now," he muttered, pressing even harder.

Maddy reached around him and caught his buttocks

and pulled him to her. He rocked back and forth, his arousal rubbing against her, driving her crazy.

"Zach!" she cried, feeling the exquisite ache that foretold orgasm. "Please, too much. Wait."

But he didn't wait. He pulled her close and continued to rock against her rhythmically until her body succumbed to his exquisite pressure. Her world exploded in a climax that caused spots before her eyes. She cried out and collapsed against him, until his arms embracing her were the only things keeping her from falling.

"Oh," she exhaled. "Oh."

He pressed his cheek against hers and nibbled on her earlobe.

"Are you—" she started, but a shake of his head stopped her.

"Don't worry about me," he said. "That was for you."

At last, she felt as though she could put weight on her legs without them collapsing. She stood shakily, but she didn't pull away from his kisses and caresses. "Do you still think this is not a good idea?" she asked him, touching his nose with the tip of her finger.

He met her gaze and nodded. "Actually…"

She covered his mouth with hers. "Don't say it," she mumbled with her lips pressed against his, then she kissed him earnestly, took his hand and led him into the nursery. She pushed him down onto the couch and climbed on top of him. When she started unzipping his pants, he groaned, but he didn't stop her. Within seconds, their clothes were gone and she was showering his face, neck and pecs with kisses.

When he lifted her above him and pushed into her, she nearly cried in exquisite pleasure. But just as she feared a tear was going to escape her eye, he turned them both over together and began to make love to her until she reached heights of pleasure she'd never experienced before. That night she came more times than she ever had in her life.

As their passion waned and they settled into the afterglow, Maddy discovered that she felt even more like crying than she had earlier. She'd never liked crying. It was a waste of time and made her nose and eyes red. So she held her breath and refused to let even one tear fall.

She didn't know what she would say if Zach asked her what was wrong. She didn't want to tell him that making love with him was the sweetest thing she'd ever known, and she was sure it was because of the connection they'd discovered.

What if he had no idea what she was talking about? What if the only time he felt their connection was when they were facing danger. What if for him, sex with her was a pastime, a fill-in because there were no elegant supermodel types in Bonne Chance? She lay there, afraid he'd notice her tears, but when several minutes passed and he didn't say anything, she lifted her head and saw that he'd fallen asleep.

Chapter Eight

Maddy woke early the next morning. She was lying close—very close—to Zach. Practically on top of him, in fact. His long, leanly muscled body was pressed against the front of her, and the back of the sofa was tight against her back. She tried to suppress a giggle. She was caught between the devil and the deep blue sofa. *Ha-ha-ha.*

Zach shifted and Maddy closed her eyes as aftershocks of the multiple orgasms he'd given her rippled through her body. His runner's muscles, normally rock hard, were still firm, but at the same time supple and loose. But even as she noticed, he tensed and they went rock hard again. And that wasn't all that was rock hard.

But Maddy's bravado from the night before had turned to shyness in the light of day. With a push, she sprang up and away from him. Or at least she tried to. Just as she pushed, his arm tightened around her.

"Whoa! Ow!" His eyes popped open and a pained expression contorted his face. "Hey!"

"Sorry," she said as she wriggled away and scrambled over to the far arm of the sofa, relieved to see that at some point during the night she'd managed to put her pajamas on. He drew in a harsh breath through his teeth. "Yeah," he said. "Watch your knees. You could really hurt someone."

"Sorry," she said again. "I was a little surprised when I woke up there." She waved her hand toward him and the sofa.

"Are you saying you don't remember last night?"

"I remember last night," she said, her face beginning to flush. "What I don't remember is going to sleep, and I certainly don't remember putting my pajamas on."

"You remember taking them off?" he asked, his mouth quirked in a half smile.

She chuckled. "I remember somebody did."

"I remember lying next to you afterward. You snuggled right into my side. Next thing I know, it's light out and you're kicking me in the—"

"Okay," she said quickly, interrupting him. "Got it." She stood and stretched, yawning. "Oh, I'm stiff."

Zach grunted as he pushed himself up off the sofa. "Yeah," he said wryly. "Me, too."

Maddy's face heated up again, so she hurried out of the room and across the hall into the master bedroom. A half hour later, when she emerged from Sandy's bedroom, having showered in the master bath, she nearly bumped into Zach, who had just stepped out of the hall bath, a towel precariously tied at his waist and his hair wet and spiky. He looked incredibly handsome, with his golden skin shining with water droplets. His eyes were brilliant green and highlighted by his long, wet lashes.

He smiled. "Sorry," he said. "I thought I'd beat you out of the shower by at least a half hour."

"I do a pretty fast shower," she said, pulling her terry-cloth robe more tightly around her. She scooted around him and into the guest bedroom.

"Hey," Zach called after her.

She turned to look at him and regretted it. The towel had slipped and appeared ready to fall any second. She focused on the corner of the ceiling. "What is it?"

"As soon as we have breakfast, I want to walk down to the water and take a look around. It's rained a good bit, but I'm hoping I can find evidence that someone has used the DuChauds' old boat dock recently. Maybe I can pick up some tracks or shoe prints. If nothing else, I can talk to one or two of the old fishermen who still go down there to fish."

"I'll go with you," she said.

"No, you won't. You're supposed to be pregnant and in bed, under quarantine. You're not leaving the house."

She pressed her lips together and shot him a look that would have worked better if she'd had real lasers behind it. "You really want me lying around in bed? That's your plan? I thought it was just a cover story for the doctor to tell the folks in town. I'm not going to stay in bed."

"How about a compromise? You don't have to stay in bed, just in the bedroom and straighten up the mess the intruders left. Maybe you can figure out what they were looking for."

She rolled her eyes. "I guess I walked into that one, didn't I? What about the sheriff? We didn't call last night. Should I call now to report the B and E?"

Zach shot her a look. "What do you think?" he said.

She evaluated his expression. "So I'm thinking no. I'll straighten everything up and see if I can find anything there. Don't worry about me. I don't mind cleaning up."

"Listen to me," he continued. "Here's something else you can do. I want you to contact the captain of the oil rig again and tell him you're really being pressured to make that *spot inspection*. Was that what you called it?"

Maddy held the robe tight at her neck and wished that Zach would put a hand on the towel that was doing a really poor job of staying up. She was sure it had slipped another inch. She averted her gaze.

"That's a complete waste of time," she said to the wall. "He's not going to let an inspector on his rig now. And he's got the perfect excuse. All he has to say is that he's in the middle of an investigation into the death of one of his employees and he's home free. Nobody would complain and nobody will force him to let me on there."

"We could sneak aboard, couldn't we?"

Maddy forgot that she wasn't supposed to be looking at him. She fixed him with a stare. "Sneak aboard? No. There are security cameras everywhere, and the communications officer and the security chief monitor them. They'd probably shoot us first and ask questions later."

Zach shrugged and the towel began to slip. He caught it and gave her a sheepish grin. "Talk to you in a minute," he said.

IT WAS AFTER NOON before Zach could get in touch with Dr. Trahill. After finally reaching him at home during Sunday dinner after church, he and Trahill met in the doctor's office. Zach wanted to look him in the eye and assure himself that Trahill still understood the importance of their secret plan to national security and the consequence of revealing it to anyone.

Then he checked in with the medical examiner to see if he had any more information regarding Tristan's remains.

Dr. Bookman told Zach that the Coast Guard was calling off the search as of that morning. "But I do have stomach contents of two sharks that I'm sending off for DNA matching."

Zach swallowed hard, feeling a little queasy at the ME's words. "Will you call Mrs. DuChaud and let her know about the search?" he asked. "I'd really appreciate it." The ME agreed.

So it was noon by the time Zach got down to the small dock that Tristan's grandfather had built to tie up his fishing boat and his pirogue. As Zach approached the dock, the ground got muddier. At least he'd had the foresight to grab Tristan's rubber knee-high boots and binoculars as he'd left the house. The gumbo mud was already sucking at the boots. Wet from the rain, it was as greedy as quicksand.

Taking what appeared to be the driest path, Zach stepped onto the first creaky boards of the dock. He stood there for a short while, gazing out over the Gulf, orienting himself not only in space but also in time. It had been thirteen years since he'd stood here with Tristan and fantasized about setting out to sea to become pirates or privateers or stowaways on a ship headed for a faraway land.

A deep sadness, mixed with a poignant sense of loss, enveloped him as he looked out on the same waters, the same sky and maybe even the same trees as they'd gazed at all those years ago.

"Ah, Tristan," he muttered. "You were always such a freaking hero. Why'd you have to go and get killed for? I always thought I'd come back, man." He shook his head. "I'm sorry, Tris. I'm sorry I wasn't here to help you."

After a long time, Zach rubbed his eyes and surveyed the water that was brown near the shore but began to reflect the blue of the sky that stretched out to meet it at a distant horizon he couldn't even distinguish. To him it looked as if the whole round world was spread out before him. A beautiful, treacherous world that could steal friends, enemies and loved ones as easily as it could yield up nourishing food to a hungry world.

Then, as he shaded his eyes from the sun, he thought he saw a tiny dark dot way out on the water. He used the binoculars to try to see it closer. When he finally zeroed in on the dot, he saw that it was a cruise ship, either coming into or leaving the Port of New Orleans.

For a moment, he'd thought it might be the *Pleiades Seagull*. He'd learned it was one of the closest rigs, probably no more than twenty to twenty-five miles out from shore. Of course, the horizon didn't stretch that far.

Maddy had told him that the *Seagull* was located on top of a deep canyon on the floor of the Gulf, much deeper than one might expect so close to shore.

A pang of something pricked him in the chest. He wasn't sure what the feeling was. Excitement, anxiety or more grief. He lowered the binoculars and pressed his knuckles into the middle of his chest, where the ache had settled.

"Hey, you!" a voice called out. "Whacha doing here, you?"

Zach whirled. For an instant his mind made the voice Tristan's. He'd often affected the strong Cajun accent of his grandfather and father.

"Hold on!" the man shouted. "You stay, you!"

Zach froze because the man he saw standing at the edge of the cypress swamp was holding a big shotgun. A 12 gauge. It was an old gun that cocked by hand. As he watched, not breathing, the man cocked the right barrel, then the left, and aimed them both right at him.

Something familiar about the man played at the edge of Zach's mind as he held his hands up, palms out. He'd probably met him before, back when he and Tristan explored the overgrown paths and hiding places in the swamp. But he couldn't be sure. It had been a long time, and to his recollection, Woodrow, or Boudreau or whatever his name was, had been old back then.

"Boudreau?" he said, his tongue sliding over the *B* in a way that could have been interpreted as either name. "Is that you?"

The man's chin lifted and he eyed Zach with eyes as black and fiery as coals on fire. "Who that?" he said.

"I'm Zach Winter. I was a friend of Tristan's." Zach didn't move, but he nodded in the direction of Tristan's house.

The man's eyes seemed to glow with more fire. "Tristán?" He used the French pronunciation with the accent on the second syllable. "Who you to know young Tristán? He ain't here no more, him. You know what happen to Tristán, you? Or you just here to try an' trick me?"

Zach noticed that the old man's mouth only moved on one side when he talked, and now he also noticed that his left eye was a little more squinty than the right. Also that his left hand, which was holding the gun by the stock, was trembling. Had he had a stroke? He decided he didn't want to give the man any information that he didn't already have, so he answered his questions with a question.

Shaking his head, he said, "I'm not here to trick you. Don't you know what happened?"

Boudreau stared at Zach for a long time. It was beginning to feel uncomfortably long by the time he spoke. "You the *chef menteur*, you. The chief liar round these parts. I might be a little tetch'd in the head, but I ain't that bad. I know *le diable* when I meet him." He held up a hand to cover his eyes. "I can't look at you, no. Can't look at the devil."

"Boudreau, I'm not the devil. I'm Tristan's friend, from school," Zach said.

"You no friend of Tristán, you. No sirree. You a devil." He lifted the shotgun, his left hand trembling more.

"Okay, okay, Boudreau—" Zach started.

"Don't call me that, you hear?" the old man said. "You call me M'sieu Boudreau, you."

"Monsieur Boudreau, have you seen any folks back in here that shouldn't be here? Maybe coming from one of the oil rigs or from another town?"

"Oil rigs? Is that where you from? You *are* the devil, then. They need to be burned, those nasty things. They make the water poison." Boudreau nodded. He kept nodding until Zach thought maybe he'd drifted off to sleep with his eyes open. The shotgun's barrel drooped a little, a little more and a little more.

Zach took a tentative step toward his car.

Boudreau's head stopped nodding and the barrel of the gun raised. "Whoa there, you," he said. "I ain't exactly decided what to do with you."

"Monsieur Boudreau," Zach said respectfully. "I wondered if you'd seen anybody around here who wasn't supposed to be here. Anybody who disturbed you or woke you at night or anything."

For an instant Boudreau's eyes lost their fire and went opaque. "Nah sirree," he said. "There been some sneaky bastards in the woods, but they don't come near me, them. Nah sirree. I guarantee they know better than that. Yeah." The fire reignited. "Now, you, you go on and get out of here. You got no business on DuChaud land, you. I don't know you. Nobody know you. You don't look like nobody I ever knew."

The old Cajun stood staunchly, holding the gun in his good right hand and his trembling left hand, and waited. When Zach didn't move immediately, Boudreau gestured with the barrel of the gun.

"Monsieur?" Zach tried one more time.

"Go on, you. Go on. Leave us alone down here. Folks gotta heal. Don't need nobody like you coming in and upsetting 'em."

Zach walked to his car, acutely aware of the shotgun pointed at his back.

ON HIS WAY back to the house, Zach called the priest. "Duff?"

"Yes?" Duff said in a subtly disapproving voice. "Who is this? Zach? Is that you?"

"Yeah," Zach said. "I mean, yes, Father Michael."

"What can I do for you?"

"Is old Boudreau still around? The old man who used to live on Tristan's property way back when we were kids?"

There was a pause. "Actually, I don't know. I don't think I've heard anybody mention Boudreau in years. I'm not sure anybody's seen him around in all that time. How old would he be now?"

"I don't know," Zach said. "Tristan and I thought he was older than dirt back when we were about ten or eleven. But now that I think about it, he might not have been more than sixty or so. What do you think? When was the last time you saw him?"

"It's been a long, long time. Why?"

"I think it was Boudreau who ran me off Tristan's boat dock just a few minutes ago. He wouldn't tell me his name, but he had an old 12-gauge shotgun like I remember he used to carry. No dog, but then that old bluetick hound that followed him around was probably eight or nine years old back then."

"Boudreau ran you off Tristan's property? I declare I'd have said he was dead. What do you think he's been living on all this time? He never, and I mean seriously *never*, comes to town. If he ever gets coffee or sugar or even beans, I don't know where he gets 'em."

Zach pulled into the driveway and parked near the French doors. "I remember Tristan was always fascinated with him. He used to tell me that Boudreau ate dandelion and chicory greens and ground up the chicory root and roasted it to make coffee. Said he ate possum and gator and rabbit. And sometimes he might kill a wild pig. Tristan said he could smell it roasting and he'd go over there with potatoes and carrots and onions and eat with him."

"Over where?" Duff asked.

"I'm not sure. I followed Tristan into the swamp to Boudreau's stick house a few times, but I couldn't have gotten there by myself back then, much less now. Okay, well, thanks. I guess he's just old and kind of crazy now. I asked him a few questions, but he didn't make much sense."

"Well, I do recall him having a stroke a few years ago. Tristan took him to the doctor but he wouldn't go to the hospital. Zach, what are you doing snooping around here?"

"Just helping Sandy out. I'm helping her with Tristan's papers."

Duff was silent and Zach knew he didn't believe him. He took a breath to try and convince him that what he was telling him was true, but Duff spoke first.

"Don't get involved in this, whatever it is, Zach. Take some advice from someone who knows. All it'll do is engulf your every waking and sleeping thought."

Zach knew Duff wasn't talking about Tristan's death. He was talking about Fox Moncour's death years ago. "Don't worry, Duff. I'm fine. I can handle it."

Zach said goodbye and hung up, thinking about what Duff had said about Boudreau. Maybe Boudreau had suffered a stroke, but his eyes burned like fiery coals and his voice had been clear. Zach was still half-convinced that the Cajun was crazy. He was more than half-convinced that if Boudreau saw him again, he'd shoot him with that 12 gauge.

"Maddy?" he called out when he entered the house after taking off the rubber boots outside the door. "Is the alarm on?"

Maddy came out of Sandy's bedroom with her newly colored hair damp and waving around her face. She blew a strand out of her eye. "No. I didn't turn it on. It's been deathly quiet. I was wishing for an MP3 player or a TV."

"They don't have a TV?" Zach asked.

"Not in the bedroom."

"Oh. Find anything?"

"You mean, did I find anything *missing*? No. But then, it's kind of hard to find something missing. I did find a partial footprint right under the window."

"Inside the room? I looked. I didn't see a footprint."

Maddy smiled. "No, you didn't because it was mostly water with just a faint bit of mud to color it. It was almost totally dry. I went over the floor with a flashlight, looking for something like that. Of course, I couldn't pick it up because I don't have the equipment. It might have come from the kind of boots the guys wear on the platform, but even if we were able to make a plaster cast or even just lift the print onto some sticky paper, we're talking about over four hundred men. Not to mention the men in town—which would be what?—twice or three times that many or more."

Zach grimaced. "No fingerprints, either?"

"Again, I don't have the equipment. I've heard of using soot from a candle, a makeup brush and cellophane tape, but I've never tried it."

"Try it. I'm not ready to let the sheriff know anything about us smuggling Sandy out of town, but you could get Homeland Security to run the print, couldn't you? If your method works, we can photograph it and send it to your lab."

"We use the FBI, but yes. We can do that. I'll talk to my handler."

Chapter Nine

"Okay, then," Maddy said. "Um, thanks, Brock." She pressed the off key on her phone with a finger that felt numb. All her fingers felt numb. She sat on the bed, trying to go over in her head what Brock had just told her. But her brain felt as numb as her fingers. He'd warned her, but she hadn't really believed him, she supposed.

"Maddy?"

Zach's voice floated across the hall from the nursery, where he'd set up Sandy's laptop. He'd spent all morning trying to find something—anything—that would give them a clue about what had gotten Tristan killed and put Sandy's life in danger.

"Yeah?" she answered Zach without even trying to raise her voice enough that he could actually hear her.

"Maddy!" She heard chair legs scraping on the hardwood floors and, sure enough, within a second, there he was at the door. Unconsciously, she smiled when she saw him. It was such a pleasure just to look at him, to let her eyes rest on his handsome face or allow her gaze to travel over his lean masculine body.

"Come here for a minute, will you? I want to show you something."

She nodded. "Sure."

"Maddy?"

She looked up. "Mmm?"

"What's wrong?"

"What?" she asked. She hadn't really heard what he'd said. She was still a little stunned by what Brock had told her.

"You're still sitting there. Come look at Sandy's laptop."

She got up and followed him into the nursery. Her gaze went immediately to the shiny blue mobile Sandy had bought a couple of weeks ago to hang over the crib. She'd gotten it on the day the doctor had told her that although it was early, he was pretty confident that she was having a boy, based on what he'd seen on the ultrasound.

"Take a look at this. Does it mean anything to you?" Zach asked.

"What am I looking at?" she asked.

"This file name. It's a shortcut for an audio file."

"That one? Named SD? Have you listened to it?"

Zach shook his head. "The file's not on the computer. Just the shortcut. It was opened from removable media, like a flash drive."

"Is there a backup or a sampling somewhere on the hard drive or in memory?" Maddy asked.

"Not that I can find." Zach hit the arm of the computer chair with his fist. "Damn it."

"It's probably around here somewhere."

"I don't know," he said. "There are a million places Tristan could have hidden it. Anywhere in the house. In his car or Sandy's car. Somewhere in town. Hell, he could have hidden it somewhere on the rig."

"Do you think that's what the guys who broke in were looking for?"

"I don't know about that, either. Do they *know* that he recorded something? And even if they know that, do they know he put it on a flash drive? Or did somebody order them to search the house, just in case?"

Maddy sighed. "For that matter, how do we know the file is even Tristan's? SD probably stands for Sandy DuChaud. What if Sandy was making a recording of songs to play for the baby? Or recording herself doing karaoke? Or recording a daily journal for Tristan while he was offshore?"

Zach stood, sending the computer chair rolling back to slam against the side of the crib. "You're right. We don't even know it's Tristan's. Hell, we don't know anything."

Maddy stood, too. "I know you're frustrated. I am, as well. I wish I knew something, but Sandy didn't mention anything about recording songs or a journal or anything to me. She never said anything to Tristan on the phone, either, if that's any consolation. So the flash drive is probably Tristan's."

"A lot of good that does us, since we have no clue where he might have hidden it. I made coffee if you want some." He stalked out.

Maddy wished she didn't have to tell him what Brock had told her, but she did, so she might as well get it over with. She followed him into the kitchen, where he was pouring a mug of coffee. She got some, too, with her usual three teaspoonfuls of sugar. She sat down at the kitchen table opposite him.

"Zach," she said once he'd had a couple of swallows. "I talked to my handler just a few minutes ago."

His gaze, which had been on the cup in his hand, met hers. "Yeah? Will he run the fingerprints for us?"

She took a sip of sweet, hot coffee. "I didn't get a chance to ask him. Zach, I'm being pulled off this case." Her voice cracked.

Zach's jaw worked, but that was the only sign that what she'd said had even penetrated his consciousness. He took another swallow of coffee, then stood and tossed the rest into the sink and set the mug down on the counter. "Are they replacing you?" he asked flatly, as if all that mattered to him was that they send someone here to help him.

"Brock didn't say anything about that. All he said was that the director had decided that there was no more need for my services here." She took a breath. "I'm thinking no. They're not replacing me."

Zach went to the French doors and looked out, then looked at his watch. "I'm going to walk back down to the dock. I didn't get to look at everything earlier. I ran into an elderly Cajun man who's lived in the swamp near Tristan's house probably all his life." He reached for the doorknob.

"Zach, wait," she said. "I wanted to tell you that I'm not leaving. I'm taking vacation days, too, so I can stay here. I may not officially be on the case, but I can still help."

He turned around and looked at her, frowning. "What? Why?"

The question surprised her. "Why? Because I want to stay here. I want to help figure out what happened to Tristan."

"No."

The single word sparked her anger. She stood and walked around the table and stuck her forefinger into the middle of his chest. "I am Sandy's guest. You can't tell me no."

"I just did," he said calmly.

"You may have tried to, but you didn't, because you *can't*. I don't have to listen to you. I'm staying right here. Tristan's death is on my hands and I'm not walking away—"

Zach grabbed her wrist. "His death was not your fault. If it's anybody's fault, it's Homeland Security's for not getting him off that oil rig in time. You did your job and it sounds like you did it well. So stop blaming yourself and go home to New Orleans, where you're not in danger. I'll take care of this. It's not your problem."

"The hell it's not. You came barreling in here, bossing me around and getting in my way and making me—" She stopped. She couldn't say everything she wanted to say. She couldn't tell him how much she'd come to depend on him being there during the past three days. Or how safe she felt with him here.

"And making you what, Madeleine Tierney? And what? Getting in your way and what?"

She shook her head. "Nothing."

"Nothing?" he mocked. "Nothing?" He stepped closer and looked down at her. "Are you sure you weren't going to say something else? Like this?" He put his hand on her cheek, with his thumb beneath her chin, and lifted it, then bent his head and kissed her, gently at first, then harder and deeper. His fingers slid from her cheek around to the nape of her neck, and he held her there, kissing her until they were both breathless. Then he kissed her some more. He used his tongue like a weapon, thrusting and parrying and thrusting again until she was light-headed with excitement.

Zach wished he hadn't started this because he was pretty sure that nothing could stop him now, short of Maddy shooting him or at least coldcocking him. He loved to kiss her. So much that he thought he could spend the rest of his life doing that. Her beautiful turned-down mouth was the most sensual and delicious mouth he'd ever kissed. He pulled back for a moment to look at her and trace the shape of her lips with a finger. Then he bent and kissed her again.

She moaned deep in her throat, and he felt the low, sexy vibration all the way through him, down to his groin. He almost smiled. He liked keeping her off guard, keeping her enthralled, while holding himself in control until he could no longer stand it. He liked watching her as she became more and more turned on by him until she finally gave in to the pleasure he gave her.

He wanted to be the one who mastered the situation, the dominant one. He wanted to kiss her senseless, knock her off her feet, make her world tilt. From the moment he'd realized that he wanted her, he'd longed to give her all the romantic clichés. Every one of them, from *opposites attract* to *happily-ever-after*, because he was sure that Madeleine Tierney didn't deal in clichés very often. She blazed her own trail and was and would always be the first one to take it.

She was an odd mix of fearlessness and vulnerability, and he had the feeling that he would never figure her out completely, not in fifty years or five hundred. He knew, though, that he'd be happy to spend all that time trying.

His own thoughts were turning him on to such an extent that he was having trouble controlling himself. Just as he was about to slow things down, Maddy turned the tables and took the aggressive role. She took his mouth in a passionate kiss that was as deep and intimate as any he had ever given or received. He pulled her to him, molding her body to his, amazed, just as he was the last time, at how well they fit together.

He was dying to rip his mouth away from hers and taste her cheek, her ear, her neck and that sexy little bump on her shoulder, the space between her breasts and the soft, firm globes themselves. But he knew he had to stop at least for a moment to get his breath, so he wouldn't embarrass himself.

When he pulled away, Maddy moaned again and crumpled handfuls of his shirt in her fists. "Don't stop," she said on a gasp. "What are you doing? Don't stop now."

But he held her there as he did his best to regain his breath. She was panting, too, her breath sawing in and out, in and out. "Ah," she said, frustrated, then looked up at him, pushing her hair out of her eyes.

He wrapped his arms around her and lifted her and set her on the kitchen table. Then he stepped between her legs and ran his palms up her thighs, across the rough material of her jeans. She wrapped her arms around his waist and pulled him closer, arching her back against his lower belly.

He bent and let his tongue trail down her neck to her collarbone and farther, tasting her between her breasts, one of the places he'd been dying to taste ever since he'd seen her in that little blue pajama top.

Spreading his hands, he wrapped his fingers around her ribs and placed his thumbs beneath her breasts, where he caressed the underside of them until she was panting. Then he pushed her shirt up and saw that she didn't have on a bra. With a soft gasp he lowered his head. His tongue and teeth found the nipple of her right breast beneath the thin cotton of the shirt. It sprang to erectness as he licked it and grazed it with his teeth.

"Oh," Maddy said. "Oh, please. Zach!"

He pulled back and blew on the nipple, feeling a thrill arrow through him when the tiny nub tightened and extended even more. Then he moved to the other breast and did the same. He'd known this was going to happen. He was on the edge. If he didn't slow down, at least long enough to get her jeans off, he was definitely going to embarrass himself in a big way.

He reached for the button on her jeans and, following his lead, she reached for the zipper and button on his pants.

Something banged against the door. Zach sprang away, whirled and drew his gun within a fraction of a second.

"What was that?" Maddy said.

Zach gulped in air as he scanned the patio through the paned windows. "I don't know," he said. "I don't see anything. Relaxing minutely, he opened the door and looked out, leading with his weapon. Then he saw it, on the concrete patio floor.

"Oh, no," he said. "A bird flew into the window." He stepped outside and took a closer look at the bird, which looked like a female robin. He put a tentative finger out and touched it and it fluttered its wings.

"I think she's only dazed," he said. He crouched down and watched the bird until it started trying to get up. Then he picked it up gingerly in his hands and carried it over to the edge of the patio and set it on the grass. It took it a couple of minutes to decide that it could fly. As soon as it flew away, he came back inside.

"She was terrified. But once she decided I wasn't going to kill her, she relaxed and caught her breath and finally was able to fly away." He was babbling because he didn't know what to say to Maddy.

While he'd been watching the bird, he'd thought about what he'd almost done. Again. It was a damn good thing the robin hit the door when it did, because every second he indulged himself with Maddy was another second he wasn't spending trying to find out who killed Tristan. Never mind that his resistance to her was crumbling like a stilt shack in an earthquake. Never mind that although he had no idea why, he was beginning to care for her in a deep, deep way he'd never cared about anyone before.

He couldn't afford to let her get to him. He needed to devote all his strength and focus to figuring out why Tristan was murdered and by whom. He didn't have enough of either to spare for selfish pleasure.

He turned to Maddy and thought about what she'd said just a few minutes before. "You said I got in your way," he said, his voice hard.

Maddy looked up at him in surprise. "I was mad," she began.

"What else were you going to say? That I got in your way and kissed you? That I got in your way and made love with you? I guess you're thinking that all that's distracting." He scowled at her. "Well, guess what, Maddy. You're getting in my way, too. You think I like it that I think about having sex with you when I ought to be figuring out what happened to Tristan? You think I enjoy being distracted by you while my oldest friend's killer goes free? I've only got until the end of this week before I have to be back at my job and I know little more than I did when I got here. All I've got is speculation."

He turned and looked out the French doors, knowing that if he kept looking at her while he tried to make her believe he didn't want or need her there, she'd see through him immediately. "So it works out perfectly that you're being taken off the case. In fact, it's a relief."

"A relief?" she said, the hurt in her voice evident. "Is that what you said?"

He didn't turn around. "Yes," he said just as her phone rang.

"Oh, hi, Brock. Thanks for calling me back." She listened for a moment. "I see. Sure. That makes sense. Of course. I'll be ready." She clicked the phone off and stood staring at it."

"Maddy?" Zach said. "What was that?"

"They denied my request. I can't stay. They've made a reservation for me for tomorrow morning on a commercial flight to DC. I have to drive to New Orleans this evening."

And that easily, he was let off the hook. He didn't have to explain that he didn't want her here, or that she was mistaken if she thought he needed her. He didn't have to look her in the eye and tell her the biggest lie of all, that it would be a lot easier to find out the truth about how Tristan died without her around.

She uttered a nervous laugh. "But I don't have a car."

He looked at her. "You can drive mine and leave it at the airport," he said.

Chapter Ten

When Maddy came out of her room a couple of hours later, after packing her clothes while tears streamed down her cheeks, Zach wasn't in the house. She figured he'd gone down to the dock as he'd said before he'd driven her half-crazy with need then told her he wanted her gone.

She still had on jeans and a T-shirt, so she decided she'd walk down to the dock, too. She wanted to see what was so interesting about it. Zach had told her to stay inside, but she had no further obligation to do anything he told her to except leave. So if he got upset because she went to the dock, then he could just lump it.

She headed down the path she'd seen him walk the other day. It wasn't much of a path. It was so overgrown with weeds and vines in a lot of places that it was difficult to tell whether there was a path there at all. She'd told him the truth when she'd said she'd never been in the swamp. This overgrown ground didn't exactly qualify as swamp, but as she walked, she could hear leaves rustling, twigs snapping and other sounds that had to come from animals. The sounds, coupled with her imagination, made her nervous. But she was determined.

Finally, just as the path seemed to disappear totally

into tangled underbrush and she was two steps away from giving up and turning around, she saw a clearing up ahead. Relieved, she hurried toward it, then stopped, nervous about seeing Zach now that she was here. What would she say if he confronted her? Would he be mean to her again?

It was too late now. She was already here. She walked through the last of the undergrowth and out into the clearing and gasped. It was beautiful. She knew that cypress trees and oleander bushes were pretty, but she'd never paid that much attention to them. The rickety, weathered dock, the odd plants and flowers growing in the water and on land, air plants nestled in the crooks of the cypress limbs and the cypress knees forming gargoyle-like shapes in the water gave the small area an alien look. It was rustic and beautiful, and something, maybe the oleander, lent a sweet scent to the air.

Maddy stepped onto the weathered boards of the dock and walked out a little way, so that when she crouched down she could see the patterns in the mud made by at least one boat that had tied up to the dock recently. There wasn't much room on either side of the wooden boards to pull a boat aground. The vessel would have to be small. But in contrast, the water at the end of the dock was deep enough for a fair-size motorboat.

Straightening, she shaded her eyes and looked out over the Gulf, thinking about the *Pleiades Seagull*. It was about twenty-five miles offshore. A relatively small rig, it employed about four hundred workers, including the captain and his crew. It was in fairly shallow water and was drilling very deep. She wasn't familiar with the drill being used, but she did know that it was a proprietary design that was specially tooled to work on such a small platform in shallow waters.

Looking back at the mostly dried mud near the edge of the water, she wondered how deep it was and how hard. If she could walk out from shore just a yard or so, or maybe not even that far, she could get a better look at the patterns made by the boats and see if up close they looked as much like the textured bottom paint used on oil rig lifeboats as she thought they had from a distance. She needed to get a sample of the pattern, whether it was a broken crust of the hardened mud or a photo, so she could compare it closely with the lifeboats' bottom-paint texture.

She sat down on the dock and started to untie her sneakers.

"You oughtn't do that, you," a gruff voice said.

Maddy jumped and jerked her head around. "Who—" She saw an old man in worn pants and shirt, wearing a bedraggled fishing hat and carrying a shotgun that was as highly polished as any firearm in a museum. "Wh-who are you?" she asked.

"That's not important," the man said. "You best leave your shoes alone and get down off that dock. Anybody lives around here knows you can't get outta the gumbo mud once you get into it, I guarantee. So you ain't from here, you."

The man's words were sort of slurred and run together, but she didn't think it was from drinking. His hand trembled on the shotgun and he only talked out of one side of his mouth. His left eye looked as if it was permanently half-closed, too. He must have had a stroke.

"I don't live here," she said, trying to keep her voice steady as she slowly rose to her feet. She didn't think he would shoot her, but she couldn't be totally sure.

"That's right," he mumbled. "So what you doing

down here trying to get yourself stuck in the gumbo mud, you?"

She wiped her hands on her jeans and turned to step off the dock.

"You stay right there while we talk," he said.

She nodded. "Yes, sir. I came down here to look at the marks made by the boat that pulled in here, probably two days ago," she told him, gesturing back toward the mud.

"Three," he said.

"What? Excuse me?"

"Three days ago. Not days, nights. It was around midnight. The boat got its motor stuck in the mud. That motor's gone, I guarantee." The man chuckled. His shoulders shook with his muffled laughs.

"I could see that it had gotten stuck. It stirred up the mud a lot. Do you know who they were or what they were doing?" Maddy asked, hoping that his chuckling meant he'd tell her what she wanted to know.

"Nah," he said. "Nah. Me, I never saw them folks before. But I guarantee they don't know much about Louisiana mud nor Gulf water."

She nodded, smiled and glanced down at the ground, but thick, green grass was growing down to within a foot of the waterline.

"No footprints," the old man said. "You got some training, you?"

"I know a little bit about boats. You said the men didn't know much about mud or Gulf water?"

"That's right. They pulled and pushed and moaned and groaned to get them bags outta the boat and into the wagon, just a-sinking in the mud and slipping on the grass and them a-talking the whole time."

"What bags? What were they talking about?"

The man chuckled. "The bags, they was dark green. Looked like body bags. That tough canvas, you know?"

She nodded.

"What'd they talk about? Everything. Said something about a dry run. Dry run on water," he said and chuckled again. "Said if it went okay and the cap'n was happy, they'd bring two boats, maybe more, next time. The one guy, he said they gotta bring 'em during the new moon. The other man, he say the bogeyman come out in the dark of the moon. The one man, he laugh at him and say shut up and push the wagon."

"What kind of wagon?"

"Me, I don't know. A wagon's a wagon. See, the road now, it's so grown over that a truck can't get down here like it used to. So those men, they got to drag those heavy bags with a wagon all the way 'thout no help." He chuckled again. "The ground is rough and they lost some of their booty."

"Booty? What was the booty? What was in the bags?" Maddy had a hard time keeping her voice steady. Had the boat come from the oil platform and had the old man seen what was in the bags?

"They was heavy, I guarantee you that. They's probably smart to use body bags. I saw them boys sink to their ankles in the mud, and it was a treat to watch them try and get out. But they ended up okay."

"Did you pick up something that fell out of the bag?" Maddy asked, trying to draw the man's attention back to her without angering him.

"I guarantee you I did. You want to guess what they was carrying?"

"I'm sure I can't," she said sweetly, then held her breath. Would he tell her what they were smuggling?

The man let the shotgun's barrel drop as he reached into the pocket of his pants and drew out a handgun.

Maddy nearly gasped. From where she was standing, she didn't recognize the make, but she knew that she'd never seen a gun like it before. The handle was longer by at least an inch than any handgun she'd ever seen. It also had what looked like a long magazine sticking out of the handle. Extra bullets? She did her best to memorize what she saw. "Is that the only one you have?" she asked him.

"Nah. I picked up three."

"Would you let me have one?" she asked shakily. If she could get her hands on one of those guns, she just might have the answer to what Tristan had stumbled upon that had gotten him killed.

The old man stared at her, his head angled so he could see her with his one good eye. "What you want with a gun, girl?"

"I can shoot," she said. "I'm pretty good, and I'd love to have a gun like that. Have you shot it?"

He shook his head. "Nah. Ain't got no bullets. You got bullets?"

"No. I don't know what kind it takes, but if you'd let me have one, I can find some bullets for it. Then you and I can do some shooting at targets. Would you like to do that?"

He shrugged. "I ain't too keen on little guns," he said.

Maddy smiled at him again. "I can get you some shells for that shotgun, too, if you want me to."

"Yeah?" He thought a minute. "That'd be nice, I reckon." He looked at the handgun, then tossed it at her feet.

She bent and picked it up. A quick glance didn't help her at figuring out what it was, but it was heavy and not very well balanced. She could tell that just from holding it.

"Don't shoot yourself, girl."

"Hard to do without bullets," she threw back at him as she turned to leave.

"Hey," he said.

She stopped.

"You didn't ever tell me why you came down here, you. How'd you get down here to this old dock?" he asked, looking bewildered. "You looking for something?"

Maddy studied the man for a moment before she spoke. "I'm trying to find out why Tristan DuChaud was killed."

The old man took a step backward and raised his shotgun. "Girl oughtn't be down here. You don't go stirring up an alligator nest if you don't want to run into the mama gator. You understand me, you?"

Maddy didn't, but she nodded her head anyway. "Yes, sir," she said.

"Now, take that evil little gun and go on, you. Get outta here, and don't come back. Pretty *chér* like you get yourself hurt if you don't watch out." He sounded angry, but he lowered the gun. "Go on."

"Yes, sir," she said again, and half walked, half ran back into the undergrowth. She kept jogging as long as she could without tripping over branches and vines. When she made it back to the house, she locked the French doors and took a long hot shower. To her dismay, she found three ticks crawling on her skin, looking for a place to dig in and feed.

By the time Maddy slipped on a pink-and-white caftan, there was a delicious aroma in the air and it was driving her tummy nuts. She hadn't eaten anything all day and she was starving. When she walked into the kitchen, Zach was stirring something in a pot on the stove.

"Mmm, do I smell jambalaya?" she asked, taking a deep whiff of the air.

He put the lid on the pot and turned around deliberately. "Where were you?"

She pointed vaguely back toward the bedrooms. "In the shower."

He growled under his breath. "I mean earlier. Around two o'clock."

"I went down to the boat dock. It's really beautiful down there, but a few ticks decided to have a picnic on me." She shuddered.

"I told you not to leave the house," he said. "When I couldn't find you I thought you might have left, until I looked in your room and saw your suitcases and your clothes."

"You must have been so angry that I didn't listen to you," she said blandly.

He glowered. "I wondered if you'd been kidnapped or hurt."

She shook her head. "Nope. Just exploring. I met the most interesting man."

"Man? Who?"

"I don't know his name. He wouldn't tell me. But he was an old Cajun man with a shotgun. He told me all about the gumbo mud and how I shouldn't step in it or I might not get out again."

"You talked to Boudreau?" Zach asked, sounding disbelieving.

"Is that his name? He told me some other things, too, very interesting things, and I found out a few things for myself."

Zach turned his back and stirred the pot again.

Maddy peeked around him to see what he was cooking. "Wow that smells good. Jambalaya is one of my favorite dishes in the entire world."

"It's from a mix," he said.

"Trust me. I do not care. It smells wonderful."

He banged the lid onto the pot, balanced the spoon on top of the lid, then turned back around. "Well? Are you going to tell me what you found?"

"Oh, right." She went to the kitchen table, trying not to think about what they'd just recently done on it, and turned on her tablet. "I've been checking the Gulf of Mexico sea charts for this area."

"Yeah?"

"Right there where Tristan's dock is, there is a long shallow shelf, then a drop-off."

"Yeah? That's not news. I grew up playing and boating around that dock."

"Right. Well, as it turns out, the lifeboats on the *Pleiades Seagull* could clear the shelf with one passenger, maybe two."

Zach's brows drew down. "How do you know that and what exactly does it mean?"

"I know because I'm an oil rig inspector and I know the specs of the *Seagull*'s lifeboats and I can read charts."

"Okay," he said, looking a little confused. "And it means…?"

"It means that the same boat, full of cargo, would run aground if someone tried to put its bow in to shore."

"I think a boat ran aground there last week, based on what I saw down at the dock," he said, looking more interested now that he was probably beginning to understand what she was getting at.

She nodded. "I think so, too."

"You think it was loaded with cargo?"

She nodded again.

He checked the jambalaya, stirred it one last time, then turned off the gas. "We can eat in a few minutes," he said. "I wish I knew what they were carrying and why they brought it to Tristan's little dock."

"Do you?" she asked. "Because I could make that wish come true."

Chapter Eleven

"What the hell are you doing, Maddy. If you know something that would help figure out what really happened to Tristan, tell me."

"I'm getting to it. Boudreau told me."

Zach crossed his arms and shook his head. "Boudreau? You met Boudreau? You need to understand that he's not exactly running on all cylinders."

"I didn't get that impression at all."

"When I talked to him he was talking to himself. When he finally said something to me it didn't make a whole lot of sense. You noticed the way his mouth and eye droops, didn't you? Duff told me he's had a stroke."

"Why don't you listen to what he said to me, and then you can tell me what you think. Boudreau told me that some folks who didn't know what they were doing tried to bring a boat up onto shore at Tristan's dock, but it got stuck and they didn't have any better sense than to get out in the gumbo mud and try to pull it up onto shore."

"He saw them?"

"That's what he said. But according to him, they finally got the bags onto shore with some help. They put the bags on a wagon."

Zach uncrossed his arms and started pacing between the table and the French doors. After about three round-trips, he stopped. "Did he tell you anything about the bags?"

"He said they were heavy, like body bags, and stuffed full."

"Heavy," Zach said, rubbing a hand across his cheeks and chin. "Did he see what was in them?"

Maddy got up to fetch the weapon. As she picked up the small bag, a lump grew in her throat. She was about to show Zach what Tristan had died for. She presented it to him solemnly. "This," she said. "This is what they're smuggling."

He took the bag and she could tell by his face that he knew immediately what he was holding. He pulled out the handgun and looked at it, then at her, then looked at it again more closely. He studied it, ejected the magazine, checked that it was empty, reinserted it, then laid it down on the table. "That's an automatic," he muttered.

Maddy nodded. "I finally figured that out," she said.

"I mean an *automatic*," he repeated. "Not a semi-automatic. If you pull that trigger, you'll fire at least three rounds."

"I know," she said.

He looked up at her from beneath his brows. "How did Boudreau get this?"

"He said it fell off the wagon. From what I understood him to say, he had three, until he gave me this one."

Zach sat there and stared at the gun for a long time. He blinked occasionally and once or twice he cleared his throat and rubbed his eyes. Finally he looked up at her again. "He gave it to you? Did he know who you are?"

"Yes, he did, and no, he didn't."

"Do you know what this means?"

She nodded, pressing her lips together and blinking her stinging eyes. "Yes. I do."

He shook his head. "This is why Tristan was killed. This is what he heard. He heard them talking about smuggling automatic handguns into the US." He slammed a fist down on the table. "Why couldn't he have told someone?" he shouted. "Damn it, Tristan. Why?"

LATE THAT AFTERNOON, Maddy was finishing packing to leave and Zach was sitting on the picnic table arguing with himself about the best thing to do regarding the automatic handguns, when his phone rang. When he answered, it was his boss, Bill. He didn't even give Zach a chance to say hello before he launched into a tirade. In fact, Zach missed the beginning.

"—if I'd thought that was what you were doing. Damn it, Winter. What the hell's going on down there? As soon as I get off this phone I'm ordering a helicopter to pick you up and you're going to wish you'd never heard of NSA. Your butt is going to be stamped NSA, Non-Secure-Ass."

Zach groaned inwardly at the old inside joke. "Bill, what are you talking about?"

"You shut up and listen to me."

There was a lot of static on the line and Zach was afraid he was going to lose the connection. "Bill. Bill! Hold on. There's only one place around here I can get a signal. Hold on!" He hurried inside and went into the nursery. "Okay. I can hear you now. I missed most of what you said after you told me to shut up."

"Listen to me, Zach. I want you to get down to the sheriff's office right this minute because I don't want to have to go over it all again with you. You can get it from the sheriff."

"Get what?"

Bill went on as if Zach hadn't spoken. "I've been on the phone all day, first with the Coast Guard, then with the sheriff, and then with Homeland Security."

Zach winced. He knew that there had been a rivalry between Bill at NSA and one of the chief deputy directors at Homeland Security for years, and he knew how seriously Bill took that rivalry. He hadn't told Bill about Maddy. So who did? Hell, it was probably his archrival deputy director, trying to one-up him.

"The next time you decide to take a vacation and climb into bed with Homeland Security, could you please give me a heads-up?"

"Into bed?" Zach said hoarsely before he realized that Bill was using the term metaphorically.

Bill obviously heard Zach's tone. "Oh, come on, Zach. Please don't tell me you've been—"

"Bill!" Zach interrupted. "Slow down. I have no idea what you're talking about." He heard plastic rattling as Bill pulled a cigarette out of the ever-present pack in his pocket. Then he heard a match strike and Bill's long inhalation. He knew that within a few seconds his boss would be a little more calm and a lot more rational.

"Okay. Yeah. We've been picking up chatter from some rigs in the Gulf of Mexico for months now. There are oil rigs that are doing double duty as smuggling rings for domestic terrorist groups, survivalists and other fringe organizations and, of course, organized crime. At least one of those rigs has access to automatic handguns. *Automatics*, Zach. Think about that. Word is they're starting to show up in some metropolitan areas in the South, in the hands of *kids*."

"Yeah," Zach said with a sigh.

Bill kept talking. "According to Homeland Security, a couple months ago they zeroed in on the *Pleiades Seagull* as the primary source for the chatter. Zach, your friend DuChaud must have discovered that the talk about the weapons was coming from the *Pleiades Seagull*."

"I know."

"I knew it!" Bill cried. "For Pete's sake. Are you the one who called in the tip to the Coast Guard? Have you found any evidence in DuChaud's house? What have you been doing—"

"Bill," Zach said.

"I don't get it, Zach. You could have requested the assignment. You wouldn't have gotten it. It's a conflict of interest, but you had an obligation as an NSA agent to let me know what you'd discovered. Why didn't you? I'd have assigned an agent—"

"Bill!" Zach yelled. "Shut up!"

"I— What?"

"Shut up for a minute. First of all, no! I did not call in any tip. I don't know anything about a tip. And I didn't know anything for certain about smuggling until just two hours ago. I heard, secondhand, that someone witnessed a boat coming ashore and off-loading two large bags that apparently contained firearms. And yes, they are automatics. Judging by what I've been told, I'm guessing there could be scores of them, maybe even hundreds. The sketchy information I got didn't mention where the boat came from nor where they took the bags. I have a good idea where they were taken, but I can't verify it because *I just found out!*"

"Okay, okay," Bill said. "Who gave you the information? And do you know if they called the Coast Guard? Are you sure you didn't know anything about this?"

"I got the information from a—" Zach decided not

to bring up Homeland Security or Maddy. Not until he had to. He didn't want Bill to know his metaphor about being in bed with Homeland Security was literally true. Not yet.

It was obvious that within the past few hours a lot of stuff had hit the fan. He was going to need some time to separate the facts from the speculation. So he kept his explanation generic, with no names. "From a woman who heard it from an old Cajun man who's old and probably has had a stroke, so not the most reliable witness of anything. I haven't talked to the Coast Guard or the sheriff because I have no evidence of anything. Least of all whether Tristan fell off the rig or was pushed."

There was a long pause, during which Zach listened to Bill inhale. "Well, what the hell are you doing down there if you're not investigating this smuggling thing? Why were you so hot to take a week's vacation?"

"Because I needed to find out the truth about how Tristan died. It looks like I'm the last one to know." He looked up to see Maddy at the door, her eyes wide. *Are you okay?* she mouthed.

He nodded and turned away from her.

"So what now?" Bill asked.

"I guess I'm going to go down to the sheriff's office. Tell me about the tip."

Bill sighed. "Can't you ask the sheriff? I already—"

"Bill!"

"Okay, okay. The call came in from an unknown cell phone that was tracked to a tower near Bonne Chance. Do you know how few towers there are in that area?"

"Tell me about it. I'm standing in what may be the only place on this side of Bonne Chance where I can get a signal. But you're saying the phone call came from around here?"

"That's what I was told. They couldn't get a reliable triangulation. I doubt we'll ever figure out who called unless they come forward. Of course, all our calls to NSA are recorded and reviewed. The ones that may have to do with national security are flagged."

"I know," Zach said through clenched teeth. "I work there."

Maddy was still standing at the door, damn her. If she had decent hearing at all, she could hear Bill. The man had a shrill tenor voice. He'd never had a private conversation in his life because his voice carried as if it were being broadcast over gigantic loudspeakers.

"This was one of those calls. It came in around eight o'clock this morning. I'm going to play it. Listen."

"Put it on speaker," Maddy said.

Too irritated to argue, Zach punched the speaker button.

After several clicks and some static, he heard a voice. It was raspy and low. Zach listened closer. It was a lot like Boudreau's voice, except that it didn't sound old or crazy. *Don't hang up. I got good information. There's an oil rig*—Pleiades Seagull. *The captain is planning to…smuggle guns. Can't say when or where, but he's got to be stopped. People going to die. People already died.* There was another, final-sounding click on the line and it went dead.

"Well?" Bill said.

"Well what?" Zach retorted.

"Do you know who it is?"

"It sounds like the Cajun man I mentioned, but that guy isn't responsible for his actions. He's had a stroke. You can't trust anything he says."

"That's not true!" Maddy cried.

Zach held up his hand and glared at her.

"I'm going to assume that's Homeland Security in the background and I'm going to ignore her."

Zach didn't comment.

"So what are you going to do?"

"Well, Bill, you're my boss. What do you want me to do?"

"I want you to go see the sheriff and then I want both of you to talk to the Coast Guard and figure out the best course of action. Figure out how to find out whether the guns are on the rig yet and when and how they're going to be moved ashore and where they're going after that. And then I want you to *stop them*!"

Zach shook his head. His jaw hurt, he'd been clenching it for so long. "No problem, boss, I'll get right on it," he said grudgingly. "I guess I'm off vacation." And he hung up.

As soon as he hit the off button, Maddy was on him. "Boudreau is not crazy. Have you forgotten what I told you he said about the guns and the boats? He was right. Why didn't you tell your boss that Boudreau thinks the guns will be moved tonight."

"Because Boudreau is not competent. I talked to him, Maddy."

"Well, where do you think he got those guns?"

"In the first place, you don't know if he has more than one. And I'll grant you, it's entirely possible that he found it somewhere around the dock. You and I both know that someone in a heavy boat got grounded there."

"What he said makes sense," Maddy insisted.

Zach shook his head. "I can't go by the word of an old man who at best has had a major stroke. He stood there holding that shotgun on me and telling me I'm the devil and he can't look me in the eye. And he didn't know me. Said he'd never seen me before. No. He's a crazy old man who has no idea what he's talking about."

"Who was that on the recording?" she pushed.

"How the hell do I know. Like I told Bill, it sounded like Boudreau if Boudreau wasn't a hundred years old, sick and, by the way, crazy."

"So what did he say?" she asked. "Your boss."

"You heard most of it. He told me about the tip. That's basically it. Apparently, they'd already brought in a small load of guns, which is where Boudreau got the one he gave you. Kind of a dry run. We've been hearing chatter for months about automatic handguns. The idea is to give them to everybody from organized crime to punk kids and who knows who else. I hate to think about what will happen to New Orleans or Galveston or Houston if those guns are distributed all over. It could be devastating for the lower-income neighborhoods." He rubbed his forehead. "I can see it now. Teens getting shot. Little kids. Those streets will turn into bloodbaths."

"Oh, no. It could be catastrophic," Maddy said with a gasp. "Zach, do you have any idea how many guns were in each of those bags? Boudreau said two guys struggled with the weight. Each bag probably had fifty guns or more."

Maddy was pale, and Zach knew exactly how she felt. Fifty per bag, two bags per boat, who knew how many boat trips. That many small automatic weapons could raise gun violence in the United States dramatically. Enough boatloads of them and the dynamic between the criminal community and law enforcement could be changed forever. Or at least until every cop and every criminal was carrying an automatic. He shook his head. "We've got to stop the guns."

"But how? We need to catch them in the act."

Zach nodded. "The call said the *Pleiades Seagull*'s captain is involved."

She nodded. "That's exactly what Tristan thought. He said the incriminating conversations he heard were between the captain and someone who was apparently very high up in the company."

"Did you say Boudreau heard what the two men were saying while they unloaded the guns?"

She nodded. "They said if the trial run went well and if the captain approved, they'd bring the big shipment in two boats or maybe more. He said they planned to do it during the new moon, which is tonight. We should go talk to him. He gets around in that swamp without making a sound. He's probably seen or heard something else."

Zach looked up, his face haggard. "*We* aren't doing anything. *You* are leaving."

Maddy felt as though he'd slapped her. She shouldn't have expected him to change his mind, but she had. That's how naive she was. She'd actually thought for a little while that he cared for her. She knew better now and she would know better for the rest of her life.

Men like him didn't fall for women like her. She'd been a convenient distraction. That was all. "Oh. Don't worry. I am," she said stiffly. "In just a few minutes. I guess you're going to see the sheriff and talk to the Coast Guard?"

He grimaced and ran his thumbnail along the corner of his bottom lip, as she'd seen him do time after time when he was thinking or if he was unsure about something. "Maybe," he said.

"Zach," she said, wiping her hands down the sides of her jeans. "Thanks."

He looked up at her from beneath his brows. "For what?"

She shrugged. "Oh, you know, everything." Then she turned and headed for her room. As she turned the doorknob, she looked back over her shoulder. He was closing the door to the nursery, Sandy's car keys in his hand.

"Be careful, Zach," she said.

His gaze slid from hers down to the keys he held, then back up. He nodded and right at the end of the nod, the corner of his mouth turned up. "I will." He strode up the hall. At the kitchen door, he stopped and turned.

"Maddy? You, too," he said, then headed through the French doors out to Sandy's car.

Maddy stood there at the door to the guest room until she heard the car's smooth engine rumble to life, then hum as Zach put it in gear and drove away. As she listened to the sound fade in the distance, she closed her eyes and bit her lip.

She was not going to cry anymore. Who was Zach Winter that he deserved her tears? Nobody. That was who. So why was she wasting them on him? A small voice deep inside her whispered, *Because you know he's worth all the tears you can cry.*

"Oh, shut up," she snapped at that small voice. She pushed the guest room door open and saw her suitcases on the bed. Sighing, she remembered that she had to finish packing and get out of here. Zach had told her to leave. She looked around the room, trying to figure out what she'd forgotten. Then she remembered that she'd left her shampoo and conditioner in the master bath. She'd been showering in there to avoid Zach, who was using the hall bath.

When she pushed open the door to the master bedroom, she came face-to-face with a stranger. He was holding one of the automatic handguns.

WHEN ZACH WALKED into the sheriff's office, Sheriff Baylor Nehigh, or Barley, as he was called in high school, turned and shook his head at Zach, every bit as if he were the disappointed principal whom the teacher had sent Zach to for punishment. "Zach, you and me, we know each other." Barley had a plug of tobacco in his cheek and he paused to spit into a coffee can. "I was in the same grade as your sister, Zoe, back when you were a skinny kid with a big chip on your shoulder. Seemed like no matter what you did, you were always trying to do it better than anybody else. I guess you still are. How come I had to find out who you work for from your boss instead of you?"

"I'm sure he told you I came down here for Tristan's funeral. I wasn't on assignment or in any kind of official capacity."

"You saying you didn't have to notify me?"

Zach sighed. "No, I'm not saying that. I'm saying all I was doing was trying to find out if there was any proof that Tristan didn't accidentally fall and drown."

"All right. What have you found out?"

"Not much. But I can tell you Tristan didn't fall."

"But can you prove it?"

Zach shook his head.

"So how much of what your boss told me did you already know?" Barley spit again.

"None of it. I mean, I did find out that there was chatter being picked up about some of the oil rigs down here. Apparently, Homeland Security—"

Barley held up his hand. "I know that Madeleine Tierney is with Homeland Security and that Tristan was, too. I'm disappointed in Tristan that he didn't let me know what he was doing. I'd like to think I could have done something to help."

"Have you talked to the Coast Guard?" Zach asked. "Have they picked up the captain or started the evacuation of the platform?"

"They're going to start evacuating the platform sometime this afternoon. I got a report about an hour ago that they can't find the captain. I reckon he jumped ship. They said there was one lifeboat missing. But apparently, not one person saw or heard him leave. Not one."

Zach closed his eyes as the sound of chewing tobacco hitting the side of the metal can rang in the air. "The captain's not on the rig? We've got to find him. Maddy said that Tristan had talked about overhearing and/or recording at least one, maybe more, telephone conversations between the captain and some big shot who was apparently giving the orders about moving the weapons."

Barley nodded. "Well, that figures. So he and Miss Maddy knew that the captain was involved and yet they didn't come to me?"

Zach stood and started to pace. "What are you getting at, Barley? Why all the complaints that nobody came to you?"

"Look, Winter. I'm more than willing to help out. But you got to remember, this is a small town. I don't have but one deputy and today he's off up to Houma, taking them some papers and picking some up." Barley spit, then held up his hands. "I know what you're thinking. But the reason I can't send that stuff by email is them not us. It's the parish clerks. They don't have their data on the computer yet."

Zach turned on his heel and started back toward the sheriff. "The only thing I'm thinking is what's the Coast Guard doing and when are the smugglers going to bring more guns in? Maddy thought it might be tonight."

"Tonight, eh? What's Homeland Security's plan?"

"My boss told me they're sending a couple of people to help us out, but they won't get here until tomorrow."

"Tomorrow? What's the holdup?"

"I get the feeling they're sending them via commercial airliner. They could send them down here in no time in a helicopter, but that's a lot more expensive."

"That's the government for you. They don't give a rat's ass that one of their own got killed?"

"I'm sure they do," Zach said, ignoring the fact that he'd thought the same thing. "Homeland Security has to consider more than just the life of one agent. They are, as you know, responsible for the safety of the entire country. Look, Barley, I'm going to head over to Tristan's dock. That's where they're going to bring the guns in because that dock is closest to the seafood warehouse.

"What's that got to do with anything?" the sheriff asked.

"The warehouse is the perfect place for them to bring the guns to load them for shipment. They could have an eighteen-wheeler in there and nobody would know. I need to know who your contact is with the Coast Guard."

Barley looked at his phone. "Captain David Reasoner. Here's his cell number. You can reach him if he's not too far out from shore."

"Thanks. Keep the smuggling thing quiet if you can."

Barley sent him a glowering look. "I can. See that you do."

As he drove back to Tristan's house, Zach dialed Captain Reasoner.

"Reasoner." The name was clipped, the tone slightly impatient.

Zach told him who he was and what he wanted to know. "If you need to, you can call my immediate superior. NSA Deputy Assistant Director Bill Wetzell."

"No need. We've already spoken," Reasoner said. "We radioed the *Pleiades Seagull* this morning at 0800. I asked to speak with Captain Poirier just to see how things were going. I do that routinely. The captain was unavailable, according to his first mate. When I asked if there was a problem, he said that they'd had an internal issue yesterday that had kept the captain up all night and that he was sleeping."

Zach didn't interrupt. He just listened.

"One of my crew noticed that there was a lifeboat missing. I asked the first mate about that and he said that was part of the incident. That it had been damaged and they'd taken it down so no one would try to use it in an emergency."

"What do you think, Captain?" Zach asked when he'd finished.

"I don't think the captain is aboard. I also don't think the lifeboat was damaged. I started to ask to see the damaged boat but decided not to push it at that time. However, I am considering going back there, boarding the platform and having a look for myself. I don't like the evasion. Particularly since their communications expert died last week. Your boss, Deputy Assistant Director Wetzell, told me that the *Pleiades Seagull* has been targeted as a source for some anti-American chatter."

"That's the word I got," Zach agreed. "In fact, judging by several factors, including some anecdotal evidence,

I'm expecting there to be contraband moved from the platform to shore tonight. Think you'd be able to spare any men to help catch these guys in the act?"

"It would be my pleasure, Agent Winter."

Chapter Twelve

Maddy tried to scream, but no sound came out of her mouth. She clutched at her throat and tried to catch her breath as the man came closer. "Who—" she rasped, still not able to force much sound past her fear-constricted throat.

"Shut up," the man said and slapped her face with his empty hand.

Maddy fell sideways, onto one knee and one palm. She gasped, partly in pain and partly in outrage, and vaulted to her feet. The side of her face stung and tingled, but the shock of the blow loosened her throat. "Who are you and what are you doing in this house?"

She took a closer look at the man. "Wait a minute. I know you. You're Captain Poirier from the *Pleiades Seagull*. What are you doing in here? Get out. This is a private residence and you need to—"

He swung at her again. She ducked, but the edge of his hand caught her chin. She staggered but stayed on her feet. Stars danced before her eyes and the anger inside her exploded. "Stop it!" she snapped. "Do *not* hit me again."

"Then stop talking," he said, taking a threatening step toward her and raising his hand again. "I need you to do something for me."

"What's going on here? How did you—" As she took

another step backward, she glanced toward the window and saw that it was open. He'd opened it through a hole the intruders had cut. "You sent them, didn't you?"

"I told you to—"

"I know," she said, smiling in spite of the ringing pain in her head. "I'll be quiet, but please, don't hit me again." Silently she added, *Or I might have to hurt you.* She was contemplating what she could do to either take the man down or talk him into letting her go. "Captain, is there something I can do for you?" she asked as she used her peripheral vision to search for something in Sandy's room that could be used as a weapon.

She realized he was going to grab her about a fifth of a second before he lunged toward her, which wasn't quite enough time for her to react. He grabbed her by one arm, squeezing inside the elbow until it went limp and throbbed with pain. "Now, see if you can keep that mouth shut for a few minutes or I'll have to find a rag to stuff in it." He twisted her arm a little. Just enough to make her cry out.

Digging into his pocket again, he came out with a large plastic tie that looked like the ones on food bags, except about a hundred times the size. He grabbed her right wrist and looped the tie around it. "Now turn around. *Slowly.* Don't try anything or I'll make you think that so far we've been having a picnic. Got that?"

Maddy nodded meekly and turned around slowly. If she had her gun, or a pair of scissors or even a nail file, she could defend herself and possibly even manage to get away. But she had nothing. All she could do was stand there as he fastened her wrists together behind her.

"That's too tight," she said.

"I told you to *shut up!*" he groused and shook her,

hard. He half dragged, half walked her up the hall to the kitchen. "Where are your car keys?"

"Car keys?" Maddy repeated.

Poirier whirled and punched her in the stomach so fast and so hard that she doubled over, then collapsed onto the floor in pain. With her arms tethered behind her, she couldn't sit up or stand. All she could do was lie there and cough and try not to throw up.

Poirier lifted her up by her arms, nearly pulling them out of their sockets. He held on to her upper arms and shook her hard. Her eyes watered with pain and nausea. "Stop," she whispered. "Stop."

"Listen to me. I know that you are not as dumb as you're pretending to be. If you keep acting like a child, I will treat you like a child. Do you understand what that means?"

Maddy blinked hard. She didn't know what he wanted her to do. Should she answer him or just move her head without speaking?

"Do you? Look at me. I'm tired of hitting you with my hands. I've got a nice heavy buckle on my belt. I can use it on you until you can't move. It's how I disciplined my own kids until my wife left me. And it's how I'll discipline you. Got it?"

She nodded, which made her head hurt.

"I don't like to do that, you understand. But sometimes it has to be done. Now." He straightened his jacket and shot his shirt cuffs as if he were wearing a tuxedo. "Where are your car keys?"

Maddy was still having trouble breathing. Her throat and lungs were spasming from the shock and pain of his latest blow. She gestured shakily in the direction of the kitchen counter. She didn't bother to tell him they were Zach's keys, not hers.

Poirier picked up the keys and glared at her. "Let's go. You're riding in the trunk."

She walked outside on shaky legs. When he pressed the remote unlock on the car, then looked at the electronic key for a second and pressed the trunk release, she just stood there, staring at the car's trunk and trying to think. What did she know about the trunks of cars these days? Newer cars had a trunk release on the inside.

She averted her eyes from the trunk and from Poirier. But when he grabbed her by the arm and pulled her toward him, causing her to stumble, he laughed.

"You don't think I'm going to let you get into the trunk until I've taken care of the interior release, do you?" He took the gun he still held and slammed the butt into the small lever, then did it again. The little piece of metal broke and skittered along the metal wall of the trunk with a tinkling sound.

Then he jerked her over to stand in front of the open trunk. "Get in," he said.

She looked at the high interior edge of the trunk, which came to her hips, then looked at him.

"Lift your leg and throw it over the edge, you idiot," he said. When she didn't move immediately, he pushed the barrel of the gun into her side. "Did you notice what kind of gun I have? If not, I'll tell you. It's an automatic. That's right. Can you imagine what it will do to you if I pull the trigger and hold it?"

She nodded. She lifted her left leg, trying to brace her tethered arm against the fender.

With a frustrated growl, Poirier pushed her in and shoved her right leg inside, then slammed the trunk lid.

Maddy closed her eyes. Her left arm hurt where she'd hit the edge of a metal tool case as she landed.

Poirier had twisted her knee when he'd stuffed her

inside. It throbbed with pain. But while they hurt, her arm and leg were not what she was concerned about. She was afraid that wherever Poirier was taking her, he intended to kill her. And she didn't want to die.

She wanted to live. She regretted giving up so easily when Zach told her he didn't want her there with him. She wanted to go back there. Wanted one more chance. Next time, she'd fight to stay. She'd tell Brock that she wanted vacation and she'd glue herself to Zach's side until he couldn't deny that they had a connection that could not be ignored—*if* she had another chance.

She and Zach could be working together right now to bring Poirier down. She smiled at the image that rose before her vision of the two of them together, perfectly in tune. Two days ago, she hadn't even known Zach Winter. But now she knew that they were better together than either of them were alone. When they stood together, they were unstoppable. They always would be. She knew that. And so did he.

They would win, as long as they fought together.

Then she tried to move her leg, which was cramping, but she had no room since she was stuffed into the trunk of the car. She almost laughed. Sure. How easy was it to rethink the things she'd done. Easy to convince herself that Zach would have acquiesced, now that there was no way to find out. No way to ever go back and make things different.

All she knew for sure was that the end of this ride was probably going to be the end of her.

AFTER ZACH HUNG UP, he dialed Maddy's cell phone, but she didn't answer. When he got back to the house, his car was gone. Zach parked and stared at the empty space, then looked at his watch. If she'd showered and dried her hair before she left, she might not have been gone but about five or maybe ten minutes. He remembered her telling him she did a pretty fast shower. He smiled and tried her phone again.

"Come on, Maddy. Answer." Maybe she was one of those people who were adamant about not talking on the phone while driving. This time, he left a message. "Call me as soon as you get this, Maddy. If you haven't gone too far, you might want to turn back. It looks like it will all go down tonight, and I'd—I'd like to have you here, with me, if you want to be. Call me."

He hung up and put his phone in his pocket. For a second, he thought about going inside and waiting, in case she called right back. But there wasn't much time and he wanted to find Boudreau and get some answers about what he'd seen, then talk to Captain Reasoner again to nail down specific plans before it got dark. So he walked on down to the dock.

He looked around and called for Boudreau, but he didn't hear or see anything. So he examined the ground and the mud. There, in the few places where the overgrown grass and vines gave way to a muddy patch right around the water's edge, he saw recent tracks of a skinny, possibly metal, wheel. He turned and walked directly away from the dock, searching the ground. Sure enough, there were more wheel marks. He took a few flash photos of the marks with his phone and labeled, dated and initialed them in the device. He knew the courts were strict on entering digital photos into evidence, and at least he had them saved and annotated, just in case.

When he looked at one of the photos, the flash had produced shadows, enough that he could see the faint outline of a footprint alongside the metal wheel track.

He took another couple of shots before he continued following the wheel tracks. Within another couple of hundred yards, he was out of the underbrush and in the sparsely grassed back of the old seafood warehouse.

He nodded. That's what he'd thought. The way that Maddy described what Boudreau had told her, the two men had pushed the wagon through the underbrush toward the warehouse. Boudreau had been convinced that's where they were going.

He walked around the building, checking out the entrances and looking at the ground. Sure enough, the thin metal wheel tracks went around to the freight door in front. He crouched down and looked at the door-lift mechanism. A few tufts of grass were caught there. Then Zach touched them. They were supple and nearly fresh. They must have gotten caught within the past two days.

Satisfied that he had enough information to let Captain Reasoner and the Coast Guard know what was likely going down in a few hours, Zach called him back and explained the layout. Reasoner immediately fired back with a simple and effective plan that was very close to what Zach was thinking and told Zach he'd be able to give him three Coast Guard officers to capture the smugglers.

Reasoner told Zach he'd arranged for an ambulance with paramedics hidden in an empty car repair shop near the warehouse, if needed. A Coast Guard helicopter was also on call.

After arranging to meet Reasoner just after dark at the dock, Zach walked back that way and called Maddy again. He was able to hear her phone ring four times before the connection was lost. He walked out to the end of the dock, out from under any overhanging trees, and tried again.

That time, the phone rang until voice mail picked up. "Maddy, call me back," he said, standing perfectly still. He didn't want to lose the connection until he'd left his message. "I want to make sure you're okay. Try to call before dark, okay? We're hoping to catch the smugglers tonight. The Coast Guard's working with me."

He paused, rubbing his thumb across his lower lip. He knew how badly he'd hurt her when he'd told her he didn't need or want her around. And he knew how much of a bold-faced lie it was.

He still didn't want her here, for her own safety, although he knew he wasn't giving her the credit she deserved as a trained Homeland Security agent. But he couldn't help it. He wasn't sure what he'd do if something happened to her.

Without understanding his reasoning, he said, "Truthfully, I'd feel better if you were here beside me. We make a good team."

He hung up, but he stood there for a minute, looking at the phone. *Call, Maddy. I know it's silly, but I'm worried about you.*

MADDY FELT AS THOUGH she couldn't breathe. It wasn't rational. But then, she was locked in the trunk of the car. What about that made sense?

There was plenty of air. She could feel it on her face. She could *see* the waning sunlight shining through the glass of the taillights. At least he hadn't blindfolded her or put a sack or a cloth over her head or gagged her. Thank goodness for the small stuff.

On the other hand, she was trussed and stuffed into

the trunk of a car, everything hurt except her hands and that was *not* a good thing, and she was terrified.

Her eyes began to sting and she sniffed. "Oh, damn it," she whispered. She was crying. Why did she always have to cry? She hated it. There was no point to it. Crying was just a reflex left over from infancy, when it was the only way to get attention or food or a diaper change. And now her nose was running and it was even harder to breathe. Every time she sniffed she got a nose full of dust, carpet fibers and dirt.

It was almost funny. She was very likely about to die and what she was wishing for was a tissue.

She forced the whirling, panic-driven thoughts out of her brain. She had to focus. She zeroed in on the pale light coming through the red glass of the taillights. *Glass.* She'd heard of people locked in trunks kicking out taillights and waving and shouting until someone called the police and saved them. Had she seen that on a news show or a sitcom? Didn't matter. It was still worth a try. But when Maddy tried to scoot around to get her feet in position to kick the taillight out, she discovered that she really could not move. Her slight claustrophobia began to grow into full-blown panic.

At that very instant, the car stopped.

A rush of adrenaline streaked through her. It was a combination of relief and terror. But it did its job. They called it the fight-or-flight response. Her mind was suddenly clear and focused. Gone was the whimpering, helpless child.

Her knowledge and training, along with the innate human fight for survival, gave her the determination she needed. She had to figure out a strategy for dealing with Poirier if she wanted to survive.

She concentrated on her hands. They were totally

numb and cuffed behind her back, so she had no idea whether her fingers were moving or not, but she willed them to flex and move and strain against the plastic strip. A searing pain in her wrists made her gasp and echoed through every muscle in her body. She'd seen characters in cop shows contort their bodies to get their hands under their legs and in front of them, then use friction to get out of a plastic handcuff. Just as she reminded herself that she couldn't move, the car door slammed, sending a shudder through the whole vehicle.

So much for Houdini-like escapes. If she'd wanted to do this the easy way, she'd have been sawing the plastic against one of those sharp edges sticking into her back the whole time Poirier was driving. It was too late now.

Poirier opened the trunk. Sunlight blazed in, forcing Maddy's burning eyes shut. She tried to squint, but the brightness was too much. Where was so much glare coming from? Her eyes still didn't want to open, so she had to force her eyelids to part for a fraction of a second at a time. Something in front of her—a huge building or wall—was reflecting the full strength of the sun.

Poirier grabbed her under her arms and dragged her bodily out of the trunk and set her upright. She swayed and took a stumbling step to lean against the fender while her head labored to adjust to being upright. The muscles in her legs cramped and she nearly fell. Just one more crippling pain to add to all the rest.

"Let's go," Poirier growled. "I don't want to take a chance on somebody seeing us. And if you try to scream, I'll knock all your teeth down your throat. Understand?"

Maddy nodded, her mind still working to figure out where they were. As her eyes adapted to the brightness, she saw that the glare was coming from a large, rust-streaked metal building.

Poirier stepped up to a garage door and pulled on the handle. It screeched and grated as metal slid over metal.

Maddy yawned to pop her ears after the auditory onslaught. Behind her back, she was still working her fingers and wrists. At least she hoped her hands were obeying her brain. She didn't want them to be numb when and if she was able to escape the plastic tie and needed to defend herself.

"Get in here," he ordered her. She hurried through the open freight door, unwilling to anger him again. She didn't think he would shoot her, but at this point she had no doubt that he would beat her with his belt buckle, and she couldn't stand the thought of that.

When she stepped inside the building, the smell overwhelmed her. She gagged and coughed. It smelled like rotting shrimp shells and dead fish and iodine. It had to be the seafood warehouse. Boudreau had told her this was where they were bringing the guns. He was right.

Her eyes started watering and she coughed again. Blinking, she did her best to push past the smell so she could concentrate on taking in and remembering everything.

The first thing she noticed was the wagon Boudreau had described to her the other day. It had two large bags in it. Boudreau had said they were body bags. *The guns.*

Poirier jerked her over to the opposite wall and opened a door. Inside the dark room, Maddy thought she could make out a glint of pale light on porcelain. A toilet. It was a bathroom.

He shoved her inside and she heard a metallic rattling then a click, like a padlock. With the door closed, the room was pitch-black. And again, Maddy was trapped in a dark closed space. But this was worse by far than the car's trunk and the warehouse combined. Not only was it almost totally black, but it was hot and the smell had her gagging again. Right now, she'd be happy to breathe in the disgusting but identifiable odor of the warehouse.

This tiny closet should be giving off acid-green steam, the smell was so bad. It actually burned her throat and nose and eyes. And with her arms behind her back, there was nothing she could do about it. She did her best not to cough, because it would cause her to suck in even more putrid air.

Rather than give in to the nausea and pain and hope-lessness of her situation, she worked on narrowing the focus of her existence down to one goal. One thing. Finding some light in the unrelenting darkness. She searched until finally, between the bottom of the door and the floor, she saw a needle-thin glow. It was only a couple of millimeters thick and was almost too pale to be seen, but it was enough. Her head quit whirling and she was able to orient herself in the world.

Unwilling to touch anything around her, she stood, trying not to sway or lose her sense of balance in the dark, fetid space. In desperation, she turned her con-centration to a game she'd invented during DHS train-ing, when she was forced to sit or hide in a bunker for long periods of time. She called it Name That Sound. It was an exercise aimed at using all her senses. Right now, she couldn't use her eyes or her sense of touch, so she concentrated on her hearing and her sense of smell.

She heard a car being cranked, heard the engine rev, then listened as it got louder. Poirier, or someone, was pulling a vehicle into the warehouse. It had to be Zach's car. The next sound after the engine stopped and a car door slammed was that metallic screech of the freight door being opened or lowered. She made an educated assumption that it was being lowered, since the only time she'd heard it before was when Poirier raised it.

Soon she smelled car exhaust. It actually surprised and dismayed her that she could smell the exhaust over the resident smell of the bathroom. She didn't like the idea that she'd gotten used to that smell.

After a few minutes of identifying a bunch of innocuous sounds outside the bathroom door and a couple of ominous rustling sounds that came from inside the bathroom, Maddy heard footsteps coming toward her. She froze, partly like a child who thinks being still would render her invisible and partly in real, identifiable fear.

The footsteps stopped right outside the bathroom door. Maddy waited, breathing through her mouth, hoping that the raspy sawing of her panicked breaths wasn't audible to the man standing on the other side of the door.

Then she heard the sound of a key sliding into a padlock.

Chapter Thirteen

Back when he and Tristan were kids, Zach had known where Boudreau lived. Now he wasn't sure. He stood in the middle of the clearing with his eyes closed, trying to remember back all those years. The pier was behind him, the path to Tristan's house was to his left and the seafood warehouse was about a mile straight ahead. So the path to Boudreau's stilt shack had to be to his right. But he'd already examined the ground in that direction. There was no hint of a path in the grass and weeds and vines that covered the ground. He'd also examined the branches of the trees and shrubs, but he couldn't find even one broken twig or branches to tell him that people had passed that way recently.

The way Boudreau had appeared, practically out of thin air, he had to have come that way. But how did he move through the thick brush of the bayou without breaking branches?

A cool breeze blew in off the Gulf, causing Zach to shiver. He had on the same short-sleeved pullover shirt he'd worn to the sheriff's office. The temperature had been warm today, in the eighties, but on the coast, as the sun went down, the air cooled, especially if the breeze was off the Gulf. He figured by dark it might be as cool as sixty degrees. Not cold by any means, but he was sunburned after being outside without sunblock and he knew that he would feel chilly.

Dismissing those inane thoughts, he started in the direction he was sure Boudreau's cabin lay. That meant he'd be walking through brush and brambles and vines, but if he wanted to enlist Boudreau's help capturing the smugglers, which he did, then he had no choice. About three feet beyond the clearing, the heavy tangles of branches and vines thinned out and he finally could make out the path. It wasn't exactly as he remembered it, but it was heading in the right direction.

He pushed on until he finally came to a small clearing that was mostly hidden on all sides by swamp. Zach glanced around, looking for some sign that would tell him that this was Boudreau's place. But there was nothing except the stilt house itself.

Zach took one step toward the house and heard a shotgun being cocked. "Boudreau?" he called, holding his hands up. "It's me, Zach. Tristan's friend. I just want to talk to you. Nothing else. I need your help with something."

He heard the second barrel of the shotgun cock. "Boudreau. Listen to me."

A shotgun blast hit just close enough to Zach's feet to knock dust up into his face, but not so close as to send a stray piece of shot toward him. He backed up a few steps and stood still, his hands still out and up. "I'm not moving, Boudreau. Sorry to disturb you. But I need this for Tristan's sake."

The large, thick wooden door swung open and Boudreau's face, dark and angry, appeared. He held his shotgun pointed right at Zach's midsection. Zach's belly contracted. "You a careless man, come here like this, you."

"I need your help, Boudreau, to stop the men who killed Tristan. Can I talk to you for just a minute?"

"There ain't no such thing as *just a minute*," the old man yelled. "Besides, this is my place, and you had to walk through M'sieu Tristán's place to get here. You ain't got business either place, his nor mine."

"You're right," Zach said, his hands still raised. "I shouldn't have come. I'll work for you. I'll give you money for your time. Anything, if you'll just listen to me for—for five minutes."

There was a long pause as Boudreau studied Zach and muttered unintelligibly to himself.

Zach was worried about the man. The last time he'd talked to him he'd seemed happy enough to babble on about things Zach had no clue about. But he was seriously talking to himself now. Zach was sure that if he could hear him clearly, the words wouldn't make sense.

"Boudreau?"

"I can listen for free," Boudreau said. "You got five minutes."

"I know you told Maddy—the woman you talked to—that you thought the smugglers would come tonight. I think they will, too. When they do, I'd like to have your help to catch them and stop them from selling those guns. The Coast Guard will help us."

"Coas' Guard?" Boudreau said. "Why you done brought the Coas' Guard in to mess everything up?" He muttered to himself some more and shook his head. "I guarantee you," he said, his voice rising, "I don't want no Coas' Guard."

"I'm afraid you don't have a choice there," Zach said. "We can't do it by ourselves, Boudreau, and we need to do it tonight. It's the last new moon, you know. The night starts getting brighter after this."

"You ain't got to tell me that, you."

"Will you come down to the clearing with your shotgun and help me?"

Boudreau stepped back inside his shack. Zach waited. After at least three minutes, he began to get worried that Boudreau had dismissed him or forgotten about him. But finally the old Cajun emerged with his shotgun and wearing a stained vest that Zach could see was stuffed with extra shells.

Zach himself had his government-issue weapon, but he also had the automatic that Maddy had given him. He had a full magazine of bullets. But if he ran out of them, he wouldn't be able to reload. He'd have to switch to his own semiautomatic gun. "You ready to go?" Zach asked Boudreau.

"I reckon," the Cajun said. "I don't like this, me. Never took much truck with killing, animals nor men, but if that's what we have to do to stop those guns getting spread all over hell and creation, then that's fine, yeah."

When the two of them got to the clearing, it was beginning to get dark. "I don't know what time they'll get here, and I don't know how long we'll have to wait," Zach said. "But if we can, I want all the evidence I can get against them. So we should wait until they load the bags onto the wagon and push them all the way up to the warehouse. Then we'll nab them there. Hopefully, they'll think they're home free and that nothing can touch them.

"Home free," Boudreau said with a grin. "Olly olly oxen free."

Zach groaned inwardly. Boudreau had been comparatively rational so far, except for the muttering. But now he was sounding crazy again. "Boudreau, listen to me. Captain Reasoner will be here. He's going to tell us where he wants us to hide and what he wants us to do. Is that okay with you, Boudreau?" Zach asked. "He's a good guy and he knows what he's doing. We can count on him to help us catch these guys."

"Captain? He one of those oil rig captains?"

Zach shook his head. "Nope."

"That's good," Boudreau said before Zach had a chance to say anything else. "'Cause if it was that captain from that rig where M'sieu Tristán worked, I could of already caught him a while ago. When he come up here in one of them boats. He looked mean and mad."

"What? What are you talking about?"

"That captain on that rig. Couple hours or so. He let that boat go, just like it were nothing. It's probably tangled up in brush and weeds around one of them bends by now, where ain't nobody can see it. That ain't right, to let a boat go like that."

Zach's head was spinning. The captain of the *Pleiades Seagull* was there at the dock? And he let his boat go? He had no idea if Boudreau knew what he was saying, but if even half of it was true…

Zach's stomach knotted. "Where did the captain go?"

"Me, I don't know. I didn't stick around to watch. All I know's he didn't come down my path today."

What Captain Reasoner told him about what he'd found on the *Pleiades Seagull* came back to him. He thought the captain might have abandoned ship using one of the lifeboats. But why? To Captain Poirier, the plan to smuggle the guns into the United States via Tristan DuChaud's old boat dock should be right on track. So what possible reason would he have to sneak ashore unannounced and alone, at that exact same spot. "I've got to get in touch with the captain," Zach muttered.

"What captain? Where? Not that one," Boudreau snapped in a panic. "I don't want him anywhere near—" he spat out a wad of tobacco "—anywhere near me," he finished sullenly, kicking up a rock with his toe like a scolded schoolkid.

"This is Captain Reasoner, remember? With the Coast Guard, Boudreau. He's a good guy."

"Coas' Guard. Me, I don't like the Coas' Guard, neither. They ride up and down here and scare the fish and spill oil from those ugly boats."

"But then, you said it was okay if Reasoner helped us figure out where to hide until the men brought the guns ashore. Remember?" If he couldn't count on Boudreau, Zach was afraid their plan would fail. He needed the old man and his stealthy silence in the swamp to spot the boats and let the rest of the team know that they were docking. "We've got to stop the guns."

Boudreau shook his head. "You think I care about all them guns and such? You think that's what's bothering me? Naw. That don't bother me none. I don't care who got what guns. Why I wanna care about that? Ain't none of them coming after me. I just care about keeping the water clean and making sure nobody hurts M'sieu Tristán's land. That's all."

Zach stared at the Cajun. "I don't believe that," he said. "You said before you don't like killing."

Boudreau looked down at the ground and kicked a pebble. "Maybe I don't. I shoot when I got to, but I don't when I don't. So, when they get to where they getting, then what? We just going to shoot 'em?"

"No. Not at all. The Coast Guard is going to be waiting outside the seafood warehouse to grab them and their contraband as soon as they start loading the guns."

"Yeah. That's good. I don't want to shoot nothing—animal or person, unless there's a damn good reason," Boudreau said, nodding.

MADDY WISHED SHE could back away from the door, but there was no room in the tiny bathroom. She listened to the rattling of the padlock, then the metallic rasp as a key was inserted into the lock and turned. If she'd been able to see, she'd have watched the knob on the door turn, but she couldn't see the knob well enough, so she waited, tense and frightened, as the door opened and Captain Poirier's face appeared in her dark-adapted vision.

"Let's go," he said.

She stepped forward, wobbling. "I can't," she said. "I'm shaky and sick. I can't balance with my wrists cuffed."

With a growl, the captain grabbed Maddy's arm and pulled her along with him. She tried to walk steadily, but she'd told him the truth. She did feel sick from the awful odors. Sick and shaky. Maybe from lack of water or the suffocating, fetid heat in that tiny room. Poirier paid no attention, though. He just dragged her over to where a nail barrel sat on the ground.

"Sit. There." He made her sit on the barrel, with her hands still cuffed behind her.

She stared up at a tractor-trailer rig that barely fit into the warehouse. "What are you going to do with an eighteen-wheeler?" she asked.

"Don't worry about what I'm going to do," he said. "Worry about what's going to happen to you—" he bent over and got in her face "—if you don't *shut up*! Do you want me to stick a rag in your mouth—or something else?" He held up the gun, then pushed the barrel of it against her lips. "Open up," he said, his lips curling in what Maddy thought looked like a devil's mask but what he must have thought was a smile.

She sat there, unmoving. She couldn't open her mouth. If she let him stick the barrel of the gun into her mouth, the dynamic of their relationship would change and she'd be defeated. He was struggling for dominance right now because so far she'd managed to push him just enough to irritate him without going too far. But if she let him do this, he would know that she wasn't strong. Not in the way that courageous people are. He would find out that she would do anything to stay alive.

So she pressed her lips together, wincing at the soreness in her jaw, and shook her head without speaking. She had to keep quiet, although it went against her nature. She'd always talked her way out of things, but she had never faced a life-and-death situation before.

"I said, open your mouth." He pushed the barrel, pressing her lips hard against her teeth. "Or this gun barrel will go somewhere else."

She pulled her head back, trying to ease the pressure on her already bruised mouth. She still didn't say anything, didn't open her mouth and didn't look him in the eye.

Neither one of them moved for what seemed like a long time to Maddy. Then finally, Poirier took the gun away from her mouth with a disgusted grunt. She held her breath, praying he wasn't going to make good on what he'd said he would do if she didn't open her mouth.

But when she finally dared to lift her gaze, he was looking at his watch and starting to pace. He still held the gun, and she saw on the side where the lever was that he hadn't switched it from single-shot to multiple-shot.

Maddy waited, willing herself not to speak. Her hands were numb and swollen. Her arms ached from being pulled backward. There were too many sore and aching places on her face and mouth to count, and when she moved a certain way, something in her midsection, where he had punched her, hurt a lot.

She tried to flex her fingers and move her hands, but they were barely responsive. She wasn't sure how long circulation had to be cut off in the hands before they were permanently damaged. She was pretty sure it wasn't very long, and she was also pretty sure that if that short deadline had not already passed, it would soon.

As she tried to distance herself from the pain in her face and stomach and hands, her thoughts turned to Zach. She hoped to high heaven that he had gone back to the house and seen her clothes and suitcases still there. He would know she wouldn't take off in his car without her things. He'd know there was something wrong.

Please, Zach. Find me.

She felt her eyes filling with tears again, and despite her efforts, a quiet moan escaped past her throat.

Poirier looked up at her. His expression at first was dark and angry, but when he saw her crying, he smiled. Maddy had never seen anything as diabolical as that smile. She cringed as he walked over to her and, using the barrel of the gun, wiped a single tear off her cheek.

She shuddered and he smiled again. And she now knew with dreaded certainty that he was going to kill her, and her death would not be easy.

Chapter Fourteen

Captain Reasoner handed Zach a wireless earpiece.
"This will let us talk hands free," Reasoner said, indicating the one in his ear. "Much more reliable than cell service around here."

Zach examined it. "Doesn't have to go far to be better than a cell phone in this area," he said wryly. "It can't be very long range, though, can it?"

"It does pretty well. Farther with line of sight, but we can easily stay in communication for eight to ten miles in this terrain."

Zach positioned the small device in his ear and took a second one to Boudreau. It took less explanation than he expected for the elderly Cajun to figure it out. Then the three of them, plus three Coast Guard officers, went over the plan one more time in order to make sure everyone, including Boudreau, knew exactly what was going down.

"Monsieur Boudreau," Reasoner said, "I'd like you to stay here at the dock. You'll be the best man to know when the boats are coming. You let my men know as soon as you hear or see something. Then you back off and my men will do what they've been told."

"I got my shotgun, me, Captain," Boudreau said. "Ain't never shot nobody," he said, then spit on the ground. "But I can take down a dozen birds with one shot—in season, of course." He scowled, then muttered, as if to himself, "Don't like to shoot 'em, but a man's gotta eat."

Zach exchanged a look with Reasoner.

"I don't think you'll have to shoot, *monsieur*," Reasoner said. "We don't want to alert the smugglers before they're inside the warehouse with the transport truck. It's better for evidence." Then he turned to Zach and reiterated what he'd told him earlier. "I'll stay in the dock area with Boudreau. You'll be with my men outside the warehouse. The sheriff will be there, too, with a couple of deputies. The takedown and arrest will be a multidepartmental cooperative effort, including the Coast Guard, NSA and local law enforcement. That way, the anti-American contingent will see a united front for the US."

Zach nodded. Boudreau kept fiddling with the earpiece in his ear, seeming preoccupied with, or maybe fascinated by, it. But when Reasoner stepped up to shake his hand, he straightened and held out his right hand, which did not tremble, and nodded like a seasoned military man.

Everyone took their assigned places and prepared for the most difficult part of the entire operation. The waiting.

ZACH HAD NO IDEA how much time had passed, when a voice spoke in his ear, rousing him from a near-drowsing state.

"Boat approaching." It was Reasoner. "Everyone ready. Officer Carter will take over from here. No noise. Out."

Zach tensed and took a deep breath, working on his focus. He waited for the feeling he called his SWAT

Mode, where his mind and body worked together to keep him alert and confident. He felt it coming over him. He was ready, his weapon felt good in his hand. But for the first time ever, there was something missing.

When he and Maddy had worked together, they had melded together and formed a perfect pair, perfectly in sync, almost able to read each other's minds. Zach's SWAT Mode didn't even compare.

"The wagon is moving toward the warehouse," Reasoner spoke again. "Men on the path, be ready. Do not. Repeat. Do not engage. Defense only. Let them pass. Wait for my orders. Out."

Zach felt his muscles straining with tension. He breathed slowly and steadily in a conscious effort to stay in his heightened state of readiness. He couldn't forget how different and more complete he'd felt when teamed with Maddy. They'd shared each other's energy and passion and felt the sheer thrill of moving in such tightly woven sync that they might as well have been one entity.

He glanced to his right at the one Coast Guard officer he could see. The man looked back at him. They nodded at the same time. Then Zach heard the creak of metal against metal. It was the wagon, and the wheels sounded burdened, as if they were straining under a very heavy weight. He pulled back farther into the shadows. Under a sky with no moon, it was easy to hide. He'd just gotten situated and regained his focus when he saw the wagon.

He needed to know how many men were with it. There were two men in front of the wagon, pulling it as if they were oxen. Another man was behind, pushing the heavy vehicle. A fourth man appeared to be the lookout.

He also retrieved any weapons that dropped onto the ground through tears in the canvas or a broken zipper.

The wagon passed without incident. Zach didn't move. He listened to the squeaky wheels until they'd gone around the warehouse. He heard a banging on the metal freight door and a voice calling out. These guys weren't very subtle. They acted as though they'd done this before. Maybe their dry runs hadn't been so skeletal after all. Light flared as the freight door opened to let the wagon in. Zach could see nothing but the light and shadows from where he was.

He knew that Captain Reasoner was in position across the street from the warehouse and was filming what was going on. He just wished Reasoner would get his assessment of the inside of the warehouse done and give them their orders.

Then he heard the little click that meant that Reasoner had turned on the microphone. "Tractor-trailer rig. White BMW rental car, 300 series. It appears the only people inside the building are a man, presumably the captain, and a woman, probably Agent Tierney of Homeland Security. She appears to be tied up or handcuffed."

Zach froze. Maddy was in there? Poirier had her tied up? He had to get to her.

"Winter, acknowledge." Reasoner's voice penetrated his thoughts and he realized the man had been talking for several seconds.

"Sorry, sir. Repeat?" Zach's face burned.

"Move in. Stay low. They have automatic weapons. Use deadly force only if unavoidable. Carter's in charge. Winter, acknowledge."

"Yes, sir," Zach responded.

"Out."

Zach made sure the small automatic handgun was ready and that the large magazine was full of bullets. Then he started moving toward the freight door, staying in the underbrush and following alongside the Coast Guard men.

As he rounded the corner of the warehouse and was able to see in the door, he spotted Maddy. She was sitting on a barrel with her hands behind her back. She looked miserable and dejected, but there was something else not right about her.

Zach looked closer. Her cheek and forehead were an angry red, and there was a blue shadow on her jaw. "You son of a bitch," he whispered under his breath. He'd like to kill Poirier or whoever had done that to her.

He looked closer, trying to see if she had any other contusions. Then he did a double take. What was she doing? She was rocking back and forth, just slightly. Had she been drugged or hit so many times that she was dazed? Before he had time to puzzle out what she was doing, Captain Poirier came into view.

Poirier was directing the men to get the wagon all the way inside the warehouse and close the door.

"Get ready," Reasoner's voice came in Zach's ear. "Don't let the door lock you out. Carter, engage your helmet camera. On your signal."

Carter was the man next to Zach. Out of the corner of his eye, Zach saw Carter press his earpiece to turn on the microphone and his helmet to switch on the camera. Just as Carter opened his mouth to speak, loud, angry shouts split the silence.

For an instant, everything stopped. The men in the warehouse froze, as did Poirier. Zach didn't move. Nor did Carter. Everyone waited to see who had been shouting.

Then Zach saw him. It was Murray Cho, the fisher-man who'd bought the warehouse. He was holding a rifle at his waist, like any decent cowboy, and he walked steadily toward the open freight door. Once he gained the doorway, he adjusted the position of the rifle so it was pointing at Poirier.

"You!" Cho shouted. "All of you. Put your hands up." He had a faint accent, which served to make his words sound more ominous. "Hands up! This is my warehouse. I buy it when I moved here. Want to make a living fishing and selling shrimp. Now you are making my warehouse into den of thieves. I want to shoot all of you and make you stop."

Zach waited, holding his breath, wondering whether Cho would actually shoot. He tried to estimate how many men Cho could kill before one of them shot him. He was pretty sure the number wouldn't be high—maybe the fisherman might get off two rounds.

Zach looked at Carter, who looked back at him. Carter was caught between the proverbial rock and hard place. If he called for his men to attack, Cho and Maddy could be killed. If he told them to wait, Cho would certainly be killed and Maddy might be shot accidentally.

Just as Carter took a deep breath to speak, another man stepped out of the darkness on the shadowed side of the building, holding a shotgun. Zach realized it was Boudreau.

"No," he whispered. He had little faith in Boudreau, but he didn't want the man to be killed because he was doing Zach a favor.

"You too nice, Mr. Cho," he said. "Captain Poirier, I never took much truck with killing. But this is for M'sieu Tristán." He fired two shotgun blasts straight at

Poirier. Both hit the middle of his chest. He went down in a double explosion of blood.

There was an instant of total silence, then Carter spoke a single word. "Go." Carter and the other two Coast Guard officers started firing. Zach started shooting, also. The four men who had been loading guns into the eighteen-wheeler took cover and began firing back. At the same time, Boudreau and Cho somehow disappeared.

In between shots, Zach tried to find Maddy, but the spot where he'd thought her barrel had been was empty. His heart and belly contracted. Had she been shot? Or had she had sense enough to throw herself onto the ground and duck away behind the boxes that lined the back third of the warehouse?

Zach took another precious few seconds to see if he could spot Boudreau and Cho. During that unguarded instant, two bullets slammed into his right shoulder. He'd never been shot before, but he had no doubt that what had hit him were bullets.

He tried to raise his hand and fire back but it didn't work. He couldn't move it. All he could do was drop to the ground right where he stood to keep from being hit again.

People were yelling, and the sound and smoke of gunfire filled the air. Zach thought he heard somebody say his name, but he was too busy trying to pick up the gun with his left hand and figure out how to hold it. But that hand was too clumsy. Back to the right hand. His arm had thick, red blood dripping down it, all the way down to his fingertips.

Chapter Fifteen

Maddy's numb hands fell apart as she succeeded in her efforts to saw through the cuff using the broken metal wheel on the barrel she'd been sitting on. The first thing she did was dive down behind the car, hoping that no one would sneak up behind her and shoot her before she had a chance to find a weapon.

She was able to get the strips off her wrists, but her hands were useless. She wrung them, then tried to flex her fingers, but they wouldn't move. Not a single one. Rubbing her hands together felt like watching someone else. It was surprisingly confusing, because her brain kept insisting that those totally disconnected hands were hers.

Then, when the feeling finally started to return, a hot, burning pain engulfed them. It felt as though someone had stuck them in a fire that was tended by a swarm of angry bees.

Outside of her pain, people were still shooting at each other and Zach had been shot. She'd seen it all. The spray of blood that turned the air pink when the bullet hit his shoulder, or had it hit his chest? Maddy's first instinct was to get up and run to him, but she couldn't. Her hands didn't work. If she tried to reach him, she could be shot, too.

Her hands were still on fire, but it seemed as though the burning pain had lessened. The swelling was going down, too. She could flex her fingers about halfway. She wrung them and shook them some more, moaning quietly the whole time because of the pain.

Something tickled the side of her nose. She tried to scratch it, but of course her fingers wouldn't work right. The tickle was about to drive her insane. Finally, she used her wrist to rub at the itchy spot and it came away streaked with blood.

Blood? Maddy clumsily wiped a finger across her forehead and felt a tender place. She must have gotten a scratch that was now bleeding. What had happened? Then she remembered. Poirier was shot and killed. She'd been close enough to him to be spattered with some of his blood, and one of the birdshot from the shotgun must have struck her on the forehead.

Poirier had been holding a gun, a loaded gun. She needed that gun. It would be on the floor somewhere near him. Pulling herself across the concrete floor by her elbows, she sneaked around the back of the car until she could see Poirier's body. It was obvious that he was dead. There was a lot of blood everywhere, but mostly in the hole in his chest. His face looked even more like a death mask, with his mouth stretched back into a horrible grin.

And there was his gun, only about three feet in front of her. She took a deep breath and crawled out into the open to get it.

ZACH CROUCHED AND PEEKED out from behind the tree where he'd fallen when the bullets had hit his shoulder. He had to find Maddy and see if she was okay. That damned barrel had rolled to one side up against the car.

If she was close to it, she took the chance of being shot by either side.

The gunfire had slowed and in Zach's ear, Carter was talking to Reasoner about the situation.

"The captain of the *Pleiades Seagull* is down. Two shotgun blasts to the chest. He has four men with him. Two of them are injured. The other two have retreated into the cab of the eighteen-wheeler, but they haven't cranked it. Apparently, don't have keys."

"Can you rush the cab?"

"Plan to, sir, just as soon as they're out of ammunition. Right now, they're in the equivalent of an armored truck."

"Our men?"

"Winter is down. Two to the shoulder, I believe. My other two are okay. Still firing at the truck occasionally, to let the two men know we're here and to draw fire. As soon as I feel their ammunition is depleted, we'll move in."

"I'll have the ambulance standing by," Reasoner said. "And the sheriff's men. Out."

Zach looked at his right hand, which was streaked with blood that had dribbled down from his shoulder to his fingertips. He tried moving his fingers, tried wiping them on his jeans. For some reason, although the shoulder was hurting a lot more, his hand was working better. He picked up the gun. Tried holding it. Not half bad.

Using the tree to steady himself, he got up from his crouching position and stood there for a few seconds. Once he'd decided that he wasn't going to pass out, he crouched down and headed back the way they'd come around the warehouse. If he remembered correctly from when he was a kid, there was an old wooden door on the back side of the building that had rotted at the bottom.

There had been about a third of the door missing when he was young. Old man Beltaine had put a dirty piece of cloth over that bottom part and probably had never thought about it again.

Zach made it around the side of the building and found the old door, which looked exactly as he remembered. But he was breathing hard and feeling completely drained. He kicked at the bottom with his toe. Thank goodness Beltaine hadn't replaced the door. He got onto his hands and knees, feeling as if half his blood had drained out of him, and crawled through the bottom of the door into the warehouse.

Aware of what Carter had said about the men in the cab of the eighteen-wheeler, Zach lay flat on the concrete inside the door. Luckily, there was a pile of boxes near the door that hid him from the two men in the truck's cab. He wound through the boxes and stayed in the shadows until he'd worked his way around the perimeter of the building and was just about even with the back of his car. Just as he ducked and ran from the last box to hide behind the car, she crawled around the back tires on her elbows and knees, balancing a gun in the crook of her elbow.

She jumped when she realized there was someone there. Then she looked at him and immediately tears glistened in her eyes. She set the gun down and reached for him. "Oh, my God, Zach," she whispered. "I saw you get hit. Is it your shoulder? You're covered in blood."

"I'm okay. My hand's giving me some trouble, but I think I can hold a gun. Maybe even shoot it," he said, giving her a smile, then leaning down to kiss her.

She kissed him back, but the kiss didn't last very long because it was interrupted by the sound of a very big diesel engine trying to crank.

"They're going to get away!" Maddy said.

"I think they're trying to hot-wire the engine. I'm not sure they can do it."

The engine fired again, but coughed and died.

Maddy smiled at Zach. "Are you thinking what I'm thinking?"

He looked at her in bewilderment for an instant, then smiled back at her. "I'll bet I am. Hang on a sec." He pressed the send button on the earpiece he wore. "Winter to Carter. Maddy and I are going to arrest the two men in the truck cab. Don't shoot us."

He heard Carter's voice saying no, so he removed the earpiece and stuck it in his pocket.

"He said go ahead," he told Maddy and leaned in to give her a peck on the cheek. "Partner."

Maddy gestured that she would take the driver's side of the truck cab and let Zach have the passenger side. That side was closer and, for Zach's sake, she was betting that the stronger, better man had taken the driver's seat.

Her hands were almost back to normal. They felt tender and every so often fire would sear through a finger or her wrist, but they were working well enough for her to hold and operate her weapon.

As she crept toward the door, staying so close to the fender and tires of the cab that she was sure the men couldn't see her, she took a long breath and reveled in the feeling of power and connection she felt, now that she was with Zach again.

From those first few minutes when they'd moved together to make sure Sandy's bedroom was clear of intruders, she'd felt an intense and intimate bond with him. As if each of them knew what the other was about to do.

She waited to open the door to the cab until she was sure Zach was in place. It didn't take him long. Once she felt that he was ready, she took hold of the cab door, shouted, "Federal officers!" and yanked it open.

In unison with her shout, Zach yelled, "Drop your weapons. Now! Hands up!" And he opened the passenger door of the cab.

The man sitting in the driver's seat dropped the cables he was trying to twist together and reached for his weapon, which was lying on the floor near his right foot.

"Don't move!" Maddy yelled.

He pushed at her with his left hand and groped for the gun with his right. Maddy didn't anticipate his shove and barely reacted in time to avoid being pushed off the edge of the driver's-side door. However, she regained her balance instantly and coldcocked him on the back of the head with her pistol. "I said don't move," she said to him as he collapsed, dazed, back into the driver's seat.

While she handled the driver, Zach wrestled with the man on the passenger side. When he'd flung the door open, the man had pointed his automatic handgun directly at Zach's head. Or where he'd figured Zach's head would be.

But Zach had anticipated that possibility, so when he swung the door open, he stayed behind it. The man started firing before the door was completely open.

Once the burst of fire stopped, Zach ducked under the door and aimed his weapon directly at the man's groin. "I wouldn't move if I were you. And you really ought to drop your weapons. All of them. Otherwise…" He paused as he prodded the man's thigh. "I might miss and take out your femoral artery. I understand bleeding to death is a scary way to go."

Chapter Sixteen

"Zach? Are you all right?" It was Maddy.

"I'm fine. I'm calling the others." He slapped his ear then remembered that the earpiece was in his pocket. So he just yelled.

"Carter!" he shouted. "We've got 'em. Want to come and take them off our hands?" Yelling made him light-headed, so he backed up until he hit the fender of the car and leaned against it.

As he saw Carter and the other two men emerge from the trees where they'd taken cover, he called out to Maddy, "Good job, Tierney." But his voice didn't sound good to himself. It sounded weak and kind of thready.

"Same to you, Winter. How's your arm?"

"Oh, it's...okay."

The last thing he remembered was Carter relieving him of his weapon while another Coast Guard man ordered Zach's prisoner out of the truck and up against it, arms out and legs apart, to be frisked.

ZACH WOKE UP in a hospital bed with tubes and wires and bandages everywhere. It took him a few moments to orient himself. Once he did, he took a look at all the stuff that was attached to him. He was trussed up like a Thanksgiving turkey. His right arm was bandaged from shoulder to below the elbow, which made it impossible for him to move any part of it except his fingers. His left hand had an IV cannula stuck in the back. Zach saw black-and-blue marks on the hand where the nurses had apparently tried to insert the IV and failed. He couldn't move either hand. He was totally helpless.

He looked toward the door. It was closed. Nobody would hear him if he yelled. For a few moments, he lay there, willing himself to fall back to sleep. Instead, the events that had put him here kept rolling around in his head.

Boudreau shooting Poirier in cold blood, as if that had been his mission all along.

The man in the truck who had gone ghoulishly pale when Zach told him where he was going to shoot him.

Maddy, her hands swollen and blue and her wrists bisected by raw scrapes from some sort of restraint, crawling around the car, holding one of the automatic guns.

He shook his head. He didn't think he'd ever get over being amazed by her. She was the bravest person he may have ever known, with the possible exception of Tristan. In the whole time he'd known her—three days?—she'd never backed down from any challenge.

Actually, he amended, she had backed down once. When he'd told her he wanted her gone.

That had surprised him. He'd thought, hell, he'd *expected* a knock-down, drag-out fight that would likely end with him agreeing to let her stay. But she'd given up way too easily.

He closed his eyes. He'd had only one thing on his mind when he'd told her to leave. Her safety. He'd had to give her the choice, and he'd had to make it as easy as possible for her. This was not her fight. It was his. Tristan was his friend.

She had no reason to stay once her assignment had been terminated. The only thing that would accomplish would be to put her in danger, and for what? To help him. He'd done it to keep her safe, and he'd understood that she might take it as a rejection.

And she had.

His thoughts weren't particularly consecutive, connected or even coherent, he realized. He kept drifting off to sleep, waking up and drifting again. At some point during his sleep-driven musings, he was aware of someone telling him that the doctor had finished operating on his shoulder and that the anesthesia, plus something to help with the pain, might make him sleep. He nodded slowly. That was why he felt so tired.

He jerked awake suddenly. What was that? Something was beeping. He peered around. To his right and a little behind his head was an IV pole with a blue box on it with a flashing red light. That was where the beeping was coming from.

Damn it, if he could just move. Where was the nurse and why had they made it impossible for him to do anything for himself? He must have fallen asleep again, because the next thing he knew, someone was hanging a new bag of fluid and talking to him.

"Don't worry about that, Mr. Winter. Your IV pole beeps at the nurse's station as well as here in the room."

"What?"

The nurse laughed. "Not fun to fall asleep while you're talking, is it? You'll feel more alert and you'll start remembering things better within the next few hours. You're still under the effects of the sedation."

"What about if I'm thirsty, or my hand starts bleeding?" he said irritably.

"I'll just move the buzzer right here by your hand," she said, putting a white controller beside him. "You can reach it fine there."

"Thanks," he said ungraciously.

"I'll check on you in a little while," she said, heading for the door.

"What about my water? I'm thirsty."

"I'll send it in as soon as I get back to the nurse's station," she said cheerily as she walked out and shut the door.

"Send it in," he mocked, trying to swallow against his dry throat. Within a few seconds, he drifted off to sleep again.

MADDY SAT BESIDE Zach's bed and picked at the bandages on her wrists as she watched him sleep. She wasn't sure if being here when he woke up was a good idea.

His mother was driving over from Houston and would be here within the hour. And Maddy had a first-class ticket on a flight from New Orleans to DC that was leaving at 11:05 a.m., so if she was going to get a chance to talk to Zach alone, it had to be now.

The bandage on his right shoulder looked massive. The nurse who'd agreed to let her sit with him while he slept had explained to her that he'd taken two bullets in the shoulder. One had passed through muscle without too much damage. It would heal naturally. But the other bullet had torn through his rotator cuff. He needed surgery to repair the large tear and he would need physical therapy to regain full use of his shoulder. The nurse had acted as if it was no big deal, but to Maddy, it sounded as if Zach was going to have a difficult and painful recovery ahead of him.

She looked at the time on her phone. His mother would be here in about forty minutes. Her time was running out. She didn't want to wake him. According to the nurses, he'd been sleeping a lot and he was pretty grouchy when he was awake. But she'd been called to DC for debriefing and reassignment and she had no idea where she might end up. She needed to talk to him before she left and possibly never saw him again.

A quiet gasping sob escaped her lips. Her hand shot to her mouth immediately, too late, of course, to stop the sob, but possibly in time to keep any others from escaping.

Zach stirred and mumbled something.

Maddy froze, staring at him, confusion tearing at her insides. Should she wake him or not? She wanted to see him, but what if he didn't want to see her? What would she say then? *Sorry, wrong room, sorry, wrong guy, sorry, wrong life?*

She shook her head and rubbed her temple. This was probably a big mistake. And now his mother would be here in thirty-five minutes.

"Maddy?"

She jumped. "Zach?" she said in a strangled voice. "I didn't mean to wake you." He turned his head on the flat hospital pillow, trying to see her around the bed rails and the IV pole.

"Come here," he whispered.

With her heart throbbing in her throat, she stood and walked around the bed. "Hey," she said, trying to smile. The trouble was that when she saw his intense green eyes looking so weak and tired, she wanted to cry. "How're you feeling?"

"I'm thirsty as hell," he croaked. "Can't even talk."

"I'll get you some water," she said, turning toward the door.

"Don't leave."

She stopped. "O-okay." She came back to the side of the bed. "Do you want me to call someone to bring it?"

"Maybe later."

"Are you hurting?"

He shook his head, then craned his neck, trying to look behind him. "Do you see that stupid controller back there? It's white, with a cord that's thick as a rattlesnake."

Maddy saw a white cord and followed it. "Here. It fell off the side of the bed. Do you want me to call for water now?"

He looked up at her. "No. What are you doing here?"

"I was— I just—"

"Damn it, Maddy." He tried to reach for her hand with his left hand, the one with the IV in it. "Let me see your hand."

"What? Why?" She didn't move. She didn't know what he wanted, but then that had been the problem all along, hadn't it? She'd known she wanted him from the first time she'd laid eyes on him, but she'd never been able to figure him out. As in sync as they were, she always knew he was holding something back. One part of himself that she'd never been able to penetrate.

"Let me see your hand," he repeated.

She held her right hand close to his left. He took it and turned it over, looking at the palm, then turned it to examine the back. Letting it go, he looked up at her again. "What about you?" he asked, running his tongue across his dry lips.

"I'm fine," she said. "I'm good."

"No," he said, shaking his head. "No, you're not. There's something wrong. What is it? Is it something about the case?"

She didn't answer.

"Something about Boudreau? Or Tristan?"

She shook her head. "No. Nothing like that. Boudreau is out on bail. One of the sheriff's deputies arrested him for shooting Poirier, but it sounds like he'll get off with simple manslaughter and time served."

"Then it's you." He rested his head back on his pillow and licked his lips again. "What is it, Maddy? You want to tell me something. Go ahead. Spit it out. I can take it. Is it about Poirier? What did he do to you? I know he hurt you."

"I'm fine, Zach," she said, then took a long breath. "He hit me in the face and once in the stomach. But that was nothing. I'm tough."

Zach nodded. "Yeah."

Maddy had never felt so out of her element. She would never forgive herself if she got this far and didn't say what she needed to say, although right that instant she felt as if she'd rather be shot and punched in the stomach than to tell him. No. She had to tell him. She might end up living out the rest of her life never knowing what might have been. And she didn't like not knowing. Anything, no matter how bad, was better than the unknown.

"Zach, I got your message on my phone."

He frowned, then opened one eye. "My message?" he repeated as a question.

She nodded and lifted her chin. "You said, 'I'd like to have you with me, if you want to be.'"

"Did I?"

"Zach, can you look at me, please?"

He opened his eyes and scowled at her. "What?"

"Did you mean it?"

"Mean what?"

Maddy felt the tears swelling up in her throat, getting ready to pour from her eyes. "You know what. Do you have to be like this?"

He closed his eyes again. "I'm tired, Maddy. What is it you want?"

She sighed, it was a halting, hiccuping sound. "I just wanted to tell you something before I leave to go back to DC."

He lay there for a long time with his eyes closed. Then about the time Maddy had decided he'd fallen asleep, he opened his eyes and looked at her. He wasn't scowling or glaring or frowning or even looking at her blandly. His green eyes had turned dark and his mouth had thinned. "DC? You're leaving me, Madeleine Tierney?"

She blinked and the first of what she knew were going to be a lot of tears slid down her cheeks. She tried to smile. "I'm afraid I have to. I'm being called to DC for debriefing and reassignment."

He nodded and looked down at the IV in his arm. "I understand," he said. "Was that it?"

She swiped tears from her cheeks with the back of her hand. "Sorry?"

"Was that what you wanted to tell me?"

"No," she said, shaking her head. "No." She laughed shortly. "No. I just wanted to tell you— I wanted to say…" she said, her voice fading.

Could she tell him what she really needed to say? Was she even capable of opening enough to him to tell him that she'd never felt the way she did when he looked at her with that faintly bewildered expression that told her he wanted her and he wasn't sure why? Could she tell him all of that, or any of it?

After a few moments of utter silence in the room, Maddy took a deep breath. "I love you, Zach Winter. I don't need you to say anything or do anything or… anything. I just needed to say it." She swiped at her tears one more time. Then she adjusted her cross-body purse and turned to leave.

"Maddy?"

She looked back at him. "Yes?" she said cheerily.

"Come here."

"I really ought to be going. I've got a plane to catch in New Orleans tomorrow."

"Please?"

The tone of his voice was odd. Maddy turned to look at him and saw the glimmer of tears in his eyes. "Zach? Are you okay? Is something hurting? Should I call a nurse?"

"Yes. Yes. No." He smiled. "There's only one cure for what's hurting me. You have to stay here. Otherwise my heart's going to shatter."

Maddy blinked. "What? Your…heart?"

"Give me your hand."

Maddy didn't hesitate this time. She held out her hand to him. He took it and pulled on it gently.

"Kiss me, Maddy," he said, and she did.

The door to the room swung open and a woman walked in.

Maddy jumped backward as if she'd been pushed. She sent Zach a look, then turned to face the woman, who looked to be in her early fifties. She was not as tall as Maddy, but she had a regal bearing, and her clothes and makeup were impeccable. She was holding a glass of water and there was something in her green eyes that told Maddy immediately who she was.

His mother, Maddy thought. And she'd seen them kissing. This could get awkward.

"Mom?" Zach said. "What are you doing here?"

"Zach, my goodness, look at you. You look like a mummy with all those bandages. Please tell me that you're all right. Otherwise I'm going to start crying and my makeup will get all streaky."

Zach laughed, then moaned. "Oh. Don't make me laugh, Mom. Hey, is that water?" Zach demanded. "Give it here. I'm dying of thirst."

His mother put the water in his hand and he turned it up and drank half of it. "Ah," he said. "Thank you." He turned the glass up again.

"Zach?" his mother said. "Who is this?" She turned to Maddy. "Hello. Are you a social worker or…?"

"Mom!" Zach snapped, then winced in pain. "What have I told you about grilling my friends?"

"What?" she said. "What did I say?"

Maddy opened her mouth to answer, but Zach's mother had turned away.

Zach talked around gulps of water. "This is Maddy, Mom. She's not a social worker. She works for Homeland Security. I'm going to marry her."

He finished the last of his water while Maddy and his mother stared at him, speechless.

Epilogue

Two months later, Sandy was in her kitchen in Bonne Chance, when the phone rang. It was Maddy Tierney. "Maddy, hi. I was just thinking about you. How are you? How's Zach?"

"I'm fine and Zach's doing really well. He's almost a hundred percent. But I called to find out how you are. I called Mrs. DuChaud's number, but she said you were back in Bonne Chance."

Sandy cradled her belly in one hand while she held the phone with the other. "I just got here yesterday. I couldn't stay away any longer. This is my home. It was our home, Tristan's and mine, and it will be mine and the baby's."

"Speaking of the baby. What's the latest? Did that little thing ever fall off?"

Sandy laughed. "No. He's definitely a boy, a big boy, according to the doctor. Oh, Maddy, I wish—"

Maddy was silent for a beat, then she said, "I know, honey."

Of course Maddy knew what she was thinking. It was heartbreaking that Tristan would never see his son, and even more so that his child would never know him. "You didn't call to hear me whine. Tell me what's going on with you. I suppose you've heard all the news from here."

"I'm not sure if I've heard everything," Maddy said, as good at evading questions as she'd ever been.

Sandy poured herself a glass of purple juice and sat down at the kitchen table. "First of all, Boudreau didn't go to trial, but he didn't go to jail, either. I'm not sure what happened there, but he's back at his cabin. Mr. Cho and his son moved to Gulfport to try their hand at netting shrimp. Mr. Cho decided there was something wrong with Bonne Chance if smugglers could shoot up his warehouse. Oh, but listen to this. He came by to see me before he left. He wanted to apologize for his son peeking in my window and making me scream," Sandy said. "I told you I didn't dream that."

"Oh, Sandy, I believed you. I promise I did."

"I know, I know. So is there any more information from your end? Has anyone officially said that my husband's death wasn't an accident?"

Maddy didn't speak for a beat. "They're looking into it. I'm not in the loop, but Zach told me that the men who were taken into custody are being offered deals if they'll talk about who their boss was working for. So far, none of them have taken the offer. Also, they're investigating the company that owned the oil rig."

"So your answer is no. There's nothing official that says Tris's death was anything but an accident."

"That's true," Maddy said with a sigh. "But don't give up."

"Don't worry," Sandy responded. "Oh! I do have some good news. Speaking of the company that owned the oil rig. They set up a trust fund for the baby."

"Lee Drilling? Wow. Vernon Lee is one of the wealthiest men in the world. He probably did it for the publicity, so I hope the trust fund is huge."

"Huge doesn't begin to describe it. I'm having to get lawyers to help me figure out what to do with it. The company sent a lovely letter saying how much they mourned Tristan's death and—" She stopped and cleared her throat. "You know. All the usual stuff."

"I'm so glad. That will be a relief for you. Now you won't have to worry about you and the baby, and you won't have to go through all the pain and heartache of suing them."

"Yeah," Sandy said absently, looking outside. The sun had gone down and the sky was darkening. It was the gloaming of the day. The one time when Sandy could become maudlin if she wasn't careful. She sat back in the kitchen chair and patted her tummy where she knew the baby's little behind and legs were. "You're going to make me ask, aren't you?" she said.

"Make you ask what?" Maddy said innocently.

"Don't give me that innocent tone. I can hear you laughing. I'm not proud. Please tell me what's going on with you and Zach."

Maddy started talking about her plans to move from New Orleans to Fort Meade, Maryland, where Zach was, and that a few weeks ago he'd visited her and given her an engagement ring.

Sandy squealed. "That's so wonderful! Congratulations. You two were meant for each other. When's the wedding?" The baby kicked her. He was restless, so Sandy stood up and walked over to the French doors and looked out.

Yesterday, she'd walked over to the dock just before sundown. About the time the sun disappeared below the horizon, she'd spotted something diving and swimming in the water. It was hardly more than a silhouette in the waning light, but before she could tell whether it was a fish, a dolphin or maybe even a person, it had disappeared.

"Sandy?"

"Hmm? What? Oh," Sandy said. "I'm sorry. I guess I was thinking about the baby."

"Anyway, as I was saying, we want you and the baby up here for the wedding."

"Of course!" Sandy replied. "I wouldn't miss it for the world. When and where is it?"

"Sandy, are you okay? I just spent, like, five minutes talking about when and where. Are you okay?"

"Sure. Just daydreaming, I suppose. I'm sorry."

"Please. You're pregnant. You get a pass. Okay, I've got to go. The pizza guy is ringing the doorbell. Zach will be calling in a minute. He and I are having pizza together in different cities."

Sandy smiled. "Tell him I said hi. You two take care of each other, okay?"

Maddy said they would and hung up.

The day was waning into night. The sun had set. It was gloaming. It was too late to walk to the dock, or to see anything in the water if she did. With a sad smile, Sandy cradled her tummy and watched the last of the light fade into darkness.

* * * * *

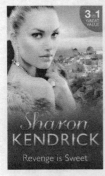

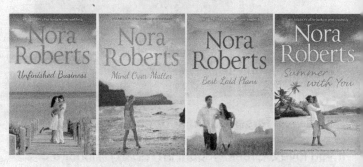

MILLS & BOON®

The Thirty List

* cover in development

At thirty, Rachel has slid down every ladder she has ever climbed. Jobless, broke and ditched by her husband, she has to move in with grumpy Patrick and his four-year-old son.

Patrick is also getting divorced, so to cheer themselves up the two decide to draw up bucket lists. Soon they are learning to tango, abseiling, trying stand-up comedy and more. But, as she gets closer to Patrick, Rachel wonders if their relationship is too good to be true…

Order yours today at
www.millsandboon.co.uk/Thethirtylist

MILLS & BOON®
INTRIGUE
Romantic Suspense

A SEDUCTIVE COMBINATION OF DANGER AND DESIRE

A sneak peek at next month's titles...

In stores from 15th May 2015:

- **To Honour and to Protect** – Webb & Black
  and **Navy SEAL Newlywed** – Elle James

- **Untraceable** – Janie Crouch
  and **Security Breach** – Mallory Kane

- **Cornered** – HelenKay Dimon
  and **The Guardian** – Cindi Myers

Romantic Suspense
- **Cowboy of Interest** – Carla Cassidy
- **Colton Cowboy Protector** – Beth Cornelison

Available at WHSmith, Tesco, Asda, Eason, Amazon and Apple

Just can't wait?
Buy our books online a month before they hit the shops!
visit www.millsandboon.co.uk

These books are also available in eBook format!